Kate Hardy lives in Norwich
husband, two young childre
many books to count! When sh
researching local history, she helps out at her children's schools. She also loves cooking—spot the recipes sneaked into her books! (They're also on her website, along with extracts and stories behind the books.)

Kate's always delighted to hear from readers, so do drop in to her website at www.katehardy.com

Louisa Heaton first started writing romance at secondary school, and would take her stories in to show her friends, scrawled on lined A4 paper in a big red binder, with plenty of crossing out. She dreamt of romance herself, and after knowing her husband-to-be for only three weeks shocked her parents by accepting his marriage proposal and heading off to Surrey to live with him. Once there, she began writing romance again and discovered the wonderful world of Mills & Boon Medical Romance.

Visit Louisa on Twitter, @louisaheaton,
on Facebook, www.facebook.com/Louisaheatonauthor,
and on her website: www.louisaheaton.com

Amber McKenzie's love of romance and all the drama a good romance entails began in her teenage years. After a lengthy university career, multiple degrees and one formal English class, she found herself happily employed as a physician and happily married to her medical school sweetheart.

Amber currently lives in Canada with her husband. She does her best to juggle her full-time medical practice with her love of writing and reading and other pursuits—from long-distance running to domestic goddess activities like cooking and quilting. Multi-tasking has become an art form and a way of life.

in the east of England, with her
one bouncy spaniel and too
many books to count. When she's not busy writing romance or

The Baby That Changed Everything

KATE HARDY
LOUISA HEATON
AMBER McKENZIE

MILLS & BOON

First Published in Great Britain 2018
by Mills & Boon, an imprint of HarperCollins*Publishers*
1 London Bridge Street, London, SE1 9GF

ISBN: 978-0-263-27457-8

0918

MIX
Paper from
responsible sources
FSC™ C007454

This book is produced from independently certified FSC™ paper to ensure responsible forest management.

For more information visit: www.harpercollins.co.uk/green

Printed and bound in Spain
by CPI, Barcelona

A BABY TO HEAL THEIR HEARTS

KATE HARDY

To C.C. Coburn and Cathleen Ross—
hope you enjoy Herod!

CHAPTER ONE

'SHE'S A BONNY LASS, our Bailey,' Archie said.

Jared's heart sank at the expression on the coach's face. Clearly Archie had taken a fancy to the researcher. And Jared had a nasty feeling that this might be a case of the coach's libido taking over from his common sense.

Allegedly, this 'bonny lass' researcher had a system that could reduce soft-tissue injuries among the players. So far, so good—but the figures being bandied about were crazy. In Jared's experience, when something sounded too good to be true, it usually was. And he could really do without some pretty, flaky girl distracting the players and getting in the way when he needed to treat them. Especially when he'd only just started his new job as the doctor to the youth team of a premiership division football club.

He'd been here before, when a manager's or player's head had been turned by a pretty girl, and the outcome was always messy. Worse still, it tended to have an impact on the rest of the team. With a bunch of teenage lads, this could get very messy indeed.

But he kept his thoughts to himself and gave the coach a polite smile. 'That's nice.'

Hopefully this Bailey woman would get bored quickly, or her system would be debunked, and they could go back to a more sensible way of preventing soft-tissue injuries—like sport-specific training, after he'd assessed each of the players and taken a proper medical history.

In the meantime, he'd have to grit his teeth and be as polite and as neutral as possible.

'Bailey—oh, good, you're here. Come and meet Jared Fraser, the new team doctor,' Archie McLennan called over from the side of the football pitch as Bailey walked through the players' tunnel.

Bailey smiled at the youth team's coach, but she made sure that she stood just far enough away so that Archie couldn't put his arm round her shoulders. She liked him very much as a colleague—he was at least prepared to listen to new ideas and he'd been more than fair with her on the research project so far—but she really wasn't in the market for a relationship.

Particularly with someone who was recently divorced and with a lifestyle that really didn't work for her; that was just setting things up to fail. And Bailey had failed quite enough in her relationships, thank you very much. She wanted life to be simple in the future—full of her family, her friends and her work, and that was enough for her. She didn't need anything more.

'Jared, this is Bailey Randall—the doctor whose research project I was telling you about,' Archie said.

For a moment, Jared looked as if he'd seen a ghost. Then he seemed to pull himself together and gave her a brief nod of acknowledgement. 'Dr Randall.'

But he didn't smile at her. Did he not approve of women being involved with a football team? Was he not good at social skills? Or—given that his accent was quite distinctive—was he just living up to the stereotype of the slightly dour, strong-and-silent Scotsman?

It was a shame, because he had the most gorgeous eyes. A deep, intense blue—the colour of a bluebell carpet. If he smiled, she'd just bet his eyes would have an irresistible twinkle.

Which was crazy. Since when did she think so fancifully? Bluebells, indeed.

'Pleased to meet you,' she said, giving him her brightest smile, and held her hand out for him to shake.

He gave another brief inclination of his head and shook her hand. His grip was firm, brief and very businesslike. He still didn't smile, though. Or say any kind of social pleasantry.

Oh, well. It wasn't as if she'd need to have that much to do with him, was it? Her project—to test a monitoring system to see if it could help to reduce the number of soft-tissue injuries in the team—had been agreed by the football club's chair of directors. She'd been working with Archie, the youth team coach, at training sessions and on match days when they played at home, and so far the system's results were proving very interesting indeed.

'Hey, Bailey.' John, one of the players, came over to the side and high-fived her.

'Hey, John. How's the ankle?' she asked.

'It's holding up, thanks to you,' he said with a smile.

'And you're still wearing that support?'

He nodded. 'And I'm doing the wobble-board exercises, like you showed me last time,' he said.

'Good.'

'Bailey helped out on a couple of sessions when she was here and your predecessor called in sick,' Archie told Jared. 'John sprained his ankle a few weeks back.'

'Sprained ankles are the most common injury in football,' Bailey said, just so Jared Fraser would know that she did actually understand the situation—maybe he was the dinosaur kind of man who thought that women knew next to nothing about sport. 'He was running when he hit a bump in the field, the sole of his foot rolled under and the movement damaged the ligaments on the outside of his ankle.' She shrugged. 'The wobble-board training we've been doing reduces the risk of him damaging his ankle again.'

Jared gave her another of those brief nods, but otherwise he was completely impassive.

Oh, great. How on earth was he going to connect with the players? Or maybe he was better at communicating when he was in work mode, being a doctor. She certainly hoped so, because the boys were still young enough to need encouragement and support; they weren't likely to respond to dourness.

'I ought to give you each other's mobile phone numbers and email addresses and what have you—in case you need to discuss anything,' Archie said.

'I doubt we will,' Jared said, 'but fine.'

Oh, what was *the guy's problem?* She itched to shake him, but that wouldn't be professional. Particularly in front of the youth team. Doctors, coaches and managers were supposed to present a united front. OK, so strictly speaking she didn't work for the football club—she was here purely as a researcher—but she still needed to be professional. 'Give me your number,' she said, 'and I'll text you with my email address so you have all my details.'

Once that was sorted out, she took her laptop out of its case. 'OK, guys, you know the drill. Let's go.' As the players lined up, she switched on her laptop, then called each team member by name and handed him a monitor with a chest strap, checking each one in with the laptop as she went.

'So what exactly is this system?' Jared asked when the players had filed onto the field to warm up. 'Some kind of glorified pedometer, like those expensive wristband gadgets that tell people they woke up three times during the night, but don't actually tell them why they woke up or what they can do about it?'

He sounded downright hostile. *What was his problem?* she thought again. But she gritted her teeth and tried her best to be polite. 'It does measure the number of steps the players take, yes,' she said, 'but it also monitors their average speed, the average steps they take per game, their heart rate average and maximum, and their VO2.' VO2 measured the amount of oxygen used by the body to convert the energy from food into adenosine triphosphate; the higher the VO2 max, the higher the athlete's level of fitness.

He scoffed. 'How on earth can you measure VO2 properly without hooking someone up to a system with a mask?'

'It's an estimate,' she admitted, 'but this system is a lot more than just a "glorified pedometer".' She put exaggerated quotes round the phrase with her fingers, just to make the point that she wasn't impressed by his assessment. Sure, once he knew what the system did and how it worked, she'd be happy to listen to him and to any suggestions he might have for improving it. But right now he was speaking from a position of being totally uninformed, so how could his opinion be in the least bit valid?

'The point is,' she said, 'to look at reducing the number of soft-tissue injuries. That means the players get more time to train and play, and they spend less time recovering from injuries. This particular system has been tested with a rugby team and it reduced their soft-tissue injury rate by seventy per cent, and my boss thinks it's worth giving it a try on other sports.' She gave him a grim smile. 'Just so you know, I'm not trying to put you out of a job. If anything, I'm trying to make your life easier by taking out the small, time-consuming stuff.'

'And you're actually a qualified doctor?' he asked, sounding sceptical.

Give me strength, Bailey thought, but she gave him another polite smile. 'Remind me to bring my degree certificate in with me next time,' she said. 'Or you can look me up on the Internet, if you're that fussed. I run sports medicine clinics three days a week at the London Victoria, so you'll find me listed in the department there, and I spend the other two working days each week on a research project.'

'So you're using this system of yours with other teams as well?' he asked.

'No—this is the only team I'm working with, and I only do one research project at a time. My last one was preventative medicine,' she explained. 'Basically I worked with patients who had high blood pressure. The aim was to help them to lose weight and maintain lean muscle mass, and that reduced both their blood pressure and their risk of cardiovascular incidents.' She couldn't resist adding, 'And by that I mean heart attacks and strokes.'

'Right.' Jared stared at Bailey. Archie had called her a 'bonny lass', but she was so much more than that. She was truly beautiful, with a heart-shaped face and huge brown eyes—emphasised by her elfin crop. She looked more like some glamorous Mediterranean princess than a doctor.

But, in Jared's experience, beautiful women spelled trouble and heartache. His ex, Sasha, had used her stunning looks to get her own way—and Jared had fallen for it hard enough to get very badly burned. Nowadays he was pretty much impervious to huge eyes and winsome smiles. But he'd already seen how Archie was following Bailey round like a lapdog; he had a nasty feeling that Bailey Randall had used her looks to get her own way with her ridiculous bit of computerised kit, the way Sasha always used her looks.

Still, at least this system of hers wasn't something

that would actually hurt the players. It wouldn't be of much real use—like the pricey fitness wristbands he'd referred to earlier, it wouldn't give enough information about what was actually wrong or how to fix it—but it wouldn't do any real harm, either.

Jared spent the session on the side of the pitch, ready in case any of the players had an injury that needed treating. But there were no strains, sprains or anything more serious; and, at the other end of the scale, there wasn't even a bruise or a contusion.

Half a lifetime ago, he'd been one of them, he thought wryly. A young hopeful, planning a career in the sport and dreaming of playing for his country. He'd actually made it and played for the England under-nineteen squad, scoring several goals in international matches. But Bailey Randall's bit of kit wouldn't have done anything to save him from the knee injury in his final game—the tackle that had stopped his football career in its tracks. Jared had ended up pursuing his original plans instead, studying for his A-levels and following in the family tradition by taking a degree in medicine.

The lure of football had drawn Jared to work with a club as their team doctor, rather than working in a hospital or his parents' general practice. And he still enjoyed the highs and lows of the game, the camaraderie among the players and hearing the supporters roar their approval when a goal was scored.

At the end of the training session, Archie turned to Bailey. 'Over to you.'

Jared watched in sheer disbelief as Bailey proceeded

to take the youth team through a series of yoga stretches and then breathing exercises.

What place did yoga have on a football pitch? In his experience, the players would do far better working on sport-specific training. As well as ball control, they needed to focus on muscular endurance and lower-body strength, and also work on explosive acceleration and short bursts of speed. If Archie wanted him to do it, Jared could design a training programme easily enough—either a warm-up routine that would work for the whole team, or some player-specific programmes to help deal with each player's weak spots—and it would do a lot more for the players' overall neuromuscular co-ordination than yoga would.

But having a go at Bailey Randall in front of the team wouldn't be professional, so Jared kept his mouth shut until the lads had gone for a shower and she was doing things on her laptop. Then he walked over to her and said, 'Can we have a quick word?'

She looked up from her laptop with an expression of surprise, but nodded. 'Sure.'

'What *exactly* does your box of tricks tell us?' he asked.

'It analyses each player's performance. For each player, I can show you a graph of his average performance over the last ten matches or training sessions, and how today's performance compares against that average.'

So far, so good. 'Which tells us what?'

'The system will pick up if a player is underperforming,' she said. 'Maybe he's coming down with a cold but isn't showing any symptoms yet—and if he's sick he's more at risk of sustaining injury and shouldn't be playing.'

He gave her a sceptical look. 'So you're telling me you can predict if a player's going to get a cough or a cold?'

'No, but I can predict the likelihood of the player sustaining an injury in his next match, based on his performance today and measured against an average of his last ten sessions.'

'Right.' Jared still wasn't totally convinced. And then he tackled the subject that bothered him most about today's antics. 'And the yoga?'

'As a football team doctor—someone who's clearly specialised in sports medicine—you'd already know that dynamic stretches are more useful than static stretches.' She held his gaze. 'But if you want me to spell it out to prove that I know what I'm talking about, dynamic stretches means continuous movement. That promotes blood flow, strength and stability. It also means you can work on more than one muscle group at a time—so it's more functional, because it mimics what happens with everyday movements. And you only hold the stretch for a short period of time, so the muscle releases more effectively and you get a better range of movement with each repetition.' She raised her eyebrows, as if challenging him to call her on it. 'Happy?'

He nodded. She did at least know her stuff, then. Even if she was a bit misguided about the computer programme. 'So you're a qualified yoga teacher?'

'No. But a qualified teacher—the one who's taught

me for the last five years—helped me put the routine together.'

'Right. And the breathing?'

She put her hands on her hips and gave him a hard stare. 'Oh, for goodness' sake! Are you going to quiz me on every aspect of this? Look, the project's already been approved by Mr Fincham.' The chairman of the club's board of directors. 'If you have a problem with it, then maybe you need to speak to him about it.'

'I just don't see what use yoga is going to be to a bunch of lads who need sport-specific training,' he said.

'"Lads" being the operative word,' she said. 'They're sixteen, seventeen—technically they're not quite adults, and most of their peers are either still in education or starting some kind of apprenticeship. I won't insult them by calling them children, because they're not, but they still have quite a lot of growing up to do. And, in the profession they've chosen, they're all very much in the public eye. The media hounds are just waiting to tear into the behaviour of overpaid footballers, whipping up a frenzy among their readers about how badly the boys behave.'

'That's true,' he said, 'but I still don't get what it has to do with yoga.'

'Discipline,' she said crisply.

'They already have the discipline of turning up for training and doing what Archie tells them to do.'

'Holding the yoga poses also takes discipline, and so does the breathing. So it's good practice and it helps to underline what Archie does with them. Plus it's good for helping to deal with stress,' she said.

That was the bit Jared really didn't buy into.

She clearly saw the scepticism in his expression, because she sighed. 'Look, if they get hassled by photographers or journalists or even just someone else in a club when they're out—someone who wants to prove himself as a big hero who can challenge a footballer and beat him up—then all they have to do is remember to breathe and it'll help them to take everything down a notch.'

'Hmm,' he said, still not convinced.

She threw her hands up in apparent disgust. 'You know what? You can think what you like, Dr Fraser. It's not going to make any difference to my research. If you've got some good ideas for how the data can be used, or about different measurements that would be useful in analysing the team's performance, then I'd be very happy to listen. But if all you're going to do is moan and bitch, then please just go and find someone else to annoy, because I'm busy. Excuse me.'

Bailey Randall clearly didn't like it when someone actually questioned her. And she still hadn't convinced him of the benefits of her project. 'Of course you are,' he said, knowing how nasty it sounded but right at that moment not caring.

As he walked away, he was sure he heard her mutter, 'What an ass.'

She was entitled to her opinion. He wasn't very impressed by her, either. But they'd just have to make the best of it, for as long as it took for Archie and the team director to realise that her 'research' was all a load of hokum.

CHAPTER TWO

'HE'S IMPOSSIBLE. TALK about blinkered. And narrow-minded. And—and— Arrgh!' Bailey stabbed her fork into her cake in utter frustration.

To her dismay, Joni just laughed.

'You're my best friend,' Bailey reminded her. 'You're supposed to be supportive.'

'I am. Of course I am,' Joni soothed. 'But you're the queen of endorphins. You always see the best in people, and to see you having a hissy fit about someone—well, he's obviously made quite an impression on you.'

'And not a good one.' Bailey ate a forkful of cake and then rolled her eyes at the plate. 'Oh, come on. If I'm going to eat this stuff, it could at least reward me with a sugar rush.'

'Maybe it just makes you grumpy.'

Bailey narrowed her eyes at her best friend. 'Now you're laughing at me.'

Joni reached over the table and hugged her. 'I love you, and you're in an almighty strop. Which doesn't happen very often. This Jared Fraser guy has really rattled you.'

Bailey glowered. 'Honestly. He quizzed me on every single aspect of my project.'

'Which is better than just dismissing it.'

'He *did* dismiss it, actually. He thinks the players should be doing sport-specific training.'

Joni coughed. 'You're the sports medicine doctor, not me. And I seem to remember you saying something about sport-specific training being the most effective.'

'But it's not the only kind of training they should be doing,' Bailey said. 'Yoga means dynamic stretches, which are more effective than static ones. And there's the discipline of holding the pose and doing the breathing. It's really good for the boys, and it helps them to focus.'

'Maybe you should make Jared do the stuff with the boys,' Joni suggested. 'And you can make him do extra planks.'

'Don't tempt me.' Bailey ate more cake. 'Actually, Joni, that might be a good idea. He needs to chill out a bit. Downward dog and breathing—that would do the trick.'

'I'd love to be a fly on the wall when you suggest it to him,' Joni said.

'No, you wouldn't. You hate people fighting—and he really doesn't like me.'

'You don't like him, either,' Joni pointed out.

'Well, no. Because he's rude, arrogant and narrow-minded. With men like him around, I'm more than happy to stay single.'

They both knew that wasn't the real reason why Bailey was resolutely single. After her life had imploded two and a half years ago, her marriage had cracked beyond repair. And Bailey still wasn't ready to risk trying another relationship. She didn't know if she ever would be.

'I don't know what to say,' Joni said, giving her another hug, 'except I love you and I believe in you.'

'You, too,' Bailey said.

'And I worry about you. That you're lonely.'

'That's because you're all loved up. Which is just as it should be,' Bailey said, 'given that it's just under two months until you get married to Aaron. And he's a sweetie.'

'Even so, I worry about you, Bailey.'

'I'm fine,' Bailey said, forcing herself to smile. 'Just grumpy tonight. And don't breathe a word of this to my mum, or she'll say that I'm attracted to Jared Fraser and I'm in denial about it.'

'Are you?' Joni asked.

Bailey blew out a breath. 'You're about the only person who could get away with asking that. No. He might be nice looking if he smiled,' she said, 'and to be fair he does have nice eyes. The colour of bluebells. But even if he was as sweet as Aaron, I still wouldn't be interested. I'm fine exactly as I am. I don't need anyone to complicate my life.'

Her words were slightly hollow, and she was pretty sure that Joni would pick up on that. But to her relief Joni didn't push it any further, or comment on that stupid remark she'd made about bluebells.

She wasn't attracted to Jared Fraser. She wanted to give him a good shake and tell him to open his mind a bit.

And bluebells were out of the question.

* * *

Before the next match, Bailey had a meeting with Archie to discuss the latest results from her software. As she'd half expected, Jared was there. Still playing dour, strong and silent. Well, that was his problem. She had a job to do.

'Travis is underperforming,' she said, showing them the graph on her laptop screen. 'It might be that he's had too many late nights over the last week, or it might be that he's coming down with something—but I'd recommend that he doesn't play as part of the team today.'

'I've already assessed the squad this morning, and they're all perfectly fit,' Jared said.

'A player who's underperforming is at a greater risk of soft-tissue injury,' she reminded him.

'According to your theory. Which has yet to be proven, because if you pull a player off every time they do a few steps less per game, then of course he won't get a soft-tissue injury, because he won't actually be playing. And if you follow that through every time, you'll end up with a really tiny pool of players. And the rest of them won't have had enough practice to help them improve their skills.'

'If they're off for weeks with an injury, that's not going to help them improve their skills, either,' she pointed out.

'Travis is fine.' He folded his arms. 'You're making a fuss over nothing.'

'Travis *isn't* fine.' She mirrored his defensive stance. 'But it isn't our call. It's Archie's.'

'Fine,' Jared said.

Archie looked at them both and sighed. 'I'll have a word with the lad.'

Clearly Travis was desperate to play, because Archie came back to tell them that the boy was in the team.

If Jared said 'Told you so', she might just punch him.

He didn't. But it was written all over his face.

Cross, Bailey sat on the bench at the side of the pitch and texted her best friend: Jared Fraser has to be the most smug, self-satisfied man in the universe.

A few seconds later, her phone beeped. She glanced at the screen, expecting Joni to have sent her a chin-up-and-rise-above-it type of message, and was surprised to see that the message was from Jared Fraser. Why would he be texting her? He was sitting less than six feet away from her. He could lean across and talk to her. He didn't need to resort to texting.

Curious, she opened the message. Herod?

What?

Don't understand, she texted back. Ridiculous man. What was he on about?

Her phone beeped a few seconds later. Your message: <<Herod Fraser has to be the most smug, self-satisfied man in the universe.>>

Then she realised exactly what had just happened.

Oh, no.

She'd been typing so fast that she obviously hadn't noticed her phone autocorrecting 'Jared' to 'Herod'. And Jared's name was right next to Joni's in her phone book. When Bailey had tapped on the recipient box, she'd clearly pressed the wrong name on the screen.

So now Jared Fraser knew exactly what she thought about him.

Which could make life very awkward indeed.

Sorry, she typed back. Not that she was apologising for what she'd said. She stood by every word of that—well, bar the autocorrected name. She was only apologising for her mistake.

Didn't mean to send that to you.

I'd already worked that one out for myself.

She sneaked a glance at him to see if she could work out how much he was going to make her pay for that little error, and was shocked to realise that he was actually smiling. He wasn't angry or even irritated; he was amused.

There was a sudden rush of feeling in her stomach, as if champagne was fizzing through her veins instead of blood. Totally ridiculous. But when the man smiled, it changed him totally. Rather than being the dour, hard-faced, slightly intimidating man she'd instinctively disliked, he was beautiful.

Oh, help. She really couldn't afford to let her thoughts go in that direction. For all she knew, he could be married or at least involved with someone. She knew nothing about the man, other than that he was the new youth team doctor and he didn't believe in her research at all.

'Sir, are you *the* Jared Fraser?' Billy, one of the substitutes, asked, coming over to sit in the pointedly large gap on the bench between Bailey and Jared.

The Jared Fraser? Why would there be something special about a football team's doctor? Bailey wondered.

'How do you mean?' Jared asked.

'Me and the lads—we saw it on the Internet. We weren't sure if it was you. But if it is—you were one of the youngest players ever to score a goal in the England under-nineteen team. And on your debut match,' Billy added breathlessly. 'And you scored that goal in the championship, the one that won the match.'

'It was a long time ago now. I haven't played in years,' Jared said.

Bailey couldn't quite work this out. Jared had been a star football player as a teenager? Then how come he was a doctor now? He didn't look that much older than she was—five years at the most, she reckoned—so surely he could still play football. Or, if he'd retired from football, it was more likely that he would have become a coach or a manager. Footballer to medic was quite a career change. Especially given that you needed four years at university followed by two years' foundation training, and then you had to work your way up the ranks. To be experienced enough to have a job as a football team doctor, Jared must have been working in medicine for at least ten years. Maybe more. So why had he switched careers?

Feeling slightly guilty about being so nosy—but she could hardly ask the man himself, given how grumpy and impossible he was—she flicked onto the Internet on her phone and looked up 'Jared Fraser footballer England team' in a search engine.

The photograph was eighteen years old now, but the

teenager was still recognisable as the man she knew. Jared Fraser had indeed been a footballer. One of the youngest players to score a goal for his country, at the age of seventeen. He'd played in several international matches and had scored the winning goal in a championship game. All the pundits had been tipping him to be one of the greatest players ever. But then, according to the online biography she was reading, he'd been involved in a bad tackle. One that had given him an anterior cruciate ligament injury that had ended his playing days.

So his dreams had been taken from him and he'd ended up in a totally different career. Poor guy. It would, perhaps, explain the dourness. She'd be pretty grumpy, too, if she was no longer able to do her dream job.

Maybe she'd give Jared Fraser just a little bit of slack in future.

Though not from pity. She remembered what it felt like, being an object of pity. It was one of the reasons why she'd moved departments. She might've been able to stick it out, had it not been for the guilt—the knowledge that people felt they had to be careful around her instead of beaming their heads off about a piece of personal good news, the kind of joy everyone else would celebrate with. Because how did you tell someone you were expecting a baby when you knew they'd lost theirs, and in such a difficult way?

Yeah. Bailey Randall knew all about broken dreams. And how you just had to pick yourself up, dust yourself down and pretend that everything was absolutely fine.

Because, if you did that, hopefully one day it *would* be just fine.

Halfway through the match, she noticed Travis lying on the ground, clutching his leg. Jared was already on his feet and running towards the boy; play had stopped and Jared was examining the player as she joined them.

'What's wrong?' she asked.

'Let me finish the SALTAPS stuff,' Jared said.

'SALTAPS?' It was obviously some kind of mnemonic, but not one she'd come across before.

'Stop play, analyse, look for injury, touch the site, active movement, passive movement, stand up,' he explained swiftly. 'Travis, what happened?'

'I don't know—there's just this pain down the back of my left leg,' the boy said, his face pale with pain.

Gently, Jared examined him. 'Did you hear a pop or a crack before the pain started?'

'I'm not sure,' Travis admitted. 'I was focusing on the ball.'

'OK. Does it hurt when you move?'

Travis nodded.

'I want you to bend your knee. If it hurts, stop moving straight away and tell me.'

The young player followed Jared's instructions and winced. 'It really hurts.'

'OK. I'm not even going to try the last bit—getting you up on your feet. I think you've got a hamstring injury, though I need to check a couple more things before I treat you. Archie's going to need to substitute you.'

'No, he can't!' Travis looked devastated. 'I'll be all right in a second or two. I'll be able to keep playing.'

Jared shook his head. 'Play on when you're injured and you'll do even more damage. You need treatment.'

Bailey had been pretty sure it was a hamstring injury, too, given Travis's symptoms. Hopefully it would be a partial rupture and wouldn't affect the whole muscle. 'Dr Fraser, you need to be on the pitch in case there's another injury,' she said. 'I'll take Travis to the dressing room and finish off the assessments for you.'

He looked at her and, for a moment, she thought he was going to refuse. Then he gave a brief nod. 'Thank you, Dr Randall. That would be helpful.'

'I'll talk to you when I've assessed him,' she said. Even though she was pretty sure that they'd recommend the same course of treatment, strictly speaking, Jared was in charge and Travis was his patient, and she was only here for research purposes. She didn't have the right to make decisions for Jared.

She supported Travis back to the dressing room. There was a wide, flat bench that would do nicely for her purposes; she gestured to it. 'OK. I want you to lie down here on your back, Travis, so I can go through the assessments and see how much damage you've done.'

'There's no need, really. I'll be all right in a few minutes,' Travis said, but she could see that his mouth was tight with pain.

'I still have to assess you, or Dr Fraser will have my guts for garters,' she said with a smile. 'OK. I'm going to raise your legs one at a time, keeping your knees straight. Tell me as soon as it hurts, OK? And I'll stop immediately.' She took him through a range of tests, noting his reactions.

'I'll put a compression bandage on—that'll stop the pain and the bleeding inside your ligament, which causes the inflammation—and an ice pack,' she said when she'd finished. 'And now I'm going to make you a cup of tea, and I want you to sit there with your leg up and the ice pack on the back of your thigh for the next ten minutes or so, while I go and talk to Dr Fraser, OK?'

'Yes, Doc.' He sighed. 'Am I going to be out of the team for long?'

'For at least a couple of weeks,' she said. 'I know it's hard and I know you want to play, but it's better to let yourself recover fully now than to play on it too soon and do more damage.' She finished making the tea. 'Sugar?'

'No. You're all right.' He gave her a rueful smile. 'Thanks, Doc.'

'That's what I'm here for. And painkillers,' she said. 'Are you allergic to anything, or taking any medication for anything?'

'No.'

'OK. I'll give you a couple of paracetamol for now—you can take some more in another four hours—and I'll see what else Dr Fraser suggests.' She patted his shoulder. 'Chin up. It could be worse.'

'Could it?' Travis asked, looking miserable.

'Oh, yes. Imagine having an itch on your leg in the middle of a really hot summer day—except your leg's in a full cast and you can't reach the itchy bit.'

That earned her another wry smile. 'OK. That's worse. Because I'd be off even longer with an actual break, wouldn't I?'

'Yes. But you're young and fit, so you'll heal just fine—as long as you do what Dr Fraser says.'

'I guess.'

She left him miserably sipping his mug of tea while she went to find Jared.

Jared knew the very moment that Bailey stepped out of the tunnel onto the field, even though his back was to her. The fact that he was so aware of her was slightly unnerving. They didn't even like each other—he'd known that even before she'd accidentally sent him that text saying exactly how she felt about him, in very unflattering terms. Dressed in a hooded sweatshirt, baggy tracksuit pants and flat training shoes, Bailey Randall should've looked slightly scruffy and absolutely unsexy—the complete opposite to his über-groomed ex-wife.

The problem was, Bailey was gorgeous. And those unflattering baggy clothes just made him want to peel them off and see exactly what was underneath them.

Not good. He didn't want to be attracted to her. He didn't want to be attracted to anyone.

Work, he reminded himself. This is work. You have an injured player, and she's helped you out. Be nice. Be polite. Be professional. And stay detached.

'How's young Travis?' he asked when she reached him.

'Pretty miserable,' she said.

Yeah. He knew how it felt, being taken off the pitch with an injury when you were desperate to keep playing. And, even though Travis's injury was relatively minor and he'd make a full recovery, Jared knew that the inactivity would make the boy utterly despondent. He'd been there himself. 'So what's your verdict?' he asked.

'I got him to do a straight leg raise and resisted knee flexion, then did a slump test and palpation,' she said. 'I'd say it's a grade two hamstring strain. I've put an ice pack on and a compression bandage for now and explained to him about standard RICE treatment. He's having a cup of tea while I'm talking to you and seeing what treatment you want him to have.'

'Thank you,' he said. He was impressed by the quiet, no-fuss way she'd examined the boy and reported back. There was no 'Told you so' or point-scoring against him, even though he probably deserved it; all her focus had been on making her patient comfortable. She'd also come to talk to him about a treatment plan instead of telling him how to treat his patient, despite the fact she was obviously more than capable of doing her own treatment plan, so she'd respected his position in the club, too. Maybe he'd been unfair to her about her project, because she'd been spot on about the actual medicine she'd discussed with him. If she was that competent, she was unlikely to be working on a project that had no merit.

'The poor lad's going to be gutted about missing training and matches, but he needs to do it properly or he'll end up with another tear in the muscle on top of this one, and it'll take even longer to heal,' she said.

Jared nodded. 'He needs cold therapy and compression every hour for the first day, and to keep his leg elevated while he's sitting, to reduce the swelling.'

'I gave him some paracetamol—he said he's not on any other medication and he's not allergic to anything.'

'Good. That'll help with the pain during the acute stage, over the next couple of days,' he said.

'I told him that you'd come up with a rehab programme,' she said, 'but if he was my patient I'd suggest a sports massage at the end of the first week, and strengthening exercises in the meantime—standing knee flexion, bridge and seated hamstring curls with a resistance band. Nothing too strenuous, and he has to stop as soon as it hurts.'

'Good plan,' he said. Exactly what he would have suggested. They might not get on, but in medical terms they were definitely on the same page. 'He can also do some gentle walking and swimming, then introduce running gradually. Though it'll be several weeks before he's ready to come back to full training.'

She nodded. 'Look, I know you don't believe in the stuff I'm doing, and I'm not going to rub your nose in it and say "I told you so". But I do want some time to talk you through what I'm doing and—well, I suppose I really want to get you on board with the project,' she admitted. 'Can we have a meeting to talk about it—I mean *really* talk?'

If he'd listened to her and supported her argument that Travis was underperforming, the boy might not be sitting in the dressing room right now with a hamstring injury. Guilt made him sharp. 'The only free time I have is before breakfast.'

He knew he was being obnoxious, but he couldn't seem to stop himself. What was it about Bailey Randall that made him behave like this? Something about her just knocked him off balance, and he liked things to be in perfect equilibrium nowadays.

'Before breakfast,' she mused. 'I normally train at the gym then—but OK. I guess I can skip my session in the gym for once.'

'Or we could train in the gym together.' The words were out of his mouth before he could stop them. What on earth was wrong with him? Panic flooded through him. This was *such* a bad idea.

'Train together, and then talk about my project over breakfast? That works for me. As long as your partner doesn't mind,' she added quickly.

'No partner.' Though he appreciated that she'd tried to be considerate. In the world of football, there was a lot of jealousy. Sasha definitely wouldn't have been happy about him having a breakfast meeting with a female colleague. Then again, Sasha had had meetings of her own with his male colleagues. In hotel rooms. He pushed the thought away. 'Will yours mind?' He tried to extend the same courtesy to Bailey.

'I'm single,' she said, 'and I like it that way.'

Which sounded to him as if she'd been hurt, too.

Not that it was any of his business. And he wouldn't dream of asking for details.

'One last thing to sort—my gym or yours?' she asked.

'So you don't go to a women-only gym?' Oh, great. And now he was insulting her.

She smiled. 'I'm not intimidated by anyone, regardless of their gender or their age or how pretty they are. I go to a place that has equipment I like and staff who can push me harder if I want a one-to-one training session. And it happens to be reasonably close to the London Victoria, so I can train before work.' She paused. 'There's a café there, too. The coffee's not brilliant, but they do a pretty good Eggs Florentine—which they don't serve in the hospital canteen, or I'd suggest breakfast there because their coffee's slightly better.'

There was no way he could back out of this now. 'OK. Your gym, tomorrow. Let me know the address and what time.'

'Seven,' she said. 'And I'll text you the address.' And there was a tiny, tiny hint of mischief in her eyes as she added, 'Herod.'

CHAPTER THREE

AT FIVE TO SEVEN the next morning, Jared walked down the street towards Bailey's gym. She was already waiting outside for him, wearing another of her hooded sweat-shirts and baggy tracksuit pants, and she raised her hand to let him know she'd seen him. He acknowledged her with a nod.

'Good morning,' she said as he walked up to her. 'Are you ready for this?'

'Bring it on,' he said, responding to the challenge in her gaze and trying not to think about how gorgeous her mouth was. This was a challenge of sorts, not a date. They were supposed to be discussing business. And the fact that they were meeting here right now was his own fault—for being deliberately awkward and not trying to fit their meeting into normal working hours.

They walked into the reception, where she signed him in as her guest, and took him through to the changing rooms. 'I need to put my stuff in my locker. Meet you back outside here in five?'

'Sure.'

'Oh—and do you have a pound coin for your own locker? I have change if you need it.'

'Thanks, but I'm good.'

It didn't take him long to stow his things in the locker.

When Bailey came out from the women's changing rooms, Jared's jaw almost dropped. Clearly she'd been wearing the hoodie and the tracksuit pants just for warmth outside, because now she was wearing form-fitting black leggings and a bright cerise racer-back crop top. And he was horribly aware of just how gorgeous she was. Curvy, yet with fabulous muscle definition. Bailey Randall was a woman who looked after herself. She was utterly beautiful and could easily have held her own with any of the glamorous WAGs he'd known at the football clubs he'd worked at. And yet he didn't think she'd be the sort to go to endless spa days and nail parlours.

This was beginning to feel like the most enormous mistake. They were supposed to be training together and then discussing her project over breakfast, and all he wanted to do right now was to scoop her up and carry her to his bed. Even though it was actually a Tube ride away.

It was obvious that, like Sasha, Bailey was aware of her effect on men. She was gorgeous. So was Bailey like his ex-wife in using her physical attributes to get her own way? The idea made him pull himself together. Just. 'So what's your normal workout routine?' he asked.

'Today is a weights day,' she said, 'so that means a quick cardio warm-up and then a resistance routine. You?'

He shrugged. 'I'll join you and adjust the weights to suit me. Just tell me what we're doing and when.'

She nodded. 'Any injuries I should know about?'

Jared had no idea whether Archie had told her anything about his past, but it was irrelevant now. 'A very old knee problem,' he said. 'But I know my limits and I'm certainly not going to be stupid about it.'

'Good. Then let's do this. How about using the elliptical as a warm-up, then through into the back room with the free weights?'

'Fine by me.'

Why on earth had she agreed to train with him? Bailey asked herself. Jared was wearing baggy tracksuit pants and a loose sleeveless vest, like all the other men in the gym. She barely took any notice of them other than to smile hello, acknowledging the fellow athletes in her time slot. But Jared Fraser was different. She was horribly aware of the hard musculature of his body. Particularly his biceps.

He was an ex-footballer. A sports team doctor. He shouldn't have biceps that beautiful and that well defined.

Worst of all, she had a real thing about biceps. Bailey always dragged Joni off to the cinema whenever her favourite actor had a new movie out—and Joni still teased Bailey about the time she'd said, 'Ohhh, just look at his biceps,' really loudly, in the middle of the cinema. The actor was incredibly handsome, perfectly built, but so was Jared Fraser.

She sneaked a sideways look. He was concentrating on putting the time and intensity settings into the elliptical machine, and right at that moment he looked incredibly sexy. It made her wonder what it would be like to have that brooding concentration completely focused on her, and she went hot all over. This training thing was a very bad move. She wished now that she hadn't challenged him. How on earth was she going to be able to concentrate on talking to him over breakfast? Even if he changed into something with long sleeves after his shower, she knew now that he had gorgeous biceps and that could seriously distract her. Right at that moment, she really wanted to reach over and touch him.

Well, she was going to have to make a lot more of an effort, because no way was she acting on that pull of attraction. She liked her life exactly as it was, with no complications—and Jared Fraser could be a real complication. If she let him. Which she really didn't intend to do.

When they'd finished warming up, Bailey talked him through her planned routine, the large compound movements that worked several muscle groups at once. 'I thought I'd do a full-body workout today, if that's OK with you, rather than an upper or lower split.'

'It's a good balance,' he said. 'I notice you're doing hams and then quads.'

'You need to balance them out properly or you'll end up with a back injury,' she said, 'and you wouldn't believe how many patients I have to explain that to.'

Funny how easy it was to talk to him when they were both concentrating on doing the right number of reps and keeping their form correct.

'What made you specialise in sports medicine?' he asked.

'I started off in emergency medicine,' she said, 'but then I found myself doing more of the sporting injuries, especially at the weekends or on Monday mornings. I did think about maybe working in orthopaedics, but then again I like the preventative stuff, too—it's great being able to make a difference. Then I had the chance of a secondment in the new sports medicine department. I liked my colleagues and I liked the work, so I stayed.'

That was the brief version. She had no intention of telling Jared the rest of it—how that secondment had saved her sanity, just over two years ago, and given her something else to concentrate on when she'd desperately needed an escape. OK, so in sports medicine there wasn't the speed and pressure that could take her mind off things as there was in the emergency department; but she also didn't have to walk into her department again after first-hand experience of being treated there, knowing that everyone in the department knew exactly what had happened to her and trying to avoid the concern that shaded too far into pity.

'What about you?' she asked. 'Why did you become the doctor of a football team?'

She wondered if he was going to tell her about his past as a footballer, but he merely said, 'I enjoy working in sports medicine, and this job means I get to travel a bit.'

Surely he must've guessed that she'd looked him up and knew what had happened to his knee? Then again, it had been a life-changing accident, and he was on a completely different path now. She didn't blame him for not wanting to talk about the injury that had wrecked his career—just as she didn't want to talk about the ectopic pregnancy that had shattered her dreams and then cracked her marriage beyond repair. No doubt he, too, knew what it felt like to be sick and tired of pity. They didn't have to discuss it.

'How did you get involved in this research project, or have you always been a football fan?' he asked.

'I ought to admit that I'd much rather do sport than watch it, and football isn't really top of my list,' she said. 'My boss was asked if someone on his team would work on the project, and he thought I'd enjoy it because...' She felt her face heat. 'Well, I like techie stuff,' she confessed. 'A lot.'

'You mean gadgets?' He zeroed in on exactly the thing she knew he'd pick up on. 'And would I be right in guessing that you've got one of those expensive wristband things?'

'Um, yes,' she admitted. 'I use it all the time in the gym. I didn't wear it today simply because I knew you'd be really rude about it.'

He burst out laughing. It was the first time she'd actually heard him laugh and it was gorgeous, rich and deep. Sexy, even. *Oh, help.*

'Oh, come off it—are you trying to tell me that you don't like game consoles and whatever?' she asked. 'My brothers are total addicts and so are Joni's—my best friend,' she explained.

'I'm not so much into game consoles,' he said, 'but I do like music—and that's where my techie stuff comes in. I bought one of those systems where the sound follows you through the house.' Then he looked surprised, as if he hadn't meant to tell her something so personal.

'What kind of music?' she asked.

'What do you think?' he parried.

She looked at him as she put the barbell down. 'I'd say either dinosaur rock or very highbrow classical.'

'The first,' he said.

She almost—*almost*—told him about Joni's brother's band and invited him along to their next gig. But that would be too much like asking him out on a date. She and Jared Fraser most definitely weren't on dating terms.

'I'm assuming you like the stuff you can sing along to,' he said.

'Musicals,' she said. 'I'm pretty much word perfect on the soundtracks to *Grease*, *Cats* and *Evita*.'

'Uh-huh.'

But there was a tiny hint of superciliousness in his expression, so she added, 'And Dean Martin. Nonno's favourite. He taught me all the famous songs when I was tiny—"That's Amore", "Volare" and "Sway".' Just in case Jared had any intention of mocking *that*, she said, 'And, actually, it's great stuff to salsa to. It's not old-fashioned at all.'

'Nonno?' he asked, looking confused.

'My grandfather in Milan. My mum is Italian,' she said.

'That explains it.'

'Explains what?' She narrowed her eyes at him.

'Why I thought you were a bit like a pampered Mediterranean princess when I first met you.' Then he looked really horrified, as if he hadn't meant to say that.

'A pampered princess,' she said, and glowered at him. 'You think I'm *spoiled*?'

He stretched out a foot and prodded the floor next to the mats. 'Ah. The floor's obviously not going to open up and swallow me.'

It amused her, though at the same time she was a bit annoyed at what he was implying. 'Princess,' she said again in disgust.

'Hey. You called me Herod,' he pointed out.

'That was an autocorrect thing on my phone, and it wasn't meant for you in any case. You know what they say about eavesdroppers hearing no good of themselves,' she said loftily.

'You didn't actually take it back, though,' he reminded her.

'No, I didn't—I do think you have tyrant tendencies,' she said, 'given how you wouldn't even listen to what Archie or I said about the project.' She paused. 'And the fact that you could dismiss me as princessy just now, when you barely even know me. That's definitely Herod-like behaviour.'

'I think,' he said, 'we just got back onto the wrong foot with each other—and this morning's meant to be about listening to each other's point of view and finding a bit of common ground.'

He had a point. Maybe she should cut him some slack. 'So you're actually going to listen to what I say? And you'll admit that you were wrong about Travis?'

'*Possibly* wrong,' he corrected. 'That injury might still have happened to one of the other players—one who was performing around his normal average on your charts.'

It was much less likely, she thought. But at least he

was admitting the possibility that he was wrong. That was a start. 'What about the yoga?' she challenged.

'No. I'm not convinced. At all,' he said.

'So you think yoga is easy?'

'It's simple stretching.'

Remembering the conversation she'd had with Joni, Bailey smiled. 'Right. So we can finish this session with a bit of yoga, then.'

He rolled his eyes, but muttered, 'If you must.'

When they'd finished the weights routine, she said, 'Yoga will be the cool down and stretch. Have you ever done any before?'

He stared at her. 'Do I look as if I do yoga?'

'Actually, there are a couple of men in our class. They recognise the importance of flexibility training as part of a balanced exercise programme,' she pointed out. 'But OK. I'll talk you through the poses.' First, she talked him through the downward dog. She noticed that he seemed reasonably flexible, and she was impressed that he managed both the warrior pose and the tree without any difficulty. He had a strong core, then.

'So far, so easy?' she asked.

'I can tell which muscle groups each one works,' he said.

'Good. Now for the plank,' she said, and showed him the position. She moved so she could see the clock. 'And we'll start in five. Hold it for as long as you can.' She counted them down, then they both assumed the position.

Jared managed to hold it for a minute before he flopped.

Bailey took it to three—even though that was pushing it, for her—just to make the point.

* * *

It looked effortless, though Jared could see Bailey's arms just beginning to shake and he knew that her muscles were right on the verge of giving in. But, when she stopped the pose, he knew he was going to have to be gracious about it—especially given that her performance had been so much better than his.

'OK,' he said, 'I admit that was hard. And clearly you've done that particular one a lot.'

She grinned. 'I have. That one usually shuts people up when they say yoga's an easy option. Though, actually, you did well. A lot of people cave after twenty seconds, or even before that.'

He appreciated the compliment, particularly as it sounded genuine and as if she was trying to meet him halfway.

'So you do a lot of yoga?' he asked.

'Every Monday night with my best friend. Any decent training regime needs flexibility work as well as resistance and cardio.'

He agreed with that. 'So what do you do for cardio?'

She actually blushed.

And he started to have all kinds of seriously impure thoughts about her. He really wished he hadn't started this discussion. The fact that she'd blushed meant she must be thinking something similar. So the attraction was mutual, then? Heat zinged through him. If she felt the same pull, what did that mean?

Then again, he didn't want to get involved with anyone. Sasha had hurt him badly—not just with the affair, but the bit she'd really lied to him about—and Jared wasn't sure he was ready to trust again.

'Cardio. I like dance-based classes,' she said. 'Also there's a salsa night at a local club. I quite often go to that. I like the music, and the dancing's fun. I'm a great believer in endorphins.'

For a moment Jared thought she was going to challenge him to go with her—and he wasn't sure if he was more relieved or disappointed when she didn't. He'd hated clubbing with Sasha in any case; a salsa club was probably just as much of a meat market as any other kind of dance club, and that didn't really appeal to him. Though the idea of dancing with Bailey Randall, up close, hot and sweaty, with her body pressed against his…

Focus, he told himself. Work, not sex.

'I assume you run?' she asked.

'Intervals,' he said, 'and rowing—it's more effective than hamster-wheel cardio. No offence to your warm-up today, because that was fine—it's just that it would bore me stupid if it lasted for more than ten minutes, even with a decent playlist to keep me going.'

'Each to their own,' she said. 'I don't mind doing a whole session on the elliptical if I have a good playlist. There are programmes on the machine that change the resistance and make it a bit more interesting.'

He just grimaced.

'So, rowing, hmm? That would explain your biceps.'

And then she blushed again.

Now he was really intrigued. She liked his biceps?

Well, he liked the muscles in her back. They had

beautiful definition. And he really, really wanted to touch them. No. More than that. He wanted to kiss his way down her spine.

'Would that be proper rowing on a river, or machine?' she asked.

'Machine,' he admitted.

'And I assume you're careful with your knee.'

'I'm wearing a knee support under my tracksuit pants,' he said. 'I'm hardly going to nag my players about looking after themselves properly and then not take my own advice.'

'I guess.' She held out her hand to shake his, and his palm tingled where their skin touched. How long had it been since he'd been so aware of someone? 'That was a good session. I enjoyed working with you, Jared.'

'I enjoyed working with you,' he said, meaning it; he was surprised to realise just how much he'd enjoyed it.

'Let's hit the shower and have breakfast.'

He went hot all over again at the thought of sharing a shower with her. He knew perfectly well that wasn't what she'd meant, but now the idea was stuck in his head. And he was glad they had temperature settings on the showers in the male changing rooms, because he needed a blast of cold water to get his common sense back and the fantasies out of his mind.

When he met Bailey outside the changing rooms, he noticed that she was wearing a black tailored suit for work. This was yet another side of her; he'd seen the slightly scruffy scientist on the football pitch and the sculpted goddess in the gym, and now she was the calm, confident medical professional.

He wished that he was wearing something a bit more tailored, too—but then again he was off to work himself after this and that meant dressing appropriately. A sharp suit wasn't what you needed when you were working on a football pitch.

Clearly the staff knew Bailey well here, because the waitress didn't bat an eyelid when Bailey ordered Eggs Florentine without the hollandaise sauce. 'And a rich roast latte?' the waitress asked.

It was obviously Bailey's usual, because she smiled. 'That'd be lovely, thanks.'

He ordered porridge with blueberries and cinnamon, paired with a protein shake.

'Not a coffee fiend?' she asked.

'I had mine before my workout. It gets the best use out of the caffeine,' he said. 'I'm balancing my protein and my carbs now, post-workout.'

She nodded. 'Good point.'

'So, are you going to take me through this system of yours while we wait for breakfast to arrive?'

'Sure. The idea behind it is that you're more likely to end up with a soft-tissue injury if you play while you're under par. You'll be slower and your reactions won't be as fast. So if you look at your performance during training or a game and your VO2 is down, you're doing fewer steps, your resting heart rate is up and your average speed is down, either you've had a slow game—and that's where Archie comes in, to tell me if playing conditions on the field have been different and affected anyone's performance—or you're under par and you're more likely to be injured in your next game.'

He asked her various questions about the measurements she used, and he was impressed that she didn't have to look up a single answer. Bailey Randall wasn't the glib salesman type, able to put a spin on her answers; she really knew her stuff. And she clearly believed in her research project. He liked her enthusiasm; it was one of the reasons why he'd chosen to look after the youth team, because he loved the enthusiasm that young players brought to the job, unjaded by internal politics.

And he also liked the way Bailey talked with her hands, completely animated when she was caught up in the subject. Now he knew she was half-Italian, he could really see it. Everything from her classic bone structure, to the slightly olive colour of her skin, to the rich depths of her eyes. Naturally stylish, she was like an Italian Audrey Hepburn, with that gamine haircut and those huge eyes.

'OK,' he said. 'I still think those wristband things are ploys to extort money out of the gullible with too much disposable income and too little common sense, but the stuff you're doing has a point.'

'Thank you,' she said. 'So do you take it back about my system being a glorified pedometer?'

'I'll reserve judgement until I've seen a month of results,' he said, 'but I will agree that it's better than the wristband things. Especially because you do at least use a proper heart-rate monitor strap with your system.'

'And the yoga?'

He shook his head. 'Even though the plank was hard, I'm not convinced that yoga's going to do what you think it will. Not for a bunch of seventeen-year-old boys.'

'It's still worth a try.'

'Do you make them do the plank?'

She laughed. 'No. That was just to prove a point to you.'

He liked the fact that she'd admitted it.

And it worried him that he liked it. Now that he was getting to know her, he quite liked Bailey Randall. Which was a very dangerous position. He couldn't afford to think of her in terms of anything other than a colleague, but she seriously tempted him. To the point where he could actually imagine asking her out on a date.

Bad, bad move.

He had a feeling that he was going to have to resort to a lot of cold showers to keep his common sense in place. Dating Bailey Randall was absolutely not on the cards. He'd only just finished gluing the pieces of his heart back together, and he had no intention of putting himself back in a position where it could shatter again.

CHAPTER FOUR

OVER THE NEXT couple of weeks, working at the football club was easier, Bailey thought. Jared was at least showing some interest in her research project rather than being an insurmountable bulwark, and he'd even come up with a couple of suggestions that she was trying to incorporate into her data.

Then she noticed that he was favouring his right knee when he went onto the pitch to treat one of the players. She waited until he'd come back to sit next to her on the bench, and then asked, 'What did you do?'

'For Mitch?' He shrugged. 'It was just a flesh wound—some studs scraped against his shin, so I cleaned it and dressed it. He shouldn't have too much trouble with it.'

'No, I meant what did you do to your knee?'

He looked away. 'Nothing.'

'Jared, I'm a doctor, so don't try to flannel me. I could see you were favouring your right knee,' she said.

He sighed. 'It's an old injury. I guess I might have overdone the running a tad at the weekend.'

'Tsk. And you're a sports medicine doctor,' she said.

He gave her a crooked grin that made her libido sit up and beg. 'It'll be fine. It's strapped up.'

'So you didn't actually see anyone about it?'

'I didn't need to.'

She tutted. 'What a fine example to set the team—*not.* Let me have a look when they've gone, so they don't know what an idiot you are.'

He shook his head. 'It's fine. You don't have to do that.'

'You're my colleague. You'd do the same for me.'

Jared thought about it. Would he? Yes, probably. And he'd nag her if she was being stubborn about it, just as he'd nag Archie. Just as she was nagging him. 'I guess,' he admitted.

'Are you icing it? Because obviously you're not resting it or elevating it.'

'No. I'm taking painkillers,' he said. 'And not strong ones, either. Just normal ibuprofen to deal with the inflammation.'

'Hmm,' she said.

After the training session, Jared said to Archie, 'I'll lock up if you need to go. I want to discuss a couple of things with Dr Randall.'

'Cheers,' Archie said. 'It'll give me a few extra minutes to make myself beautiful for my date.'

'What, another one?' Bailey teased. 'I'm sure she'll think you look beautiful.' She blew him a kiss.

Archie grinned and sketched a bow.

'Why didn't you just tell him that your knee hurts?'

Bailey asked quietly when Archie and the players had gone, and she and Jared were alone in the dressing room.

'Because it isn't relevant.'

'Of course it's relevant. If you have to kneel on the pitch to treat one of the players, it's going to hurt you.' She rolled her eyes. 'Men.'

'Women,' he sniped back.

'Just shut up and lose the tracksuit bottoms.'

Oh, help. The pictures that put into his head. To clear them, he drawled, 'Fabulous bedside manner, Dr Randall.'

Except that made it worse. Bed. Bailey. Two words he really shouldn't have put together inside his head, because now he could imagine her lying against his pillows and giving him a come-hither smile…

She just gave him a dry look. He shut up and removed his tracksuit bottoms. He knew she wasn't thinking of him in terms of a man right now, but in terms of a patient. What she saw wasn't six foot two of man; she saw a sore knee. An old injury playing up that needed to be looked at and soothed.

Gently she examined his knee. 'Tell me where it hurts, and don't be stubborn about it—because I can't help you if you're not honest with me.'

'Do you talk to all your patients like this?' he asked.

'Just the awkward ones.'

He guessed he deserved that. 'OK. It hurts there. And there.' He gave a sharp intake of breath. 'And there.'

'All righty.' She grabbed a towel and spread it across her lap. 'Leg. Here. Now.'

His bare leg astride her body.

Uh-oh. How on earth was he meant to stop his thoughts doing a happy dance?

'Yes, ma'am,' he drawled, hoping she didn't have a clue what was going through his head right now.

Her hands had been gentle when she'd examined his knee. Now they were firm. There wasn't anything remotely sexual about the way she touched him, and he had to grit his teeth on more than one occasion.

But when she'd finished the deep-tissue massage, he could move an awful lot more easily.

'You're very good at that,' he said when she'd finished and he'd put his tracksuit bottoms back on. 'Thank you.'

'Better?' she asked.

He nodded. 'Sorry for being snippy with you.'

She shrugged. 'You were in pain. Of course you were going to be snippy. It's forgotten.'

'Thanks. I owe you one,' he said lightly, expecting her to brush it aside.

To his surprise, she looked thoughtful. 'I wonder.'

'Wonder what?'

'I do need a favour, actually, and you'd be perfect.'

He still wasn't following this. 'For what?'

She took a deep breath. 'My best friend's getting married in three weeks' time. And I'm under a bit of pressure to take someone to the wedding with me. My family's convinced that I need someone in my life, and I can't get them to see that I'm perfectly happy just concentrating on my career.'

'You want me to go to a wedding with you?'

'Yes.'

'As your partner?'

She grimaced. 'I'm not asking you on a date, Jared. I'm asking you to do me a favour.'

'To be your pretend boyfriend.'

'For one day. And an evening,' she added.

Go with her to a wedding.

She'd just made his knee feel a lot better. And this would be payback.

But…a *wedding.*

Where people promised to love, honour and cherish, until death did them part.

Vows he'd taken himself, and had meant every single word—although it turned out that Sasha hadn't. For all he knew, Tom hadn't even been her first affair. He'd been so clueless, thinking that his wife was happy, when all the time she'd been looking for something else.

Sasha had broken every single one of her vows.

She'd lied, she'd cheated—and then she'd made a crucial decision without talking it over with him. A decision that had cut Jared to the quick because he really couldn't understand her reasoning and it was totally the opposite of what he'd wanted. Even *if* the baby hadn't been his, it would still have been hers. They could've worked something out.

Except she hadn't wanted to. The only person she'd thought about had been herself. Not him, not the baby, not the other man who also might've been the baby's father—as she'd been sleeping with them both, she'd had no idea who the father of her baby was.

To go and celebrate someone else making those same vows when he'd lost his faith in marriage…that would be hard.

'If it's a problem…' her voice was very cool '…then forget I asked.'

He didn't want to tell Bailey about the mess of his divorce, Sasha's betrayal and the termination. He didn't want her to pity him. Besides, he owed her for helping him with his knee. 'OK. I'll do it.'

He knew it sounded grudging, and her raised eyebrow confirmed it. He sighed. 'Sorry. I didn't mean to sound quite so—well—Herod-ish.'

That netted him the glimmer of a smile. 'Knee still hurting?' she asked.

It would be an easy excuse. But he thought she deserved the truth. 'Let's just say I've seen a lot of divorces.' He'd been through a messy one, too. Not that she needed to know that bit. 'So I guess my view of weddings is a bit dark.'

'This one,' Bailey said, 'is definitely going to work. My best friend used to be engaged to a total jerk, but thankfully she realised how miserable her life was going to be with him, and she called it off.'

Interesting. So Bailey was a realist rather than seeing things through rose-tinted glasses? 'I take it you like the guy she's marrying?'

She nodded. 'Aaron's a genuinely nice guy. And he loves Joni as much as she loves him. It's equal.'

Did that mean Bailey had been in a relationship that hadn't been equal, or was he reading too much into this?

'Plus,' she said, 'I happen to know the food's going to be good—and the music. Joni's brother has a band, and they're playing at the evening do.' She paused. 'Dinosaur rock. They're seriously good. So I think you'll enjoy that.'

'You don't need to sell it to me. I've already said I'll go with you, and I keep my word.'

Funny how brown eyes could suddenly seem so piercing. And then she nodded. 'Yes. You have integrity. It's better to be grumpy with integrity than to be charming and unreliable.'

That *definitely* sounded personal. And it intrigued him. But if he asked her any more, then she'd be able to ask him things he'd rather not answer. 'Let me know when and where the plus-one thing is, then,' he said instead.

'Thanks. I will.'

Bailey couldn't stop thinking about Jared on the way home. The world of football was pretty high profile—as much as the worlds of music and Hollywood were—and the gossip magazines were forever reporting divorces and affairs among sporting stars. But something in Jared's expression had made her think that it was a bit more personal than that. Was Jared divorced? Not that she'd pry and ask him. But it made her feel a bit as if she'd railroaded him into agreeing to be her partner at the wedding. And that wasn't fair.

When she got home, she texted him: You really *don't* have to go to the wedding.

The answer came back promptly: I said I'd do it. I'll keep my word.

Typical Jared. Stubborn.

Well, she'd given him the chance to back out. But

hopefully he wouldn't hate it as much as he seemed to think he would. OK, thanks, she texted back, and added all the details of the wedding.

The next day was one of Bailey's clinic days at the London Victoria. Her first patient was a teenager who'd been injured playing tennis.

'Viv landed awkwardly in training,' Mr Kaine said. 'She said she felt her knee give and heard a popping sound. And her knee's started to swell really badly.' He indicated his daughter's knee. 'It hurts to walk.'

'It's just a sprain, Dad. It'll be fine,' Vivienne said. 'Let's stop wasting the doctor's time and go home.'

'No,' he said firmly. 'You're going to get this checked out *properly*.'

It sounded as if Mr Kaine was putting his daughter's welfare first and would support her through any treatment programme—which was a good thing, Bailey thought, because what he'd just described sounded very like the injury that had finished Jared's career. Damage to the anterior cruciate ligament.

She pushed Jared to the back of her mind. Not here, not now. Her patient came first.

'Thank you for giving me the background, Mr Kaine. That's very useful,' she said cheerfully. 'Vivienne, would you mind if I examine your knee?' she asked.

The girl rolled her eyes, as if she thought this was a total waste of time, but nodded. She flinched when Bailey touched her knee, so clearly it hurt to the touch and Bailey was very, very gentle as she finished examining the girl's knee.

'I'm going to send you for an MRI scan to confirm it,' she said, 'but I'm fairly sure you've torn your anterior cruciate ligament. I'm afraid you're going to be out of play for a little while.'

Again, she thought of Jared. He must have had a similar consultation with a doctor at a very similar age.

'What? But I *have* to play! I've got an important tournament next week,' Vivienne said, looking horrified. 'I've been training for months. I can't miss it!'

However bad the girl felt about it, she had to face up to the severity of her injury. She wouldn't even be able to have a casual knockabout on the court for a while, let alone play an important match on the junior tennis circuit. Not even if her knee was strapped up.

'Viv, you have to listen to the doctor. She knows what she's talking about,' Mr Kaine said. 'I'm sorry, Dr Randall. You were explaining to us what Vivienne's done to her knee.'

Bailey drew a couple of diagrams to show Vivienne how the ligaments worked and what had happened to her knee. 'You have a complete tear of the ligament—it's the most common type, and I'm afraid it also means you've damaged the other ligaments and your cartilage.'

'Will it take long to fix?' Vivienne asked. 'If I miss this tournament, can I play in the next one?'

'I'm afraid that's unlikely,' Bailey said. 'You're going to need surgery.'

'Surgery?' The girl looked totally shocked. 'But—but—that means I'll be out for ages!'

'The injury won't heal on its own and unfortunately you can't just stitch a ligament back together. Vivienne,

I'll need to send you to a specialist surgeon. I know Dr Martyn here quite well, and he's really good at his job, so I promise you'll be in the best hands.' She looked up at Vivienne's father and gave him a reassuring smile, too. 'He'll replace your torn ligament with a tissue graft, which will act as a kind of scaffolding for the new ligament to grow on. You'll be on crutches for a while afterwards.'

'Crutches. I can't play tennis with *crutches*.' Vivienne shook her head. 'This can't be happening. It just can't.'

'Crutches will stop you putting weight on your leg and damaging the structure of your knee further,' Bailey said. 'I can also give you a brace to protect your knee and make it more stable. But I'm afraid it's going to be at least six months until you can play sports again. After the surgery, you'll need a rehab physiotherapy programme—that means exercises tailored to strengthen your leg muscles and make your knee functional again.'

'Six months.' Vivienne closed her eyes. 'Oh, my God. My life's over.'

'Viv, it's going to take six months for you to get better. I know it feels bad, but it's not the end of the world. You'll come back stronger,' Mr Kaine said.

It was good that her dad was so supportive, Bailey thought. But Vivienne was clearly finding it hard to adjust.

'If you go back to playing too soon, you might do more damage to your knee and you'll be out of action for a lot longer,' Bailey said. 'The good news is that the way they do surgery today is a lot less invasive. It's keyhole surgery, so that means you'll have less pain, you'll spend less time in hospital and you'll recover more quickly.'

'When will the surgeon do it?' Mr Kaine asked. 'Today? Tomorrow?'

'Not straight away,' Bailey said. 'We need the inflammation to go down a bit first, or there's a risk of scar tissue forming inside the joint and you'll lose part of your range of motion.'

'And that means I won't be able to play tennis the way I do now.' Vivienne bit her lip. 'Not ever.'

'Exactly,' Bailey said. 'What you do next is going to make the biggest difference. For the next seventy-two hours you need to remember RICE—rest, ice, compression and elevation.' She talked Vivienne through the treatment protocols.

'What about a hot-water bottle to help with the pain?' Mr Kaine asked.

Bailey shook her head. 'Not for the first three days—and no alcohol, either.'

Vivienne rolled her eyes. 'Fat chance of that. Dad's part of the food police. We were told in sixth form that as soon as you're sixteen you're allowed a glass of wine with your meal in a restaurant. But Dad won't let me.'

'Alcohol slows your reactions and you can't play tennis with a hangover,' he said. 'At least, not well—and I should know because I've tried it.'

Bailey smiled at him. He was definitely going to need a sense of humour to help coax Vivienne through the next few months of a total ban from tennis. 'No running or massage, either,' she said. 'But I can give you painkillers—ones that will help reduce the inflammation as well as the pain.' She looked at Mr Kaine. 'Are there any allergies I need to know about?'

'No,' he confirmed.

'Good.'

'Six months,' Vivienne said again, making it sound like a life sentence.

'Better to make up a bit of ground in a couple of months,' Bailey said softly, 'than to go back too soon, do more damage and then have to spend even more time recovering.'

'She's right, love.' Mr Kaine rested his hand briefly on his daughter's shoulder. 'So what happens after the operation?'

'For the first three weeks the physio will concentrate on increasing the range of motion in the joint but without ripping the graft,' Bailey said. 'By week six Vivienne should be able to use a stair-climber or a stationary bike to maintain the range of motion and start strengthening her muscles, and then the plan will be to work to full rehab over the next few months. You need a balance between doing enough to rehabilitate the knee,' she said gently to Vivienne, 'but not so much that you damage the surgical repair and make the ligament fail again.'

'Six months,' Vivienne said again, looking totally miserable.

'There are other things you can work on that won't involve your knee,' Mr Kaine said cheerfully. 'Chin up.'

Vivenne just sighed.

Once Bailey had sorted out a compression bandage and painkillers, she said, 'I'll see you again in a couple of days and then we'll see the surgeon. Reception will make an appointment for you. Call me if you're worried about anything. But we'll get your knee fixed and you'll be back to playing tennis again.'

And, some time before their next appointment, there was someone she needed to talk to who might just be able to give her some really, really good advice to help Vivienne cope with the next few months.

She hoped.

CHAPTER FIVE

THERE WAS NEVER going to be a perfect time to ask Jared, Bailey knew, and she certainly wasn't going to ring him outside office hours to talk it through with him. But once the next training session with the team was under way and she was seated on the bench next to him, she turned to him.

'Can I ask you for some professional advice—something that's a bit personal?'

He looked completely taken aback. 'Why?'

She'd known before she asked that this was going to be difficult; Jared had never talked to her about his injury. But he was the only one who might be able to help. 'I have a patient, a teenage female tennis player. She landed awkwardly from hitting a ball.'

'And?'

'She, um, has a complete tear to her ACL.'

He went very, very still and guilt flooded through her.

'I know I'm being intrusive,' she said, 'and I apologise for that. I really don't mean to dredge up bad memories for you about your own injury. And, yes, I did look you up, so I know what happened. I could hardly ask you, could I?'

'I guess not.'

Talk about inscrutable. Jared's voice and his face were completely expressionless, so she had absolutely no idea how he was feeling right now. Worrying that she was risking their newfound truce, but wanting to get some real help for her patient, she said, 'The reason I'm asking you is because when it happened you were about the same age as she is now, so you know how it feels. Her dad's really supportive and he's trying to get her to rest her knee sensibly so she'll recover well from the operation, but she's distraught at the idea that she's going to lose a lot of ground over the next year. So I guess what I'm asking you is if there's anything I can tell her to help her deal with it a bit better.'

For a moment she thought Jared was going to blank her, but then he blew out a breath. 'That really depends on whether she's going to recover fully or not.'

Clearly he hadn't recovered fully enough to be able to resume his sports career. But she knew that if she tried to give him a hug—out of empathy rather than pity—he'd push her away, both literally and figuratively. So she kept the topic to a discussion about her patient. 'I think there's a very good chance she'll recover fully. The surgeon's brilliant,' Bailey said.

'Good.'

A complete tear to the anterior cruciate ligament. Jared knew exactly how that felt. Like the end of the world. When all your dreams had suddenly exploded and there wasn't any meaning in your life any more. You couldn't do the one thing you knew you were really good at—the thing you were born to do. In a few moments it was all gone.

At seventeen, it had destroyed him. Knowing that his knee wouldn't hold up in the future—that if he played again he was likely to do more damage to his knee and eventually he'd be left with a permanent limp. Knowing that he'd never play for his country again. He'd been so sure that nothing would ever be that good for the rest of his life.

Although it hadn't actually turned out that way. He enjoyed his job, and he was still involved with the game he loved.

He blew out a breath. 'It's a lot to deal with. Especially at that age. Tell her to take it one day at a time, and to find someone she can talk to. Someone who won't let her wallow in self-pity and will talk her into being sensible.' He'd been so, so lucky that the team's deputy coach had been brilliant with him. He'd let Jared rant and rave, and then told him to look at his options, because there most definitely *would* be something he could do.

What goes around comes around. It was time to pass on that same advice now. 'Tell her there will be something else. At first it'll feel like second best, but she'll find something else she loves as much. Even if it doesn't look like it right now.'

'Thank you,' Bailey said quietly. 'I appreciate it—and I'm sorry I brought back bad memories. That really wasn't my intention.'

He shrugged again. 'It was a long time ago.'

She said nothing, simply waited, and he was surprised to find himself filling in the gap. 'At the time, it was bad,' he admitted. 'I wanted someone to blame for the end of my dreams—but I always knew that the tackle wasn't deliberate. It was just something that went wrong and it could've happened to anyone. The guy who tackled me felt as guilty as hell about it, but it wasn't his fault. It wasn't anyone's fault. It was just an accident. Wrong time, wrong place.' He paused. 'And I found something else to do.'

'Did you think about coaching?' She put a hand across her mouth. 'Sorry. You don't have to answer that.'

He liked the fact that she wasn't pressuring him. There was no malice in Bailey Randall. She just wanted to help her patient, and he'd had first-hand experience of what her patient was going through right now. Of course she'd want to know how he'd coped. 'I thought about it,' he said. 'Though I knew I was too young to be taken seriously when my knee was wrecked. At seventeen, you don't really have enough experience to coach a team.'

'So why did you choose medicine? That's—well, a huge change of direction.'

'My family are all GPs,' he said. 'I'd always thought I'd join them. I guess it was a surprise to everyone when I was spotted on the playing field at school and the local team took me on for training.' He shrugged. 'Then I had to make a choice. Risk trying for a career in football, or do my A-levels. My parents said to give it a go—I could always take my A-levels later if it didn't work out. And when I was picked for the England squad…they threw one hell of a party.'

He smiled at the memory. 'When my knee went, it hit me pretty hard. But I was lucky in a way, in that I could fall back on my original plans—I just took my A-levels two years later than I would've done if I hadn't tried for a career in sport.'

'So you trained as a GP?' she asked.

'No. I ended up training in emergency medicine,' he said. 'I liked the buzz. Then, like you, I had a secondment to a sports medicine department. And then it occurred to me that I could have the best of both worlds—I could be a doctor in the sport I'd always loved.'

'That's a good compromise,' she said.

Again, to his surprise, he found himself asking questions and actually wanting to know the answers rather than being polite. 'What about you? Is your family in medicine?'

'No—my family has a restaurant. Mum's the head chef, Dad's front of house and my brothers are both kitchen serfs.' At Jared's raised eyebrows, she added swiftly, 'Joke. Gio is Mum's deputy—he's going to take over when she retires. And Rob's probably the best pastry chef in the universe and he makes the most amazing wedding cakes. They're planning to expand the business that way, too.'

'Didn't your parents expect you to join the family firm?'

She shook her head. 'Mum and Dad always said that we should follow our hearts and do what we love, and that they'd back us whatever we decided. Rob and Gio were always in the kitchen making stuff, so it was obvious what they wanted to do. And I was always bandaging my teddies when I was a toddler.' She grinned. 'And the dog, if I could get him to sit still.'

He could just imagine that. He'd bet she'd been the most determined and stubborn toddler ever. 'A born doctor, then?'

'I've no idea where it came from. It was just what I always wanted to do,' she said. 'And I guess I was lucky because my family's always supported me. Even when I nag them about healthy eating and saturated fat.' She laughed. 'Though the nagging has at least made them put some super-healthy options on the menu—that's gone down really well with the customers, so I feel I've made some kind of contribution to the family business, apart from volunteering to taste-test any new stuff.'

Clearly Bailey was very close to her family and Jared had a feeling that they adored her as much as she obviously adored them. And she cared enough about her patients to do something outside her comfort zone; he knew that it must've been daunting to ask him about the injury he didn't talk about, but she'd asked him to see if he could help her patient rather than because she wanted to pry into his life.

'Your patient,' he said. 'When are you seeing her next?'

'Friday morning.'

'I could,' he suggested, 'come and have a word with her, if you like.'

'Really?' The way she smiled at him made him feel as if the sun had just come out at midnight.

'It might help her to talk to someone who's been there and come out just fine on the other side,' he said.

'I think it would help her a lot. If you're sure.' She bit her lip. 'I mean, I don't want to rip open any old scars.'

He smiled. 'It was a long time ago now. And I was lucky—I had someone who helped me. It's my chance to pay it forward.'

She rested a hand on his arm; even through his sleeve, her touch made his skin tingle. 'Thank you, Jared. I really appreciate it.'

'No worries,' he said.

On Friday, Bailey saw Vivienne in her clinic at the London Victoria and examined her knee. 'Obviously you've followed my advice about rest, ice, compression and elevation,' she said.

Vivienne nodded. 'I want to play again as soon as possible. That means doing what you say.'

Bailey smiled. 'Well, you'll be pleased to know you're good to go for surgery and you can see the surgeon this afternoon.'

'That's great news,' Mr Kaine said, patting his daughter's shoulder. 'Thank you.'

'Actually, there is something else,' Bailey said. 'Obviously I wouldn't dream of breaking patient confidentiality, but I happen to know someone who had an ACL injury at your age, and I asked him for some advice for someone in your position.'

'Was he a tennis player?' Vivienne asked, looking interested.

'No, he was in a different sport,' Bailey said, 'but the injury and the rehab are the same. Actually, he offered to come and have a chat with you. He's waiting outside, if you'd like a word.'

Vivienne turned to her father, who nodded. 'That'd be great. Thanks.'

Bailey opened her office door and looked out; Jared glanced up, caught her eye and came to the door. 'She'd like to talk to me?' he asked.

'Yes. And thank you. I owe you,' she said.

'No. I'm just paying it forward,' he reminded her. 'Just as your patient will pay it forward, one day.'

It was a nice way of looking at it, Bailey thought. She brought him into the room and introduced him to Vivienne and Mr Kaine.

'Well, I never. Jared Fraser—the England footballer. I remember watching you play years ago. You were amazing.' Mr Kaine shook Jared's hand. 'It's very good of you to come in and talk to us.'

'My pleasure,' Jared said.

'So do you still play for England?' Vivienne asked.

'No. Unfortunately, they couldn't fix my knee. Though that's *not* likely to be the case for you,' he emphasised, 'because Dr Randall tells me that you're a really good candidate for surgery. If you follow the rehab programme to the letter you'll be fine. Dr Randall asked me for my advice, and I thought it might be better for you to have it in person, just in case you have any questions.'

Vivienne nodded. 'Thank you very much, Mr Fraser.'

'Right now,' he said gently, 'it probably feels like the end of the world and you're worrying that you're going to lose so much ground against everyone else.'

She bit her lip. 'That's exactly how it feels.'

'So you need to take it one day at a time, and find someone you can talk to—someone who won't let you pity yourself, but will make you be sensible and get the right balance between doing enough work to strengthen your knee, but not so much that you damage it again and end up back at square one,' Jared said.

'That's good advice,' Mr Kaine agreed. 'I'll always listen, Vivi, but he's right—you do need someone else to talk to.'

'I was lucky,' Jared said. 'I had a great coach. And he made me see that although my knee wouldn't hold up enough for me to play at international level again, I had other options. I could learn to coach, or I could do what I ended up doing—I trained as a doctor, and I'm still part of the sport because nowadays I work with the youth team of a premiership division club. So even if there are complications in the future and you don't end up playing at this level again, you'll still have options—you can still be part of tennis.'

'I don't mean to be rude,' Vivienne said, 'but I don't want to be a coach or a doctor. I just want to play tennis. It's all I've ever wanted to do.'

'And you will play again,' Bailey said. 'But, as Dr Fraser said, you need to follow your rehab programme.'

'Waiting is the worst bit,' Jared said. 'You'll want to push yourself too hard. But don't. Use that time to study instead. Look at different techniques, look at the way your opponents play and use that to hone your strategy. To really succeed at a top level in sport you need just as much up here…' he tapped his head '…as you need the physical skills.'

'Vivi picked up a racket practically as soon as she could walk,' Mr Kaine said. 'I used to play—nothing like at her level—just at a club on Sunday afternoons, and her mum would bring her to watch. And she ended up joining in.' He ruffled her hair. 'When she started beating us hollow and she wasn't even ten years old, we knew we were seeing something special in the making. And you'll get that back, love. We just have to make sure we do everything the doctors tell us, OK?'

'OK,' Vivienne said.

Bailey smiled at them both. 'And I'll do my very best to help you get that knee back to how it was, so you can go and get those grand slams.'

'Can I be rude and ask, Mr Fraser, do you miss playing?' Vivienne asked.

'Sometimes,' Jared said. 'But I'm thirty-five now, so I'd be near the end of my professional playing career in any case. And I'm lucky because I really enjoy my job. It means I get the chance to help players fulfil their potential. If someone had told me that when I was your age, I would have laughed at them—but I really do feel I've achieved something when I see them grow and improve. So don't rule it out as something you might do when you're ready to retire from playing.'

Vivienne looked thoughtful, and Bailey could see that Jared's words had given her a different perspective—something that would make all the waiting during her rehab a lot easier. 'Thank you, Mr F—*Dr* Fraser,' she amended.

When the Kaines had left, Jared was about to follow

them out when Bailey stopped him. 'Thanks for doing that, Jared—you've made a real difference to her.'

'No worries.'

'If I wasn't up to my eyes in paperwork and appointments,' she said, 'I'd offer to take you for lunch to thank you properly. Or dinner—but I'm doing bridesmaid stuff for Joni tonight. So please consider this a kind of rain check.' She took a plain white patisserie box from her desk drawer and handed it to him.

'What's this?' he asked.

She smiled. 'A little slice of heaven. Don't open it now. Tell me what you think later.'

'OK.' He looked intrigued. 'I'll text you. Good luck for tonight.'

'Thanks.'

Later that evening, she had a text that made her laugh.

Best chocolate cake in the universe. Would very much like to help with more patients. Quite happy to be paid in cake.

I'll see what I can do, she texted back.

Funny, when she'd first met Jared, she'd thought him grumpy and surly and a pain in the neck. Now she rather liked his dry sense of humour and the quiet, sensible way he went about things.

But she'd better not let herself get too close. After the way her marriage to Ed had splintered, she just didn't trust herself to get it right next time. It was best to stick to being colleagues. Friends, too, maybe; but she'd have to dampen down the attraction that sparkled through her veins every time she saw him. To keep her heart safe.

CHAPTER SIX

'JONI, YOU LOOK BEAUTIFUL,' Bailey said, surveying her best friend.

'So do you.' But Joni also looked worried. 'Bailey, are you sure you're OK?'

'Of course I am—why wouldn't I be?'

'Because I remember the last time that one of us was in a bridesmaid's dress and the other was the bride,' Joni said softly.

Bailey's wedding day. A day so full of promise. A day when she'd thought she couldn't be happier… And then, two short years later, she'd discovered that she couldn't be any more unhappy when her whole world crashed down around her. 'I'm fine. More than fine. Don't give it another moment's thought,' she said brightly. Even if she hadn't been fine, no way would Bailey rain on her best friend's parade on her wedding day.

'I can't believe you're actually bringing Herod as your plus-one.'

Bailey groaned. 'Please don't call him that when you meet him—he'll be mortified.'

'You've been very cagey about him. So you're getting on OK together now?'

'We've reached an understanding.'

Joni raised an eyebrow. '*That* sort of understanding?'

'Absolutely not. Even if I was looking for someone, Jared Fraser wouldn't make my list of potentials.' That was a big fat lie—Jared Fraser was one of the most attractive men she'd met, particularly when he smiled—but hopefully Joni would be too distracted by all the bridal stuff going on to call her on it. Bailey hoped. 'No, he's just doing me a favour and taking a bit of heat off me where my family's concerned.'

'As long as you're OK.'

'Of course I'm OK,' Bailey reassured her. 'I'm thrilled that my best friend's getting married to the love of her life, and I get to follow her down the aisle in the most gorgeous bridesmaid's dress ever. Now, the car's going to be here at any second, so we need to get moving.'

Jared took a deep breath and walked down the path to the church. He hadn't been to a wedding since his own marriage to Sasha. And, despite Bailey's assurances that the bride and groom were right for each other, Jared still felt awkward. A cynic who'd lost his belief in marriage really shouldn't be here to celebrate a wedding. He half wished Bailey was going to be there with him to take his mind off it, but as she was Joni's bridesmaid he knew that she would be the very last person walking into the church, and she wouldn't be sitting with him, either.

He really should have asked if he could at least meet the bride and groom before the wedding, so he would know someone there. Right at that moment he was really regretting the impulse that had made him offer to be Bailey's 'plus-one'.

His only consolation had been the text she'd sent him that morning: See you at the church. And thank you. I appreciate it.

And being appreciated was nice. It had been a while since he'd last felt appreciated.

The usher greeted him with a smile. 'Bride's side or groom's?'

'Bride's,' Jared said, feeling a total fake.

'Sit anywhere on the left except the front two pews,' the usher said with a smile, handing him an order of service booklet.

Jared remembered the drill: anywhere except the front two pews, where the bride's and groom's immediate family would be sitting.

Over the next few minutes the church filled up. Two men walked down to the front of the church; one of them was obviously the groom and the other the best man, Jared thought.

A wedding.

A room full of hope, with everyone wishing the bride and groom happiness until the end of their days. But how often did that hope turn sour? How many people did he know who'd actually stayed together, apart from his parents and two of his siblings? Not that many.

The organist started to play the wedding march, and the bride walked in on her father's arm, looking gorgeous and deliriously happy. Behind her, carrying the long train and a bouquet of deep red roses—to match her knee-length dress and incredibly high-heeled shoes—was Bailey.

Jared had never seen her wearing make-up before, not even on that morning when they'd trained together and she'd come to breakfast in a suit. It was barely there—mainly mascara and a hint of lipstick, from what he could tell—but it served to show him that she was jaw-droppingly beautiful and didn't need anything to enhance her looks. Right now, she looked incredibly glamorous, a million miles away from the slightly scruffy doctor he was used to—the one who walked around the football pitch in tracksuit pants and a hoodie.

He caught her eye as she walked by and she actually winked at him.

And all the blood in his body rushed south.

Oh, help. They hadn't set any ground rules, so this might just be one of his biggest mistakes ever. God. He really should've agreed it with her beforehand. At the very least they should've agreed on no touching and no holding hands. And yet he was supposed to be her fake boyfriend. Everyone would expect him to hold her hand, put his arm round her, gaze at her adoringly, maybe even kiss her...

The idea of kissing her sent him into such a flat spin that he was barely aware of the marriage ceremony. But then the registers were signed and the bride and groom walked down the aisle, all smiles.

The usher handed him a box of bird-friendly confetti on the way out. Jared lined up on the side of the path to the church with everyone else and waited until the photographer directed them all to throw confetti over the happy couple.

He took a couple of photos on his phone and managed to catch one of Bailey with her head tipped back, laughing. The kind of picture that would make a rainy morning feel full of sunshine.

She came over to him while the bride and groom were being photographed on their own. 'Hey. Thanks for coming.'

'Pleasure.' And, actually, it was now. 'You, um, look very nice.'

'Thank you. So do you. I've never seen you in a proper suit before.' She grinned. 'I would say a suit "suits" you, but I need to find a better way of saying it.'

Funny, her easy manner put him at his ease, too. It suddenly didn't matter that this was a wedding, and all the darkness associated with the end of his own marriage just faded away—because Bailey was there and she *sparkled.*

'I'll introduce you properly to everyone at the reception,' she promised. 'Sorry, I should have organised this a lot better so I was travelling with you or something.'

'It's fine. You're the bridesmaid and you have things to do. I'll see you at the reception.'

She gave him another of those incredibly sexy winks. *'Ciao, bello.'*

The Italian side of her was really coming out today. He'd never really seen this before; but then again she'd never flirted with him before, either.

Oddly, he found himself looking forward to the reception—and what he really wanted to do was dance with her. Which was crazy, because he didn't even like dancing very much; but he had a feeling that Bailey did and that she'd be good at it.

He made his way to the hotel where the reception was being held, and joined the line-up of people waiting to kiss the bride and shake the groom's hand. Bailey came and found him in the line. 'Hey, there.'

'Hey.' How ridiculous was it that he should feel suddenly intimidated?

But Bailey took charge, making small talk until she could introduce him to the bride and groom. 'Jared, this is Joni and Aaron. Joni and Aaron, this is Jared Fraser.'

'Very pleased to meet you, Jared,' Joni said with a smile. Jared caught the meaningful look she gave Bailey, and wondered just what Bailey had told her best friend about him. 'Thanks for coming.'

'Thanks for inviting me. It was a lovely service, and you look gorgeous,' he said.

She kissed his cheek. 'You're too sweet. I knew Bailey was lying when she said you were grumpy.'

He laughed. 'I can be.' He gave Bailey a pointed look. 'Though so can she.'

'No way—she's the endorphin queen,' Joni said. 'Bailey believes endorphins are the answer to absolutely everything.'

Jared went hot all over, thinking just how endorphins could be released and how much he'd like to do that with her. He really hoped nobody could read his thoughts. But he managed to pull himself together and shook Aaron's hand. 'Congratulations, both of you, and I hope you'll be very happy together.'

They exchanged a glance, and he could see just how much they adored each other. So maybe Bailey was right and this would have a happy ending. Maybe he should start to believe in love again.

'Righty.' Bailey tucked her arm into his. 'Let's get this over with. Come and meet my lot. They're the nicest family in the world, but I'm going to apologise in advance because they're a bit—well—full on.'

'Italian,' he said.

She nodded. 'Even though Dad's English, living with my mum and the rest of us has kind of made him Italian.'

'That's nice,' Jared said, and let her lead him over to her family.

'Jared, this is my mother, Lucia, my brothers, Roberto and Giorgio—Rob and Gio for short—and my dad, Paul.'

Jared shook hands and kissed cheeks as expected, and then turned to Bailey. 'How come you don't have an Italian first name?' he asked.

'Because I was born on Christmas Eve, and in my family it's tradition to watch *It's a Wonderful Life* every single Christmas Eve—including the year I was born, because Mum had me at home. So she really had to call me Bailey, after George's family.'

'It could be worse,' Lucia said with a grin. 'I could have called you Clarence.'

'Clarrie. Yes. That's *so* me.' Bailey flapped her hands in imitation of an angel's wings and laughed.

'She's kept you very quiet, Jared,' Lucia said.

'Because we haven't known each other very long, and I know what you're like, Mamma,' Bailey said. She switched into rapid Italian; clearly she was asking her mother not to interrogate him or embarrass her, Jared thought. Mischief prompted him to ask her if she realised that he spoke Italian, just to tease her; but, knowing Bailey, she'd call his bluff and speak in Italian for the rest of the evening, so he resisted the temptation. Just.

'Sì, sì, bambina mia.' Lucia pinched Bailey's cheeks, and then continued her interrogation. 'So where did you meet, Jared?'

'At work,' he said carefully.

'So you're a doctor?'

'For a football team, yes.'

Bailey's dad smiled at him. 'Which one?'

Jared named the premier division club. 'I work with the youth team—and they've got real potential.'

'Oh, the team Bailey's testing her box of tricks on?' Paul asked. 'I thought you said the team doctor was about to retire, Bailey?'

'He did. Jared took over from him,' Bailey said. 'Are you going to grill the poor man all night, or can we talk about something else—like how gorgeous my best friend looks in her lovely floaty dress?'

'She does indeed.' Paul gave her a hug. 'And so do you, darling. We don't see you dressed up like this very often.'

'If you came to see me with a sports injury and I looked like this when I treated you, you'd be worried that I didn't have a clue what I was talking about and think that you were going to be injured and in pain for the rest of your life,' she said with a grin. 'That's why I don't dress like this very often.'

It turned out that they were at a table with Bailey's family for the wedding breakfast, and Jared was surprised by how easily they included him in the conversation, as if they'd known him for ever. In turn, he got them to talk about the restaurant—and learned a lot about Bailey as a child. Her family was merciless in telling tales; but they clearly adored her, because she was laughing along with the rest of them and giving just as good as she got by telling tales about them, too.

He discovered that Bailey, when she was with her family, was incredibly tactile, so it was just as well they hadn't agreed a no-touching rule, because she would've broken it several times a minute. He already knew that she talked with her hands, but this was something else. She touched his arm, his shoulder, his face, his hair. He wasn't used to that at all, but he was surprised to discover that he liked it. That he wanted more.

Though that wasn't part of the deal. He was her fake partner for tonight, not her real one, he reminded himself.

The food was excellent, but best of all was the cake. 'This has to be the best cake I've ever had in my life,' he said.

Rob looked pleased. 'I'm glad you like it. Actually, it's one of mine,' he said diffidently.

'Bailey said you were good—but she didn't say you were *this* good. And I'm going to beg for seconds.'

'You weren't listening properly,' she said, cuffing his arm. 'I told you Rob was the best pastry chef in the universe. And who do you think made that chocolate cake I gave you?'

'Oh, now, with those two pieces of evidence, I agree completely,' Jared said with a smile.

Funny, he'd been faintly dreading the reception. But it was all easy, from chatting at the tables to listening to the speeches. And then finally the band started playing and the dancing began. The bride and groom danced together first, followed by Bailey and the best man. Jared couldn't take his eyes off her. The way she moved was so graceful, so elegant. This was yet another side to the clever, slightly acerbic doctor he was used to. She'd turned out to be full of surprises.

And then she came over to him. 'Dance with me?'

How could he say no? Especially when he'd been wanting to hold her close all day, and this was the perfect excuse.

When he danced with her, it was the first time he'd ever noticed her perfume; it reminded him of an orange grove in full bloom, yet with a sweet undertone. Sparkly and warm, just like her personality. And he could feel the warmth of her body against his.

To keep his mind off that fact, he asked, 'Why do I recognise the guy playing guitar with the band?'

'That's Olly, Joni's brother—he was one of the ushers, so you would've met him at the church,' she explained.

'Oh.'

'Sorry about my family earlier. As I said, they're a little intense.'

'Don't apologise—I like them. They love you,' he said, 'and it's pretty clear they worry about you.'

She rolled her eyes. 'I'm thirty years old. I can look after myself.'

'Families are supposed to worry about you,' he reminded her.

'Does yours worry about you?' she challenged.

He smiled. 'When I let them, yes.'

'So you're as bad as I am—except I bet you keep yours at bay by being grumpy.'

'And you keep yours at bay by sparkling,' he fenced.

'Sparkling?'

'Like vintage champagne in candlelight,' he said.

Oh, for goodness' sake. Anyone would think he'd been drinking way too much of the vintage champagne. He simply didn't wax poetic like that. But something about Bailey made the words flow and he couldn't stop them.

She smiled. 'You think I'm sparkly?'

'Very,' he admitted.

'Thank you—that's a really lovely thing to say. Especially as I've pretty much neglected you today, and you're doing me a huge favour by being here in the first place.'

'You haven't neglected me.' And he was suddenly really glad that he'd agreed to do this. Because he was seeing a new side to Bailey Randall—a side he really liked. Sweet and playful and totally charming; yet it was totally genuine.

He held her closer. Somehow they were dancing cheek to cheek, and his hand was splayed at the top of her dress. He could feel the warmth of her skin against his fingertips and it sent a thrill right through him. Right at that moment it felt as if it was just the two of them on the dance floor, with nobody else around for miles and miles and miles.

'Your back is perfect,' he murmured.

'Why, thank you, Dr Fraser.'

'Sorry.' He sighed. 'I didn't mean to say that. Ignore me.'

She pulled back slightly to look him straight in the eye. 'I wasn't being sarcastic—and I wasn't offended. Seriously, Jared, thank you for the compliment.'

Her mouth was beautiful; her lower lip was full and he itched to catch it between his.

Oh, this was bad.

Why was he thinking about kissing her?

'I noticed how perfect your back was when we trained together,' he said. And now he was making things much worse. He really needed to shut up.

She ran one finger down his sleeve. 'And I noticed your biceps when we trained together.' Her voice had grown husky. 'I like your biceps. They're perfect, too.'

He knew that he was supposed to be just playing the part of her partner, but right now he wanted to make it reality. So he dipped his head. Just a little bit. Just enough that his mouth could brush against hers.

She tasted of champagne and wedding cake—and he liked it. A lot.

He pulled back so he could look her in the eye and take his cue from her. If she wanted him to back off, he'd do it.

But her lips were ever so slightly parted and there was a sparkle in her eyes that he'd never seen before.

'Bailey, I really want to kiss you,' he whispered.

'I want you to kiss me, too,' she whispered back.

That was all the encouragement he needed. He dipped his head again and took his sweet time kissing her. Every brush of his mouth against hers, every nibble, made him more and more aware of her. And she was kissing him back, her arms wrapped as tightly round him as his were round her.

He wanted this to last for ever.

But then he became aware that the music had changed and become more uptempo, and he and Bailey were still swaying together as if the band was playing a slow song. He broke the kiss, and he could see the exact moment that she realised what was going on, too. Those gorgeous dark eyes were absolutely huge. And she looked as shocked as he felt. Panicked, almost.

This wasn't supposed to be happening.

'I, um…' she said, and tailed off.

'Yeah.' He didn't know what to say, either. What he really wanted to do was kiss her again—but they were in a public place. With her best friend and her family in attendance. And doing what he really wanted to do would cause all kinds of complications. He didn't want to get involved with anyone. Apart from that one awful evening when his best friend had persuaded him to try speed dating—an experience he never wanted to repeat—Jared hadn't dated since his divorce. No way was he setting himself up to get hurt again, the way he he'd been with Sasha—even though he knew that Bailey wasn't a bit like Sasha.

'I guess I ought to do some chief bridesmaid stuff and get the kids dancing,' she said.

And he ought to offer to help her. Except there was just a hint of fear in her eyes. He didn't think she was scared of him; maybe, he thought, she was just as scared of getting involved as he was. Especially given that she'd asked him to be her fake partner to keep her family happy. Bailey had obviously been hurt at some point, too, and they clearly worried about her.

'I guess,' he said. 'Do you, um, want a hand?'

'Do you like kids?'

That was an easy one. 'Yes, I do.' And he'd always thought he'd have children of his own one day. Sasha had taken the choice of keeping the baby away from him, and at that point he'd realised just how much he wanted to be a dad. But unless he took the risk of giving someone his heart—the right woman, someone he could really trust—that wasn't going to happen.

He pushed the thought away and concentrated on helping Bailey organise the children. She was a natural with them—they responded to her warmth. Just like him.

'If you could dance with some of the wallflowers,' she said quietly to him, 'that would be kind.'

Kind wasn't what he was feeling right now, but kind would be a hell of a lot safer. 'Sure,' he said.

Even though he was polite and made conversation with the women he danced with, he was totally aware of Bailey throughout the entire evening. Her smile, her sparkle, her warmth. And she made him ache.

He wanted her. Really wanted her. But he knew she'd panicked as much as he had when they'd kissed, so it was a bad idea. They needed to go back to being strictly colleagues. Somehow.

At the end of the evening he said his goodbyes to Bailey's family, trusting that she'd manage to get him out of a promise to see them soon.

'I guess this is it, then,' she said as she walked him to the door of the ballroom.

'I'll call a taxi and see you home first,' he said.

She shook her head. 'You don't have to do that.'

He smiled. 'Yes, I do. I'm old-fashioned. So let's not argue about it—just humour me on this one, OK?'

She didn't argue and let him organise a taxi. She didn't say much on the journey back to her place; although Jared desperately wanted to reach for her hand, he kept a tight rein on himself and simply joined her in sitting quietly.

When the taxi stopped, he paid the cabbie.

'Isn't he taking you home now?' Bailey asked, and he could see the panic in her eyes. Did she really think that he expected her to invite him in for a nightcap—or more?

'No. I'm seeing you to your doorstep and waiting until you're safely inside, then I'm taking the Tube home,' Jared said. 'And, yes, I know you can look after yourself, but it's been a long day and you're wearing incredibly high heels.'

'Point taken.' Her expression softened. 'Thank you.'

She let him escort her to her doorstep.

'Thank you for today,' she said. 'I really appreciate it.'

'No worries.' He leaned forward, intending to give her a reassuring—and strictly platonic—kiss on the cheek. But somewhere along the way one or both of them moved their head, and the next thing he knew his lips were skimming against hers.

What started out as a soft, sweet, gentle kiss quickly turned to something else entirely, and he was kissing her as if he was starving. She was kissing him right back, opening her mouth to let him deepen the kiss. And this felt so right, so perfect.

When she pulled away, his head was swimming.

'No,' she said. 'We can't do this.'

The panic was back in her face.

Her ex, whoever he was, must have really hurt her badly, Jared thought.

And he had no intention of making her feel worse.

'It's OK.' He took her hand and squeezed it. Just once. The way she'd squeezed his hand when he'd talked about his knee injury. Sympathy, not pity. 'You're right. We're colleagues, and *just* colleagues.'

And he needed to keep that in mind. He didn't want the complication of falling for someone, either. The risk of everything going wrong. Been there, done that and learned from his mistakes.

The fear in her eyes faded—just a fraction, but she'd clearly heard what he'd said.

'I'll see you at work,' he said.

'Yeah. I'll see you.' She swallowed. 'And I'm sorry.'

'There's nothing to be sorry for,' he said.

He waited until she'd unlocked her front door and closed it again behind her, and then he left to find the Tube station. It was better this way. Being sensible.

Wasn't it?

CHAPTER SEVEN

BAILEY SLEPT REALLY badly that night. Every time she closed her eyes, all she could see was Jared in that wretched suit, looking totally edible. Worse, her mouth tingled in memory of the way he'd kissed her.

OK, she'd admit it. She was attracted to Jared Fraser. Big time.

But, after the way her marriage had imploded, she wasn't sure she could risk getting involved with anyone again. Letting herself be vulnerable. Risking the same thing happening all over again. After the ectopic pregnancy she'd ended up pushing Ed away—physically as well as emotionally—because she'd been so scared of getting pregnant again.

So, as much as she would like to date Jared—and to take things a lot further than they had at the wedding—she was going to be sensible and keep things between them just as colleagues. Because she didn't want to hurt him, the way she'd hurt Ed.

Do you like kids?

And he'd said yes. She could imagine him as a father, especially after she'd seen him with the children at the wedding. And that was another sticking point. She wanted children, too. But the ectopic pregnancy had shredded her confidence. What if it happened again and her other tube ruptured, leaving her infertile?

She'd been terrified of getting pregnant again, and that had made her scared of sex—a vicious circle she hadn't been able to break. Technically, Ed had been unfaithful to her; but Bailey blamed herself for it, because he'd only done it after she'd pushed him away and refused to let him touch her. She knew that the break-up of her marriage was all her fault.

Since her divorce, until Jared, she hadn't met anyone she'd wanted to date. But how could she expect him to deal with all her baggage? It wouldn't be fair.

So, the next morning, she sent Jared a text to clear the air—and also to make it very clear to him how she felt. And hopefully it would ease any potential awkwardness at work.

Sorry. Too much champagne yesterday. Hope I haven't wrecked our professional relationship.

Jared read the message for the fourth time.

Too much champagne? Hardly. He'd been watching Bailey. She'd had one glass, maybe two. With a meal. Most of the time she'd been drinking sparkling water—as had he.

It was an excuse, and he knew it. She'd looked so scared. As panicky as he'd felt. But why?

Next time he saw her, he decided, he'd get her to

talk to him. For now, he'd try to keep things easy between them.

Medicinal recommendation of a fry-up for the hangover, he texted back. See you on the pitch later in the week.

Facing Jared for the first time since the wedding made Bailey squirm inside. In the end, she decided to brazen it out. Hadn't he said she was sparkly? Then she'd go into super-sparkly mode. So she chatted to all the players, gave Archie a smacking kiss hello on the cheek—while making quite sure she was out of grabbing reach half a second later—and gave Jared a lot of backchat about being too old and too stuck in his ways to do yoga with the boys in the team.

To her relief, he responded the same way, and things were back to the way they used to be. Before he'd kissed her.

Almost.

Because during the training session she looked up from her laptop and caught him looking at her; those amazing blue eyes were filled with wistfulness.

Yeah.

She'd like to repeat that kiss, too. Take things further. But she just couldn't take the risk. She knew he'd end up being just as hurt as she was. She couldn't destroy him, the way she'd destroyed Ed.

'Can we have a word?' Jared asked at the end of the training session.

'Um—sure.' Bailey looked spooked.

He waited until the players and Archie had gone into the dressing room. 'Are you OK?' he asked gently.

'Of course. Why wouldn't I be?'

'You and me. Saturday night,' he pointed out.

'Too much champagne,' she said swiftly.

'I don't think so.' He kept his voice soft. 'I think you're running scared.'

She lifted her chin and gave him a look that was clearly supposed to be haughty, but instead he saw the vulnerability there. 'I'm not scared.'

'That,' he said, 'is pure bravado. And I know that, because this thing between us scares me, too.'

The fight went out of her. 'Oh.'

'So what are we going to do about it?' he asked.

'I'm not looking for a relationship. I'm fine being single.'

'That's what I've been telling myself, too.' He paused. 'Maybe we could be brave. Together.'

'I…' She shook her head. 'I'm not ready for this.'

'Fair enough.' He held her gaze. 'But when you are…'

She swallowed hard. 'Yeah. I, um, ought to let you get on.'

He let her go. For now. And he could be patient, because Bailey Randall was definitely worth waiting for.

Everything was fine for the next week, until Bailey's system picked up a marked problem. Maybe it was a glitch in the system, she thought, and decided to keep it to herself for the time being. But when the same result showed after the next session, and after she'd caught the tail end of the lads gossiping outside the dressing room, she knew that she was going to have to do something.

'Jared, can we have a quick word?' she asked quietly.

He frowned. 'Is something wrong?'

'I think so.' She gestured to her laptop, so he'd know that it was to do with the monitoring system and one of the players.

'Hadn't we better talk to Archie if you want to pull someone from the team?' he asked.

She shook her head and kept her voice low. 'This is a tricky one, and you're the only person I can talk to about it.'

'OK,' he said. 'I assume you mean somewhere quiet, away from the club.'

'Definitely away from the club,' she said. 'Yes, please.'

'Are you free straight after training?'

She nodded.

'We'll talk then.'

'Thank you.' And just knowing that she could share this with him and he'd help her work out what to do made some of the sick feeling go away.

After the session, Jared took Bailey to a café not far from the football club. 'Sit down, and I'll get us some coffee.' He remembered what she'd drunk at the gym. 'I take it you'd like a latte?'

She smiled. 'I'm half-Italian. You only drink lattes at breakfast. Espresso for me, please.'

He smiled back. 'Sure.'

'And can I be greedy and ask for some cake, too?' she asked. 'I don't care what sort, as long as it's cake.'

'It's not going to be up to your brother's standards,' he warned.

'Right now, I don't care—I need the sugar rush.'

Worry flickered down Jared's spine. Whatever she wanted to discuss with him was clearly something serious if she needed a sugar rush. And he'd noticed that she'd been much quieter than normal during the training session.

He came back with two coffees, a blueberry muffin and a double chocolate muffin. 'You can have first pick.'

'Thank you.' She took the blueberry one.

He sat down opposite her. 'Spit it out. What's worrying you?'

'You know how my system picks up if someone's underperforming?'

'Yes.'

'I'm worried about one of the players. I've heard the rumours that he's in danger of losing his place on the team because he hasn't been playing well for a while.'

'Darren,' Jared said immediately.

She nodded. 'And I heard the boys talking. He's not coping with the pressure.' She sighed. 'It's hearsay and I don't want to accuse him of something when he might be perfectly innocent, but…' Her eyes were huge with concern. 'I think he's drinking. Apart from it making his performance worse, he's not even eighteen yet—he's underage.'

Jared blew out a breath. 'I've known a few players

over the years who started drinking to handle the pressure, and it finished their careers.'

She looked miserable. 'I don't know what to do. If I tell Archie, then Darren will definitely lose his place. He'll be kicked out.'

'For breaking his contract,' Jared agreed.

'But if he *is* drinking, then it needs to stop right now, Jared. He's going to damage himself.'

'Agreed.'

'Maybe I'm being a bit paranoid and overthinking it. Have a look and see what you reckon.' She opened her laptop and drew up the graphs. Darren's performance had been very near his average in every session apart from the last two, where there was a marked difference.

'So you suspected it last time as well?' he asked.

She nodded. 'I wanted to monitor a second performance, just in case the first one was a one-off—a glitch in the programme or something.'

'No, I think your analysis is spot on. We need to tell Archie and Lyle Fincham.'

'But they'll kick him out.'

'Not necessarily. We can both put in a good word for him. He's not a bad kid—he's just made a mistake and he needs some help.' Jared shrugged. 'Extra coaching might make things easier for him, and I can design a workout programme tailored to his needs.'

'You'd do that for him?' She sounded surprised.

'Everyone makes mistakes. And everyone deserves a second chance,' he said. 'A chance to put it right.'

He hoped she'd think about it. And that she'd give them a second chance, too.

* * *

Mr Fincham wasn't available, so Jared and Bailey tackled Archie.

'So there's a problem with one of the players?' Archie asked.

Bailey nodded and talked the team coach through the computer evidence.

Archie frowned. 'So you think he's drinking?'

'You know as well as I do, some players do when they can't cope with the pressure,' Jared said.

'And it only makes things worse. Plus he's underage. If he can't cope, then he'll have to leave the team,' Archie said with a sigh. 'I can't have him being a bad influence on the rest of the lads.'

'Or,' Bailey said, 'you could give him another chance. We could talk to him and tell him what damage he's doing to himself—in graphic enough terms to make him stop.'

'And I can give him an extra training programme to help him brush up his skills and make him feel that some of the pressure's off,' Jared said.

'If the papers get hold of this, the muck will really hit the fan,' Archie said, and shook his head. 'No. He'll have to go.'

'Archie. It's happened *twice*. That's not so bad—he'll be able to stop. Give the boy a chance to come good,' Bailey urged.

'And what message does that give the others? That I'm soft on the kind of behaviour that destroys a team?'

'No. It tells them that you understand they're still

very young and some of them need a bit more guidance than others,' Jared said.

'Lyle won't be happy about it,' Archie warned.

'But you can talk him round. You're the team coach. He'll listen to you,' Bailey said.

Archie didn't look totally convinced. 'And what if Darren does it again?'

'Then there are all kinds of disciplinary options,' Jared said.

'But if we all give him the right support,' Bailey added, 'he won't do it again.'

Archie went silent, clearly thinking about it. 'All right,' he said. 'I'll square it with Lyle. But I'm going to read young Darren the Riot Act and make sure he knows that if he puts a single toe out of line from now on, he'll be out.'

'Thank you,' Bailey said.

'Everyone deserves a second chance,' Jared added. 'I think he'll make the most of it.'

Everyone deserves a second chance.

Could that be true for them, too? Bailey wondered.

Jared had clearly been thinking about it, too, because later that evening he called her. 'Are you busy?'

'I'm studying,' she said.

'Have you eaten yet?'

'Yes.' A sandwich at her desk. But it counted.

'Oh.' He paused. 'I wondered if you'd like to have dinner with me.'

Was he asking her on a date? Adrenalin fizzed

through her veins. Strange how Jared made her feel like a teenager. 'As colleagues?' she asked carefully.

'No.'

So he *did* mean a date. Excitement was replaced by skittering panic. 'I'll think about it.'

'Is my company really that bad?' he asked.

'No—no, it's not that, Jared. Not at all.' She sighed. 'It's complicated.'

'I can take a hint.'

She *would* like to have dinner with him; it was just that the whole idea of dating again scared her. How could she tell him, without dumping all that baggage on him? Telling him what had happened to her, and why her marriage had ended? She couldn't. She just couldn't. 'I, um, haven't dated in a while,' she said.

'Me, neither,' he said, surprising her. 'I'm seriously out of practice, too.'

Something else they had in common. Who, she wondered, had hurt him?

'I was thinking,' he said, 'we were a good team, this afternoon.'

'Yes.'

'And I was thinking,' he said, 'maybe we should give ourselves a chance to see if we could be a good team outside work.'

'Maybe,' she said.

'I could,' he suggested, 'cook dinner for you.'

'You can cook?'

He coughed. 'Don't be sexist. Especially as your brothers are both chefs.'

She smiled wryly. 'Yeah, I guess.'

'So—how about it?'

'If I say yes,' she said, 'then it's just between us?'

'You want to keep it a secret?' He sounded slightly hurt.

'I want to keep life simple,' she said. 'Can I think about it?'

'It's just as well I'm a sports doctor. My ego could really use some liniment right now,' he said dryly.

And now he'd made her laugh. He was the first man to do that in a long while. Maybe, just maybe, she should give this a try. Maybe everyone was right and it was time she learned to live again. And Jared might just be the man to help her do that.

'All right. Thank you, Jared. I'd like to have dinner with you. I don't have any food allergies and I'm not fussy about what I eat.'

'That was a quick decision.'

And she still wasn't sure it was the right one. Part of her really, really wanted to do it; and part of her wanted to run. 'When do you want to do it?' Oh, and that sounded bad. She felt her face heat. Worse still, that was a definite Freudian slip. Because any woman with red blood in her veins would want to go to bed with someone as sexy as Jared Fraser. 'Have dinner, I mean,' she added hastily.

'Tomorrow night?' he suggested.

'That's fine.' Big, fat lie. Now they'd actually set a date, the panic was back. In triplicate. 'I'll need your address.'

'Got a pen?'

'Give me two seconds.' She grabbed a pen. 'OK, tell

me.' She scribbled down his address as he dictated it. 'What time?'

'Seven?'

'Seven,' she confirmed. 'Can I bring anything? Pudding, maybe?' She could get Rob to make something special. Then again, Rob would tell their mother, and Lucia would go straight into interrogation mode. OK. She'd cheat and buy it from a top-end supermarket instead.

'No, that's fine. Just bring yourself,' he said.

And how scary that sounded.

Bailey was feeling antsy the next morning, and she was really glad that she was busy all day in clinic. There were the usual sprains and strains, although she did feel a bit sorry for the middle-aged woman who'd managed to give herself tennis elbow from taking her weightlifting training too hard and was horrified to learn it could take several months of rest before the tear in her ligament healed.

'Rest, ice it every couple of hours, take painkillers and use a support bandage when you exercise and whenever it's really sore,' Bailey said. 'And when you do go back to using weights, you'll need to drop the weights right down and take it very steadily. And don't do anything above your head before it's healed fully, or your rotator cuff in your shoulder will overcompensate for your elbow and you'll have to get over the damage to that, too.'

Mrs Curtis grimaced. 'I knew I shouldn't have done that last set. I just wanted to finish the last few reps, but I should've just admitted that I was tired and stopped there.'

'You'll know next time,' Bailey said. 'Come back and see me if it's not any better within a couple of weeks. It should heal on its own, but if it doesn't then a corticosteroid injection could help.'

'Thank you.' Mrs Curtis smiled wryly. 'That'll teach me to remember how old I am, not how old I feel.'

Bailey patted her shoulder. 'We all do it. Don't beat yourself up about it.'

She bought wine and chocolates on the way home, and changed her outfit three times before deciding that smart casual was the way forward—a little black dress would be way too much. Black trousers and a silky long-sleeved teal top would be better. She added her nice jet earrings to give her courage, put on a slightly brighter shade of lipstick than she would normally and then stared at herself in the mirror.

How long had it been since she'd gone on a first date? Or since someone had cooked for her? How did you even behave in these sorts of situations? She thought about calling Joni and asking for help—but, then again, it would make Joni think she was really serious about Jared, and… No, it was all too complicated. She had no idea how he made her feel, other than that he put her in a flat spin.

'It's dinner. Just dinner,' she told her reflection. 'Treat him as a friend. A colleague. And then everything will be fine.'

Except she knew she was lying. Because since that kiss, she hadn't thought of Jared as a colleague—or as a friend. And he hadn't asked her to dinner as a colleague or friend, either.

Would he kiss her again tonight?

And she wasn't sure if the shiver down her spine was anticipation or fear.

CHAPTER EIGHT

BAILEY'S PANIC GREW as she walked up the path to Jared's door. She almost didn't ring the bell and scuttled home to safety instead, but she knew that would be unkind and unfair. He'd gone to the effort of cooking her a meal, so the least she could do was turn up to eat it—even if she did feel way more jumpy than the proverbial cat on a hot tin roof.

She took a deep breath and rang the bell.

When he answered the door, she was glad she'd opted for smart casual, because he'd done the same. He was wearing black trousers and a dark blue shirt that brought out the colour of his eyes. She could feel herself practically dissolving into a puddle of hormones, and her social skills had all suddenly deserted her.

How had she forgotten just how gorgeous the man was?

And his biceps.

Don't think about his biceps, she told herself. Concentrate. Friends and colleagues.

She handed him the wine and chocolates. 'I forgot to ask you if I should bring red or white, so I played it safe—and I should've asked you if you like milk, white or dark chocolate.' Oh, help. Now she was gabbling and she sounded like a fool.

'These are just fine, and you really didn't need to bring them—but I appreciate it,' he said.

And, oh, that smile was to die for. The butterflies in her tummy went into stampede mode.

'Come in.' He stood aside and gestured for her to enter.

How come he didn't look anywhere near as nervous as she felt? How could he be so cool and relaxed when she was a gibbering wreck?

She followed him inside, her tension and anticipation growing with every step.

'We're eating in the kitchen. I hope that's OK,' he said, obviously trying to put her at ease.

'That's very OK, thanks.' His kitchen was gorgeous: a deep terracotta tiled floor teamed with glossy cream cabinets, dark worktops and duck-egg-blue walls. There was a small square maple table at one end with two places set. 'I really like the way you've done your kitchen,' she said.

'I'm afraid it's all my sister's idea rather than mine,' he confessed. 'When I bought this place and did it up, she offered to paint for two hours a day until it was done if I would let her choose the kitchen.'

It sounded as if he was as close to his family as she was to hers. 'So you're not really a cook, then?'

'Given that you come from a family of restaurateurs and chefs, I wouldn't dare claim to be a cook,' he said.

She smiled. 'I promise I won't go into food critic mode.'

He pretended to mop his brow in relief, making her smile. 'Can I get you a drink?'

'Yes, please—whatever you're having.'

He took a bottle of Pinot Grigio from the fridge and poured them both a glass. Bailey noted that all his appliances were built-in and hidden behind doors to match the rest of the cabinets. Efficient and stylish at the same time. She liked that. It was how she organised her own kitchen.

'Have a seat,' he said, indicating the table.

'Thanks.' She bit her lip. 'Sorry. As I said, it's been a while since I dated.'

'Me, too. And it's hard to know what to say. We could make small talk about the team and work—but then it wouldn't be like a date.'

'And if we ask each other about ourselves, it'll feel like—well—we're grilling each other,' she said.

'Or speed dating.' He grimaced. 'I let my best friend talk me into that one six months ago. Never, *ever* again.'

Speed dating was something she'd never done—along with signing up to an online dating agency or letting anyone set her up on a blind date. She'd made it clear to everyone that she was just fine as she was. 'Was it really that bad?'

'Probably slightly worse,' he said. 'But how do you meet someone when you get to our age?'

'You make us sound middle-aged.' She laughed, even though she knew what he meant. By their age, most people had already settled into a relationship or had a lot of baggage that made starting a new relationship difficult. It wasn't like when you were just out of university and there were parties every weekend where most of the people there were still single.

'I'm thirty-five—and sometimes I feel really middle-aged,' he said wryly, 'especially when I hear the seventeen-year-olds talking in the changing room about their girlfriends.'

She raised an eyebrow. 'They don't do that in front of me. Probably because they think I'll tell them off.' Then she groaned, 'Which means they think I'm old enough to be their mother, and at thirty I'm not *quite* that old.'

'Or maybe they've got a secret crush on you and don't want to sound stupid in front of you,' Jared suggested.

'I think,' she said, 'that might be a slightly worse thought. They're still practically babies!'

He laughed and raised his glass. 'To us,' he said, 'and finding some way to talk to each other.'

'To us,' she echoed, feeling ridiculously shy.

'I forgot to ask you if you like fish,' he said.

'I do.'

'Good. Though I'm afraid I cheated on the starter,' he admitted. 'Which is ready right now.'

He took two plates from the fridge: baby crabs served in their shell with a salad garnish, and served with thin slices of rye bread and proper butter.

'I don't care if you cheated. This is lovely,' she said.

The main course was sea bass baked in foil with slices of lemon, rosemary potatoes, fine green beans and baby carrots. 'This is fabulous,' she said. 'Super-healthy and super-scrumptious.'

He inclined his head in acknowledgement of the compliment. 'Thank you.'

Pudding was a rich dark chocolate mousse served in a tiny pot with raspberries.

'Now, this,' Bailey said after the first mouthful, 'is what you'd use to make any woman say yes.'

And then she realised what she'd said.

She put one hand to her face in horror. 'Please tell me I didn't say that out loud.'

'I'm afraid you did.' His voice had grown slightly husky, and his pupils were huge, making his eyes look dark.

She blew out a breath. 'Um. I don't know what to say.'

'If it helps, I didn't actually make it with the intention of using it to seduce you,' he said. 'Only…you've put an image in my head now.'

'An image?'

He nodded. 'Of me feeding you this, one spoonful at a time.'

So much for telling herself to treat this as just dinner with a friend. Right now, he'd put exactly the same image in her own head and she could hardly breathe. Especially as she could vividly remember what it had felt like when he'd kissed her.

What would happen if she held out her spoon to him? Would he let her feed the rich chocolate mousse to him? Or would he lean forward and kiss her?

Time hung, suspended.

Which of them would make the first move?

Dark colour was slashed across his cheekbones. And she could feel the heat in her own face. The beat of desire.

Would he kiss her again?

'I think,' he said, his voice even huskier now, 'we probably need coffee.'

And some distance between them so they could both calm down again. 'Yes,' she whispered.

Though she couldn't help watching him while he moved round the kitchen. For someone who was over six feet tall and so muscular, he was very light on his feet. He'd moved lightly when he'd danced with her, too. What would it be like if he…?

No.

Do not think of Jared Fraser naked, she told herself.

Except she couldn't get the idea out of her head.

What would it be like, making love with Jared?

Her face heating even more, she tried to push the thought to the back of her mind and concentrated on her pudding. He did likewise when he'd finished making them both an espresso.

Silence stretched between them like wires, tighter and tighter.

They needed to break the tension now. Right now. Before they did something stupid. Like kissing each other until they were both dizzy. Right at that moment it was what she really wanted him to do. And she didn't dare look at him in case he didn't feel the same—or, worse, in case he did. She wasn't sure which scared her more.

She sipped the coffee. 'This is good,' she murmured. Oh, for pity's sake. Where was her stock of small talk when she needed it? Why couldn't she talk to him about books and films and theatre?

Probably because her tastes were on the girly side and his would be decidedly masculine.

'I'm glad you like the coffee.' He paused. 'Would you like to sit in the living room?'

'Can I help you wash up first?'

'No. That's what a dishwasher is for,' he said.

Actually, it probably wouldn't be a good idea to work with him in the kitchen. It would be way too easy to brush against each other. Turn to each other. *Touch each other...*

She followed him into his living room. Everything was in neutral tones and comfortable. There were several framed photographs on the mantelpiece and she couldn't resist putting her coffee down so she could look at them more closely. His graduation, three more graduation photographs of what had to be his brothers and his sister as they looked so like him, wedding photographs of his brothers and sister, and various family portraits—including one of him with a small child.

His daughter? Or maybe she was his niece or his godchild. If he'd had a daughter, he would've mentioned it when they talked about kids at Joni's wedding, surely?

'Your family?' she asked.

'Yes. Also known as the doctors at Lavender Lane Surgery.' He smiled. 'They try to poach me onto the team every so often, but I like what I'm doing now.'

Then she came to a picture of a football team. Judging by the haircuts, she'd say the picture was nearly twenty years old. So it was pretty obvious what that represented. His first ever international match. But something had puzzled her for ages. 'So how come, given that you have a Scots accent and a Scots surname, you played for England?'

'I was born in London,' he said, 'and my mum's English—so technically I could have played for either team, but as I lived in London I guess it made more sense to play for England.' He smiled. 'Dad said if my team ever played the under-twenty-one Scotland team, his loyalties would've been really divided.'

'Like in our house. Whenever England plays Italy in the World Cup the boys end up cheering both sides.'

She picked him out immediately in the middle of the photograph. Mainly because that was the one she'd seen when she'd snooped on the Internet—not that she was going to tell him that. 'That's you at seventeen?'

'Yes—the first time I played for England.' He smiled. 'It was an amazing feeling. And when I scored that goal, it felt like all my birthdays and Christmases at once.'

'I bet.' On impulse, she turned round and hugged him.

Big mistake, because then his arms came round her, and he dipped his head to kiss her. His mouth was warm and sweet and tempting, and she found herself responding, letting him deepen the kiss.

He picked her up and carried her over to the sofa, still kissing her, then settled down with her on his lap.

Right at that moment she really wanted him to carry her to his bed. To take her clothes off, bit by bit, and kiss every inch of skin as he uncovered it. And then to touch her again, make her forget about everything in the universe except him…

But then reality rushed back in. She wasn't on the Pill. She hadn't needed to be, because she'd steered clear of relationships, let alone sex. Condoms weren't always effective. If they made love, what if she got pregnant, and what if…? She swallowed hard. She could still remember being rushed into the emergency department, the crippling pain in her abdomen followed by an even worse pain in her soul. And it froze her.

Jared was aware that Bailey had stopped kissing him back. He pulled away slightly and he saw she looked incredibly panicky. Something had clearly happened in her past, something that had put absolute devastation in her eyes.

He stroked her face. 'Bailey, it's all right. We can stop right now and I'm not going to push you.'

But the fear didn't seem to go away. She remained where she was, looking haunted.

'If you want to talk to me,' he said, 'I'll listen, and whatever you tell me won't go any further than me.'

'I don't want to talk about it,' she muttered.

'That's OK, too.' He kept holding her close. He had a few trust issues, too, thanks to Sasha cheating on him and then not giving him any say in keeping the baby. But he really liked what he'd seen of Bailey. It would be worth the effort of learning to trust and teaching her to trust him. They just needed some time.

Maybe it would help if he opened up a little first.

'I used to be married,' he said.

Bailey still looked wary, but at least she hadn't pulled away.

'I loved her. A lot. Sasha.' Funny, saying her name didn't make him feel as if he'd been put through the shredder any more. 'We were married for three years. I thought we were happy, but I guess she wanted more of a WAG lifestyle than I could give her—so that meant seeing a footballer rather than the team doctor.'

Bailey looked surprised. 'She left you for a footballer?'

Sasha had done a lot more than that, but Jared wasn't quite ready to talk about that bit. About how she'd totally shattered his world. How she'd had an affair, got pregnant, decided she didn't actually know who the father of her baby was as she'd been sleeping with them both, and had a termination without even telling him. 'Yes,' he said. 'She'd been seeing him for a while.'

'That's hard,' Bailey said.

He shrugged. 'It was at the time. But it was a couple of years ago now and I'm over it. We could probably just about be civil to each other if we were in the same room.'

'It's easier when you can be civil to each other,' she said.

'You're on civil terms with your ex now?'

It was her own fault, Bailey thought. She'd practically invited the question.

And she had to be honest with Jared. 'It wasn't Ed's fault that we broke up.' She'd shut her husband out and pushed him away. Sex had been out of the question because the fear of getting pregnant and having another ectopic pregnancy had frozen her. Ed had tried to get through to her, but her barriers had been too strong. And so he'd given up and turned elsewhere for comfort. She couldn't blame him for that. She hadn't been in love with him any more, but the way her marriage had ended still made her sad. 'Jared, I don't want to talk about it.

Not right now.' She wriggled off his lap. 'And I think I ought to go home.'

'I'll drive you. I only had one glass of wine so I'm under the limit.'

'I'll be fine on the Tube,' she said. 'To be honest, I could do with a bit of a walk to clear my head.'

'Would you at least let me walk you to the Tube station?'

She shook her head. 'I'll be fine. But thank you—that was a really nice meal, and I appreciate it.'

And she needed to get out of here now, before she did something really stupid—like resting her head on his shoulder and crying all over him. It wouldn't be fair to dump her baggage on him, and it really wasn't fair to lead him on and let him think that this thing between them was going anywhere, because it couldn't happen. She wasn't sure she was ready to get that involved with someone again—especially someone who'd been hurt in the past and had his own baggage to deal with. She was attracted to Jared, seriously attracted, but that just wasn't enough to let her take that risk. She didn't want it all to go wrong and for him to get hurt because of her.

When Bailey still hadn't texted him by lunchtime the next day, Jared knew that he'd have to make the first move.

But what had spooked her?

She'd flatly refused to talk about it, so it had to be something huge. He wasn't sure how to get her to talk to him without making her put even more barriers up.

In the end, he called her. He half expected her to

let the call go through to voicemail, but she answered. 'Hi, Jared.'

'How are you doing?' he asked softly.

'OK. Thanks for asking.'

'Want to go and get an ice cream or something?'

'Thanks, but I have a pile of work to do.'

It was an excuse, and he knew it. He could hear the panic in her voice, so he kept his tone calm and sensible. 'So if you have a lot of work to do, a short break will help refresh you.'

She sighed. 'You're not going to let this go, are you?'

'Nope,' he agreed.

'OK. What time?'

'Now?' he suggested. 'It's a nice afternoon.'

'Are you standing outside my flat or something?' she asked.

He laughed. 'No. I'm sitting in my kitchen, drinking coffee. Which is the alternative offer if you don't want ice cream.'

'You're pushy.'

'No. I'm not letting you push me away, and it's a subtle but important difference. I like you, Bailey,' he said. 'I think you and I could make a good team.'

There was a pause, and for a moment he thought he'd gone too far. But then she said, 'I like you, too.'

It was progress. Of sorts.

'I'll see you here in, what, an hour?' she asked.

'An hour's fine,' he said.

Jared turned up with flowers. Nothing hugely showy, nothing that made a statement or made Bailey feel under pressure; just a simple bunch of pretty yellow gerbera. 'They made me think of you,' he said.

Funny how that made her feel warm all over. 'Thank you. They're lovely.' She kissed his cheek, very quickly, and her mouth tingled at the touch of his skin. 'I'll put these in water.' Which was the perfect excuse for her to back away, and she was pretty sure he knew it, too.

They ended up going for a walk in the nearby park. And when Jared's fingers brushed against hers for the third time Bailey gave in and let him hold her hand. He didn't say a word about it, just chatted easily to her, and Bailey knew they'd turned another corner. That she was letting him closer, bit by bit.

Everything was fine until they walked past the children's play area.

'I used to take my niece to the park when she was small. Before she grew into a teen who's surgically attached to her mobile phone,' Jared said. 'The swings were her favourite. That and feeding the ducks.'

So that picture back at his place was of his niece. Even though Bailey's mouth felt as if it was full of sawdust, she had to ask the question. She needed to know the answer. Clearly he loved being an uncle—but would that be enough for him? 'Do you want children of your own?'

'Yes,' he said. 'I'd love to have kids—someone to kick a ball round with and read bedtime stories to. One day.'

Was it her imagination, or did he sound wistful? She didn't quite dare look at him. Besides, panic was flooding through her again.

He wanted children.

OK. So this thing between them was new. Fragile.

There were no guarantees that things would work out. But it wouldn't be fair of her to let things go forward without at least telling him about her ectopic pregnancy. If he wanted kids, he needed to know that might not be an option for her. Yet, at the same time it felt too soon to raise the subject. As if she were presuming things.

She'd have to work out how to tell him. And when.

'What about you?' he asked.

How did she even begin answering that?

It was true. She did want children. But that would mean getting pregnant, and the whole idea of that terrified her. It was a vicious circle, and she didn't know how to break it. 'One day,' she said. Wanting to head him off the subject, she added, 'The café's just over there. The ice cream's on me.'

To her relief, he didn't argue or push the subject further. But he didn't let her hand go, either. He was just *there*. Warm and solid and dependable, not putting any pressure on her.

So maybe, she thought, they might have a chance.

She just had to learn to stop being scared.

CHAPTER NINE

EVERYTHING WAS FINE until the following Monday, when Bailey was having her usual chicken salad with Joni after the yoga class.

Joni had been a bit quiet all evening, looking worried.

'Is everything OK?' Bailey asked.

'Ye-es.'

But she didn't sound too sure. Bailey reached across the table and squeezed her hand. 'What? You've had a fight with Aaron? It happens. One or both of you is being an idiot, one or both of you will apologise and it'll be fine.'

'It's not that.' Joni bit her lip and there were tears in her eyes. 'Bailey, I don't know how to say this—I mean, it's good news, but I also know that…'

At that moment Bailey knew exactly what her best friend was going to tell her. And, even though it was ripping the top off her scars, no way in this world was she ever going to do anything other than smile—and she was going to try and make this easy for Joni, because she knew exactly why her best friend was worried about telling her. 'Joni, are you about to tell me something really, really fantastic—that you and Aaron are going to be…?'

The sheer relief in Joni's eyes nearly broke her.

'I've been dying to tell you since before the wedding, but…'

Yeah. Bailey could remember how it felt. The moment she'd suspected she was pregnant, the moment she'd done the test and seen the positive result, the way Ed had scooped her up and swung her round when she'd shown him the test stick. The sheer joy and happiness of knowing that they were going to have a baby, start their own family… She'd managed to keep the news to herself for four whole days before it had been too much to keep it in any more; she'd sworn both her mum and her best friend to total secrecy and had burst into happy tears when she'd told them. And whilst Ed had been worried about her jinxing it by telling everyone too early and not waiting until the twelve-week point was up, she'd been so happy that she just couldn't contain her news any longer.

Maybe Ed was right—maybe she *had* jinxed it by telling everyone too soon.

She pushed the thought away. Not now. This was about her best friend's future, not the wreck of her own past.

'Oh, Joni, I'm so pleased for you.' And she was, she really was. Just because it had gone bad for her, it didn't mean that she couldn't appreciate anyone else's joy. 'That's fantastic news. How far are you?'

'Ten weeks. I went for the dating scan today,' Joni said almost shyly.

'Good.' So Joni definitely wasn't going to go through the pain and fear of an ectopic pregnancy. Bailey almost sagged back in her chair in relief. 'So do I get to see a photograph, then?'

'Are you sure you want to see it?'

At that, Bailey got up, walked round to the other side of the table and hugged her friend. 'Don't be so daft! Of course I want to see the scan picture—I'd be really upset if you didn't show me.'

Joni blinked away tears. 'Sorry. I just didn't want to bring back…you know. And I'm being so wet.'

'Hormones,' Bailey said with a grin. 'You'll be crying at ads with puppies and kittens in them next.'

She sat down again as Joni reached into her bag for a little white folder and handed it to her. She studied the ultrasound photograph. 'You can see the baby's head, the feet, the spine—this is incredible, Joni.'

'And the heart—it was amazing to see the baby's heart beating.'

Bailey hadn't even got to do that bit, so it wasn't as if this was bringing back memories; it was more the shadow of what might have been. And she wasn't going to let any shadows get in the way of her best friend's joy. She was fiercely determined to share that joy with her.

'Bailey, there's something else I wanted to ask you,' Joni said. 'Will you be godmother?'

'Of course I will! I'd be utterly thrilled.' Bailey blanked out the fact that she'd wanted Joni to be godmother to her baby, too. 'So that means I get to do all the fun things, all the cuddles and the smiles and the messy toys, and then I hand the baby back to you for nappy changes and the night feeds. Excellent.'

She could see in Joni's eyes that her best friend knew exactly how much effort this was costing her and how much she was holding back, but to her relief Joni didn't say it. She simply smiled and said, 'Bailey Randall, you're going to be the best godmother in the history of the universe.'

'You can count on that,' Bailey said. 'And you can still do yoga during pregnancy, though maybe…' She took a deep breath. 'Maybe you need to switch to a water-aerobics class, one of the special antenatal ones. And I'll do it with you for moral support.'

She meant it, she really did—even though it would be hard seeing all those women with their bellies getting bigger each week and trying not to think about how that hadn't happened for her.

Joni reached across the table and squeezed her hand. 'I know you would. This is yet another reason why I love you. But I'm not going to make you do that. I'll stick to yoga—I'll talk to Jenna before the next class and ask her where I need to take it down a notch.'

Bailey kept it together at the restaurant, but all the way home she could feel the pressure behind her eyes, the sobs starting down low in her gut and forcing themselves upwards. Once her front door was closed behind her, she leaned against the wall and slowly slid down until she was sitting with her knees up to her chin and her arms wrapped round her legs. Then and only then did she let the tears flow—racking sobs of loss and loneliness, regrets for what might have been.

She didn't hear the doorbell at first. She was dimly aware of a noise then recognised the sound. Who was it? She wasn't expecting anyone. She scrubbed at her face with her sleeve and took a deep breath. Right at that moment she wished she hadn't cut her hair short, because then at least she could've hidden her face a bit. As it was, she'd have to brazen it out. She opened the door just a crack. 'Yes?'

'Bailey, are you all right?'

'Jared?' She frowned. 'What are you doing here?'

'We have a meeting to discuss Darren, remember?'

She remembered now. Joni's news had knocked the meeting completely out of her head.

She couldn't let Jared see her in this state. 'Can we do it tomorrow?'

'Are you all right?' he asked again, and this time he pushed the door open. He took one look at her and said, 'No, you're not all right.' Very gently, he manoeuvred her backwards, closed the door behind them and cupped her face between his hands. 'You've been crying.'

'Give the monkey a peanut,' she muttered, knowing that she was being rude and unfair to him but hating the fact that he'd caught her at a weak, vulnerable moment.

But he didn't pay any attention to her words. 'Come on. I'll get you a drink of water.' He put one arm round her. 'Your kitchen's at the end of the corridor, yes?'

'Yes.'

She let him lead her into the kitchen and sit her down at the bistro table. He opened several cupboard doors before he found where she kept her glasses, then poured her a glass of water; she accepted it gratefully.

* * *

Jared waited until Bailey had composed herself for a bit before he made her talk. He knew she'd been to yoga with Joni and then out for dinner; it was their regular Monday night catch-up. But he'd wanted to have a quick chat with Bailey about Darren, their problem player, so she'd agreed to be home for nine o'clock and meet him at her place. Jared had been caught up in a delay on the Tube after a signal had broken down, so he'd been all ready to apologise for being twenty minutes late for their meeting, but that didn't matter any more. Clearly something bad had just happened.

'What's happened? Is Joni all right?'

'She's fine.' Bailey dragged in a breath. 'It was good news.'

'Good news doesn't normally make you cry or look as if you've been put through the wringer,' he pointed out.

'I'm fine.'

They both knew she was lying.

'It's better out than in,' he said softly. And he should know. He'd bottled it up for a while after Sasha, until his oldest brother had read him the Riot Act and made him go to counselling. And that had made all the difference.

'I can't break a confidence.'

'Under the circumstances, I think,' he said softly, 'that Joni would forgive you. Or maybe I can guess. Good news, from someone who's just got married—it doesn't take a huge leap of the imagination to know what that's likely to be.'

And it didn't take a huge leap of the imagination to put the rest of it together, either. What would make someone bawl their eyes out when they learned that their best friend was going to have a baby? Either Bailey couldn't have children or she'd had a baby and lost it. Miscarriage, stillbirth, cot death…a loss so heartbreaking that she'd never really recovered from it. And neither had her marriage.

Was that why she'd been so adamant that the break-up hadn't been her ex's fault? And was that why she'd suddenly been so antsy at the park, when she'd asked him if he wanted children?

The way she looked at him, those beautiful dark eyes so tortured, was too much for him. He came round to her side of the table, scooped her out of her chair, sat in her place and settled her on his lap, his arms tightly wrapped round her. 'I'm not going anywhere until you talk to me. And whatever you say isn't going any further than me, I promise you.'

She didn't really know him well enough to be completely sure that he wouldn't break his promise, but he hoped that she'd got to know him enough over the time they'd worked together to work out that he had integrity.

'What happened, Bailey?' What had broken her heart?

'I was pregnant once,' she whispered.

He stroked her face. 'When?'

'Two and a half years ago. I was so thrilled. We both were. We wanted that baby so much.'

He said nothing, just holding her close and waiting for her to tell him the rest.

'And then I started getting pains. In my lower abdomen. It hurt so much, Jared. I was worried that I might be having a miscarriage. And my shoulder hurt—but I assumed that was because I was worried.'

Jared knew that when you were stressed and tense you tended to hold yourself more rigidly and the muscles of your shoulder and neck would go into spasm, causing shoulder pain. Clearly that hadn't been the reason for the pain in this case.

'I went to the toilet,' she said, 'and there was spotting.' She closed her eyes. 'I felt sick. Light-headed.' She dragged in a breath. 'Then I collapsed. Luckily one of my colleagues found me and they got me in to the department. I told them I was pregnant, but I knew what was happening. I *knew*.'

A miscarriage? Heartbreaking for her.

'They gave me a scan. I was six weeks and three days. The pregnancy was ectopic.'

Even harder than he'd guessed. The fertilised egg hadn't implanted into the uterus, the way it should've done. Instead, it had embedded in the Fallopian tube and stretched the tube as it had grown, causing Bailey's lower abdominal pain.

'My Fallopian tube had ruptured. They took me straight into Theatre,' she said, 'but they couldn't save the tube.' Her voice wobbled, and then a shudder ran through her. 'I wanted that baby so much. And I—I...'

'Shh, I know.' He stroked her hair. 'And it wasn't your fault.' It happened in something like one out of eighty pregnancies. Often it sorted itself out and the woman hadn't even known she was pregnant in the first place. But Bailey had been unlucky, caught up in one of the worst-case scenarios.

And clearly the fact her best friend had just shared the news of her pregnancy had brought it all back. Joni had doubtless been one of the first people that Bailey had told about her own pregnancy, and Jared would just bet that Joni had agonised over telling her best friend the news, knowing that it would bring all these excruciating memories back. And he was equally sure that Bailey had gone into super-sparkly mode to reassure her that it was fine, all the while her heart breaking into tiny pieces again.

'The ectopic pregnancy wasn't my fault,' Bailey said, 'but the rest of it was.'

The rest of it? He'd obviously spoken aloud without meaning to, or maybe the question was just obvious, because she started talking again.

'I pushed Ed away afterwards. I—I just couldn't cope with the idea of it happening all over again.'

Jared knew that a second ectopic pregnancy was more likely if you'd had a first. He'd never worked in obstetrics, but he was pretty sure that the statistics weren't shockingly high. Bailey's fears had obviously got the better of her.

'I was so scared of getting pregnant again. So scared of losing another baby. So scared of losing my other Fallopian tube, so I'd never be able to have a baby without medical intervention. I wouldn't let Ed touch me. I knew he was hurting and he needed me, but I just *couldn't* let him touch me. I couldn't give him the physical comfort he wanted.' She leaned her head against his shoulder. 'I was such a selfish bitch.'

'You were hurting, too, Bailey,' he reminded her softly. 'You weren't being selfish. You were hurting and you didn't know how to fix it—for yourself or for your husband.'

'In the end, Ed found comfort elsewhere. But he—he wasn't like your ex,' she whispered. 'He wasn't out there looking for someone else. He would never have done it if I hadn't pushed him away and made him feel as if I didn't care. It was all my fault.'

And now he understood why her family worried about her so much and were so keen for her to meet someone. Not because she was 'on the shelf', but because they knew how much she'd been through and they wanted her to find someone to share her life with and to cherish her, someone who'd stop her being lonely and sad.

If she'd let him, maybe he could do that. Maybe they could both help each other heal.

But Bailey had pushed her husband away, terrified of getting pregnant again. She'd ended her marriage rather than risk another pregnancy going wrong.

And that explained why she'd responded to him and then backed off again so swiftly. She'd felt the pull of attraction between them just as much as he had, but she was too scared to act on it. Too scared to date, to grow intimate with him, to make love with him—in case she became pregnant and she ended up having another ectopic pregnancy.

'It takes two to break a marriage,' he said. 'Your ex gave up on you.'

'You gave up on your marriage,' she pointed out.

He knew she'd only said it because she was hurting. Clearly she thought that sniping at him would make him walk away and leave her to it. Maybe that was one of the tactics she'd used to push her husband away, but it wasn't going to work on him. 'Yes, I did,' he said. 'I'll take my share of the blame. Just as long as you accept that not all the blame of your break-up is yours.'

'It feels like it is,' she said, sounding totally broken.

If only he had a magic wand. But this wasn't something he could fix. The only one who could let her trust again, let her take the risk of sharing her life with someone, was Bailey herself. Until she was ready to try, it just wouldn't work.

So he said nothing, just held her. If necessary, he'd stay here all night, just cradling her on his lap and hoping she'd be able to draw some strength from the feel of her arms around him.

Eventually, she stroked his face. 'Thank you, Jared. For listening. And for not judging.'

Unable to help himself, he twisted his face round so he could drop a kiss into her palm. 'No worries.'

'I'm sorry I cried all over you.'

'It probably did you good,' he said.

'And we were supposed to be talking about Darren,' she said.

He smiled. 'Don't worry about it. Darren can wait. We'll talk about him tomorrow, maybe. Right now, this is a bit more important.'

'I don't normally cry over people.'

No. He'd guess that normally she sparkled that little bit more brightly, pretending everything was fine and waiting until she was on her own before letting her true feelings show. 'It's fine. Really.'

'I, um, ought to let you go. It's getting late.'

'I'm not going anywhere,' he said softly.

'But...'

'Bailey, do you really think I can walk away and just leave you here alone, upset and hurting?' he asked.

She just looked at him, those huge, huge eyes full of pain.

'It's your choice,' he said. 'I can sleep on your sofa tonight—just so I know you're not alone, and I'm here if you need anything. Or...' He paused.

'Or?' she whispered.

'Or I can hold you until you fall asleep. Sleep with you.'

Even though she tried to hide it, he could see the panic flood into her face. 'I said *sleep*, Bailey,' he reminded her quietly. 'Which isn't the same as having sex.'

'I—I'm sorry.'

He kissed the corner of her mouth. 'You're upset, you're trying to be brave and all your nightmares have come back to haunt you. Some people might use sex as a way of escaping it all, but you're not one of them. And I would never push you into anything you're not happy with.'

'I know.' She swallowed hard. 'I'm a mess, Jared. And you've been hurt in the past, too. I'm the last person you need to get involved with.'

'Let me be the judge of that,' he said gently. 'And let me be here for you tonight.'

Bailey knew it was a genuine offer. It would be, oh, so easy to take him up on it. To lean on him. To take comfort from the warmth of his body curled round hers.

But it would also make things really complicated.

'You're going to be stubborn about this, aren't you?' he asked wryly.

She nodded. 'And you said I had a choice.'

'Sofa?' he asked.

'Go home,' she said. 'Really. I'll be fine.'

'How about we compromise?' Jared suggested. 'You let me hold you—on the sofa—until you're asleep. Then I'll tuck you in and I'll leave—though if you wake at stupid o'clock and you need to talk, then you call me.'

So, so generous. She stroked his face. 'I'm sorry I called you Herod.'

He smiled. 'That was the autocorrect on your phone.'

'But I never took it back. And you're not a tyrant at all. You're more like Sir Galahad. A knight on a white charger coming to the rescue.'

He laughed. 'Hardly. I'm just a man, Bailey.'

'There's no "just". You're a good man, Jared Fraser. Kind. You do all that gruff, dour Scotsman stuff—but that's the opposite of who you really are.'

'Thank you,' he said. 'Now lead me to your sofa.'

'Don't you want a drink or anything? I've been horribly rude and haven't even offered you a coffee.'

He kissed the tip of her nose. 'In the circumstances, that's not so surprising. And I don't want a coffee. I just want to hold you until you fall asleep.'

'Yes,' she said softly, and led him through to the sofa in her living room.

CHAPTER TEN

THE NEXT MORNING, Bailey woke to find herself still fully clothed on the sofa, with her duvet tucked round her.

Falling asleep in Jared's arms last night had felt risky—but it had also felt so, so good.

She grabbed her phone, but a wave of unexpected shyness stopped her calling him. What would she even say?

Instead, she sent him a text: Thank you for last night.

Her phone pinged almost immediately with his reply: No worries. Sleep well?

Yes. Thank you.

Good. See you at work. And this time he'd signed his text with a kiss.

Maybe this was going to work out after all. Jared made her feel brave. And his ex, Bailey thought, really needed her head examined. Why would you throw away the love of a kind, decent, thoughtful man for a shallow, publicity-obsessed lifestyle?

Then again, unhappiness made you do stupid things.

Cruel things. Bailey knew she was just as guilty when it came to the way she'd pushed Ed away. And didn't they say you shouldn't judge someone until you'd walked a mile in their shoes?

She showered, changed and headed for the football pitch. But when she got there she was surprised to find that the players weren't warming up as usual on the field. Instead, they were sitting in the dressing room, and the mood was extremely subdued.

'What's the matter, lads?' she asked.

'You need to go in and see Mr Fincham in his office,' Billy said. 'Archie and Jared are already there.'

Mr Fincham? Why would the football club's chairman of directors want to see her? 'Why?' she asked.

'I can't say.' He bit his lip. 'But there's trouble, Bailey.'

Worried, Bailey hurried along to the office. Mandy, Lyle Fincham's PA, was typing furiously on her keyboard. 'Mandy, what's going on?' Bailey asked.

Mandy shook her head. 'That's for Mr Fincham to say, not me.' She inclined her head towards the door. 'They're in there, waiting. You'd better go in.'

Bailey knocked on the door out of courtesy and walked in. 'Sorry I'm a bit late. There was a delay on the Tube.'

Then she saw Darren sitting between Archie and Jared. And Jared was looking every inch the dour, unsmiling Scotsman.

'It's in all the papers this morning,' Lyle said, indicating the stack of newspapers on his desk. 'And all over the Internet.'

'What is?' she asked.

'The video of laddo here.' Lyle jerked his head towards Darren. 'In a club, getting drunk. Underage.'

She looked at Darren, who was white-faced and looked utterly guilty. So much for making the most of his second chance. Or maybe they just hadn't given him enough support. After all, Jared had originally wanted to talk to her last night about the boy; they hadn't got round to discussing the situation, because she'd been in meltdown.

And yet…something didn't quite stack up. The last couple of weeks, since she'd picked up Darren's under-performance and she and Jared had persuaded Archie to give the boy another chance, his stats had all been back to normal. 'When did all this happen?' she asked.

'Last night,' Archie said grimly.

Darren shook his head. 'I wasn't out last night. You can ask my mum. She'll tell you.'

'Actually, my stats show that Darren's performance has been normal ever since we talked to you, Archie,' Bailey said. 'If he'd still been drinking, it would've shown up on my graphs.'

'Graphs, schmaphs,' Lyle Fincham said, flapping a dismissive hand. 'Archie should never have let that box of tricks of yours cloud his judgement. This is a total mess, and I can't afford to let this affect the club. As from today, you're out, Dr Randall. I don't care how much of your research project's wasted. It's over.'

'Actually, I agree with Bailey,' Jared cut in. 'It would show on the graphs. And if she goes, I go.'

No. No way was she letting Jared risk his career. For

her, this was a research project. Yes, there would be repercussions about the way it had ended, but it would eventually blow over. For Jared, it would be his whole career on the line. This wasn't fair.

'I was the one who talked Archie into giving Darren another chance, so don't take this out on Jared,' she said swiftly. 'Don't make him leave because of me.'

'And that video's from weeks back, I swear. I haven't touched a drop since you said I could stay, Mr McLennan,' Darren added desperately, giving Archie a beseeching look. 'I know I was stupid to do it before.'

'But you've still dragged the club's name into disrepute.' Lyle shook his head. 'No. You're out, boy, so go and pack your things.'

'That's not fair—he's owned up to his mistakes, and this is just bad timing,' Bailey said. 'Nobody's perfect. Can you honestly put your hand on your heart and say that you've never, ever made a decision you haven't later regretted?'

Lyle gave her a speaking look.

'We all have the potential to make the wrong choice somewhere along the way. It's hard to own up to it. But Darren admitted his mistake and he's doing something about it.' Bailey grimaced. 'Look, can Darren just go and wait in another room while we talk about this like the professionals we are? It's horrible, all of us standing round like vultures pecking at the poor lad.'

'I agree,' Jared chipped in. 'And I also think we can turn this around so the club can make this a positive. We'll need your PR manager to help us, but we can do it.'

For a moment, she thought Lyle Fincham was going

to refuse, but then he tightened his mouth and nodded. 'Darren, go and wait next door with Mandy. You don't move a muscle, you don't phone anyone or talk to anyone and you don't go anywhere near the Internet, do you hear? Leave your phone with us.'

Looking hunted, the boy handed over his phone and went to wait with Lyle's PA next door.

Lyle picked up his phone. 'Max? My office. Now. There's a situation that needs handling.' He put the phone down again. 'Right. So we'll sort this out between us.'

'Darren's only seventeen. He's still just a kid, really. He's not going to think things through properly, the way someone more mature would do. Instead of coming to you to ask about extra training, Archie, he got drunk to blot out how he felt. You agreed to give him a second chance. He's stayed clean since then—and I bet if you ask any of the other lads they'll be able to tell you that, too,' Bailey said.

'I let you persuade me into giving him another chance, yes,' Archie said. 'But if one player goes wrong, then all the players get tarred with the same brush. You know what the press is like about how much money is in football. They'll have a field day with the kid—and with the club. This isn't fair to the rest of the players, or to the fans.'

'Or the shareholders,' Lyle added. 'His behaviour's put everything at risk.'

'But we can turn this round,' Jared said. 'Really.'

There was a rap on the door and Max Porter, the PR manager, came in. 'So what's this situation?'

'Darren. There's a video of him drunk and underage.' Lyle's colour was dangerously high again, and Bailey was really beginning to worry that the chairman of directors was about to have a heart attack or a stroke.

'Right,' Max said calmly. 'Talk me through it.'

'We picked it up on Bailey's system,' Jared said. 'He admitted he'd been drinking. Archie agreed to give him another chance.'

'And he hasn't touched anything since,' Bailey said. 'All his stats since we talked to him about it match his average. And it would show up if he was still drinking.'

'I've analysed the way he plays and designed a training programme to help him improve his weak spots,' Jared added.

'So you both obviously think he should stay,' Max said. Then he looked at Archie and Lyle. 'And I take it you both think he should go?'

'And not just him,' Lyle said with a pointed look at Jared and Bailey.

'We can turn this around,' Jared said again. 'This is a classic example of what the pressures of professional football can do to young players. We brought Darren into the club. We set the bar high. And what do we do with the players who can't handle the pressure? Do we just abandon them, in a cold-hearted business decision? Or do we treat them like a family member—knowing he has flaws, knowing he's human and helping him to get over the problem?'

'That's a good spin,' Max said. 'I do hope you're not planning to change career and go after my job, Jared.'

The joke was just enough to dissipate some of the tension in the room. *Just.*

'We don't just need to teach our young players ball skills,' Jared said. 'We need to teach them life skills, because this is a kind of apprenticeship and we're responsible for the way our players develop as people, not just as players. We need to show them how to own up to their mistakes and how to start to make things right.' He paused. 'When my knee was wrecked by that tackle, I was the same age as Darren and it felt like the end of the world, knowing I was never going to be able to play professional football again.'

Knowing how rarely he spoke about this, Bailey held her breath for a moment.

'I could so easily have gone off the rails,' Jared continued. 'But my family and my coach were brilliantly supportive. They stopped me doing anything stupid. And we need to do that for Darren.'

'Actually, Darren could be a good ambassador for the club,' Max said thoughtfully. 'We could get him to talk about his mistakes to kids at school, how he's overcome them and how he managed to get back on the right path with our help. They can learn from his mistakes rather than making those mistakes themselves.'

'So he gets away with it?' Lyle asked, his nostrils flaring in disgust.

'No. Because you could always fine him,' Bailey suggested. 'Donate the fine to a charity specialising in alcohol abuse among kids. Then his mistake will help people who also made mistakes.'

'Making the punishment fit the crime,' Archie said. 'I like that. And he's not a bad lad, Lyle. He's not wild. We need to give him a bit more pride in himself.'

'And what's the press going to think? That I condone all sorts of nonsense at the club?' Lyle demanded.

'No. They'll think that you expect the best from people, but you don't just throw them to the wolves if they get it wrong. You help them be the best they can be,' Max said. 'You're going to get all the mums on your side.'

'Mums don't buy season tickets,' Lyle grumbled.

'Maybe, but they can talk their partners into buying a season ticket for a club that gives a damn about the kids and doesn't just see them as future cash cows,' Jared said.

Lyle threw his hands up. 'I give up. All right. The boy gets a second chance. But you make sure everyone knows we fined him for doing wrong, and that we donated that money to help kids who made the same mistake.'

'Thank you,' Bailey said. 'And I'm sorry I didn't talk it over with you and Archie. I understand why you don't want me here again after today.'

'You know, it would be a shame to lose all that PR—it shows that we care so much about our players' well-being, we've worked with them using the latest technology to help reduce soft-tissue injuries,' Jared said, looking at Max and then Lyle.

'He's right,' Max said. 'It's a brilliant story and it would be a real pity to lose it.'

This time, Jared looked straight at Bailey. 'Everyone deserves a second chance,' he said softly.

She knew he didn't just mean Darren, or their work on the team. He meant them. A second chance to get it right. And it made her go hot all over.

'All right, all right,' Lyle grumbled. 'You can finish your research, Dr Randall. But one foot out of line from you in future...or you,' he warned, gesturing to Jared, 'and that's it.'

'I promise,' Bailey said.

'Me, too,' Jared said. 'Should we send Darren back in to learn his fate?'

'Do that,' Archie said, clapping them both on the back. 'And we'll postpone training until this afternoon. Two-thirty, sharp. Tell them for me, will you?'

Bailey and Jared went next door into Mandy's office. 'Darren, you can go back in now,' Jared said.

'What did Mr Fincham say?' Darren asked, looking anxious.

'He'll listen to you and be fair about it. Just go in, tell the truth and you'll be fine,' Bailey advised him.

Then they went into the dressing room to see the rest of the players. They were full of questions, all talking together and not giving anyone a chance to answer them.

'Has Darren been sacked?'

'Is the boss mad because of all the stuff that happened in that nightclub?'

'Are the rest of us going to be sacked?'

'Shh—calm down,' Bailey said. 'Archie will be in to see you later and he'll explain everything. In the meantime, training today has been postponed until two-thirty. I'm sure you lot have stuff you can get on with in the meantime—and stay out of trouble, OK?'

'Nicely done,' Jared said when they left the dressing room.

'I've got everyone into quite enough trouble as it is,' she said ruefully. 'And I'm sorry, Jared. I really thought you were going to lose your job because of me back there.'

'Lyle always blows up. He'll calm down again.' Jared gave her a wry smile. 'Though I was worrying about him back there. I didn't like his colour.'

'Me, neither,' she agreed.

'Maybe you could teach him some of your yoga stuff to help him relax and reduce his blood pressure.'

'Suggesting that,' she said, 'is probably more than my life's worth right now—and yours.'

'Well, it looks as if we have some unexpected free time.' He paused. 'Want some cake?'

'I think that's a really good idea,' she said.

'My place isn't far. And there's a good patisserie on the corner.'

'That sounds good to me,' she said. 'Though I insist on buying, considering I nearly got you the sack.'

'No, you didn't—but I'm not going to turn down the offer of cake,' he said with a smile. 'Let's go.'

CHAPTER ELEVEN

THEY BOUGHT CAKE at the café and walked back to Jared's place in comfortable silence. Jared made them both a mug of coffee; Bailey was relieved that they sat in his kitchen, given how they'd ended up kissing on his sofa. She didn't quite trust herself not to repeat that, especially as the more time she spent with Jared, the more attractive she found him.

He'd hinted at a second chance. Did she dare take it?

'I was wondering,' he said, 'if you were doing anything at the weekend.'

'Nothing out of the ordinary,' she said. What did he have in mind? Adrenalin fizzed through her at the possibilities.

'I know it's ridiculously short notice, but there's this football function on Saturday night—a charity ball thing. I, um, have two tickets.'

'And you've been let down at the last minute?'

He frowned. 'Bailey, I'm not the kind of man who asks someone to go to a dinner with me and then kisses someone else stupid.'

'No, of course not.' But he was obviously remembering those kisses, too. Had he been planning to ask her to the ball all along? Or had he just bought the tickets to do his bit to support the charity, not actually intending to be there on the night?

She blew out a breath. 'Sorry. I didn't mean to insult you. Honestly. First I nearly lose you your job, and then I practically accuse you of being a philanderer… I'm not doing very well today.'

'The job thing was just as much my fault,' he said. 'And I think you and I…' He blew out a breath. 'It's complicated.'

'Just a tad.' She paused. 'So is this an official date? In public?'

He held her gaze. 'It could be. Or it could be the same deal as you had with me at Joni and Aaron's wedding.'

A fake date, to take the heat off him?

'Sasha's going to be there?' she guessed.

'Possibly.' He shrugged. 'I have no idea.'

There was something she needed to know. 'Are you still in love with her?'

'No. Actually, I don't care whether she's there or not. That isn't the reason I asked you. I only bought the tickets to support the charity,' he admitted. 'I wasn't actually going to go.'

Just as she'd half suspected.

'But I've been thinking about it. And I'd like to go.' He paused. 'With you.'

It was tempting. So very tempting. And maybe the sugar rush of the cake was to blame for her opening her mouth and saying, 'Yes.'

His smile made her feel warm all over.

'So where do I meet you, and what time?' she asked.

'I could pick you up from your place at seven?' he suggested.

'That works for me.'

And how crazy it was that this made her feel like a teenager all over again.

A second chance. If you counted the wedding, this would be their third attempt at a date. At the wedding, and when they'd had dinner together, she'd ended up panicking and backing away. Would this be third time lucky? Would she be able to get over the fear this time?

Jared was a good man. He'd stuck up for her. He'd been there for her when she'd needed a shoulder. He ticked all her boxes. All she had to do was get rid of the fears inside her head.

All.

The training session that afternoon was pretty much as usual. The lads were a little subdued but did their best, including Darren. She was busy at clinic the rest of the week.

And all too soon Saturday night arrived.

Rather than going all out for a ballgown, Bailey had chosen a black lacy dress and patent black leather high heels. Simple yet sophisticated enough for the function, she hoped. And as soon as she opened the door to Jared, she knew from the flare of heat in his gaze that she'd made the right decision. He definitely liked what she was wearing.

'Hello,' she said, feeling ridiculously shy.

'You look fabulous,' he said softly.

'So do you.' She'd seen him in a suit before, but not a dinner jacket. How crazy that something as simple as a dark red bow tie should look so incredibly sexy on him. Just to stop herself doing something stupid—like grabbing him and kissing him and dragging him off to her bed instead of going to the ball—she said, 'Though I was half expecting you to wear a kilt.'

He laughed. 'That would be a wee bit clichéd.'

But, to her relief, laughter broke the tension just enough to get her common sense back.

Jared had seen Bailey dressed up before, but it did nothing to stop the shock of how attractive he found her. Right at that moment he didn't want to go to the charity ball and share her; he wanted her all to himself. He wanted to kiss her until they were both dizzy, and then take her to bed and spend the whole night finding out what gave her the most pleasure. But he held himself in check. Just.

He ushered her to the taxi. When he reached for her hand on the way to the dinner-dance, she curled her fingers round his.

Maybe, just maybe, this thing between them was going to go right.

At the dinner, Bailey went into sparkle mode. She chatted to absolutely everyone, not in the slightest bit fazed by the incredibly glamorous WAGs there or how famous some of the players were. But Jared noticed that she didn't only talk to the famous ones; she talked to everyone and drew them out.

Bailey Randall had a gift for making people feel special.

He watched her sparkle and thought, *I could really lose my heart to this woman.* He knew she was as special as she made people feel, but he also knew that she had a protective shell round her. He wasn't sure if he'd be able to persuade her to let him past it.

He turned round to see Sasha there with her third husband in tow. Jared had expected to feel some kind of reaction at seeing her again—but he was surprised and relieved to discover he didn't. What had happened was in the past. It couldn't be changed. And it didn't matter any more—it didn't *hurt* any more.

And he knew why: because Bailey was in his life. Being with Bailey made his world a much brighter place.

After he'd introduced Bailey to Sasha and her husband, Jared made his excuses and drew Bailey towards the dance floor.

'Are you OK?' Bailey asked.

'Sure. Why wouldn't I be?'

She coughed. 'Sasha's not exactly a common name. I take it she's *the* Sasha.'

'Yes. Actually, I thought I'd find it difficult to see her,' he admitted, 'but there's just nothing there any more. It's fine,' he reassured her. But he also noticed that Bailey didn't look fine. 'What's wrong?' he asked softly.

'Well—she's incredibly beautiful.'

'And?' He didn't get it.

She shook her head. 'Nothing.'

Then he got it. And it surprised him that Bailey was feeling vulnerable. The Bailey Randall he'd got to know was incredibly together and was comfortable in her own skin, and he really liked that. 'I know you're not fishing for compliments,' he said, 'but, just for the record, you can more than hold your own with her. You're just as beautiful, except yours is a natural beauty.' He paused. 'And I'm so glad you're nothing like her as a person.'

'Hmm,' she said.

'Just to make it clear,' he said softly, 'right now I'm dating a woman I really, really like. A woman I respect for who she is.' He held her gaze. 'And whom I happen to find very, very attractive.'

Had he gone too far?

Panicking that he might make her back off, he added, 'Anyway, your hair's shorter than Sasha's.'

'I used to wear it long.'

He held her closer. He could guess when she'd cut it. After she'd lost the baby. 'No shadows tonight,' he said softly. 'This is just you and me.' He pulled back slightly so she could see his eyes and know that he was telling the truth. 'I've put the past to rest.'

'Good.'

For a moment he wondered if she was going to say that she'd put her past to rest, too.

But she didn't. And he knew he was going to have to take this at her pace.

When he'd been younger he wouldn't have had the patience to do that. But Bailey Randall was going to be more than worth his patience, he thought. So he wasn't going to push her until she was ready.

* * *

During the evening, Bailey danced with both Lyle Fincham and Archie.

Archie tipped his head towards Jared. 'Are you and Jared...you know?'

She smiled. 'I'm taking the Fifth Amendment on that one.'

He laughed. 'You can't. You're not American.'

'I'm still doing it. Anyway, under English law you have the right to remain silent, too,' she pointed out.

'I guess.' He smiled. 'He's a good man. I know you two didn't exactly hit it off at first.'

'Jared's not the grumpy Scotsman he likes everyone to think he is,' she said with a grin.

'Exactly. And I think you'll be good together.'

'It's early days, Archie,' she said softly. She wasn't quite ready to believe this was all going to work out. But she really was going to try and put the past behind her.

Eventually Jared claimed Bailey back. Perfect timing, too, because the music changed to soft and slow, which meant that she was right where he wanted her—up close and personal. And she was holding him just as tightly. He wasn't going to embarrass her by kissing her stupid in public, but maybe...

'Shall we get out of here?' he murmured into her ear. 'Go and have a glass of wine back at my place?'

He didn't realise he was holding his breath until she said yes.

He held her hand in the taxi all the way back to his place.

And once the front door was closed behind him, he was able to do what he'd wanted to do all evening and kiss her.

He could drown in her warmth and sweetness.

He broke this kiss before he did something stupid, like carrying her upstairs to his bed. Too fast, too soon. 'I promised you a glass of wine,' he said hoarsely.

'I don't really want a drink,' she said softly.

Then what did she want?

Anticipation thrummed through him. Did she want the same thing that he did? Did she want to lose herself in him, the way he wanted to lose himself in her?

'Last time I was here, you put pictures in my head,' she said. 'Do you happen to have any more of that fabulous chocolate pudding?'

'No, but I can improvise,' he said. Then he went very still as he took in what she'd just said. Not quite sure he'd got this right, he asked, 'Bailey, are you saying we can…?'

'Yes. Provided,' she said, 'we're really careful and you use protection. I'm not on the Pill. I never thought I'd…' She tailed off, wrinkling her nose and looking awkward.

He knew what she meant. When she'd told him about her ectopic pregnancy, she'd also told him how scared she was of getting pregnant again and how she'd pushed her husband away physically. And so what she was offering him now was *hugely* brave. So generous it made him catch his breath. She was going to trust him. To let him prove to her that having sex again wasn't going to make her life implode. 'I'll take care of you,' he said softly, 'and I want you so badly it hurts—but I know this is really scary for you. If you change your mind at any point tonight and say you want to stop, that's also fine. We can take this as slowly as you like.'

Tears glittered in her eyes. 'Thank you, Jared.'

He needed to ask. 'Do you want me to stop now?'

She took a deep breath. 'Yes. And no. Both at the same time. I'm scared, Jared,' she admitted.

'I know. And I understand.' He held her close for a moment. 'But maybe, just maybe, you can be brave with me. Maybe we can be brave with each other,' he said, and drew her hand to his mouth. He kissed each fingertip in turn, then her palm, folding her fingers over his kiss.

She stood on tiptoe and kissed the end of his nose. And then the corner of his mouth. And then she caught his lower lip between hers, in silent demand that they deepen the kiss.

He was more than happy to comply. And happier still when she kissed him back, matching him touch for touch and nibble for nibble.

'I want you,' he whispered. 'So very, very badly.'

'I want you, too,' she said, her voice low and husky and sensual.

He didn't need a second invitation. He scooped her up and carried her up the stairs to his bedroom. He'd already closed the curtains before he'd left that evening, so all he had to deal with was the light, once he'd set her back down on her feet.

In the soft light of the table lamp he could see the strain on her face. The fear.

'It's OK,' he said. 'We can stop.'

She shook her head. 'Not now.'

'Are you sure?'

She took a deep breath. 'I'm sure.'

He knew she wasn't yet she was clearly trying to push herself past the fear. So he'd do what he could to help. He kissed her lightly, then slid the zip at the back of her dress all the way down. He pushed the lacy material off her shoulders and the dress slid to the floor. She stepped out of it, and he hung it over the back of a chair, not wanting the dress to be spoiled. And then he held her at arm's length. 'You take my breath away, Bailey,' he said huskily.

'Right now,' she said, with the tiniest wobble in her voice that told him she was still panicking inside, 'I think I'd feel a bit better if you weren't wearing quite so much.'

He smiled. 'I'm all yours. Do what you will with me.'

She slid his jacket off and placed it over her dress on the chair. Then she checked his bow tie. He could see the moment that she realised it was a proper one. 'Very flash,' she said, rolling her eyes, and pulled both ends. The knot came apart in her hands, and she draped the tie over his jacket.

Next was his shirt, and he noticed that her hands were slightly unsteady as she undid the buttons. She pushed the material off his shoulders. 'Oh, your biceps,' she breathed, and stroked the muscles. 'I've wanted to do this since we trained together. They're so beautiful.'

And so was she. He needed to see her. Properly. All of her. 'Can I play caveman now?' he asked. Stupid, because he'd already done that by carrying her up the stairs.

'I was thinking superhero,' she said. 'One with really, really sexy biceps. Though I can live with the fact you're not wearing a cape.'

'That works for me.' At her nod, he unclipped her bra and turned her round. 'Oh, my God, Bailey. You're glorious.' He kissed his way down her spine. 'If I could paint, I'd want you to model for me.' He stroked her back. 'You're perfect.' He drew her back against him so she could feel his erection pressing against her and would know that he meant every word of what he said. He cupped her breasts and kissed the curve of her shoulder. 'Right now, I want you so badly. You make me ache, Bailey. In a good way.'

She turned round in his arms. 'Then take me to bed, Jared.'

He didn't need her to ask again. He picked her up and carried her to the bed, then laid her gently against the covers.

Time seemed to stop. Bailey wasn't sure which of them had removed the rest of his clothes and her underwear, but finally they were skin to skin.

Then she froze as she realised what was just about to happen. She wanted this—she really, really did—but supposing this all went wrong?

'Stop thinking, Bailey,' he whispered. 'Let yourself go. Let yourself *feel*.'

He kissed her again; she tipped her head back against the pillows, and he kissed the curve of her throat, lingering in the hollows of her collarbones.

She could feel her nipples tightening; he nuzzled his

way down her sternum and then took one nipple into his mouth, sucking hard. Bailey pushed her hands through his hair, urging him on, and his mouth moved lower, lower.

She almost forgot how to breathe when she felt the long, slow stroke of his tongue along her sex. And it was like a starburst in her head when he teased her clitoris with the tip of his tongue. Her climax was shockingly fast. Oh, God. She'd forgotten what this was like. Forgotten how it felt. Forgotten how good it could be. And it had been so long…

He waited until the aftershocks had died away, then came up to lie beside her and drew her into his arms. 'OK?'

'I think so,' she said. 'Which planet am I on again?'

He chuckled softly. 'I wanted that first time to be all for you.'

He cared that much? She felt a single tear leak out of the corner of her eye.

He kissed it away. 'Bailey, I think we're going to be good together.'

The panic threatened to spill over again, but she pushed it away. She'd said that she'd be brave with him. She wasn't going to back out now.

'Show me,' she whispered.

He took a condom from his drawer and handed her the packet. 'You're in control.'

She knew exactly why he'd done that—so she could be quite, quite sure that there was no chance of getting pregnant, because she'd know they'd used the condom properly—and had to blink back the tears, but she ripped open the packet and rolled the condom over his shaft. And then finally, finally, he was inside her. He held himself very still so her body could adjust to the feel of him, then began to move.

He was a concentrated lover, she discovered. One who didn't talk and who focused on his goals. And, oh, having that focus entirely on her… She was aware of every touch, every kiss, and she knew that he was exploring her and paying very, very close attention to what she liked, and what she liked even more.

It shouldn't be this good. Not their first time. It should be awkward and embarrassing and faintly ridiculous.

But then she stopped thinking as she felt a climax spiralling through her again. She clung onto him for dear life and knew the very second that he'd fallen over the edge, too.

When they'd both floated back to earth, he moved. 'I'd better deal with the condom,' he said softly, and kissed her shoulder. 'Stay there. You look comfortable.' She *was* comfortable. And even though there was a slow burn of panic deep inside her, knowing that Jared was there—that he was solid and dependable and real—helped her to ignore that panic. It was time she stopped letting what had happened to her dictate her life. Time she stopped letting it scare her away from what she wanted. With Jared by her side, supportive and compassionate, she could have everything.

That night, she fell asleep in his arms, just as she had on her sofa. But this time when she woke she was still in his arms. In his bed. Skin to skin. Warm and comfortable. She kept her eyes closed for a little while longer, just luxuriating in the feeling of being held. Of being cherished. She'd forgotten how good this could be.

'Good morning,' he said softly when she opened her eyes at last.

'Yes. It is,' she said with a smile. 'Because you're here.'

'It's the same for me. I don't care if it's raining outside, because it feels like the brightest summer day.' He stroked her face. 'So will you stay for breakfast?'

She kissed him lightly. 'Thank you. I'd love to.'

He made her pancakes with maple syrup and some truly excellent coffee. They went back to her flat so she could change from her lacy cocktail dress into something casual, and spent the rest of the day wandering hand in hand along the South Bank, enjoying the market stalls and the art installations and the street performers.

'No regrets?' he said on her doorstep when he finally saw her home.

'None,' she said. 'Today's been fantastic. Actually, it's the first time in a long while that I've felt this happy.'

'Me, too,' he said.

'So I was wondering,' she said. 'I'm not promising pancakes, but I make a mean bacon sandwich.'

His eyes widened. 'Are you asking me to stay for breakfast, Bailey?'

She took a deep breath. 'Yes.'

'Sure?' he checked.

'It still scares me a bit, the idea of having another relationship,' she admitted. 'But yes. You make me feel brave. I can do this, with you.'

In answer, he kissed her. And she opened her front door and ushered him inside.

CHAPTER TWELVE

FOR THE NEXT three weeks Bailey was really happy. She and Jared were so in tune—and she really liked the funny, kind, gentle man beneath his dour exterior. She also enjoyed the occasional sarcastic text he sent her, signed 'Herod'. He was never going to let her forget that, was he?

This was all still so new that she wasn't quite ready to share it with her family or her best friend, but she found herself looking forward to every evening that she spent with Jared, every night that she slept in his arms and every morning that she woke and he was the first one she saw.

Work was fantastic. She'd always enjoyed her clinic work, and she'd been accepted as one of the team at the football club, so both strands of her job suited her perfectly.

Life didn't get any better than this, she thought.

Until the middle of the day when she suddenly realised that her period was late. She calculated mentally. Not just late—*a whole week late*, and she was never late.

For a moment she couldn't breathe. *What if she was*

pregnant? And why, why, *why* hadn't she waited to go on the Pill and insisted on using condoms as well, before she'd made love with Jared?

She took a deep breath, knowing that she was being ridiculous. OK, so the only form of contraception that was one hundred per cent effective was total abstinence, but condoms still had a pretty good success rate. She and Jared had been really, really careful. And she was thirty years old, so her fertility level was lower than when she'd fallen pregnant last time. She only had one Fallopian tube working, making the chances of falling pregnant even lower. This was probably just a stupid glitch.

But how many other women had been caught out that way? How many teenage girls had fallen pregnant after just one time? How many women, nearing menopause and thinking that their fertility was practically zero, had taken a risk and discovered they were having a 'happy accident'? She knew of several colleagues who hadn't planned their last babies.

And what if history repeated itself? What if she was pregnant and it was another ectopic pregnancy? What if, this time, she lost absolutely everything?

There was only one way to find out. And she was going to have to be brave and face it.

At lunchtime she went out and bought a pregnancy test kit. With every step back towards the hospital her legs felt as if they were turning into lead, heavy and dragging.

The last time she'd bought a pregnancy test she'd been so excited, so hopeful. She had actually run to the bathroom, because she'd so desperately wanted it to be positive—she'd wanted to know the result that very second.

This time, taking a pregnancy test felt more like a sentence of doom. Something she had to nerve herself to do. Panic made her hands shake as she opened the box. It took her three goes to open the test kit itself.

Oh, God. Oh, God. Oh, God.

Please don't let her be pregnant.

Please don't let the nightmare happen all over again.

Please don't let that low, dragging pain start as a nag and then flare into agony.

Please don't let her lose her last chance.

Time felt as if it was wading through treacle as she washed her hands and kept an eye on the test stick. One line in the window to let her know that the test had worked.

She felt sick. The line in the next window would tell her yes or no.

'Please let it be no. Please let it be no. Please let it be no.' The words were ripped from her, low and guttural.

But she knew that begging wasn't going to change a thing. The test stick was measuring the level of a hormone in her urine: human chorionic gonadotropin, which was produced by the placenta after fertilisation.

Then again, a negative result could be just as bad because it might mean that the embryo hadn't implanted yet—or that it had implanted in the wrong place. Just as it had before.

She stared at the next window. One line formed, and then a second.

Positive.

Her knees went weak and she sat down heavily.

And then there was the window to tell her how many weeks since conception…

She stared at the window until the words finally penetrated her brain. *Three weeks plus.* She and Jared had first made love three weeks and two days ago. Now she thought about it, it had been smack in the middle of her cycle. The most fertile stage. Which would make her five weeks and two days pregnant now.

No, no, no, no, no.

Nearly three years ago, at this stage, that meant that in one week and one day's time…

Her stomach heaved, she dropped the test stick and was promptly sick in the sink.

Bailey washed her face afterwards while she tried to think about what to do.

She was going to have to tell Jared; but she had absolutely no idea what she was going to say. Or what was going to happen next. He'd said he wanted kids one day. But they hadn't been together that long. This was way too soon. She didn't think Jared was the kind of man who'd walk away, or who paid towards a child's upbringing but had no emotional involvement with the baby whatsoever—yet something else worried her. Would he want the baby more than he wanted *her*?

Panic really had turned her into a gibbering, raving idiot. She was always so together, so organised. Not knowing what to do next just wasn't in her make-up. And it freaked her out even more that she was reacting like this. That all her common sense had vanished into thin air. That she couldn't think rationally.

What the hell was she going to do?

Right now, her parents were in Italy. She knew that all she had to do was pick up the phone and her mother would get on the next plane to London to be with her but that wasn't fair; her parents deserved a chance to enjoy having a holiday around their wedding anniversary. Her brothers were up to their eyeballs running the restaurant, so it wouldn't be fair to talk to them about it, either.

Then there was Joni. But how could Bailey dump something like this on her best friend, when Joni should have the chance to enjoy her own pregnancy without any shadows?

Besides, Jared was the one she *really* needed to talk to.

Today was one of her clinic days, so she wouldn't see him during working hours. She knew she could call him—but she didn't trust herself to make any sense on the phone. She had a nasty feeling that she'd start crying as soon as she heard his voice. The last thing she wanted to do was to panic him by sobbing uncontrollably and mumbling incoherent fragments at him. This conversation needed to be face-to-face. Rational. Together.

But her brain was so fried that she couldn't even remember what they'd arranged to do this evening. Was she meeting him at his place? At hers? Somewhere else?

'For pity's sake, Bailey Randall, get a *grip*,' she told herself sharply.

But she couldn't. She felt as if she was scrabbling around in the dark, wearing oversized boxing gloves.

She grabbed her phone and texted Jared. Can you meet me at my place after work?

* * *

Jared looked at Bailey's message on the screen of his phone: Can you meet me at my place after work?

Odd. They'd planned to go out for a pizza after work and then to the cinema. He was meeting her at the Tube station. Had she forgotten? Or had something happened that meant they had to change their plans?

Sure. Is everything OK? he texted back.

OK, she replied.

That was very un-Bailey-like. She was normally much chattier than this. Or maybe she was having a rough day in clinic and she was up to her eyes in work. Being busy might explain her forgetting their plans.

He was busy that afternoon, too, and didn't think anything more of it until she answered the door to him. Then he saw that her face was pale—paler than he'd ever seen it before—and her eyes were puffy, as if she'd been crying. 'Bailey? What's happened?' he asked.

She backed away before he could put his arms round her. 'You'd better come in and sit down.'

And now he was really worried. This definitely wasn't normal for her. The woman he'd been dating was warm and tactile. She liked being hugged, and he really enjoyed the physical side of being close to her. The fact that she'd just backed away… What was happening?

He followed her into the kitchen and she indicated the chair opposite hers.

'Do you want a drink?' she asked.

'No. I want to know what's wrong,' he said, sitting down. And his worry increased exponentially when he reached across the table to hold her hand and she pulled away.

'I'm, um…' She dragged in a breath. 'Well, the only way I can tell you is straight out. I'm pregnant.'

Jared wasn't sure what he'd been expecting, but it sure as hell hadn't been this.

Pregnant?

'But—how?' He knew the question was stupid as soon as the words left his mouth. They'd had sex. Which meant the risk of pregnancy. He shook his head in exasperation at his own ridiculousness. 'I mean, we were careful.'

'I know.'

'How far along are you?'

'Just over three weeks, according to the test.' She dragged in a breath. 'Five weeks since the start of my LMP.'

'OK.' He blinked, trying to clear his head.

Bailey was pregnant.

With his baby.

He'd been here before—sort of. When Sasha had told him that she'd had a termination. Saying that she didn't know whether the baby was his or not. Saying that she didn't want a baby anyway. Saying that she didn't want to be married to him any more.

This wasn't the same thing. At all.

But it was a hell of a lot more complicated. The last time Bailey had been pregnant it had been ectopic. She'd gone through enormous physical pain—and she'd lost part of her fertility as well as the baby. And the fear of it happening again had led to the breakdown of her marriage.

Right now, she was clearly panicking, worrying that history was about to repeat itself. Would that panic make her consider having a termination even before the embryo had implanted—and would she make that decision without him?

He pushed the fears away. Bailey wasn't Sasha. And Bailey needed his full support. He had to put his own concerns and feelings aside and put her first. And he needed her to know that he'd be there. Given how she'd pushed Ed away, she was likely to do the same thing with him—he was learning that this was the way Bailey coped. She'd already begun pushing him away by not letting him hold her and comfort her when she was clearly so upset.

Well, Jared wasn't Ed, either. He wasn't going to let her push him away. The future might be tricky, but they had a lot more chance of surviving it if they faced it together.

He didn't think she'd listen to him right now—panic would've stopped up her ears. Which left him only one course of action. He stood up, walked round to her side of the table, scooped her out of her chair and sat down in her place. Once he'd settled her on his lap, he wrapped his arms tightly round her. Now she'd know for sure that he wasn't going to let her go.

She wriggled against him. 'Jared, what are you doing?'

'Showing you,' he said simply. 'That I'm here. That

we're in this together. That I'm not going to let you push me away.'

She looked utterly confused. 'But—'

'But nothing,' he cut in gently. 'Oh, and just so you know—Bailey Randall, I love you.'

CHAPTER THIRTEEN

HE LOVED HER?

Bailey couldn't quite take this in. 'But…we've hardly…'

'It's too soon. I know. We haven't been dating long, we've both got baggage and we should both be taking this a hell of a lot more slowly.' Jared shrugged. 'But there it is. I don't know when it happened or how. It just *is*. I love you, Bailey. You make everything sparkle. My world's a better place with you in it. I know the very second you walk onto the football pitch at work, even if my back's to you and I haven't heard you speak, because the world immediately feels brighter.'

It was the nicest thing anyone had ever said to her.

But still the worry gnawed at her. He'd told her he wanted children. And she'd just told him she was pregnant. Why else would he say that he loved her? 'Are you saying this because of the baby?' she asked.

'No. The baby doesn't change anything about the way I feel about you.' He blew out a breath. 'But I guess there's something I ought to tell you. It's the wrong time to tell you, but if I don't tell you now then you'll be hurt that I didn't tell you when you eventually find out, and… Oh, hell, you'll be hurt if I do tell you.' He rested his forehead against her hair. 'I don't know how to say this.'

'You and Sasha had a baby?' she guessed.

'Not exactly,' he said.

She frowned. 'I don't understand.'

'She was pregnant,' he explained, 'but she didn't know whether the baby was mine or someone else's, because she'd been sleeping with another man, too. Until she told me, I didn't have a clue that she'd been having an affair, much less anything else.'

Bailey was too shocked to say anything. So Jared had been here before. Been hurt. And she'd just brought back all the bad memories for him, too.

'She, um, had a termination,' Jared said quietly. 'When I thought she was going on a girly weekend with her mates.'

'She didn't tell you until afterwards?'

'She didn't tell me,' he corrected softly, 'until the bank statement came through and it turned out she'd accidentally used the wrong debit card to pay for it.'

'How do you mean, the wrong debit card?'

'Sasha didn't work,' Jared explained. 'I used to put money into her account every month, because I didn't want her to feel that she had to check with me or ask me for money before she went out to lunch with her mates or had her hair done. That might've been the way our grandparents did things, but I thought it was important she should feel that she had money of her own.'

So Jared had done what he'd thought was the right thing, and it had come back to bite him.

He sighed. 'When I saw the payment to a private medical clinic, I realised something was wrong.' He gave a wry smile. 'I know I'm a sports medicine doctor, but I was a bit hurt that she hadn't talked to me about whatever medical thing was worrying her. I could've reassured her and maybe helped her get the right treatment. When she came home that night I asked her about it, and that's when she told me about the affair.' He swallowed hard. 'And the reason she'd been to the clinic was because she'd had a termination. She'd got rid of the baby without telling anyone what she was doing—without telling anyone at all. Not me, and not the other guy whose baby it might have been.'

Clearly the double betrayal had cut him to the bone.

'Don't get me wrong,' he said. 'I believe there are circumstances where a termination is the right choice. But I do think you should at least talk over all the options with your partner before you make a decision as life-changing as that.'

'And it wasn't the decision you would've made?' Bailey asked.

He shook his head. 'As I said, even if the baby hadn't been mine, we could've worked it out. Or at least tried to work it out. But then she came out with all this other stuff and I realised that even if the baby had definitely been mine, she would've done exactly the same thing. She didn't want a baby at all. She didn't want the changes it would make to her body.'

'That's… I don't know what to say,' Bailey admitted. 'That was hard on you.'

'On both of us,' Jared said ruefully.

'It wasn't your fault she had an affair, Jared.'

'Maybe, maybe not. My work took me away a lot, and that wasn't fair on her.'

Sasha had taken the choice away from Jared. Did he think Bailey would do the same? Was that why he was telling her this? Or was he telling her that he definitely wanted the baby? She swallowed hard. 'You said in the park, that time, that you wanted kids.'

'I do.' He paused. 'But that's not the be-all and end-all of a relationship, Bailey. You're pregnant with my baby, but that's not why I want to be with you. I want to be with you for *you*.' He took a deep breath. 'And right now I'm guessing that you're in a flat spin, worrying that history's going to repeat itself. This must be your worst nightmare. Your biggest fear come true.'

Her breath hitched. 'Yes.'

His arms tightened round her. 'I know you've had one ectopic pregnancy, but it doesn't mean that this one's definitely going to be ectopic as well.'

Brave, she thought, but misguided. 'We both know the risks of having another ectopic are higher in subsequent pregnancies.'

'It's a *risk*, not a guarantee,' he said. 'Let's start this again. You've just told me that you're pregnant. I know you're scared. I think I am, too. It's a huge thing. But this is amazing, Bailey. Really *amazing*. We're going to be parents.'

'What if…?' Again, she couldn't breathe. Couldn't say the words that haunted her.

'If it's another ectopic pregnancy or you have a miscarriage? Then we'll deal with it if and when that happens,' he said. *'Together.'*

And then she realised that he wasn't going to let her push him away. Even if she tried. He wasn't going to repeat his mistakes, and he wasn't going to let her repeat hers, either.

The bleakness and fear ever since she'd taken the pregnancy test suddenly started to recede. Only a little bit, but it was a start. 'You reckon?'

'I reckon.' He didn't sound as if he had any doubts. 'And I'll be brave and lay it on the line. I want you, Bailey. Yes, I'd like us to have children together—whether they're our natural children, whether we need IVF to help us or whether we adopt. But the non-negotiable bit is you. I love you, Bailey, and I want to be with you.'

He meant it. She could see that in his eyes. He'd been honest with her, and she owed him that same honesty. 'I want to be with you, too,' she said. 'But I'm scared that I'm going to make the same mistakes again. My marriage collapsed because I pushed Ed away, and I know I hurt him. I feel bad about that.' She blew out a breath. 'I don't want to hurt you like that, Jared. Especially as I know you've already been through a rough time.'

'Then maybe we both need to do something different this time,' he said softly. 'Maybe we need to take that leap and trust each other—and ourselves.'

She nodded. 'This is a start.'

He took a deep breath. 'If you decide that you can't go ahead with the baby, then I'll support you. I'll be right by your side.'

Even though a termination was clearly a hot button for him, he'd support her if that was what she wanted.

But that was only one option. What about the really scary one? 'And what if—what if I *do* want to go ahead?' she asked.

'Then I'll still be right by your side. Nothing changes.'

He'd be there for her. Whatever. Regardless. Because he loved her.

'I'm not going to wrap you up in cotton wool—even though part of me wants to—because I know it will drive you insane. So I'll be whatever you need me to be. Though, to be fair, I'm not a mind reader,' he added, 'so you'll have to tell me if I get it wrong, instead of expecting me to work it out for myself. Because I'm telling you now that I probably won't be able to work it out.'

Trust him.

Take the risk.

Could she?

She thought about it. When she'd told him about her ectopic pregnancy, he'd been brilliant. He hadn't pushed her, he hadn't told her what to feel—he'd just held her and listened. He'd backed her in front of Lyle Fincham; he'd even said that if she left the club, so would he. And he'd just opened his heart to her, been totally honest with her.

She knew he'd be by her side all the way through her pregnancy. Not smothering her, not making the decisions for her—but he'd be there to discuss things, to help her see a way forward through all the worries. Just as he was here for her now—holding her, letting her know that he was there, supporting her.

So, yes, she could take the risk.

But there was something else she needed to tell him. Something important.

'I love you, too,' she said softly. 'Even when you're being stubborn and awkward and I want to shake you.'

'I'm glad we cleared that up,' he said dryly.

'And here I am, insulting you again when I'm trying to tell you something really important.' She leaned forward to kiss him. 'I didn't date anyone after my divorce. I never wanted to be with anyone again. I didn't want to take the risk of loving and losing. But I noticed *you*. Even though you annoyed me the very first time I met you, at the same time I noticed your eyes were the colour of bluebells.'

'Bluebells…' He looked amused.

She cuffed him. 'Stop laughing at me. I'm trying to be romantic.'

'Are you, now?'

She loved that sarcastic Scottish drawl. 'And then you trained with me.' She went hot at the memory and her breath caught. 'Your biceps,' she whispered.

He nuzzled her earlobe. 'Yeah. Your back. I hope you know you gave me some seriously hot dreams.'

Just as she'd dreamed about him. 'You danced with me at my best friend's wedding. You kissed me.'

'I wanted to do a lot more than dance with you. And kiss you. Except you got spooked.'

'I know. It scared me that I wanted you so much, Jared. I didn't want to be attracted to anyone. I didn't want to love anyone again. But then,' she said simply, 'there you were. And it happened. I fell for you. As you said, I don't know how or where or when. I just *did.*' She paused. 'I love you.'

'Good.'

She kissed him again. 'So what are we going to do about this?'

'Given that you're expecting my baby and we haven't had a proper courtship?' he asked. 'I guess we're just going to have to take each day as it comes. But one thing I promise you is that I'll always have your back,' he said. 'Just as I know you have mine—I haven't forgotten the way you stood up to Lyle Fincham on my behalf.'

'You stood up for me, too,' she pointed out. And then suddenly it was clear as the panic ebbed further and further away. 'You make me feel safe, Jared. And you make me feel as if I can do everything I'm too scared to do.'

'And you make me want to be a better man,' he said.

'You're already enough for me, just as you are,' she said.

He held her closer. 'So I'm going to ask you properly. I don't have a ring, but that's something we'd choose together later in any case.' He kissed her, then gently moved her off his lap and dropped to one knee in front of her. 'Bailey Randall, will you do me the honour of being my wife?'

'Yes. Absolutely yes,' she said, drawing him to his feet and kissing him. 'I think I'd like a quiet wedding, though.' Particularly as it would be second time round for both of them. Their second chance.

'We can do whatever we want,' Jared said. 'Whether you want a tiny church or a deserted island or a remote castle—whatever you want, that's fine by me. I don't care where we get married or how, just as long as you marry me.'

'I'd like just our family and closest friends there—the people who mean most to us,' she said. 'And then maybe a meal afterwards.'

'Maybe a little dancing. I quite like the idea of dancing with my bride,' he mused. 'And a wedding cake made by Rob.'

'White chocolate and raspberry,' she suggested.

He grinned and kissed her. 'Good choice. I agree.'

'When did you have in mind?'

'I would say as soon as we can, which means a fortnight, but that might be rushing it a tad,' he said. 'So how about...say...six weeks from now?'

Around the time of the twelve-week scan. *If* the baby was even viable. If she wasn't in the middle of another ectopic pregnancy.

'What if it goes wrong?' she whispered.

Luckily he seemed to realise that she was talking about the baby and not them. 'It's not going to stop me loving you and wanting to be married to you,' he said.

'But what if everything goes wrong and I can't have children?' She dragged in a breath. 'You said you wanted children.'

'There are other ways,' he said. 'Adoption. Fostering. Or even if it's just the two of us and a dog and a cat, and we just get to spoil our nieces, nephews and godchildren. We'll still be a family. We'll be together.'

He really, really believed in them.

And the strength of that belief nearly made her cry.

'Agreed. Six weeks,' she said. 'On a weekend?'

'Or a weekday. Whenever they can fit us in.' He paused. 'I need to buy you an engagement ring. Maybe we can go shopping at the weekend.'

She smiled. 'That's not important. It's not about the jewellery. It's about how we feel.'

'I know. But I still want to buy you an engagement ring.' He hammed up his accent. 'I'm traditional, you know.'

'And you're going to marry me in a kilt?'

That made him laugh. 'No.'

She rolled her eyes. 'Spoilsport.'

'It might clash with your dress. Anyway, we need a ring first. We're going to do this properly, Dr Randall.'

She laughed and kissed him. 'OK. An engagement ring it is.'

He paused. 'Though maybe you should meet my family before I give you the ring.'

'And we need to tell mine,' she said. 'Be warned, there will be a party. And nobody parties like Italians.'

'No? Try the Scots,' he said. 'Now, *we* can party all night.'

She smiled. 'So your family likes partying as much as mine? We might have a bit of trouble talking them into a quiet wedding.'

'No. They love us. They'll back us in having exactly what we want,' Jared said. 'My family's going to love you.'

'Mine already likes you.'

'Then we're going to be just fine.' He sat down on the chair again and pulled her back onto his lap. 'I love you, Bailey.'

'I love you, too.'

'And I know you're still scared—so am I,' he admitted. 'But we can talk to the experts and make sure we know what all our options are.'

'They did tell me last time,' she said, 'but I didn't really take any of it in. I guess I was a bit too shell-shocked.'

'Then we'll ask again,' he said. 'We'll get the first appointment we can and ask for an early scan—maybe even more than one, until we're sure this pregnancy definitely isn't ectopic—and the one thing I promise you is that your other tube isn't going to rupture. Because if it *is* another ectopic, we'll do something before that happens.'

She swallowed hard. 'Have a termination, you mean.'

He nodded. 'But it won't be because we don't want the baby. It'll be because the baby doesn't have a chance of survival and it's a risk to your health, which isn't the same thing at all. And I will be right by your side, holding your hand, all the way.'

Giving her courage when she faltered. And letting her give him courage in the bits he found difficult. A true partnership. The same team. That worked for her. 'That,' she said, 'is a deal.'

The next morning, Bailey booked an appointment with her GP. She texted Jared to let him know the time and where to meet her, just in case he could make it.

He made it. She was pretty sure he'd had to call in some favours to do it, but she was glad that he'd kept his promise to her: he was right by her side, all the way.

He held her hand while she told the GP about her previous pregnancy and the GP rang through to the hospital to book her in for an urgent scan.

And he was right by her side as they walked through the corridors towards the ultrasound department at the hospital later that afternoon.

'I'm scared,' she whispered.

'I know you are, but I've got a good feeling about this.' His fingers tightened round hers. 'And, whatever happens, I'm here and I'm not going away.'

No matter what she did or said, he wasn't going to let her push him away. He wouldn't let her repeat her mistakes. Funny how that made everything feel so much safer.

Jared held her hand while the trans-vaginal scan was done, and he didn't say a word about the fact that her fingers were so tightly wrapped round his that she must've been close to cutting off his circulation. He was just there. Solid. Immovable. Her personal rock.

'Dr Randall, I'm absolutely delighted to say,' the ultrasonographer said with a broad smile, 'that you have an embryo attached very firmly to the wall of your placenta.'

The picture on the screen was just a fuzzy blob to both of them; they couldn't really make anything out at all.

But it was their baby.

In her womb, not in her Fallopian tube.

And the nightmare that had happened last time definitely wasn't going to happen again. *It wasn't an ectopic pregnancy.*

Bailey felt the tears spilling out of her eyes as she

looked over at Jared; and she could see that his eyes were shiny with tears, too. 'Are you crying?' she whispered. Her big, tough, dour Scotsman, in tears?

'Yes, and I'm not ashamed of it. We're seeing our own little miracle,' he whispered back. 'I'm so happy. I want to climb on top of the hospital roof and yell it out to the whole world.'

The picture that put in her head made her smile but then the panic came crashing back in to spoil it. 'Not yet. We don't say a word to anyone, not until twelve weeks,' she said. Just in case she lost the baby. There were still no guarantees that everything would be all right. But at least they'd passed the first hurdle.

CHAPTER FOURTEEN

Jared's prediction about his family turned out to be spot on. Bailey adored Jared's family—particularly when Aileen, Jared's sister, took her quietly to one side and confided in her. 'We've all been so worried about him.'

'After Sasha, you mean?'

Aileen nodded. 'But he's seemed a lot happier lately. Now I've met you, I can see exactly why. And I'm so pleased you're joining our family.'

'Me, too,' Bailey said, and hugged her impulsively.

And her family was just as ecstatic when Jared and Bailey dropped in to announce the news of their wedding. And they insisted on having a small party with cake and champagne—including Jared's family—when Jared bought Bailey a very pretty sapphire-and-diamond knot.

To Bailey's relief, Jared didn't wrap her in cotton wool. Instead, he insisted that her life should be pretty much as it always was—only just not quite so intense on the exercise front. But he did move into her place, and he insisted on bringing her breakfast in bed every morning.

Bailey couldn't ever remember being this happy before.

It was hard not to share the news about the baby with her mum and Joni, especially as Joni was blooming with her own pregnancy, but Bailey was completely superstitious about it. She wasn't going to do anything the same this time. She wasn't even going to start looking at baby clothes, or nursery furniture, or baby name books, until they'd reached the twenty-week mark.

But she was glad that Jared had suggested getting married in six weeks' time, because planning everything would keep them both occupied. He'd already booked the register office and asked his oldest brother to be his best man. Her family had immediately offered to sort out the wedding breakfast and the wedding cake—raspberry and white chocolate, as she'd suggested. So all she had to do was sort out her bridesmaid, the dresses, the invitations and the flowers.

On Monday evening, after the yoga class—and luckily Joni had told Bailey exactly which bits Jenna had suggested to tone down during pregnancy, so she was able to do the same without having to ask—she and Joni had their usual catch-up over a chicken salad.

'There was something I wanted to ask you, Joni,' she said. 'How do you fancy being a bridesmaid again?'

Joni stared at her in shock. 'You and Jared, you mean? But…you stopped talking about him. I thought it had gone wrong. And, um—well, I thought you'd tell me about the break-up when you were ready.'

Bailey grinned. 'In answer to your questions—yes, yes, yes, and we've sorted it out so there's nothing to talk about.'

'You and Jared,' Joni repeated.

'Me and Jared,' Bailey confirmed.

Joni hugged her. 'That's the best news ever.'

'Don't cry, or you'll start me off,' Bailey warned, seeing the telltale glitter in her best friend's eyes.

'Sorry. It's hormones making me so wet and crying over everything,' Joni said.

Me, too, Bailey thought, but hugged the secret to herself.

'So when is it all happening?'

'Um, that would be…a little under six weeks.'

Joni looked shell-shocked. 'That soon?'

Bailey shrugged. 'We couldn't see any reason to wait. The reception's going to be at the restaurant, Rob's doing the cake, the register office is booked…so all I need to do is sort out flowers, dresses, and ask you if Olly's band would come and play during the meal.'

'I'm sure they will—in fact, I'll ring him now.' A couple of minutes later she hung up. 'Deal. Olly says he needs to know what the "our song" is.'

'I have no idea.' Bailey spread her hands. 'I guess I'll have to ask my fiancé what he thinks.'

'And I'll go dress-shopping with you any time.'

'Good. That means this Saturday,' Bailey said.

And by the end of Saturday she had the perfect dress—a skater-style strapless dress in deep red velvet that wouldn't let her pregnancy show, even in another five weeks' time, with matching shoes. Joni had a similar dress in ivory with red shoes and a red sash, and her mother found a champagne-coloured suit.

'Look at us. We rock,' Bailey said, when they were dressed up and standing in front of the mirror.

'Jared's going to be totally bowled over. You look so beautiful,' Lucia said. 'You both do.'

They agreed on simple flowers—ivory roses for Bailey and red roses for Joni. The invitations were written and posted. And all they had to do then was hope for a sunny day.

Finally it was the Thursday of Bailey and Jared's wedding day. Bailey had spent the previous night at her parents' house, to preserve the tradition of not seeing the groom until the actual wedding. Jared had sent her a single red rose, first thing, with the message, 'I love you and I can't wait to marry you'—in his own handwriting, she noticed, rather than the florist's.

Joni and Aaron came over to help them get ready, and finally they were ready to go to the register office. As Bailey had been expecting, she and Jared were both interviewed by the registrar—in separate rooms so they wouldn't see each other until the wedding—and then finally the guests were all seated and it was time to walk into the room itself.

They'd arranged for Olly to play a song on acoustic guitar as she walked down the aisle on her father's arm—a love song from Jared's favourite rock band, with the mushiest words in the world, and she'd nearly cried the first time Jared had played it to her.

And her dour Scotsman—wearing morning dress rather than a kilt, but with a velvet bow tie to match her dress—lit up in smiles as he turned to watch her walk up the aisle.

'You look amazing,' he said. 'I love that dress. But, most of all, I love you.'

'I love you, too,' she whispered.

Every moment of the ceremony felt as if it had been engraved on her heart—from the registrar welcoming everyone to declaring all the legal wording.

'I do solemnly declare that I know not of any lawful impediment why I, Jared Lachlan Fraser, may not be joined in matrimony to Bailey Lucia Randall,' he said, and she echoed the declaration.

He took her hand. 'I call upon these persons here present to witness that I, Jared Lachlan Fraser, do take thee, Bailey Lucia Randall, to be my lawful wedded wife.'

And then, once they were legally married, the registrar smiled. 'You may kiss the bride,' she said, and Jared took Bailey into his arms, kissing her lingeringly to the applause of their family and friends.

Once the registration was complete and they'd checked the entry was correct before signing it, there was time to take photographs on the marble staircase. And then, outside the register office, everyone threw dried white rose petals over them.

She smiled at Jared. 'This is even better than snow,' she said.

'Especially as it won't result in broken bones on the football pitch,' he said.

She grinned. 'Indeed, Dr Fraser.'

'Absolutely, Dr Fraser.' His eyes were full of love.

He helped her into the wedding car. There were some last photographs, and then the chauffeur drove them off. It was only when Jared stopped kissing her that she realised they weren't heading in the right direction for her family's restaurant.

'Um, excuse me, please?' she said to the driver. 'I think we're going in the wrong direction.'

'No, we're fine, ma'am,' he said with a smile.

'But we're going the opposite way to the restaurant. Would you mind turning round, please?'

'Sorry, ma'am, I have my orders,' he said.

'Orders?' She frowned. What orders? 'Jared, do you know anything about this?'

He looked blank. 'We already made the arrangements. We're going to your family's restaurant—aren't we?'

She frowned. 'Can I borrow your phone?'

'Sure.'

She rang her mother. Lucia made some completely unsubtle noises that were clearly meant to be static and didn't sound remotely like it. 'Sorry. This mobile phone signal is breaking up,' she said, and hung up.

'I'll try Joni,' Bailey said, but her bridesmaid did exactly the same as the mother of the bride.

'Let me try my mother,' Jared said. Bailey handed the phone back to him, but the result was the same.

'This is obviously their idea of a surprise,' he said. 'Whatever they've planned, they're all in it together.'

'I'm not very keen on surprises,' Bailey said.

'Me, neither, but right now I don't think there's anything we can do but go with it.' Jared smiled at her. 'Their hearts are in the right place.'

'I know,' she said ruefully. 'Sorry. It's hormones making me grumpy. I love you.'

He kissed her. 'I love you, too, Dr Fraser.'

Then she realised they'd pulled up outside the football club. 'What are we doing here?' she asked.

'I have no idea,' Jared said.

Bailey's father opened the door with a beaming smile. 'Dr and Dr Fraser, this way, if you please.' He helped Bailey out of the car.

There was a red carpet unrolled outside, and Jared and Bailey exchanged a glance; both of them had a glimmer of an idea now of what was happening.

They followed the red carpet into the room that the club used for functions. As soon as they walked in, there was a massive cheer from everyone in the room and a flurry of confetti in the air. The walls had been decorated with hearts, balloons and a huge banner saying 'Congratulations, Bailey and Jared'.

She could see everyone there—their families and friends, everyone from the football club, and all her colleagues at the sports medicine unit.

Archie and Darren came up to them. 'We know you wanted to keep it quiet—but we wanted to throw a party for you because you're both so special,' Darren said, and hugged them both.

Bailey had to blink back tears. 'Did you arrange all this, Darren?'

The boy nodded shyly.

'It was all his idea,' Archie said. 'He went to see

Lyle about it, and Lyle got Mandy to help him with the details. He's been talking to both sets of parents and to your best friend, Bailey.'

'I don't know what to say,' Bailey said, 'except this is fantastic—thank you so much!'

The food was fabulous, and the centrepiece was an amazing wedding cake made by her brother. No wonder he'd refused to let her see it, as it was a lot bigger than the one she'd planned—it was the same raspberry and white chocolate cake, but scaled up for many more guests.

'I can't believe you kept it all a secret,' she said to Rob. 'And that cake is just stunning.'

'Anything for my little sister,' he said, 'and the man who made her smile again.'

Finally it was time for the speeches. Jared stood up. 'This wasn't quite what we'd planned for the reception, so I don't have a huge speech. I'd just planned to thank my bride for making me the happiest man alive and I'm going to stick with my plan—well, almost.' He smiled. 'Some of you know that something quite special happened to me when I was seventeen. I thought when I scored the winning goal in the championship that it was the happiest moment of my life, but I was wrong—because today is even better than that. Today, the love of my life married me. So I'd like to make a toast to her. To Bailey.'

'To Bailey,' everyone echoed.

'And I'd also like to thank our family and friends, who managed to surprise us this afternoon as much as we surprised them with the announcement of our wedding,' he said. 'You're all fantastic and we love you.'

Jared's oldest brother gave a short, witty best-man's speech. And then it was the turn of the father of the bride; Paul was almost in tears. 'There's so much I could say—but I want to keep it short and sweet. Bailey's the apple of my eye, and I couldn't find a better son-in-law than Jared. So I want to wish Bailey and Jared a long, fabulous life together.'

Darren stood up next. 'I know I don't really have the right to do this, because I'm not family, but I wanted to make a tiny speech, too.'

'You organised our reception, so I think you earned the right,' Jared said with a smile. 'Go for it.'

Darren took a deep breath. 'I think most of you know that I got into a bit of trouble a few months back, when I wasn't doing very well and I started drinking. Between them, Bailey and Jared straightened me out and gave me a second chance, and I owe them everything. Jared's been a brilliant father figure to me and I just wanted to say thank you. To Jared.'

A brilliant father figure. Yes, Bailey thought, he's going to be a brilliant dad. She squeezed her husband's hand under the table. He caught her eye and at her raised eyebrow he gave a small nod.

'In that case, I think I need to make a speech, too,' Bailey said, standing up. 'Doing this research into soft-tissue injuries at the football club has turned out to be the best decision I ever made, because it's how I met Jared. But what Darren just said really struck a chord with me. Jared's a brilliant father figure. And we've been keeping things under wraps a bit because—well, some of you know it's been a bit tricky for me in the past. But we'd like the world to know officially that Jared's going to be a dad in about six months' time.'

And the room erupted in a froth of cheering and champagne.

EPILOGUE

Six months later

JARED SAT ON the edge of the hospital bed, one arm round his wife and the other resting on the pink-swathed sleeping bundle in her arms.

'She has eyes the colour of bluebells—just like yours,' Bailey said dreamily.

'All babies have blue eyes,' Jared pointed out. 'She'll have brown eyes like you when she's older.'

'Not necessarily—my dad's eyes are blue,' she reminded him.

Jared stroked his daughter's cheek. 'She has your mouth.'

'And your nose.'

'She's beautiful. Our Ailsa.' He leaned over to kiss his new daughter. 'I thought on our wedding day I could never be happier than at that moment, but seeing her safely here in your arms and knowing you're both OK—life doesn't get any better than this.'

She smiled at him. 'Oh, I rather think it will. We have

the first smile, the first word, the first step, the first "I love you, Daddy"—there's all that to come.'

'We're lucky. We got our second chance,' he said softly. 'And I love you, Bailey Fraser.'

'I love you, too,' she said. 'Always.'

* * * * *

THE BABY THAT CHANGED HER LIFE

LOUISA HEATON

For Nicholas, James, Rebecca, Jared and Jack xxx

PROLOGUE

CALLIE TAYLOR STARED at the pregnancy test kit. She felt the weight of it in her hands. There was no point in reading the instructions—she already knew what they said. Knew the simplicity of its words: *'One line indicates a negative result. Two pink lines indicate a positive result'.*

Simple words but such a momentous implication. Life-changing. Well, just for nine months, maybe—because, as a surrogate, she'd be giving the baby away after it was born. But even then…being best friends with the father of the baby meant the baby would *always* be in her life…

Callie opened the box, pulling out the thick wad of paper wrapped around the end of the two kits, and threw the instructions in the bin. She knew how these things worked. As a midwife, she conducted many a test—especially when she worked in the fertility clinic. She placed the second kit back on the shelf and tore through the wrapping around the first.

She had never considered for even one moment that she would be doing this test on herself, and yet here she stood.

What was she doing? Had she made the right decision to do this? To be a surrogate? What if things didn't work out? What if she fell in love with the baby?

No, course not...I'd never do that.

She splashed her face with cold water and dried her hands.

Pee on the stick. That was all she had to do and she would *know.*

Could there be any doubt? It had to be positive, didn't it? She already felt sick and tired all the time. And she kept eating biscuits.

Not much of a sacrifice, though, was it? A big waistline and labour. That was all she had to get through to give Lucas and Maggie their much wanted baby. Callie could do that. And she didn't have to worry about wanting to keep the baby because she'd never wanted kids anyway.

No biggie.

So why aren't I peeing on this stick?

She held the slim white plastic tube in her fingers, staring at it. Her bladder felt full. There was only one thing to do…

She did what she had to and put the cap on the stick, sliding it between the taps on her sink.

I'll look at it in a moment.

Just as she was finishing washing her hands her doorbell rang. They were insistent, whoever they were. Ringing constantly, a finger held on the button, determined not to stop until she answered the door.

'Oh, God… Who is it?' she called out. If it was someone she didn't know, then she wasn't going to bother answering it at all! Did they not know that she had a life-changing moment going on here?

Leaving the bathroom, she glanced around at the state of her flat. It wasn't too bad. There were cups here and there and on the coffee table, papers, magazines and an open packet of gingernuts. Clothes were draped over the back of the sofa, the radiator, and the whole place had a bit of an uncared-for air about it. It looked a mess.

Like me. Besides I'm in my pyjamas.

'Callie, it's me…Lucas!'

Lucas. The father. Maybe…

Okay, I have to answer the door for you, at least.

'Hang on.' Callie moved quickly down her hallway, grabbing stray items of clothes and tossing them all in her bedroom. She ran her fingers through her hair, hoping she didn't look too much like death warmed up, and pulled open the door, trying to seem casual.

'Hi,' Lucas said. He looked awful.

She frowned. Lucas looked pale, distracted. Not his usual self.

Callie followed him into her lounge. 'You okay?'

It wasn't like Lucas just to turn up like this. Normally he'd ring to let her know he was coming round, just to make sure it was all right and she wasn't going out.

Lucas stood in the centre of Callie's lounge, hands in his jacket pockets, looking very uncomfortable. 'No, not really—no.' He fidgeted in his pockets, bit his lip. Then, with nothing better to do, he sat down on the couch in a sudden movement, waiting for Callie to join him.

'What's up?' She hoped this was going to be a quick conversation, considering the state her stomach was in.

Lucas shrugged, unable to meet her gaze. 'Everything. Everything's up.'

Callie felt awkward. Normally in this situation a friend would reach out, lay a reassuring hand on a knee and say, *Hey, what's up? You can tell me.* But Callie didn't feel comfortable doing that. It wasn't who she was. She didn't do reassuring physical contact.

Except with her patients. Somehow it seemed okay to do it with them. It was her professional persona. It wasn't *her*. That was *Midwife* Callie, not *Real* Callie.

Lucas smiled at her, but it was strained—one of those brave smiles that people tried to put on their faces when in reality the last thing they wanted to do was smile.

Callie was even more at a loss.

'Hey…what's wrong?' She edged closer. She could manage that and resist the urge to put her arm around him.

'It's Maggie…'

'What's wrong?' she asked quickly. 'Is she sick?' Callie really couldn't imagine anything worse than that.

'No, not sick. That would be easy to deal with… No, she's worse than sick.' His voice had a tinge of anger to it now, and Callie found herself frowning.

'Then what is it?' She dreaded asking. What would he say? Had she been in an accident? Was she at death's door? In a coma? If it were any of these things, then how would the baby situation work? She'd only agreed to be a surrogate because there was no chance she'd be expected to take care of the baby…

Oh, God, I'm going to be expected to take care of the baby...

Horror and fear grabbed her in their vice and she began to feel icy-cold, almost to the point of shivering. She closed her eyes at the onslaught, hoping that when she opened them again everything would be good and Lucas would tell her something nice.

Lucas took in a deep breath. 'She left. Walked out.'

He looked at her in disbelief and waited for her reaction. His eyes were strangely empty of tears, despite the news.

'*Left*? But—'

'She's been having an affair, apparently. Some doctor in A&E. I don't know—I think that's what she said. She said I didn't love her enough, she wasn't happy, and she's gone.' He stood up then, unable to sit still a second longer, sighing heavily now that he'd told her the important news. He turned to her and did that brave smile thing again. 'Good thing you're not pregnant yet.'

His words echoed around her skull like a bully taunting her in the playground.

Of course. She'd told neither Lucas nor Maggie about feeling a bit dodgy these last few days. She'd kept it to herself so that if it *were* true that she was having a baby it would be the best surprise to give them…

Only now it was backfiring as a great idea. There was a test in the bathroom, currently marinating, about to tell them both their future. She *could* be pregnant. With Lucas's child and no Maggie to play the part of mother!

So who would be mum, then?

Callie recoiled at the thought, looking away from Lucas and shifting back in her chair. She nibbled on her nail, worrying about all the implications.

She'd never wanted to be a mother—that was the whole point! It was her gift to Lucas and Maggie: the most perfect gift you could ever give to your best friend. A baby. Ten tiny fingers and ten tiny toes…all for them to look after, allowing her to swoop in occasionally on visits and bestow a few 'oohs' and 'aahs' before sweeping out again. The perfect—and distant—godparent.

And that was all. Callie wasn't meant to have a bigger role than that!

Sitting there, she felt numb. She knew she needed to go to the bathroom. To check that result. All she had to do was excuse herself…

Callie leapt to her feet and turned to Lucas to say something, but he'd gone. Her eyes tracked a movement to her left and she saw him disappearing into her bathroom…

'No!'

The bathroom door closed and she heard him lock the door.

Oh, God...

She waited.

And waited.

She heard the flush of her cistern, then the running of her sink taps. Closing her eyes in disbelief, she could see in her mind's eye him picking up the test on the sink and finding out that...

That what? It could still be negative, couldn't it? There was every possibility that the egg salad she'd eaten last night had been off. And the day before that? Maybe that jacket potato had been past its sell-by date...

Lucas emerged from the bathroom. He held the test in his hand and came back into her lounge, looking perplexed. His every step was heavy. Then his gaze met hers. 'You're pregnant?'

She stared at him, hearing the words but needing confirmation still. 'It's positive? Two lines?'

He turned it round so she could see and, yes, there were two solid pink lines.

Callie's mouth went dry. Sinking back down onto the couch, she felt her head sink into her hands. Tears burned her eyes with a fire she'd never felt before.

'You're pregnant.'

This time it wasn't a question.

Callie sat numb, aware only of Lucas sinking onto the couch next to her, just an inch or so away.

She hoped he wouldn't put his arm around her, or tell her everything was going to be okay, because how could he? How could he know?

Neither of them had any idea.

So they sat in silence, staring only at the carpet.

CHAPTER ONE

Dr Lucas Gold sat next to Callie in the ultrasound waiting room, wishing he had something he could do with his hands. Nerves were running him through with adrenaline, and he had to fight the strong urge to get out of his seat and pace the floor.

He wasn't used to feeling out of his depth in the hospital. It was his home turf—the place he felt most secure. He knew what he was doing with work and he was looked up to and respected for it. But this situation was brand-new. Something he'd never experienced before. It was completely terrifying and he had no idea how to handle it. His insides were a mish-mash of conflicting thoughts and emotions, all jarring with each other and fighting for superiority, whilst on the outside he hoped he was maintaining an air of calm authority. As everyone was used to.

His best friend, Callie, was drinking water from a white plastic cup, an oasis of calm, whilst he sat there, rigid, a million thoughts running through his head.

'Callie Taylor?' A nurse in blue scrubs stood in a doorway.

He glanced at Callie, meeting her gaze and offering a supporting smile, although he knew he was probably just as nervous as she was. This situation was all just so… complicated! Not the way he'd imagined this time in his life being at all. But he tried not to show it. He didn't want Callie worrying. He didn't want her to think that he had any doubts at all.

Not that I *do. Have doubts, that is. Not about the baby anyway.*

And he knew that *she* just had to be as frightened of this as he was. The situation wasn't perfect, was it? For either of them. People didn't normally plan to have babies like this. But it was the situation they were in and he was going to make it work—no matter what. The important thing here was the baby, and he was determined to do right by his child as well as his best friend. After all, he was the one who'd got her into this mess. There were so many men who got a woman pregnant and then, when the circumstances changed, left them holding the baby.

Well, not me. I could never be that man.

They both stood and he reached out to touch her upper arm, just to offer her some reassurance. But something held him back and he stopped, letting his hand drop away, pretending not to have done it and hoping she hadn't noticed. She wasn't his to touch, after all.

'After you.'

He followed her into the darkened room and stood by her side. He held his hands out as she got onto the bed, to make sure she wasn't about to fall whilst she carried his precious cargo, before sitting down in the chair beside it.

The sonographer smiled at them both. 'Oh, Callie, I didn't realise it was you!' It was one of her colleagues: Sophie. 'Are you happy for me to perform your scan today?'

Callie nodded. ''Course!'

Sophie beamed. 'So exciting! Okay, can you confirm your name and date of birth for me?'

Callie gave the details.

'And it says here that this is your first pregnancy?'

'That's right.'

Callie's voice held a tremor and Lucas glanced at her, wondering what she was thinking.

'And when was the date of your last period?'

'February seventh.'

Sophie fiddled with the plastic wheel that Lucas knew was a predictor of delivery dates. 'So that makes you twelve weeks and two days today—is that right?'

'Yes.'

'Okay, so what I'm going to do is ask you to lower the waistband on your trousers. I'll put some gel on you, which might feel cold but will help the transducer move around easier and also helps with a better image. Now, do you have a full bladder?'

'Fit to burst.'

Sophie laughed. 'I'll try not to press on it too hard. So, do you want to just undo your trousers for me and lower the waist?'

Lucas glanced away, looking elsewhere to give Callie some privacy. He waited for Sophie to tuck some blue paper towel into the top of Callie's underwear before turning back. He watched the sonographer squirt on the gel, mentally hurrying her in his mind, but smiling when Callie gasped at the feel of it on her warm skin. Then he waited.

Sophie had the screen turned away from them both as she made her initial sweeps with the scanner, and Lucas had to fight every instinct in his body not to get up and go round the bed to have a look at the screen himself!

It was difficult to be the patient. To be the person on the other side. He was used to being the one who knew what was going on first. But he knew he had to wait. Sophie would be checking for an actual embryo first, then a heartbeat, before she turned the screen for them to see.

He'd have to learn how to be patient if he was going to be a good parent.

He glanced at Callie and noticed the frown on her face

in the half-light. He wanted to tell her it would be all right, to hold her hand tight in his and tell her that there was nothing for her to worry about, but he knew he couldn't. Not yet. What was the right etiquette in this situation? No one told you *that* at the clinic.

She's pregnant with my child and I daren't even touch her.

Besides, how could he tell her there was nothing to worry about? It wasn't true, was it? There was plenty to worry about. Like how this was going to work in the first place. Maggie was supposed to be by his side at this moment, both of them watching the screen with Callie, but Maggie was gone. That was still a shock. They were on their own now and he had no idea what Callie was thinking.

Then Sophie was smiling and turning the screen. 'There you are…your baby.'

'Oh, my God!'

Lucas couldn't quite believe it! After all the uncertainty—all the testing, the waiting, the drugs, the injections, the tests. After all this time… There it was. A tiny grey bean shape, nestling in Callie's womb, its tiny heart busily beating away. It was amazing. Surreal.

My child...

His eyes burned into the screen, imprinting the shape of his child, the beat of its strong heart, into his memory for ever. This was something that could never be forgotten. Pride filled his soul and he felt an instant connection and a surge of protectiveness for his little bean—and for Callie.

He'd waited so long for this moment…

To be a father...it's real...it's happening...

A laugh of relief escaped him and he reached out without thinking and grabbed Callie's hands in his, not noticing her flinch, forgetting that she wasn't good with physical contact. His prior fears were forgotten in the moment of joy.

'Can you believe it, Callie?'

She shook her head, not speaking, and he saw the welling of tears in her own eyes and was glad. He wouldn't normally be glad to see *anyone* well up with tears or cry, but this was different. They were in a difficult situation, the pair of them, thrown together into having a baby when they weren't even a couple. Now Maggie had gone they had to find a way through this situation themselves…

After Maggie had left them both in the lurch they'd initially struggled even to be in the same room as each other. It had been so hard to know what to do or say in their situation. And so wrong that they had to feel that way! They were best friends and always had been.

Maggie had been quick to see a solicitor and apply for a divorce. She'd said it was best for both of them. She'd been quick to sever all ties.

As the days had passed the atmosphere between him and Callie had got a little less awkward—though it still wasn't what it once had been. He knew Callie had as much adjustment to make to this situation as he had—if not more. It was a tough test of their friendship…one that neither of them could ever have imagined they would have to face. They were both testing the water like anxious ducklings, not knowing if they were going to sink or swim.

Each day that they worked together brought new challenges for both of them. He could sense her awkwardness each time she worked with him. Often he found himself craving the relaxed atmosphere they'd used to have with each other. The ability to laugh at the same things, to predict what the other was thinking.

Only last week he'd helped her out on a particularly difficult shoulder dystocia and, though they'd worked together efficiently for their patient, the old rapport had not been the same and he'd felt the tension between them return the second the baby had been delivered safely. When he'd left the patient's room he'd banged his fist against the wall with frustration at the whole situation.

But he was thrilled that seeing the baby meant something to Callie too. After all, he knew she'd never wanted to have a baby of her own. Not after the way she'd been treated by her own mother. Callie's childhood had been bloody awful compared to his. To see that she was just as affected as he was at seeing the baby onscreen was priceless.

'It's a baby,' she said.

Sophie laughed at them both. 'Of course it is!' She began to take measurements. She measured the head-to-rump length and then zoomed in on the nuchal fold, which was one of the measurements they took at the three-month scan to check the risk factors for Down syndrome. 'This all looks fine. Well within parameters.'

'That's good,' Lucas said, relieved.

'I had no idea you two were together. You kept that quiet,' Sophie said.

Callie glanced at him, a question in her eyes. Should they correct her?

'Actually…er…we're not…' He stumbled over the explanation, his words fading away as he recalled Maggie's impression of their relationship. '*You love Callie, Lucas! Always have! I could never live up to her, so now I'm giving you the chance to be together!*'

'We're not together,' Callie said. 'Just having a baby.'

Lucas gave a polite smile.

Sophie raised her eyebrows. 'There's no "just" about it—you two should know that. Having a baby is hard work.'

'You give all your patients this pep talk?' Lucas didn't want her attacking their decision, and he *certainly* didn't want Callie getting upset. She'd been through enough already, what with all the morning sickness and everything.

'I'm sorry. I didn't mean—'

Lucas shook his head, appalled that he'd been snappy

with her. 'I'm sorry. I didn't mean to be sharp with you/ It's just been a tough few months already.' What was he doing? He wasn't normally this prickly.

But Sophie was obviously used to the up-down moods of her patients and she smiled. 'That's all right. Here—take these.' She passed over a long strip of black-and-white scan photos.

Callie took the opportunity to pull free of his cradling hand and took the pictures first. She held them out before her, admiring each one, and then turned them so that Lucas could see. 'Look, Lucas.'

His heart expanded as he looked at each one. He could physically feel his love growing for this little bean-shaped creature he didn't yet know, but had helped create. All right, maybe not in the most ideal of circumstances, but they'd find a way to make it work. They had to. Even though he knew he and Callie would never be together *like that.*

'You okay?' He looked into her eyes and saw the tears had run down her cheeks now. He hoped they were happy tears. She *seemed* happy, considering…

'I'm good,' she said, nodding. 'You'd better take these.' She offered the pictures to him, but he sat back, shaking his head.

'Not all of them. I'll take half. You'll need some too.'

She looked puzzled, and he didn't like the look on her face. It made him feel uncomfortable to think that maybe she still didn't feel that the baby was part hers.

'It's your baby, too,' he insisted.

The smile left her face and Callie avoided his gaze, looking down and then wiping the gel from her belly using the paper towel.

He helped her sit up and turned away so she could stand and fasten her trousers. Then, when he judged enough time had passed, he turned back and smiled at her. 'Ready for work?'

'As I'll ever be.'

He thanked Sophie for her time and followed Callie, blinking in the brightness of the waiting room. He tried to avoid looking at all the couples holding hands. Couples in love, having a baby. The way *he* ought to be having a child with a partner.

Yet look at how I'm doing it.

He didn't want to think about how appalled his parents must be. He'd avoided talking to them about it, knowing they'd be sad that his marriage had failed. He was upset to have let them down, having wanted his marriage to succeed for a long time—like theirs had.

'Youngsters these days just give up on a relationship at the first sign of trouble!' his mother was fond of saying.

But I'd not given up. I thought everything was fine... We were going ahead with the surrogacy. It all looked good as far as I was concerned. And then...Maggie said it was over. That she'd found true love elsewhere because she'd had to!

Now he and Callie, his best friend in the whole wide world, were in this awkward situation.

We have to make this work.

I have to.

Callie had not expected to have such a strong emotional reaction to seeing the baby on screen. Why *would* she have suspected it? Having a baby had never been one of her dreams, had it? Not really. She'd always been happy to let other people have the babies. She just helped them along in their journey from being a woman to a mother. Others could have the babies—others could make the mistakes. Others could be utter let-downs to their children and be hated by them in the long run. Because that was what happened. In real life.

What did people say about not being able to choose your family?

So even though she'd *known* she was pregnant, logically, had *known* she was carrying a child, she'd still somehow been knocked sideways by seeing it on screen. Her hypothetical surrogate pregnancy had turned into a real-life, bona fide baby that she might have to look after! And seeing it on screen had made her feel so guilty and so upset, because she already felt inadequate. She feared that this baby would be born into a world where its mother was useless and wouldn't have a clue. Callie could already imagine its pain and upset.

Because she knew what it was like to have a mother like that.

Callie waited until the sonographer had led someone else into the scanning room and then she stopped Lucas abruptly. 'Hold this,' she said, passing him her handbag. 'I need to use the loo.' Her bladder was *killing* her! Sophie had pressed down hard, no matter what she'd said about being gentle.

In the bathroom, she washed her hands and then realised how thirsty she was and that she wanted a coffee. Her watch said that they had twenty minutes before they were due to start their shift, so when she went back outside she tried to ignore the anxious look on Lucas's face and suggested they head to the café.

'You okay with coffee?' Lucas asked with concern.

'I think so.' She'd been off coffee for weeks. But now she could feel an intense craving for one and ordered a latte from the assistant. 'This is so strange,' she said as she gathered little sachets of sugar and a wooden stirrer.

Lucas looked about them, glancing at the café interior. 'What is?'

'This.'

'Having coffee?' He smiled.

She gave him a look. 'You know what I mean! This. The *situation*. Me and you—having a baby. I mean…' She swallowed hard, then asked him the question that had been on her mind ever since Maggie had walked away. The question that had been keeping her awake at night. The question that she wasn't even sure she wanted answered. If he said he wanted her to be the mother… 'How's it going to work?'

She could tell her question had him stumped.

He was trying to decide how to answer her. After all, it wasn't an easy situation. After Maggie's big revelation they'd both been knocked for six—especially when Maggie had kept her word and disappeared out of their lives altogether. No one had heard a peep from her—not even the hospital where she'd worked. She'd really dropped them in it as they'd lost a midwife without notice!

For a while Callie had believed that at some point Maggie would call and it would all sort itself out again. That she and Lucas had simply had one giant misunderstanding and it would all be sorted easily. Because then it would be easier for *her. Callie.* And wasn't that how Lucas operated? Before Maggie there'd been other girlfriends. There'd certainly been no shortage of them during the time she'd known him. Which seemed like forever. He'd always been splitting up with them and then getting back together again.

But Maggie hadn't called. The situation hadn't changed.

Callie was pregnant with Lucas's child. But they hadn't slept together and they weren't a couple.

Lucas wanted a baby and Callie never had.

Yet here she was. Pregnant. And though she'd thought she'd be safe getting pregnant, because she wouldn't be in any danger of having to keep the baby, she was now in the predicament that she might have to. Or at least have more to do with it than she'd hoped.

It.

'Honestly, Callie…? I don't know how it's going to work. But I know that it *will*. In time. We'll sort something out.'

He stood opposite her and shook some sugar into his own drink, replaced the lid.

'But *how* do you know that?' She pressed him for more information. He was her best friend in the whole wide world and always had been—for as long as she could remember. There'd once been a moment—a brief, ever so tempting moment—when she'd considered what it would be like to go out with him, but she'd not allowed herself to do it. His friendship with her had been much too valuable and the one stable element in her wretched childhood.

Callie didn't do relationships. Not long-term ones anyway. She'd had dates, and gone out with someone for a couple of months, but once he'd started making mutterings about commitment she'd backed off.

Then one day Lucas had asked her out. On a date. In a boyfriend/girlfriend kind of way. He'd looked so nervous when he'd asked her. And though they'd been great friends, and she'd known she loved him a lot, she just hadn't been about to ruin their friendship by going out on a date with him.

Lucas had been her one stable choice through her childhood and she couldn't risk losing him if things went wrong between them. Besides, they'd both been about to go off to university—it would never have worked, would it? It had been a sensible decision to make.

She could still recall the absolute shock on his face when she'd turned him down. But then he'd left her that night and gone out and met Maggie and the whole thing had been moot, after all.

'I don't know it. But you're sensible—so am I. We're good friends. *Best* friends. I don't see why we won't be able to come to some arrangement.'

She watched him sip and then wince at his coffee. 'I wish I could be as sure as you,' she said. Because Callie wasn't used to certainties. All her life she'd felt as if she lived in limbo—nothing stable, nothing rooted, her mother going through bottles of alcohol as fast as she went through various men, all of them the latest, greatest love of Maria's life.

He put his coffee down and reached out to take her hand, knowing she didn't feel comfortable with personal touch but doing it anyway to make his point. His thumb stroked the back of her knuckles, gently caressing the skin. 'We'll be fine.'

Then he let go and went back to his coffee.

She was relieved he'd let go—relieved to get back control of her hand. Relieved the sizzling reaction to his touch—where had *that* come from?—had gone. Her hand had lit up with excited nerves as his fingers had wrapped around hers and her stomach had tumbled all over like an acrobat when he'd squeezed them tight before letting go.

She gave a little laugh to break the tension. 'Too big a subject when we're due to start work in ten minutes!' She grinned, but inside her mind was racing. She'd never reacted like that to Lucas before. Why? What was happening? Hormones? Possibly…

No, it *had* to be. No 'possibly' about it.

He smiled back, laughing too. 'Way too big.'

Callie laughed nervously. There'd been something reassuring and caring about his touch, and though she disliked physical contact something had changed since she'd got pregnant. It was as if she needed it now but didn't know how to ask for it, having gone for so long without it.

And how threatening was Lucas's touch anyhow? He was her best friend. It didn't mean anything. Not like *that*. And he knew it.

But I'd like you to protect me, Lucas. Promise me I'll be safe.

Lucas sat in his office, twiddling with a pen without really seeing it. There was plenty of work he knew he ought to be getting on with, but his mind was caught up in a whirl of thoughts and emotions. As it had been for many weeks now.

Maggie was gone. But if he was honest with himself that wasn't what was bothering him. Not at all. What bothered him was what Maggie had said on that final night before she'd walked out.

'I tried with you, Lucas, I really tried! But it was all pointless, wasn't it? You've never truly loved me. Not the way you should have.'

'Of course I love you—'

She'd half laughed, half cried.

'But it wasn't real, Lucas! You thought it was, and that was the problem. You lost your heart to Callie long ago and you can't see it!'

'Callie? No, you're wrong. She's my friend...that's all—'

'She's more than your friend and I can't be second best in your life. I need someone to love me for me. I don't want to be your substitute.'

'You're not! Maggie, you're being ridiculous. Callie and I are just friends and that's all we'll ever be!'

'But you still want more. Haven't you noticed how uncomfortable it is for me every time she comes round? How you are with her?'

He'd looked at her then, confused and still reeling from her announcement that she was leaving him.

'Well, yes, but—'

'I know you care for me, Lucas. Maybe you do love me—just not enough. And not in the way that you should.'

'But we're going to have a baby together, Maggie. Hopefully. One day soon!'

She'd looked at him then, her eyes filled with sadness.

'And look who you picked to carry your child.'

Why had he allowed Callie to get into his mess? His beautiful Callie. His best friend. That was all she was. He knew her situation, knew her background—with her awful childhood and her ridiculous drunk of a mother—and he'd stupidly let her get into this situation.

Why?

Was it because Callie always seemed to set things right? Was it because he only had happy memories with her, so he'd let her suggest the surrogacy in the hope that her involvement would somehow set his marriage right?

Maybe. He couldn't be sure.

But now his mess had got real. There was a *baby.* He'd just seen it. And though he was happy, and thrilled to be having a child—there was no disappointment in *that*—he wasn't sure how all of this was going to sort itself out.

He didn't want to pretend. As he had with Maggie. The fact that he'd hurt Maggie hurt him. Pretend to Callie that everything would be fine…? He couldn't be sure. Not really. Callie didn't think she could be a mother so it looked as if he was going to have to raise this baby by himself.

I could do that. Plenty of men are single dads.

But the realisation was there that he *did* want Callie involved. More than she had ever volunteered for.

Was that fair of him? To push her down a road she wasn't ready for? Did he want to parent a baby with someone who wasn't committed—like his father?

The pen dropped to the table with a clatter and he glanced at the clock. He needed to be with his patients.

I'll have to think about this later.

He and Callie could do this. He was sure of it.

Callie was running the booking clinic that afternoon, and there were twelve women booked in to be seen over the next four hours. Due to Maggie's unexpected absence they were still down a staff member and had had to rely on an agency midwife to step into the breach and help out.

Callie took a few minutes to show the new member of staff where everything was, and how to log into the computer system, and then pulled out the first file: *Rhea Cartwright. Sixteen years old.*

Callie checked to make sure she had all the equipment she'd need and then went to the waiting room and called out the girl's name. A young girl, who was there alone and looked far less than sixteen, stood up. Clasping a large bag in front of her stomach, she followed Callie into the clinic room.

'Hi, there. My name's Callie Taylor. I'm a midwife here at St Anne's and I'll be following your case throughout your pregnancy—hopefully right up to the birth. How are you feeling today?'

The girl was about eleven weeks pregnant, according to the notes from her GP, so Callie hoped she was no longer suffering the effects of morning sickness as she herself had done. Those few weeks when it had been at its worst had been just horrible!

'I'm all right.'

The girl answered tersely, without smiling, and didn't meet Callie's eye as she gazed about the room, taking in the breastfeeding poster, the framed black-and-white picture of a baby fast asleep surrounded by sunflowers in full colour.

Callie beckoned her to sit down and settled into a chair next to her. 'No one with you today?'

'My mum couldn't make it. She was busy.'

She nodded. Perhaps Rhea's mum *was* busy. Or perhaps Rhea's mum had no idea of the pregnancy—or, worse still, couldn't be bothered. Callie didn't *want* to jump to that conclusion, but she had personal experience of having an uninterested mother. It wasn't nice. But she couldn't judge someone she'd never met, and nor did she want to jump to conclusions.

'What about your partner? The baby's father?'

Rhea shook her head and looked at anything but Callie. 'I don't want to talk about him.'

She was going to be a closed book. Callie knew she would have to tread softly with Rhea and gain the girl's confidence if she was to learn anything. It was like this sometimes with teenage mothers. They suddenly found themselves in an adult world, living by adult rules, when all they wanted was to live by their own and be left to get on with it.

And in Callie's experience pregnant teenage mothers were often reluctant to show their trust until you'd earned it.

'Okay…well, take a seat.' Rhea still hadn't sat down. 'I'll need to run through some questions with you.'

She tried to keep her voice gentle and neutral. Nothing forceful. Nothing that would suggest Rhea was being ordered or expected to answer questions, as if she was taking some sort of test.

'Just some basic things about you and your last period… that sort of thing. Is that okay?'

Rhea sank into the chair with her bag clasped in front of her, still looking at anything but Callie. She shrugged, as if unwilling to commit either way.

'Well, we'll just start with some basics and see how we go on. Can you confirm your date of birth for me?'

Callie sensed it was going to be a long afternoon. Rhea was not going to give up any information easily. Small red flags were waving madly in her mind. Her midwife's sixth sense, developed over time, was telling her that there was something going on here that she didn't know about. She had learned that it was best to listen to it. It would be so straightforward if every couple or single mother she saw had a happy home life for a baby to be born into, but quite often that wasn't the case. There was a lot of poverty in London. There were a lot of drugs problems, lots of drink problems. Hadn't that been her own experience?

'April the first.'

April Fools' Day. Not a joke. It was confirmed in her

notes. Callie knew she didn't have the type of relationship with Rhea yet to make a joke about the date, so she kept a neutral face and voice and continued with her questions.

'And when was the first day of your last menstrual period?'

There was a moment of silence, as if Rhea was weighing up whether to give her the information or not, then she said, 'February the seventh.'

The same as me.

Callie smiled, about to say so, but decided to hold back. This young girl was so different from her in so many ways.

'Do you mind telling me whether this is a planned pregnancy, or were you using contraception?' she asked without thinking.

She'd not asked just because Rhea was a teenager. It was one of the questions that she always asked. It was important to know whether someone had planned their pregnancy. Whether they'd been actively trying for a baby, or whether the pregnancy was a complete accident and a surprise. It had a bearing on the mother's attitude to it all. Just because a mother was at her booking visit it didn't automatically mean that she wanted to keep the baby. Plus, she needed to know if Rhea had taken any prenatal vitamins.

'I don't see why that's important.'

Callie put down her pen. 'I'm sorry. I just wanted to know whether you'd planned the pregnancy or not.'

'Because I'm sixteen? Because I'm young it must have been a mistake? Is that what you're saying?'

Rhea met Callie's gaze for the first time, and now Callie could see how frightened and unsure this young girl was.

Where was her support? She was so *young*! It had to be scary for her. Callie herself was twenty-eight—a whole twelve years older than Rhea—and *she* was terrified of being pregnant. How could she even begin to imagine how this girl felt?

'No, not at all. I didn't mean that. It's a standard question—'

'Well, I don't want to talk about it. Next?'

Rhea folded her arms and closed up and didn't meet Callie's eyes again for the rest of the meeting.

It was obvious she was a troubled young woman, and if Callie was going to be there for her then she needed to get the young girl on side.

'Let's start again… Let's look at your family health. Any medical problems on your side of the family I should know about? Diabetes? Asthma?'

Rhea shook her head reluctantly. 'We're fine.'

'Again this is a standard question: any history of depression? Anything like that?'

'My mum has that.'

Right, okay—that's something.

'Do you know if your mum suffered with postnatal depression?'

'No.'

'That's okay.' Voice still neutral. Unthreatening. Soft. Rhea was answering the questions.

'What about the father of the baby?'

Rhea stiffened, still not meeting her gaze, shuffling her feet, twiddling with her bag strap with nervous fingers. 'What about him?'

'Any health issues on his side we should be concerned about?'

'I don't know.'

What is it about the father of this baby that she doesn't want me to know?

'How tall is he?'

'What?' Rhea frowned.

'His height? It can have a bearing on the size of your baby.'

Surely she can tell me his height?

'I don't know.'

Callie paused. What was going on here? How did she not know the boy's height? Or perhaps she did know but didn't want to give Callie any clues that might identify him? Perhaps he was an older man? Married? Or was he younger than Rhea? Which would be a whole different kettle of fish. Not that she wanted to think that way, but it was a possibility she had to consider.

'How did you two meet?' That *wasn't* a standard question, but Callie felt she needed to do some extra detective work on this case if she were to get any helpful answers.

'What's that got to do with anything?'

Callie shrugged. 'I'm just interested.'

'Nosy, more like. How I got pregnant has got nothing to do with you. You're a midwife. You should know how people get pregnant, yeah? So just tell me what I need to do next so I can get out of here.'

Callie shrank back from the anger, but she was getting really concerned for Rhea. The girl was so angry and scared. There had to be a way to help her. To get the young girl to trust her.

'Okay, okay… I guess what I really need to know is your intention. You're very young and I have no idea of your support system. I'm making no judgements, but I need to know what your intentions are regarding this pregnancy.'

'My intentions?'

'Yes. Are you keeping it? Are you here to ask about other options?' She didn't want to use the word abortion unless Rhea used it first.

She was quiet for a while, and Callie could see that Rhea's eyes were filling with tears. Her nose was going red and she was really fighting the urge to cry. All Callie's instincts told her to reach out and comfort her, to put an arm around her, to show her that someone genuinely cared. But it wouldn't have been professional to break that boundary—

and, besides, she wasn't comfortable being that person just yet with Rhea. Any show of affection might have the opposite effect and send Rhea running for the hills.

So she sat quietly and waited, her gaze on Rhea's face.

'I don't want it.' Her voice was quiet and empty of emotion.

'You don't?' This was what she'd suspected.

'No.'

'Then there are two options open to you, Rhea.'

Tears rolled down Rhea's cheeks. 'I can't have an abortion. I don't believe in it.'

'Right…okay.'

'I want to give it away. Get rid of it that way.'

It.

So impersonal. So unattached.

I called my baby 'it'.

There had to be personal reasons for Rhea's decision, but Callie truly felt that now was not the time to push for them. If Rhea wanted to give her baby away after it was born, that gave Callie six more months of learning about Rhea and working with her to find out what was going on and how best she could help her.

It was a big decision to give away your baby.

It was what I was going to do. Give the baby to Lucas and Maggie. Only it's not 'the' baby now. It's 'my' baby, isn't it?

Isn't it?

Callie wasn't sure. She and Lucas still hadn't discussed properly what they were going to do to sort this. But they needed to. They were on the clock now and time was ticking. Should she still give the baby to Lucas? Was it even her decision to make?

Callie decided that once the booking clinic was over she was going to call the fertility clinic and ask to speak to one of the counsellors there. She, Lucas and Maggie had each undertaken individual counselling before agreeing to the surrogacy, but the situation had changed now. Everything was different.

I was going to give my baby away. Happily. I was going to do it for Lucas and Maggie.

Who was Rhea doing it for? *What* was Rhea doing it for?

'Okay. We can talk about that. It's a big decision.'

'I know what I'm doing.'

'Have you talked to your family about it?'

'It's not their decision. It's mine. My body—my choice.'

'Of course it is. I'm not denying that.'

'Just put it in my notes that I'm giving it away. The Social can have it. I don't want to see it, or hold it. Just get them to take it away and give it to someone who doesn't know where it's come from.'

'Doesn't know where it's come from'? Why would she say that? Did Maria think that way about me? She never wanted me. Never wanted anything to do with me. Was my own mother like this young girl once?

'I'll put it in your notes. You do know that I'll be here for you throughout this, Rhea? Any time. You'll be able to call me, night or day. I'll give you my contact details.' She passed over a small card that had the hospital numbers and Callie's own personal mobile number on it too.

Rhea stuffed it into her bag. 'I don't want anyone judging me.'

'No one will do that.'

'You don't know what I've been through.'

'No. But I'm hoping that at some point you'll trust me enough to tell me.'

She meant it. Sincerely she meant it. And she hoped Rhea could sense that. It was at times like these that Callie's job meant the world to her. It was at times like these when she felt she could really help someone—and this young girl clearly needed help for something.

If only she'd let me in. If only she'd let me help her so that another baby doesn't grow up feeling like I did as a child. Unwanted and unloved.

'Don't you need to take my blood pressure or something?'

Rhea broke the silence and Callie nodded, glad that Rhea was offering her something.

'Of course. I need to take blood, too.'

'I brought this.' Rhea reached into her bag and took out a small jar with a urine sample in it. 'I washed it out before I used it.'

'That's great—thanks.' She would need another sample if this one was more than two hours old. It was hospital policy. However, she wasn't going to say that. Rhea had offered her a little something. That would have to do for now.

Rhea's blood pressure was fine, as was her urine sample. Nothing out of the ordinary and all well within parameters. Physically, she seemed fine. It was just emotionally that something was off.

'You know, I'm really looking forward to getting to know you better throughout this, Rhea.'

'Yeah, well, don't go thinking you'll get me to change my mind.'

'That's not my place.'

'No, it isn't. No one has the right to judge me for giving this thing away.'

'No, they haven't.' *I was going to give a baby away myself.* 'But please don't call the baby a "thing". Call it what it is.'

Rhea stood up to go and slung her bag over her shoulder. 'It's a *thing.* It will always be a *thing.* It'll never be anything else.' And she stormed from the clinic.

Callie watched her go, bewildered and amazed. In some ways Rhea seemed so strong, but in others she was just a tiny young girl, terrified and afraid.

And what am I afraid of?

Callie's hand went to her own stomach, as yet still unchanged in size. She didn't even know she was doing it until her phone beeped a text message alert and she was brought back into the present. As she rummaged in her bag for her phone thoughts echoed through her mind.

Don't go getting attached.

You have no idea if you're keeping it either.

CHAPTER TWO

THE NEXT DAY Callie was scheduled to work on a twin delivery. She could see that Lucas was on duty that day too, along with the senior consultant Dev Patel, though she hadn't seen him yet. They had four women in labour, most in early stages, and Callie had been assigned to a woman in her late forties, having her first babies. Callie hadn't been expecting to work with Lucas, but he was already in the room.

'There's been some decelerations,' he said, after saying hello and seeing her look of surprise.

Olivia Hogarth was on her knees, leaning over the back of the bed, panicking and almost out of control, showing real signs of not dealing with her labour at all. Every time a contraction came along a terrified look came into Olivia's eyes and she began to huff and puff on the Entonox as if for dear life. Her husband, James, stood helpless beside her. He was at a complete loss as to what to do, but kept rubbing her back for dear life as she held on to the support of the bed.

'Hi, Olivia, I'm Callie, and I'm going to be your midwife today.' Callie leant round the back of the bed so Olivia could see her face and not just hear a random voice.

'Hurgh!' Olivia's teeth gripped the mouthpiece and her frightened gaze practically begged Callie to do something. 'Help me!'

'Okay…slow, deep breaths…that's it. Slow your breathing.' Callie showed Olivia how to breathe in slowly through her nose for five seconds and then out through her mouth for five more seconds.

'I'm all tingly!' Olivia protested when the contraction was over. 'Pins and needles.'

'It's because you're not exhaling properly. Come on—practise with me whilst there's no contraction.'

As Olivia practised Callie took a moment to glance at Olivia's trace. There were some decelerations in the babies' heartbeats. Not by much, but they were definitely there. Each time Olivia's babies got squeezed by a contraction the heart-rate dipped, which meant they weren't liking labour very much.

Callie wasn't happy with the trace and glanced up at Lucas as he came to stand by her and judge it for himself.

Sometimes decelerations could be caused by there being a short cord, or a knot in the cord, or by the cord being tightly wrapped around the baby's body. It didn't mean that there was something wrong with the baby physically. But Callie knew it was never worth taking any chances. It was always best to call for help if you were working alone. If you weren't sure you got someone else. Fortunately she already had Lucas there.

He stood beside her, dressed all in black, in tailored shirt and trousers, and she could smell his aftershave. Since she'd got pregnant smells and aromas had seemed particularly pronounced, and his was delicious today.

Callie glanced at him sideways as he concentrated on the trace. Her heart skipped a beat—*palpitations?* She'd never had those before—it had to be the pregnancy. She supposed she couldn't help it, she thought wryly. He was a very attractive man after all. Hadn't she watched a multitude of women fawn over him?

He was tall, broad and handsome. It was hard to think

that the little boy she'd once known—the one with the spindly legs and constantly scuffed knees—had turned into this strong, mature, devastatingly handsome man. It never mattered what was going on in her own life—her mother letting her down yet again, her mother lying to her, someone treating her badly—she always brightened when she saw Lucas. He was her pillar. Her rock. Her safe place in stormy seas. He'd always been there for her and she hoped he always would be. Especially now. Now they were having a baby together—even if it wasn't in the traditional way.

He looked really good today. Fresher and brighter-looking than she'd seen him look these last few weeks. Maggie leaving the way she had, and admitting to an affair, had shaken them both. But even though Lucas had been shocked by the end of his marriage, he'd thankfully not been devastated. He'd coped with the change in his life amazingly well, and she couldn't help but admire him for his courage and resilience—as everyone did.

She could only assume that seeing the scan yesterday had perked him up. Either that or he'd managed a great night's sleep! His eyes were bright and blue, like cornflowers in a summer meadow, and there was colour to his cheeks. He'd even shaved! These last few weeks he'd been beginning to look like a mountain man.

She liked the fact that he looked bigger and stronger. It made her feel safe and protected, and she knew he'd move heaven and earth to do anything to help her at the moment.

Callie couldn't help but wonder what this pregnancy was *doing* to her? Her emotions and responses seemed hyper-aware, with all these hormones floating about, and she knew she needed to be careful that she didn't let them carry her away. He cared for her because they were good friends. Nothing more.

He's just my friend. Yes, he's the baby's father, but it's not like we slept together, is it? It was all done in a petri dish in a clinic—nothing romantic.

But just thinking about sleeping with Lucas made her cheeks flush with heat.

She knew she needed to focus on her patient and deliberately stepped away from him. Thoughts about sleeping with Lucas were dangerous and she'd never allow them to surface.

Olivia finished puffing on her gas and air and looked panicked, her eyes open wide. 'What's wrong? Is it the babies?'

Lucas pulled out the long white roll of paper and checked through the tracing with Callie. He gave a tiny nod. 'Olivia, Baby A seems to be a bit upset after each contraction and Baby B doesn't look too happy either. It may just be because of the reduced room in your uterus and the contractions, but I'd like to be on the safe side.' He turned to Callie. 'When was her last examination?'

She checked the notes. 'Four and a half hours ago. Would you like me to do another?' They tried to examine women vaginally every four hours during labour. This usually gave the cervix plenty of time to show the changes every midwife and mother wanted to feel.

Lucas turned the full beam of his attention on the mother. 'Sure. Olivia, we'd like to examine you, if possible, see how you're getting along. Is that all right?'

'Of course.'

Lucas looked at Callie and nodded.

'I'll be as gentle as I can…'

Callie washed her hands and then put on gloves, settling herself on the side of Olivia's bed as she did so. She felt as much as she could, her fingers sweeping the edge of the cervix, her eyes on Lucas.

He kept checking with Olivia to make sure she was all right and apologising for any discomfort she might be feeling, but Olivia was quite stoical. The most calm she'd been since Callie had met her. Perhaps she could cope better with men around, supporting her, rather than another woman?

As Callie removed her gloves she smiled. 'You're making good progress. Eight centimetres.'

'Eight!' Olivia began to suck in gas and air again as another contraction hit, so she didn't notice Callie take Lucas to one side of the room.

'I'm concerned there's some extra blood in the birth canal,' she whispered. 'I don't want to panic her, but I think we need to put a continuous CTG on her and the babies and keep it monitored.' CTG was cardiotocography—a technical way of recording the foetal heartbeats as well as any uterine contractions.

'Yes, we need to be alert for any signs of possible placental abruption.' He kept his voice low.

Placental abruption was a life-threatening condition in which the placenta detached itself from the uterine wall before birth, causing heavy bleeding and potentially fatal consequences for both mother and baby if not caught in time.

'Possibly.'

'Okay. I want to move her to Theatre, just in case.'

'I'll ring Theatre to let them know we're coming.'

And just as Callie said this blood soaked into the sheets around Olivia's legs.

Her husband, James, leapt to his feet. 'My God! What's going on?'

Callie and Lucas leapt into action. There wasn't much time. They had to act fast. They quickly unplugged Olivia from the monitors, grabbed the ends of the bed and began to wheel her from the room.

Lucas kept his voice calm, yet firm, as he gave an explanation to James and Olivia. 'Your wife's bleed may mean the placenta has detached early from the wall of her womb. We need to do an emergency Caesarean to get the babies out safely.' Lucas's controlled, assertive voice was an oasis of calm in a situation that could so easily be filled with panic or fear.

'Is she going to be okay?' The colour had gone from James's face.

Olivia looked pale and clammy and her head was beginning to loll back against the pillows.

'Just follow us. It's going to be a general anaesthetic, so you won't be allowed into Theatre, I'm afraid.'

They began to push the bed from the room and head up the corridors towards the operating rooms. Lucas called out to passing staff to help and they responded to his firm authority and helped them get Olivia to Theatre.

'And the babies?'

As they reached the theatre doors there was a large sign stating 'Staff Only Beyond This Point' and James slowed to a stop, looking lost and hopeless.

Lucas turned back briefly and laid a reassuring hand on James's arm. 'We'll do our best for all of them.' And then he and Callie pushed Olivia into Theatre, leaving James behind, bewildered and in shock.

They didn't like to do it, but James was not their first priority at this point. Time was critical now, and they couldn't waste it by stopping to talk it through with Olivia's husband. They could debrief him afterwards.

It was a mad rush of preparation. They'd not had time to call Theatre, so the first the theatre staff knew of an emergency coming was when they wheeled Olivia in. But they were such a well-oiled machine that they all knew what to do.

Within minutes, they had Olivia under general anaesthetic, drapes up, and Lucas was scrubbed and ready to go. The theatre staff were used to emergency sections, and they all liked working with Lucas, who was calm and fair and friendly—unlike some of the other doctors who operated.

Lucas could just give a look and everyone would know what he needed. His authority was not questioned, and everyone in his team looked to him for guidance.

'I'm going to perform a lower segment section.' He pointed the scalpel to Olivia's skin and in one quick yet sure movement began the emergency operation.

Callie stood by the side of the bed, her heart pounding, her legs like jelly. She really disliked occasions such as this. *Emergencies*. If she could have her way then all babies would be born normally, without danger, without the need for Theatre. Babies were meant to arrive in calm environments, with music softly playing in the background, and then to be placed in their mother's arms afterwards for that all-important cuddle and skin-to-skin contact.

General anaesthetics and emergencies took away all of that. Babies were separate from their mothers until the mother was awake enough to hold the baby without dropping it, and sometimes that initial important breastfeed was missed because the mother was unable to do it, or the baby itself was too drowsy from the cross-over of the drugs the mother had had.

Her lips felt dry beneath the paper mask. She glanced at Lucas, admiring the concentration in his gaze, his composure. Despite the emergency, he knew exactly what needed to be done and how. But as she stood there Callie realised she was beginning to feel a little bit woozy and hot.

The rush from Olivia's room and pushing the bed through the corridors wouldn't normally have taken its toll, but now that she was pregnant she felt a little more fragile than normal. She still felt out of breath from the sprint and her brow was becoming sweaty, as was her top lip. Her stomach began to churn like a washing machine, as if she was about to be sick.

It wasn't the sight of the blood. That sort of thing never bothered her. Nor was it the controlled tension in the room.

No. This was something else. She didn't feel right at all. She looked at Lucas over her mask in a panic, hoping he'd look up. See her. Notice that something was wrong.

She could feel something…a weird sensation beginning to overcome her. If she could try to focus on his calm, reassuring face she felt it might help, but her vision was going a bit blurry and the noises in the room—the beeping of machines—began to sound distant and echoing.

As she felt herself sway slightly she put one hand on the bed to steady herself. Lucas looked up from his work and frowned.

'Callie? You okay?'

But his words sounded as if they were coming from far away. She blinked to clear her eyesight, felt her heart pound like a hammer and then heard a weird whooshing noise in her ears. A black curtain descended and she went crashing to the floor, taking a tray of instruments down with her.

'Callie!'

Lucas was unable to catch her. She'd been standing on the other side of the operating table and there was a patient between them. Instead he had to stand there, horrified, his scalpel poised, as she collapsed onto the floor and lay there, despite the best efforts of the scrub nurse to try and catch her.

Her arms were outspread, her eyes closed.

I need to concentrate on my patient first. Her life is in my hands. I'll have to let the others take care of Callie.

The situation killed him, but what could he do? Just focus on delivering Olivia safely and *then* he could check on Callie.

How did I not see she looked pale? he berated himself inwardly.

The anaesthetist couldn't move either, but two other theatre assistants got Callie up onto a trolley and wheeled her from the theatre. He watched her go, his heart in his mouth, his mind whooshing with a million thoughts. But he pulled it back.

I need to be professional. Callie's in good hands. I know that. I can't do anything here but look after my patient.

The staff were great. They knew the situation—knew Callie was Lucas's surrogate, and knew how much it must be hurting him not to be with her—so they all did their best to help him work quickly, so he could be with her.

Lucas had to think fast and concentrate. All he wanted to do was leave Theatre and go and check on Callie, but he *knew* he couldn't! His professional integrity told him to stay with his patient. Her life and that of her babies were on the line.

Once into the uterus, he was able to deliver both babies quickly. They came out crying, which was great. A glance at the monitors assured him that Olivia was doing fine, despite the emergency.

A few moments later the theatre assistants returned.

'How's Callie?' he asked, busy removing the placentas.

'Coming round. We left her in the staffroom with one of the midwives looking after her,' the assistant called, her back to him as she assessed the babies at the Resuscitaires.

'How are the babies?'

'Pinking up—we'll get there,' confirmed the paediatrician, and then there was a lusty cry and Lucas was able to let out a breath he hadn't realised he'd been holding. He glanced at the anaesthetist at the head of his patient.

'Sats ninety-seven per cent, BP dropped. But she's stable…she's good.'

That was good to know. He'd expected Olivia's blood pressure to drop with the bleed, but if she was stable then it looked as if both mother and twins were going to get through this.

Once both the placentas were out Lucas began to stitch,

sewing together all the layers of muscle and fascia that made up the abdomen, finally closing Olivia's lower belly about forty-five minutes after he'd first had to open her.

It had been nearly thirty minutes since Callie's collapse and he was desperate to see her. His stomach was in knots, but he sewed quickly and efficiently. He kept clenching and unclenching his jaw as he thought of all the things that were worrying him.

Why did she faint? *Was* it a faint? Or something else? Perhaps she'd not eaten properly that morning? There had to be a reason, and he intended to do a full medical check-up on her when he got out of Theatre.

Why was everything going wrong? Having a child was meant to be one of the happiest times of his life! Yet it was all such a mess. He still didn't know what was going to happen after the birth, and now Callie had collapsed. He hated not being able to be there for her and he wanted to be. Every step of the way.

Finally Olivia was ready to go through to Recovery. The assistant and porters wheeled her away and he thanked the staff, seeing their appreciative smiles and nods, then scrubbed clean, quickly changed his scrubs and hurried off to find Callie.

He found her looking pale and ashen in the staffroom, feet up on the chairs and her hands shaking as she nursed a hot sweet tea.

He rushed straight over to her, kneeling by her side and feeling her forehead. 'Are you all right?'

She looked sheepish and slightly disturbed by his hand on her head, so he removed it.

'I'm fine.' Her voice sounded weak and shaky.

'You passed out.' He knew he sounded angry and was stating the obvious, but…

'I'm fine.'

'How do I know that?' Next he reached for her wrist and

felt her pulse as he glanced up at the clock in the room. Her skin was cool and soft, but her pulse was going quite fast. She pulled her hand free.

'Honestly, Lucas. I'm fine.' She sounded angry.

He knelt next to her, filled with concern, wanting to ask her a million questions, wanting to know if she'd hurt herself when she fell. He checked her over—skin pallor, pupil dilation, carotid pulse, respirations.

'You've no pain?'

'No. How's Olivia and the twins?'

'All doing well. Which is the least that can be said for you.'

'I missed breakfast, that's all.'

'That's *all*? You know how important breakfast is in your condition.'

'I know!'

'And yet you missed it? Why? What were you doing?' He tried his best not to sound angry, but knew she could hear it in his voice.

She shrugged, looking guilty. 'I slept in.'

'You *slept in*?'

'I was late getting up. I hit the snooze button a few times and then it was too late to eat breakfast, so I came straight to work. I was going to grab a banana or something.'

'So all you've had is that tea?'

'Yes.' She at least managed to look shamefaced.

He frowned, thinking of how he could immediately put this right. 'Wait there. Don't move.'

Lucas disappeared from the staffroom, headed for the stairs and ran down two stairwells, jumping the last couple of steps and skidding out onto the ground floor of the hospital. Women looked at him as he passed, but he didn't notice.

There was a store selling most things—mainly for visitors—and he grabbed lemon and raisin pancakes, a banana, chocolate and a snack pack of fresh strawberries, and headed back upstairs with his carrier bag full of goodies.

In the staffroom, Callie watched him thoughtfully as he arranged everything on a plate—slicing the banana and strawberries, pouring her a glass of milk and laying out the food as if it had been served at a hotel.

Then he turned to her with a smile, a towel folded over his arm as if he was a waiter. *'Voilà!'* he said with a flourish.

She laughed as she took it from him, and he grinned at her delight. Her laughter and pleasure made him feel good in a way he hadn't felt for some time. But Callie had always been able to cheer him up. She'd always been there for him. And there was something about her smile and childish delight that touched his heart.

'Now, you're not allowed to complain—in this situation I get to look after you,' he said.

Callie stabbed a strawberry with her fork and popped it into her mouth. 'I could get used to it.'

He nodded, his eyes shining with pleasure, and then a serious thought shot to the front of his head. It was a huge decision—a huge idea—but it felt so right and he just let it out.

'Then let me do it.'

'Do what?' she asked quizzically, another strawberry piece halfway to her mouth, suspended on the end of her fork.

'Move in with me. To the spare room,' he added, feeling his cheeks colour as he realised just what a huge thing he was asking.

Where had *that* idea come from? Okay, he hadn't liked the idea of not being there for every moment of her pregnancy, but he'd resigned himself to it. Hadn't he? It was what he would have had to do if Maggie had still been around. Or would it have come to this anyway? Her moving in to his spare room?

'No strings—nothing like that. Just a friend sleeping over. Just…let me look after you.' Suddenly he needed her to agree to this. And why not? They were best friends—how hard could it be? They'd spent years together, they knew each other inside out, and it wasn't romantic or anything. He knew that would never happen—she'd always been clear on that.

She slowly chewed the strawberry before swallowing. 'But why?'

'Because I shouldn't have to be worrying about you all the time!' His exasperation burst from him unexpectedly. 'I think about you constantly, Callie!' It was true. His mind was always on her just lately. Since the pregnancy, anyway. 'Whether you're okay, whether you're sick, if you're having pains, if you're bleeding and not saying anything. I worry, okay? It *is* natural—you *are* carrying my child.'

Callie stared at him, saying nothing. She wasn't used to people caring about her.

'I never wanted it to be this way.' He brought his voice down an octave or two, even though they were alone in the room. 'I thought I'd have a child the normal way, you know? Married…living with the woman who was carrying the baby…being there for everything. Missing nothing. The first kick. The first movement. The Braxton Hicks. The real contractions. The rush to hospital for the birth.' He let out a big sigh. 'I don't want to do this from a distance.'

'Do what?'

'*Fatherhood.* I can't do it from a distance, Callie. I'm not my father. At least consider it. Please?'

She stared long and hard at him and he wasn't sure whether to say any more. He decided to remain silent. He'd not meant to say *anything*! But it was tough, being a dad-to-be and not being allowed to hold the woman carrying your child. Not to be involved. He'd thought he'd be able to handle it, but what if he couldn't?

How had his own father done it? Eight kids in total, eight pregnancies, and he'd been away on duty in other countries for most of them. How had he got on with life? By not being there for it all? Easily. That was how. Because his father was a totally different creature. A man who liked to have the knowledge that his wife was forever pregnant, so other men knew she was taken, was unavailable, but without the day-to-day drudgery of being at home himself. He thought it was boring.

Callie was his best friend but the lines between them were blurring now, because of the baby she was carrying. She had always meant so much to him, but now she meant *everything.* She was precious and fragile and carrying his child—and he wanted to be there. Was that so wrong?

He couldn't think about what Maggie might have said if they'd still been together. How would she have reacted to him asking Callie to move in with them?

Not very well.

'I'll think about it,' she said, eating a slice of banana.

He nodded, satisfied with that answer for now. 'No strings. Strictly spare room stuff. Just…in the same home. That's all. Think of it as a long-term sleepover at a mate's house.'

Callie put down her fork as he reached out for her and wrapped his arms around her shoulders, holding her close, squeezing her gently, enjoying the feel of her next to him, knowing that this was as close as he would ever get.

'You worried me. I don't ever want to have to see you that vulnerable again,' he whispered into her hair. He felt her hot breath against the side of his head and realised he had to fight to not turn his face to her.

'I'm sorry.'

'Let me look after you. It'll be fun.'

She pulled back and looked at him, laughing. *'Fun?'*

It was good to laugh with her, to see the happiness in her eyes. 'Why not?'

Callie tilted her head to one side and looked at him strangely. 'I'd need to pay rent.'

He nodded. 'Fine.'

'And I'll do my own laundry.'

'Double fine.'

'And I get to cook sometimes.'

'Hmm…'

'Oy!' She gave him a prod. 'I'm not that bad!'

'Okay. Deal.' He held out his hand and she took it.

It had been a difficult time—a difficult event, seeing her collapse like that. But in these last few minutes he had his best friend back. And it felt good. Being close to her once again.

The only problem, Lucas began to realise as he sat facing her, was that he wasn't sure if he wanted to let go of her at all.

What mess had he got them both into?

CHAPTER THREE

CALLIE HAD MANAGED to get hold of Rhea on her mobile phone and persuaded her to come in. After Rhea had stormed off the other day there were still lots of things that Callie needed to do to make sure she was looking after Rhea in the best possible way. That meant doing blood tests and asking some of the questions that she hadn't got to ask in the first place.

As an incentive, she'd arranged for Rhea's first scan, hoping that the sight of her baby might make Rhea open up a bit more.

When she arrived, Callie noted that Rhea was wearing the same dowdy pink top and jeans as before, and was looking a little bedraggled. She invited her into the clinic room and offered her a cup of tea.

'I can't drink tea at the moment, thanks.'

'Me neither. Would you like coffee?'

Rhea looked at her, head tilted to one side. 'You're pregnant, too?'

'I am.' She smiled, hoping that this sharing of a confidence might provoke the same in her patient. 'Just out of that horrible first trimester. The sickness was awful—I tell you, it certainly made me think twice. How about you?'

Rhea nodded. 'I never wanted to be pregnant in the first place. The sickness was like extra punishment.'

Callie could empathise about the sickness. She smiled reassuringly. 'So the pregnancy is unplanned?'

'I didn't ask for it.' Rhea was instantly abrupt.

It was an odd response, and Callie wasn't sure what to make of it. 'What *did* you ask for?'

Again Rhea couldn't meet her eyes, but there were tears threatening again and Rhea was struggling to hold them back. Callie knew she had to offer Rhea something, in the hope that the girl would open up to her.

'Last time we met you mentioned you wanted to give the baby away. Have it adopted.'

'So?' The response was almost a challenge and Rhea glared at her, as if daring her to criticise.

'So…' Callie took a deep breath and plunged in. 'I want you to understand that adoption is a huge thing. It's difficult for the birth mother. You know…having carried the baby for nine months. Felt it kick, felt it move, gone through labour for it. I want to know that you've thought it all through.'

Callie didn't feel there was any need to mention that she was in a similar situation. For now, she needed Rhea to think hard about her choice, to look at her decision carefully. Without rushing.

Rhea looked at her with barely disguised curiosity. 'Yeah? I thought the Social would just take it away if I didn't want it.'

'Yes, they would. But they'd *also* give you the time to say goodbye. See the baby. Hold him or her. Some mothers who choose to have their babies adopted keep the baby for a few weeks, just to be sure of their decision.'

'I don't want to look after it! I don't want to see it!'

Callie frowned at such a strong, determined response. She wasn't judging Rhea's decision. She was free to make the choice to have her baby adopted. But Rhea was so young—only sixteen—and Callie knew she had to be sure that Rhea had thought this through properly and not just rushed into a decision because the pregnancy was still a shock.

'Okay, and that's fine—you don't have to if you don't want to. But, Rhea, you have to understand that, as a midwife, I know many women feel emotional after giving birth. It's such an arduous thing. It hurts, you're exhausted, but at the end of it—for most women—there's the prize, if you like, of a baby. They *need* to hold it. Need to see it. Smell it, touch it. See that after all those months of watching a bump grow their baby is real and that they're different people now. Mothers.'

'There's nothing you can say that will make me change my mind.'

Callie held up her hands. 'I'm not trying to. It's not my place and it would be totally unprofessional for anyone to do that. This is your choice, and whatever you choose will be fine by me.'

Rhea nodded firmly.

'As long as I know that you've thought through the consequences of your choice properly. It's not something you'll be able to just forget. It will always be with you.'

Rhea pulled her mobile phone from her pocket, checked the display and then put it away again. 'You're trying to make me feel guilty.'

'No. Absolutely not. But I *will* be devil's advocate and make sure you've thought through your choice—because, Rhea, you don't want to get a couple of years down the line and suddenly be filled with regret, with no way of reversing your decision.'

'You think I'll want it later on?' she scoffed. 'You've *got* to be kidding me.'

'I don't know how you'll feel later on. But I want you to think about it. I want you to imagine you give up this baby and a few years pass by, life carries on, and then you find yourself wondering about your daughter or your son.'

Rhea shook her head. 'I won't.'

'Okay, but I want you to think about it. You've got time, after all, if you're going to go through with the pregnancy.'

Rhea shrugged. 'I appreciate what you're doing, okay? You're a midwife. You must love babies to do this job. But I'm not you. I don't live in la-la land, where everything is right and beautiful. Where I come from it's tough and hard and life is cruel. I don't need to be saddled with the burden of a baby in a fourteenth-floor flat reached with a broken lift that stinks of old pee.'

'I know what it's like to have a tough life, Rhea. My childhood was no bed of roses, believe me.'

Callie bit her lip. This wasn't the time to be sharing personal information with Rhea. It wasn't professional. But she needed to get through to her somehow.

'Let me guess…your parents got you the wrong type of doll?'

'Actually, my alcoholic mother dragged me through childhood. Reluctantly.'

She regretted her words as soon as she'd said them. Callie knew better than to share that much personal information with a patient. But there was something about this young girl that called out to her.

Rhea stared hard at Callie, assessing her words, judging if she thought they were real. But she must have seen the truth in Callie's eyes, because she looked away and then apologised.

'It's okay. I'm sorry. I should never have said that.' Callie told her.

'I'm glad you did. Made you seem a bit more real.'

'Worldly-wise?' Callie smiled.

Rhea managed a small smile, the corners of her mouth turning up. 'Yeah.'

'It's easy to assume that everyone else's life is better than ours, but sometimes it just isn't.'

'No.'

Callie gathered the notes on her desk, taking a deep breath, and changed the subject slightly. 'Do you have support, Rhea? Family?'

'My mum—though she's as much use as a chocolate chisel.'

Callie smiled. Snap. Her own mother was now supposedly a *recovered* alcoholic, rather than an 'active' one, but Callie wasn't sure whether she was or not. Maria *said* she was off the sauce, but Maria was a born liar and Callie had heard enough lies to last a lifetime.

It was the one thing she couldn't stand more than anything. Liars. There was just something so horrible about them. Being untruthful. Taking you for a fool. Not respecting you enough to give you the truth. Assuming you were stupid enough to fall for the fallacy. Everything Callie's mother now said she took with a pinch of salt.

It was why she tried her hardest to have as little to do with her as she could, despite Maria's constant efforts to get in touch. The times Callie *had* bothered, the times she had made the effort, had always been in vain and dealing with the constant let-downs was just getting too much. It was easier not to try.

'Your dad? Brothers? Sisters?'

'Just mum.'

Like me. And Rhea is pregnant—like me. And both our mothers are useless and both of us are pregnant in difficult circumstances.

Tears began to prick and burn her eyes and she quickly turned away, pretending to look for something in a drawer. She felt a tap on her arm and turned back to see that Rhea was holding a box of tissues out to her. The box of tissues that Callie usually offered her patients, only now the situation was reversed.

'It's okay,' Rhea said softly. 'These hormones make you crazy, don't they?'

Callie half laughed, half cried and, nodding, she took a tissue.

What is the matter with me?

'Sorry, Rhea. This is very unprofessional.'

'Don't be. I should be the one saying sorry. I was being harsh.'

'But if you have reason to be—'

'There was no need for me to be rude. You were trying to help.'

Callie nodded, sniffing, and dabbed at her nose with the tissue. Letting out a breath, she relaxed her shoulders, sat forward and laid a hand on Rhea's knee. 'How are you coping?'

'I'm okay.'

'Are you doing this alone? Is the father in the picture?'

She couldn't help but think of Lucas, the father of her own baby. She'd agreed to move in with him! Would she regret that? Had *she* made a decision without thinking it through? What would it be like, living with Lucas for all those months, only to move out when the baby was born? Would he even want her there?

Of course not. It's the baby he's after. I'm his friend, but that's all. This was always about giving Lucas the baby—nothing's changed.

The thoughts made her feel sad again, but she bit the inside of her lip and tried to concentrate on that rather than allow herself to cry again. She'd already embarrassed herself once today…

'I need a biscuit. Something with chocolate. You?'

'Yes, please. I'm ravenous.'

'Are you eating properly?' Callie got a packet of chocolate chip cookies from her drawer and opened them, offering them to Rhea, who took three.

'I haven't got much money.'

'But you live with your mother?'

Rhea nodded.

'Does she cook for you?'

'She isn't in often.'

No. Callie knew what *that* was like. She'd lost count of the amount of times she'd come home from school to find nothing in the house but empty beer cans or discarded bottles. Plenty of empties, but not much else. She recalled one dinner time when the only thing she'd been able to find in the cupboards was an old tin of custard powder. She'd made herself custard for lunch, just to have something hot before she went back to school for the afternoon.

Callie shook her head. 'My mother was never the best.'

Rhea shrugged. 'But I bet *you'll* be.'

'Rhea! Are you trying to tell me I'd make a good mother?'

'Sure. You're a midwife. You're caring. How much better could you be?'

How about how wrong could I be? What about being in a committed relationship? Raising a child together?

But it was the first time Callie had seen Rhea smile. Properly, anyway. Perhaps they'd made a connection after all?

She laughed, thinking of Lucas. His blue eyes and the way he looked at her. The way his dark hair always looked tousled, no matter how much he combed it. The way he made her *feel*. Before all of this Lucas had been her best friend and, yes, she loved him. *As a friend.* But her pregnancy was changing things. Her hormones were changing things. Maggie leaving had changed everything and it was all up in the air now.

Callie didn't know what to think. What to feel. Before Maggie had left it had all been straightforward. Get pregnant, have the baby, give it to Maggie and Lucas and then play doting godparent or something. But now…?

'I shouldn't have told you any of that, you know. Not very professional.' She wiped her eyes dry and smiled.

Rhea nodded, seeming to be thinking deeply. Then she took a deep breath and said, 'My mum's thrown me out.'

Callie was shocked. She'd not been expecting that. 'Oh, Rhea…'

'I'm sleeping on a friend's couch. Have been for a week or two.'

'She knows about the pregnancy? That's why she threw you out?'

Rhea nodded and grabbed a tissue from the box for herself. 'She thinks I'm a tart. That I got pregnant deliberately, that it's all my fault. And it wasn't! It *wasn't…*'

Callie offered fresh tissues. 'What happened? Will you tell me?'

Rhea met her gaze and eventually nodded. 'I was at a party. At a friend's house. There was alcohol and I'd never really tried it before, so I think it went to my head quite quickly. I went to lay down in her room—try and sleep it off because I felt awful. I woke up in the dark and there was someone on top of me. I tried to stop him. I really tried. But he was stronger than me…' She sounded so matter-of-fact.

Callie stared on in horror. 'You were *raped*?'

'Mum reckons I asked for it. She's disgusted with me.'

'Did you go to the police?'

'Yes. But I'd already had a shower and they reckoned I'd washed away a lot of the evidence.'

'Oh, Rhea, I'm so sorry! Did they test you for STIs?'

'They came back negative.'

'But you were pregnant?'

'Yes. That's why I want to get rid of it.'

Callie could now understand why Rhea had been so uptight, so resistant to her prying questions. She felt glad now that she'd confided in Rhea herself, because it had shown Rhea that Callie could be trusted.

'That's why you don't want to keep it?'

Rhea shook her head. 'How could I? Every time I looked at it I'd be reminded. I'd see its eyes looking at me and—'

'And it would love you. The child. The baby would have no idea about its conception. It would just see you as its mother. It would *love* you.'

Rhea shook her head, violently disagreeing. 'No.'

Callie sat silently for a moment. They'd both shared an awful lot. She'd said something herself that she'd not meant to say. Certainly not to a patient. Even if it *had* been to get Rhea to open up and trust her.

'Let me arrange some counselling for you.'

'I don't need it.'

'It can help to have someone to talk to.'

'I've got you.'

Callie nodded. 'Okay. But I'll need to take some blood from you today. I should have done it last time.'

'What for?'

'To check your blood group. Check your rhesus status—that sort of thing.'

People could be either rhesus positive or rhesus negative, depending on their blood type.

'Right. I see.'

'I've booked you in for a scan as well. We need to do certain checks on the baby—check its growth and health. It's an ultrasound. Will you do it?'

'Do I have to look at it?'

'Not if you don't want to. But aren't you curious to see it?'

'No. I don't want to get attached to it.'

The walls had gone up again.

'In case it makes it harder to give away?'

Rhea met her gaze, nodded, and quickly looked away.

Callie could understand her reasons.

Rhea lay down on the same couch that Callie had just a few days ago and had gel smeared onto her abdomen. The sonographer spent a few moments getting her bearings and then turned to look at Callie, who was sitting in. 'Well, everything looks just fine.'

Callie reached for Rhea's hand and squeezed it. 'Do you want to see?'

'But if I see it—'

'Rhea…please…let me turn the screen. You need to see this.'

The teenager gave in and nodded, the expression on her face turning from a mix of apprehension and fear to one of confusion and wonder. 'What is that?'

Callie wasn't sure whether to smile or not. 'That's your baby.'

How would Rhea react? What would she feel?

At her own scan Callie had felt awe and a little afraid, if she were honest with herself. The pregnancy was *real*. No longer a hypothetical situation.

Rhea would have no choice now but to face facts.

Lucas sucked in a breath, then sighed heavily down the phone. 'I've asked Callie to move in with me.' He waited for the reaction from his mother, not knowing how she'd be.

'Right. Well, that makes sense.'

She still didn't sound too pleased, but then again she hadn't been happy with him ever since he'd mentioned the divorce and the surrogacy.

'And how's she doing?'

'Callie's doing well. She was a little faint at work the other day, so I suggested she move in so that I can look after her.'

'And that's all this is?'

He rubbed his forehead roughly. What *was* it with everyone suggesting there was more to their relationship?

'Yes! She's just my friend. There's nothing untoward about this.'

'Moving in together is a big deal, Lucas. You two have known each other for years and I know how you felt about her once and what it did to you when she turned you down. Are you sure there's nothing else going on?'

'Mum—'

'Maggie never liked her, did she? Always suspected your friendship was more than that?'

His mother was right. Maggie had never liked Callie very much. Or his friendship with her. It had been a difficult line he'd had to walk when he'd still been married to Maggie. Every phone call or conversation with Callie had had to be explained in minute detail, as if she'd suspected him of wanting to jump into bed with Callie at any moment.

Maybe once he'd wanted that, but they'd both been very young then. He'd adored Callie. Had been able to picture them both together as a couple and been excited to think that she'd say yes.

When he'd asked her and she'd got all upset before telling him no, they could never be together that way…*ever*…his heart had been broken. Never had he imagined that she'd turn him down. So he'd gone straight out and at the first club he'd gone into he'd met Maggie and bought her a drink.

Maggie—whom he'd treated appallingly by trying too hard to love her. Forcing feelings that had never been true…

Callie wouldn't risk their friendship back then and she sure as hell wouldn't now! So his mother had nothing to worry about. He knew where he stood with Callie. It had been clear then and it was clear now.

'Well, Maggie's not here anymore, is she? It doesn't matter. Callie and I are friends. I just thought I'd let you know what was happening.'

There was a pause. 'I see. And have you decided what's going to happen when the baby's born? Does she move out then?'

Lucas refused even to think that far. He certainly didn't like the idea of thinking of her moving out before he'd even got her moved in! 'I don't know.' He knew he didn't like the idea of her leaving.

'Well, you need to decide. Before that poor baby is born.'

'My child is not a "poor baby". It will be cherished and adored. You've no need to feel sorry for it.'

'Of *course* I feel sorry for it. It might never have a mother.' She sighed. 'Why didn't you marry Callie in the first place? You know that's what your father and I wanted for you.'

Lucas gritted his teeth. Of course he knew. Because he and Callie had been friends for so long they'd always hinted at it, or joked about it, but he'd seen the look on Callie's face every time they did. Shock…fear. Didn't they know that it had killed him to see her look that way? Didn't they know that it had destroyed him to know he couldn't have her? That she'd never contemplate it?

He refused to lose his temper. There was no point in going over old ground. Callie would never look at him in that way.

Ever.

Callie opened up the suitcase on her bed and stared at her clothes hanging in the wardrobe. She was meant to be packing. Getting ready for moving in with Lucas—just whilst she was pregnant—so that he could be there for her and the baby.

There's nothing romantic about this, so why do I feel so strange? So nervous?

She didn't want to call her mother—Maria was usually the last person she turned to—but she needed to talk to someone and it couldn't be Lucas. After her time spent discussing what had happened with Rhea, she felt as if she needed the connection that family gave. Even if Maria *was* useless, she could still be a sounding board—so she picked up the phone and dialled.

It rang for a long time, and just when she thought her mother must be out or in a drunken stupor somewhere it was answered.

'Yes?'

'Mum? It's me—Callie.'

'Oh, hi. I thought you might be someone else.' As always, her mother's regret at being connected to Callie shone through.

'Sorry. I can go if you're waiting for another call.'

'No, it's fine. I'm glad you rang. I've been wanting to speak to you.'

Well, then, you could have called me, couldn't you? Busy getting to the bottom of a bottle?

'I just wanted to talk…speak to you…let you know that…um…I'm having a baby. I'm pregnant.'

There was silence at the other end of the phone for a moment, though Callie felt sure she heard the slosh of a bottle being upended.

'A baby? Congratulations.'

Maria didn't sound thrilled. But what had Callie expected?

'I didn't even know you were in a relationship.'

You never called to find out.

She closed her eyes with dismay and hurt. What had she really expected from her? Support? Happiness? Joy at becoming a grandmother?

Who was I kidding?

'No, no, I'm not. I…er…just thought I'd tell you that you won't be able to get hold of me at this number for a while.'

'Oh?'

'I'm going to be moving in with the father… It's Lucas, by the way. This is his number, if you want to contact me there.' She read off the number, knowing in her heart that her mother would not be writing it down.

'You and Lucas? That's great. I always thought you two would end up together.'

It was too complicated to explain. 'Okay. I guess that's it. Take care.'

'Callie, wait!'

'Yes?' *What now?*

'He's been your best friend, hasn't he, all these years? I guess it was to be expected you'd have a baby with him.'

'Well, it's not straightforward.'

'What is in this life? Well, I'm happy for you both. I have some news too.'

'Yes?'

'I've met someone. Someone special to me. His name's Gareth and I'd like you to meet him.'

Callie had lost count of the number of 'someone specials' she'd had to meet over the years. This Gareth would surely be just another man in the long list of men that her mother hung around with—hangers-on, fellow drunks. She wasn't desperate to meet him at all.

'Well, I'm very busy at work.'

'Oh, I see.' Her mother sounded disappointed.

'I'll try to come over soon, I'm just not sure when.'

'Things are different now, Callie. I've changed. Gareth's helped me change. I haven't had a drink for six months.'

Lies. All lies!

Callie had heard all this before! She almost couldn't bear it—the way her mother handed out the same old patter all the time! Expecting her to believe it!

What sort of a fool does she take me for?

'Really? Well…keep it up.'

'I will. I *am*. I mean it this time, Callie. I really do.'

'I hope so. But you've said all this before, Mum.'

'I know I have, and I know it's difficult for you to believe me, but this time I'll prove it. In actions *and* words.'

Callie couldn't speak. There was too much emotion flowing through her at that moment. If she did speak, she'd cry.

'So I'll look forward to seeing you soon?'

She sucked in a deep breath and gathered herself. 'Sure. Bye.'

Callie put the phone down and shook her head at her own stupidity.

What was I thinking? She isn't going to care about a grandchild! She could barely care about her own *child! She hardly said anything when I said I was pregnant. She cares more about this Gareth person!*

'She's still drinking,' she announced to the empty room, to her empty suitcase, and she began to well up, then cry, as she pulled her clothes from the wardrobe and shoved them haphazardly into her suitcase.

Lucas would be round soon. He'd said he would be there about five to pick her up and take her to his.

It had been a long time since she'd last been at his place. She'd liked it there. It was safe. Homely. Not like her own. It would be nice to come home from work and not find an empty flat. There'd be someone to talk to. Someone to share her day with. They could each get exasperated about work and know where the other one was coming from.

Like a couple.

Now where had *that* thought come from?

Wiping her eyes, she sat down on the bed and thought about him. Did she like Lucas? In *that* way?

He is gorgeous. Kind and funny and caring and...yes, okay, he's hot.

But he was a friend. A friend she was now having a baby

with. Moving in with until it was born. She couldn't risk losing his friendship by having romantic feelings for him!

I'm not feeling that way. I'm not! It's just hormones, that's all.

Will I have to move out when the baby's born?

They hadn't spoken about it. She hadn't asked. But now she needed to know. What *did* Lucas expect of her after the birth? Anything? The original plan had been that she would be like an aunt, or a godmother or something. She'd be in the baby's life but on the edges, the fringe. *Maggie* was meant to have been the mother, but she'd gone now.

Does Lucas want me to be the baby's mother?

She knew she'd have to ask him. This was too big a deal not to get cleared up, too big a question not to ask. She couldn't assume. She'd have to ask him.

But what do I want to hear? I've never wanted to be a mother. But I know I want the best for this child.

She folded her jeans and placed them into her suitcase, absentmindedly laying a couple of reading books in the suitcase, a small toiletries case, a camera.

The clock said five past five when the doorbell rang.

It's him.

She got up and checked her reflection in the mirror. 'Bad hair, red eyes, chafed cheeks. I look great,' she muttered, and headed for the front door.

When she opened it she saw him take one look at her and read her face, but instead of the joke that she was expecting about how awful she looked he simply dropped the bouquet of flowers he was holding and pulled her into his arms, crushing her against his broad chest. He squeezed her tight and she could feel his lips in her hair, kissing the top of her head, whilst she inhaled his heavenly scent as if he was oozing pure amber nectar.

'What's wrong? Has someone upset you?'

She could hear his heart pounding through his strong

chest and it felt good to stand there, wrapped in his embrace, protected and warm and safe. He smelt amazing, and it would have been so easy just to stand there and let him hold her and never let go. So easy just to melt into him and stay there. Never moving, never letting go.

'I spoke to my mum…' she mumbled into his shirt. 'You know what she's like.' She pulled away, smiling sheepishly, and tucked a stray strand of hair behind her ear.

He walked with her into the flat, closing the door behind them. 'You told her?'

With reluctance, she nodded and sat down on the couch opposite. 'Yep. She reacted pretty much how I expected. You'll probably be pleased to know there'll be no pushy grandma from *my* side of the family.' She smiled, but the smile didn't reach her eyes. Then, as an afterthought, she asked, 'Were those flowers for me?'

'Dammit!' He leapt over the couch in one fluid movement and went back outside, picking up the flowers he'd dropped. Brushing off imaginary fluff, he presented them to her. They were beautiful! Lots of tiny pink roses, mostly still in bud. 'Flat-warming. I thought you could put them in your new bedroom.'

She lifted them to her nose and inhaled their delicate scent. 'They're lovely—thank you. You always know how to make me feel better.'

Lucas smiled. 'I try. So what did Maria say, exactly?'

'Well, I got a "congratulations" but she was too busy telling me about her new man to offer anything else.' Callie fiddled with the pink roses. 'She wants me to meet him.'

'But you don't want to?'

'I've met too many of her men. Oh, and she saw fit to inform me she's been off the booze for six months.'

'That's good, isn't it?'

'It'll be a lie.'

Lucas looked grim. 'Maybe, but what if she is telling the truth?'

Callie looked at him in disbelief and laughed. 'Hardly!'

Lucas persisted. 'But if she *is*...don't you think you should give her that chance? She's your mother. That's not a relationship you can just ignore.'

'Why not? She's done a good job of it for all these years. Why do I have to be the responsible one?'

He shrugged. 'Because you're about to be a mother yourself?'

There. He'd said it. But Callie still didn't know if she *was* going to be a mother, did she? Lucas and she hadn't discussed, yet, just exactly what her role was going to be now.

We need to clear this up soon.

'I think you ought to go and visit her. See for yourself.'

'I don't see the point, Lucas.'

'She's your *mum*.'

'Yes. She is. But only in title. I've always had to look after myself.' Her answer was final, suggesting the conversation was over where Maria was concerned.

Lucas let out a big sigh and looked around. 'Is there anything you need help with? Or are you already packed?' He was eyeing her flat, and she had to admit it didn't look as if she'd packed much.

'It's pretty much done. I was just finishing my suitcase when you rang.'

'So you're still happy to move in?'

She nodded. 'If you're happy—though I think there are a few things we still need to talk about.'

'I agree. But we've plenty of time to iron out the wrinkles in this situation. Let's not rush into making life-changing decisions straight away.'

She was glad to hear that he must have been thinking things through, too. 'Okay, so let's start with an easy one. Who's cooking tonight?'

He laughed and she smiled at the sound, enjoying the way his eyes twinkled with merriment. Glad that they were back on easier territory. Lucas had always tried to get her to be closer to her mother. Probably because he had a close relationship with his own mother. Well, he was lucky. Not everyone had that.

'Someone else will… I thought we could make it special. Our first meal together. At a nice restaurant… Because I'm damned sure I'm not going to have a baby with someone who I haven't taken out to dinner.'

It had been ages since she'd last been there, but his flat was exactly as she remembered. There'd once been a time when she'd felt she could pop round whenever she needed to, but when Lucas had got together with Maggie that freedom to visit had ended. She and Maggie had got on okay, but there had been a sense of 'stay away' that she'd got from Maggie when it came to visiting. Almost as if Maggie was laying claim to Lucas—especially after she'd married him.

Lucas had always told Callie to come round, but she hadn't called in as often as she'd used to, and she'd always made up some excuse. There was no way she would have caused problems in his marriage with Maggie.

But now she was looking forward to reclaiming her friendship with him. Regaining the closeness they'd once had.

All the photos that had once been there of him and Maggie were gone. Thankfully. It would have been disturbing if they'd still been there. At least it showed that he didn't still need her picture about, reminding him of their shared past.

Lucas gave her a quick tour, though she pretty much already knew where most things were. But she hadn't seen the spare room before. It was bigger than she'd realised, and decorated in a beautiful pale blue. A large double bed dominated the centre of the room, covered in a gorgeous crocheted creamy-white throw.

Callie raised an eyebrow at this, looking for Lucas to explain. It seemed a very girly decoration.

'Before you say anything, I bought that for you. Maggie took all the pretty covers we'd bought and left me with my old black and grey ones, and my inner interior designer made me go out and get something a little more feminine.' He grinned and heaved her suitcase into the room before depositing it on the bed. 'Want a hand to unpack?'

'I'm all right, thanks.'

'Okay. Dinner reservations are for seven-thirty.'

'Where are we going?'

'Gianni's. It's Italian—I'm sure you said you liked that once.'

She smiled. He'd remembered. 'I love Italian.'

'Great. I'll leave you to it, then.'

'Are we getting dressed up?'

He hovered in the doorway, his hands casually in his pockets. 'We can do. Might be nice. We *are* celebrating.'

'Okay.'

It would be nice to get dressed up, and she hadn't been out to eat for ages! Two months' worth of morning sickness had put paid to any appetite she'd had, but that was gone now. Callie was feeling much better, and she finally understood why some of her women were so glad to get that first trimester out of the way!

'Wow...you look...*amazing*.'

Lucas couldn't believe his eyes. Callie was wearing a gorgeous figure-hugging dress, all red and flowing, close-fitting at the hips and loose around her legs.

And what a pair of legs! Her calves were shapely and toned—and he wasn't sure why he was so surprised.

I guess I'm so used to seeing her in scrubs.

She'd obviously been keeping her figure a secret beneath the shapeless hospital garb. But there was a lovely gentle rounding around her abdomen, and he knew it was caused by the fundus of her womb spilling over the pelvic cavity and rising up as it swelled in size.

My baby.

She looked great. Blooming and healthy and…

Gorgeous!

There was no other word for it. She'd done her hair and put on make-up and he couldn't recall ever seeing her looking like this! She was glowing! As she smiled shyly at his response, her cheeks flushing, he had to fight the desire to reach out and stroke her cheek.

What's that all about?

He cleared his throat, trying to tamp down the physical response his body was having to her sensual curves.

She'd done something to her hair, too, curling it, sweeping it up, but letting small pieces hang down here and there. She looked tousled—as if she'd just had a good session in bed!

Calm yourself, Lucas, this is Callie...

Yes. It most certainly was Callie. She'd always been pretty, though she'd never played up to it as far as he could recall. But for some reason looking at her tonight, right now, she was more than just a pretty friend…she was beautiful and alluring…

'Wow…' he repeated.

'Thanks. You don't scrub up too badly yourself.'

He'd put on a dinner jacket and white shirt, though he hadn't bothered with a tie. His suit was tailored and well-fitting, and he was glad he'd put it on after seeing the effort she'd gone to.

Escorting her down to his car, he held the door open for her and waited for her to get in. He tried not to take advantage of his position, but he couldn't help getting a good view of her legs again and inhaling the scent of her perfume. He took a deep breath to try and regain control of his raging senses as he walked to his side of the car and then drove to Gianni's. He felt as if he was on a proper date.

Gianni's was a small Italian restaurant on the edge of London. It had had some excellent reviews by restaurant critics and he'd been there once before with some friends. Inside, it was dimly lit by wall sconces and individual candles on each of the tables, and a guy at a real piano played soft background music. No schmaltzy taped music here!

'Wow, this place is gorgeous,' Callie said.

'I'm glad you like it.' They went up to the maître d', who was waiting by a desk. 'Table for two under the name Gold.'

'Certainly, sir. This way, please.'

The maître d' led them to a small table for two, situated at the back of the restaurant. French doors near their table opened out onto a balcony, covered with bougainvillaea and filled with pots of flowers and a small water fountain. The view looked out over the lights of London.

'This place is amazing, Lucas,' Callie said in awe, draping her wrap over the back of her chair as he held it out for her.

He tried not to smell her hair as she stood before him, and he really struggled to keep his hands off her. He felt guilty. Maggie's words were haunting him.

When she was seated he quickly settled himself into his own chair opposite, glad to put some physical distance between them. Seeing her all done up like this was great and all, but…it was making him think crazy things! This was *Callie*! Not a date. Nothing romantic. But, by God, she was doing something crazy to his insides…

'I'm glad you like it.'

Callie wouldn't drink any wine, so they ordered soft drinks whilst they perused the menu. Lucas couldn't help but sneak peeks at her over his own menu whilst he pretended to read, and his stomach was in knots with nerves. He had to break the tension he felt inside, so he laid his menu down to reach across the table and take her hand.

He stared at her fingers within his own and played with one of her rings, pondering his question for a moment. Then he looked up at her and said, 'I've always meant to ask you something.'

She looked slightly afraid, worried about what he'd ask. 'Oh…?'

'Yes…it's something I've been meaning to ask you for a long time.'

'Yes?' Her breath sounded as if it was caught in her throat. What did she think he was going to ask?

He paused for a moment, dragging the tension out. 'What's Callie short for? Is it Calista? Something like that? In all these years we've known each other you've never said.'

She laughed with visible relief, squeezing his fingers and shaking her head as if in disbelief. '*That* was your big question?'

'That was my big question. For now.' He grinned.

'It's not Calista.'

'No?'

'No. And you don't really want to know what it's short for. There's a reason I've never told you, you know.'

'Is it something weird? Like Caligula? Be honest with me—are you named after a Roman emperor?'

They both laughed, and she took a sip of fruit juice before answering. 'I don't know why I've never told you. Actually, I *do* know—it's because I'd be embarrassed.' She took a deep breath. 'Promise me you won't laugh if I do.'

'I promise.' He mimed crossing his heart across his chest and smiled at her, loving the way she looked, so soft and gentle in the candlelight.

She looked at him carefully, weighing up his promise. 'You know what my mother was like, right?'

'Yes.'

'A drunk…an alcoholic. She never wanted me. Hardly bothered to acknowledge me sometimes. So she didn't even bother thinking of a name for me when I was born. *But…* she had to register me. Obviously she needed the child benefit money for drinking. So she went to the register office and when they asked her for my name…'

He was listening intently, wondering about the possible outcome.

'She looked about the room for the first thing she saw. There was a calendar on the wall and so she called me… Calendar. Calendar Taylor.'

Lucas didn't laugh. He'd promised. And there was something so inherently sad about the story that it didn't seem the slightest bit amusing now. He'd hoped it would be something exotic—Calliope, or something like that—something interesting. But instead it was simply a very sad story about a mother who seemed to care nothing for her child.

'I'm so sorry.' He reached out and tightened his grip around her fingers once again. He realised that he suddenly wanted to kiss her. Kiss her madly to take away the sadness and the pain that she'd experienced over the years at the hands of her mother. Crush her against his body, his lips to hers, with so much passion that neither of them would be able to breathe until it was all over and they had to break apart for air. Kiss her the way a lover might…

A lover?

The realisation startled him, so instead of holding her tightly he let her hand go. He took a sip from his drink, feeling the condensation on the glass, the drops of water, giving himself a chance to cool down. There was no way *that* was going to happen. Not with Callie. He knew that.

When he felt he might have control over his voice box he called the waiter over so they could order.

Callie had told him what she'd like and he ordered for them both: pan-fried tiger prawns in butter and chilli for a starter, *agnello* for main—which was a braised lamb shank in tomatoes and a red berry jus. When the first course arrived he heard her apologise. 'Sorry if I've ruined the evening. Mentioning my mother does that a lot.'

'I always knew you and your mother didn't get along. That she was an alcoholic. But I guess if you never have high expectations of her she can't let you down.'

'I suppose.'

'But, you know, even normal families have their issues.'

'Really? Are you trying to cheer me up?'

He smiled at her over the candlelight. 'I am. Both my parents were sober, but I had six sisters! Being the seventh child and the long-awaited son, in a family whose father was always absent for one reason or another, didn't always make for a great time either.'

'But you were the only boy. They'd wanted a son all that time. You *have* to admit you were a little spoilt!' She smiled to show she was joking.

'Are you kidding me? I had to fight for any attention that came my way. Positive attention was rare and negative was in great supply. My father, when he was there, was always quite happy to use his belt and make me into a man. My parents had all these dreams for me and they pushed me hard. *Very* hard. Sometimes nothing I did was right. All my life they'd wanted me to be a doctor and so that's what I became—just so they would be proud of me. I sometimes wonder what I might have been if they hadn't steered me in that direction.'

Callie frowned. 'But you love being a doctor, don't you?'

He nodded. 'Absolutely. I *do* love it. But that's just luck, isn't it? My parents wanted the best for me—a career, marriage with children—but only when the time was right… when my career had taken off. They didn't like Maggie, they didn't like me choosing to marry her, and they let me know about it.'

'How?'

'They initially told me they wouldn't come to the wedding. That I was making a mistake.' He chose not to explain that his parents had actually told him he was marrying the wrong woman and that *Callie* should have been the one in a veil. 'And look at how *that* turned out. They were right.'

He sipped at his drink.

'You rushed into the marriage?'

'Maybe. You turned me down!' He laughed to lighten the atmosphere, not referencing the great pain in his heart at the memory. 'So I had to look elsewhere. I met Maggie and down the aisle we went, without thinking about what we were doing until it was too late. I should have waited, maybe, but I thought I knew what I was doing. I was never in love with Maggie. Not the way I should have been. I see that now.'

Callie was listening intently, her heart saddened by these revelations. She should have known about this, but hadn't because she'd been so wrapped up in her own problems. 'I never realised.'

'Why would you?'

'Well, I'm your best friend. Perhaps I should have known instinctively? Perhaps you should have felt able to tell me?'

'Neither of us are psychic, Callie. You had too much going on in your own life to be worrying about mine. I didn't want to burden you. At the time all this was happening your mum was in hospital with that liver complaint.'

'I do feel like maybe I let you down, though. You should have been able to talk to me about it.'

But he knew that he wouldn't have. Why would he? He'd had those intense feelings for Callie, which had slowly developed over time, without him realising, and when he'd finally discovered the nerve to ask her out she'd turned him down! He'd been heartbroken. In all his imaginings he'd never expected her to say no. The let-down had been devastating and he'd reacted by going out to a club. That was when he had run into Maggie.

'People make you hurt,' she said with understanding.

Once again, she'd hit the nail on the head. She'd always understood him so well. 'I guess both of us would have changed things if we could.'

'Oh, I don't know. If my mother hadn't been the way she was then I might never have become a midwife.' She looked up and smiled. 'And we get to work together.'

'I love that we're still together. After all this time. So many people lose their childhood friends when they become adults. Move apart.'

'I'm glad too.' She looked into his eyes. 'I would like to discuss our situation, though, Lucas. We've got a lot to sort out, you and me.'

'I know.'

But he was afraid of letting her down. He'd let Maggie down by treating her badly, by not loving her the way he should have and driving her into the arms of another man. No wonder she'd gone looking for love elsewhere if she'd thought that he loved Callie. What woman would stand for that?

He'd tried so hard to make his marriage work, to make Maggie happy, to give her the child she wanted so badly—but he'd been doing it all for the wrong reasons. His heart had always been with Callie, even though he knew nothing could come of it.

Maggie had been right to leave him.

For a while they ate in companionable silence. The food was delicious—not too rich, yet full of flavour, with explosions of taste on their tongues.

'What we're doing...it's a big thing,' she said.

Lucas put down his knife and fork and dabbed at his mouth with his napkin. 'Moving in together?'

'The baby. It seemed a simple thing for me when Maggie was still going to be the mother, but she's gone now and I can't help but wonder...' She looked down at her lap, almost afraid to say her next words.

He waited for her to finish, but it seemed she couldn't say what she wanted to say. He leaned forward, looking past the candles, past the small posy of flowers on the table and deep into her eyes.

'I'd like you to be involved,' he said softly. 'As much as you'd like.' He paused for a moment before continuing. 'Actually, that's not true. I want you to be involved a hundred per cent. I know you've always said that you've never wanted to be a mother, but...'

'I never felt I could be what a child would need me to be.'

'But why not?'

He could see her eyes filling up. She was trying her hardest to blink away the tears, but couldn't stop a solitary tear from rolling down her cheeks.

He hated that she was upset. That she was hurting.

'I just...I wouldn't know *how* to be a mother.'

'Does anyone?'

'It should be instinctive. I never had that instinct. Never felt it. Never experienced it.' The tears trickled freely down her cheeks now 'Damn...I'm always crying just lately.'

He reached out with his napkin and dabbed at her cheek. There was so much he should be saying to her. That she still looked beautiful even if she was crying. But instead he went with, 'It's hormones. You can't help it.'

She hiccupped a laugh.

The waiter came and took away their starter plates and they sat quietly at the table. Lucas held her hand. How could he not? He didn't want to see her upset or crying, but he knew she must be scared because he was too. Every time he touched her now it was getting harder and harder to let her go. They'd always been close, but now that she was carrying his baby…

Moving in together, although it was just as room-mates, *was* a big deal. He was welcoming Callie into his life so that he could be there for them both, and he hoped that by doing so she would become happy and feel safe.

He knew she didn't want to be a mother. Was scared about being a mother. It was why she'd sworn off children. But she'd become a midwife—a profession where caring for others was tantamount. Could she not see that? She was one of the most caring people he knew and he felt instinctively, even if she didn't, that she would be a great mother. He knew she could be if she gave herself that chance.

He wanted his child to have a mother like Callie. For Callie to consider herself to be its mother. All his life he'd insisted that whenever he had a child it would be in a stable relationship, hopefully he'd be married, but whatever the situation it had to be stable and strong and definitely with a mother as well as a father. Parents who were around for their kids every day.

It was something he hadn't had with his own father. And when his father *had* been around he'd been angry and had had little patience with a young boy who'd craved his approval… There'd be no getting out the belt for *his* child. His and Callie's baby.

Would Callie agree to be that parent?

He wouldn't ask anything of her apart from that. There'd be no demands on them to become an actual couple. They didn't have to start 'going out'. She'd already turned him down once before and he knew she wouldn't let that happen anyway. It was totally out of the question for her. Wasn't it? And he could keep his feelings separate. Somehow. Callie could be a mother without being his partner. Although…

I wouldn't stop it. I think Callie and me would be good together. I always have.

But he knew he couldn't press her that way. She'd turn tail and run for it—as she had before when he'd tried to ask her out. That had been years ago now, and she hadn't wanted to risk their friendship. But things were different now, weren't they? They were both adults, for a start, and they knew what they were doing. Supposedly.

Their lamb shanks arrived and they tucked in with gusto. The meat was tender and just melted in the mouth. The green beans were perfectly *al dente* and the potatoes soft and full of flavour, with butter and mint melting over them.

They kept the conversation neutral for the rest of the evening. One set of tears had been enough for them both and Lucas didn't want to upset Callie any more about anything. They talked about films they'd both seen, which led to Callie announcing that a new documentary about midwifery was going to start on television and she wanted to see it.

'Should be interesting. It's meant to be real-life fly-on-the-wall stuff.'

'Could you imagine if they filmed in *our* hospital?'

She laughed. 'Oh, my God! That would be priceless!'

Their puddings came and went, the evening rolled on pleasantly, and much too soon it was time for home.

When they got back to the flat Callie kicked off her heels and stumbled onto the couch. 'I'm beat.'

'What shift are you on tomorrow?' Lucas asked.

'I've got three night shifts in a row. You?'

'A late shift tomorrow, then two nights.'

'I guess we'll run into each other, then.'

'Guess so.'

They were staring at each other. Uncomfortably so. As if each of them was expecting the other to say something or do something definitive.

But when Lucas didn't make a move Callie stood up

with a sigh and went to pick up her heels, then she turned to walk to her room. 'I'm going to bed. Thanks for tonight. It was lovely.'

Lucas stood up and nodded. 'It was my pleasure.'

She looked at him from across the room. Was there tension between them? Sexual tension?

She walked over to give him a friendly peck on the cheek, her lips caressing rough stubble. 'Good night.' She paused again, as if she was thinking of something, but then smiled and turned away before he could process it too much.

'Goodnight, Callie.'

He watched her go and he could feel the burn on his cheek where her lips had touched him. He ached with longing for more. He switched off all the lights, grabbed a drink from the kitchen and headed for bed himself. After hanging up his suit, he pulled back the duvet and slumped into bed, one hand behind his head as he stared up at the ceiling.

It had been an interesting night with his Calendar Girl.

I wanted to kiss her.

But she's my friend.

I can't lose her as a friend.

I wouldn't be able to bear it.

But what if they gained so much more?

Sleep was a long time coming, and by the time he finally drifted off into the land of nod he'd pretty much memorised exactly how his bedroom ceiling looked in the dark.

In the next room, Callie also lay staring at the ceiling. Her stomach was comfortably full with rich food and she felt a nice warm buzz from the evening. It had been good to spend some time with Lucas away from work, away from the hospital, out on a social basis. They hadn't done that for…

God...years!

They'd had a nice night. He'd looked totally amazing too! When she'd come out of her room and seen him standing there in the middle of his flat in his dinner jacket she'd practically melted with desire. Where had this *sexy* Lucas emerged from? He could have been James Bond, he'd looked so yummy!

It's just hormones. You know it is. You tell women that every day.

Didn't make it easy, though. He'd kept taking her hand at dinner and it had been *so difficult* to remember that they were just friends and nothing else.

Her hand went beneath the covers and rested on her barely-there bump. She spoke to it, whispering soft words that meant so very much.

'I'll not hurt your daddy. I'll make sure I do right by him. Even if that means I have to walk away.'

For Callie, sleep didn't come easily either.

CHAPTER FOUR

THE NEXT FEW weeks were strange as they got used to living with each other. Waking up in the morning and finding Lucas in the next room, ready to have breakfast with her, seemed odd, but enjoyable.

She liked the way he was always there when she needed someone to talk to. She didn't have to phone him and make a time to come round, she didn't have to seek permission to be with him, and she didn't have to make an appointment—like she had to if she wanted to see her mother.

He cooked her some delicious meals, and once he even rubbed her feet after she'd had a particularly exhausting day. That had been surprising. Not the foot-rub, but the thoughts that had gone through her head as he'd done it! He had a wonderful way with his fingers. His large hands had enveloped her feet individually, their warmth caressing her tired muscles as his fingertips pressed and glided and worked out the knots. Firm where they needed to be, gentle and delicate in other places.

Her thoughts had run to how Lucas might be as a lover, though it had felt strange to allow herself even to think of him that way when he'd always been her friend. He'd had a masterful way with her feet, anyway, and she could only imagine the wonderful sensations he'd produce if his hands were let loose on the rest of her body!

And every night she'd chastely wish him good-night and go to her room feeling alone.

Odd how I feel alone even though I'm living with someone.

Callie had just turned eighteen weeks in her pregnancy, and was beginning to show much more. She went into work most days feeling tired and sleepy. Sleep had evaded her for many of her nights, and she didn't think it was because she was sleeping somewhere different. The bed in her room was comfortable, the mattress firm. She was warm enough. It was just that her head was brimming with too many thoughts…

Would she be a mother?

Wouldn't she?

Where were things heading with Lucas?

What would this do to their friendship?

She hoped it would strengthen it. After all, they'd been best friends for years and now a baby was involved…half her, half Lucas.

If I had ever changed my mind about wanting a child I'd have wanted it to be with Lucas.

That was the main thought that kept spinning round her head, rattling its way into all the corners like a whirling dervish. Not that she'd admitted to that at the fertility clinic when they'd all had to go through counselling. She knew she could never admit that.

Her thoughts were spilling over into her consciousness and making her fret and worry over lots of little things. Neither of them had come up with many answers, though she now knew that Lucas would like her to be involved as much as possible.

And that's the big question for me.

Can I be involved? And by how much?

What form would that involvement take? Neither of them

had been specific, and the idea of being a full-time mother scared her still.

I don't know if I have it in me to do that. What if I get things wrong?

Originally she'd have been on the sidelines. The baby would have been Lucas and Maggie's child and Callie would only have been involved whenever she'd visited them, or if—as Lucas had once suggested very early on—she'd became a godparent to the child.

She'd agreed to that. After all, how many godparents actually ended up having to look after a child because something tragic had happened to both its parents?

Hardly ever. In fact she knew of no circumstances in which that had happened to *anyone*. So for her it had been an easy thing to agree to. A godparent could be as close as he or she wanted.

But an actual *mother*?

I wouldn't know what to do. If I get things wrong... I have no frame of reference for what a good mother is...

And now Maggie was gone. Lucas would happily raise the child on his own. She knew in her heart that he would be more than capable of doing so. She still didn't have to be involved. She could still be a godparent.

But it's different now. If I'm to be its mother, then I want it to have the best childhood. Nothing like mine. And how could I explain to that child why I walked away?

What would Lucas think of her if she *did* walk away?

Maggie was gone and Lucas wanted Callie to be involved and, damn it, her hormones were affecting her more than she'd ever thought that they would! On the scan day she'd been so determined not to get attached, not to get excited at what she might see. To keep her distance just as Rhea had wanted to.

After all, hadn't she been taught how to do that by a master? It should have been easy…

But then the baby had been there, right before her eyes, on the screen. Curled up, rounded like a bean, softly nestled safe in her womb, its heart beating away, unaware of the situation its parents faced.

Totally innocent. It had no preconceptions. It was simply a baby. A baby that would be born into the world not knowing whether it would have one, two or any parents to care for it.

Callie changed from her day clothes into scrubs, attached her name tag and filled her pockets with all the paraphernalia she carried with her at work—scissors, pens, a small notepad, tape measure… She pinned her pink fob watch to her top and clipped her hand scrub to the bottom, where it was easily accessible. Then she pulled her hair up to keep it out of her face and headed to the reception area of Antenatal, where the staff hand-over at shift-change took place.

The supervisor of midwives, Sarah, was leading the hand-over and she stood in front of a busy board. All the rooms were filled with labouring mothers and Callie sensed a hectic shift.

Sarah turned to Callie. 'Callie, I'd like you in Room Six. Dr Gold will be assisting. In fact he may already be in there. Jenny Cole—she's thirty-six and a first time mother. She's diabetic and we think it's a very large baby. She's got no birth partner. There doesn't seem to be any close family.'

'Okay.'

Callie loved working with Lucas. He was just so good and efficient. Yes, all registrars were probably the same, but she *knew* Lucas and that made it different. Though she was a very capable midwife on her own, she felt safer knowing that he was in the room, backing her up. There had been so many times when he'd been there for her. And not just for her but the whole team. Calm in a crisis, efficient, direct when he needed to be, and an absolute rock in an emergency situation. Everyone knew they could rely on him and Callie had never heard anyone say a bad word about Lucas Gold.

In Room Six, Callie nodded to Lucas as she entered and then introduced herself to Jenny. Her patient appeared to be coping with her contractions well and was simply breathing her way through them.

'I'm just going to have a quick read-through of your notes.'

Callie stood at the end of the bed as Lucas checked the trace. It all seemed to be going well. According to Jenny's notes, at her last scan just two weeks ago her baby had already been estimated to be at ten pounds. Callie had a quick feel of Jenny's abdomen. Baby was head down, engaged almost four-fifths, and definitely felt extremely large.

As Jenny put in earphones to listen to soothing music Callie stepped over to Lucas. 'What's your idea for delivery?'

'I think when the time comes we'll have everyone on standby. If this baby is as big as we think it is I want to know people will be available if it becomes an emergency.'

Callie nodded. 'How come she's not having a C-section?'

'She was offered one in clinic, but she insisted on trying for a natural birth. She was adamant.'

Fair enough. Callie felt that a mother *should* try for a natural birth if that was what she wished. Though she had reservations about that if there was a risk to either mother or baby. Still, it was not her place to make a judgement. She was there to support Jenny in her wishes.

Jenny removed one of her earbuds. 'Is that a little bump I see?' She nodded at Callie's stomach.

Blushing, Callie nodded. 'Still a long way to go yet.'

'It's exciting, isn't it?'

Exciting wasn't the word… It had been a real rollercoaster since Maggie had left. Callie made a non-committal noise. It was difficult to answer with Lucas in the room. If she said it *was* exciting would he think she was thinking of being there for the baby? If she said it wasn't, then what would Jenny think?

'I've waited an age to have a baby…' Jenny breathed out happily.

'I saw in your notes you used a sperm donor?'

'Best decision I ever made. No health problems. An academic. Similar physical attributes to me. And no worries about anyone making demands to be involved. Perfect.'

'What does everyone else think of your choice?' Callie was curious.

'Mum and Dad were very supportive once they got over the shock. They wanted me to be in a relationship, you know?'

Callie nodded. Wasn't that how everyone expected it would go?

'Lots of good friends?'

'Loads. All dying to be aunts and uncles.'

Lucas came to stand by the bed. 'It's good to have a large support network. I grew up in a big family, so I can't possibly imagine what it might be like to not have anyone.'

Jenny looked at him, blushing slightly. 'Are you married, Dr Gold?'

Since becoming pregnant with his child Callie was beginning to notice the effect Lucas had on other women. It was something she'd always been aware of but hadn't really paid any attention to. But now it was different. She could see them looking at him. Sizing him up. Noting the absence of a ring on his finger. And she wasn't sure if she liked it.

He glanced at Callie. 'I'm not, no.'

'But you have a big family? That's good.'

Callie wondered what it might be like to have a supportive parent? How did that feel? To have a parent on the other end of the phone you could just talk with or pour your heart out to? What would it feel like to know you could just call round to your parents' house and *know* that you'd be welcome? That they'd make you tea, serve you biscuits, tell you the latest about so-and-so down the street?

It was so different for Callie. She couldn't imagine having that kind of relationship with her mum at all. Maria had never, *ever* been there for her on the end of a phone.

'What about you, Callie?' Jenny asked.

Callie glanced at Lucas and saw that he was staring at her with an intense look in his face. She could see he was intrigued to hear her answer, but she felt like a rabbit caught in the headlights.

What could she say? That she had an alcoholic mother, no siblings, and no idea if she was keeping the baby she was carrying? That she was considering giving away her own child? That she might have to?

How easy it had seemed months ago to agree to that. Whilst she wasn't pregnant. Whilst Maggie and Lucas were still together and married. It had been a future event—one that hadn't actually seemed real. And what maternal instincts had Callie had? None. Zero. And she'd been happy for it to be that way. Which was what she'd told everyone.

She could still enjoy babies. Other people's babies. Which was why she'd become a midwife. Callie was fascinated by pregnancy—how a woman's body nurtured and grew a baby in order to birth it and create brand-new life. A pure life, unburdened by worry, regret, selfishness or ego.

And each baby would go home with its mother and she would help another woman. And another.

Each case was different, but mostly she got to share in the joy of creating a child. Bringing a brand-new person into the world, their pages unwritten.

It was the hope she loved. That each new baby she saw would go home with its parents and have a fabulous life. The kind of life she'd never had herself.

Callie's cheeks flushed under the intensity of Lucas's gaze, the heat searing her skin as if she was being roasted on a spit over a flaming hot barbecue.

'I…there's just me, really.' She smiled and fiddled with Jenny's bed sheet, making it lie flat on the bed.

Lucas raised an eyebrow at her and she felt her heart skip a beat. She was having palpitations over Lucas as she stood at a patient's bedside!

What was happening here with Lucas? How had he gone from just being her friend to being this *man*, this *sexy, alluring guy*, since she'd conceived his child? She'd understand it if they'd slept together, or something, but they hadn't. Their baby had been conceived in a laboratory—the most unsexy, least alluring conception you could ever imagine. The most he'd done was hold her hand as the fertility specialist had positioned the fertilised egg in her womb.

Hand-holding! That was all! But now the morning sickness had passed, coupled with the fact that he was now a single man and she was carrying his baby—which was also hers as she'd used her own eggs—it was as if her body *knew* that this was the man she should have. The man she caught looking at her oddly at times…the man whose sofa she shared, whose genes she carried. Technically she should let him take her to bed and have him make her tremble and quiver with delight…

How had that happened? One minute Lucas was her best friend, a good laugh, a dependable guy—yes, he was good-looking, but she'd always believed herself immune to those good looks of his—and then the next minute, when she was knocked up with his baby, Lucas became this scintillating, sexy, so-hot-he-looked-airbrushed kind of guy, whom she lived with, slept in the next room to…a please-can-I-get-into-your-bed kind of guy.

It was madness. Madness!

Dragging her eyes away from Lucas's steely blues, she blushed once again and smiled at Jenny.

'I'm going to be the best mum this little girl could ever have,' Jenny said.

'I'm sure of it,' Callie said. Though part of her wondered how she could be so sure for someone else but couldn't apply that certainty to herself.

Jenny delivered her baby girl some hours later. Ten pounds exactly. She gave birth beautifully and it was a very smooth delivery, even though there'd been a fear that there might be a shoulder dystocia when the baby's shoulders had got stuck in the birth canal. But everything had gone well.

Only when Jenny and her daughter, Camille, were settled on a postnatal ward, with the baby feeding well, did Callie go for a sit-down in the staffroom.

She was tired…exhausted. It would be so easy to close her eyes. But as she sat there with her feet up she felt a little something swirling around in her stomach. She laid a hand on her round abdomen.

Was the baby kicking?

She must have had the strangest look on her face, for when Lucas came into the staffroom to grab a coffee and saw her frozen, waiting for something to happen again, he asked, 'You okay?'

'I felt something.'

'Pain?' Fear was etched into his features.

'No, not pain…'

'Is the baby moving?' A beam of a smile broke out across his face and he shot across the room to join her.

'I don't know…' She moved her hand to feel again.

'Is it doing it now?'

He reached out and laid a hand on her stomach—the first time he'd done so. She could feel the heat of his hand through her scrubs and found herself hoping the baby would make one of its swishing movements.

It did.

'Oh, my God!' He pulled his hand away, his face lit up with delight. 'I felt that!'

So had she. And though she was delighted the baby had moved for him she found herself wishing he'd lay his hands on her again.

Oh, my goodness, these pregnancy hormones!

She flushed and had to use a piece of card to wave at her face and cool herself down.

'Are you all right?'

'Absolutely. Just a little hot flush.'

Putting her feet up, she lay back on the chair and ran her hands over her growing baby bump. She was quite happy with her bump. Pleased that as yet she had no stretch marks.

Inside, her baby gave her another little swirl and she gasped out loud as she felt it through her skin. She wanted to see if she could *see* the baby move, and raised her scrubs over the bump to reveal her bare belly.

This time there were no scrubs between them. This time Lucas had his hands on her bare abdomen, cupping the small mound of her growing uterus as the baby flipped and swished and generally swam about inside.

'That's amazing!'

'It knows you're its daddy.'

'Maybe.' He nestled closer to her and laid his head against her stomach. She could feel the bristles from his jaw prickling her skin. 'I can't hear it.'

'Give it a few months.'

He looked up at her, one hand still on her abdomen. 'I'm glad I'm having the baby with you.'

Callie looked back at him, shocked at his words. For weeks they'd danced around the subject, since that night at Gianni's, but now he was getting all serious again. 'Are you?'

'Yes. I couldn't have wished for it to be with anyone else.'

She gulped, her face flushing with heat and tension. 'Really?'

'You're my best friend.'

'I'm not very maternal.'

He looked deep into her eyes. 'You are. Or you wouldn't worry so much about doing the right thing.'

'You know I worry?'

'Of course. I worry too. We didn't get ourselves into this situation in the conventional way, did we?'

'I guess not.'

'I don't want that to matter anymore.'

She sat there, tummy exposed, his hand still resting on it just above the belly button, aware of his touch, aware of his nearness, and aware that his lips looked ever so kissable!

He got up off the floor and sat on the sofa next to her. He was close. Unbearably so.

Her heart began to pound as her breath caught in her throat. Her skin had come alive at his touch, tingling and yearning for more.

He's going to kiss me!

And she realised she wanted him to. Wanted it more than anything else in the whole wide world!

She sat up slightly and met him halfway, wrapping her hand behind his neck, embedding her fingers in his tousled hair and pulling his face towards hers, meeting his lips with hers, indulging in a wonderful, tentative, exploring first kiss.

Fireworks were going off throughout her body. She felt tense and relaxed and excited all at once. Her hands itched for his touch, to be holding him. Their mouths opened as the kiss deepened and his tongue took hers, and then she was breathing him, kissing him, holding him, in a way she'd never felt with a man before. His bristles scorched her face and it was a sweet agony as passion took them both by surprise and hunger for each other burned them to their very core.

This is Lucas!

Of course it was! He'd been there in front of her all this time, the man for her, and she'd let him be just a friend for all that time—not knowing, never allowing herself to think about it. *Why* hadn't she thought about it?

Perhaps I did. In fact, I know I did!

She'd once let the thought of what it would be like to sleep with Lucas occupy her mind for many a night.

But she'd not wanted to risk their friendship. She'd not allowed herself to linger on the prospect. She'd always dismissed it. It had been wrong before—he'd been with someone else, and she'd been his friend.

I need to breathe.

She couldn't remember how. Instead she continued to kiss him, to feel his soft hair in her fingers, his chest against hers, the yearning for more… She moaned softly and it seemed to increase his ardour. He mumbled her name.

For so long she'd wondered what it would be like. This moment. This kiss. Yet never in her wildest dreams had she thought she'd be thinking about ending it.

She knew she had to stop it. Knew she had to let him go. Because this wasn't meant to happen! If she lost him as a friend they would endanger everything they'd held dear about their friendship. And if she let things continue in this vein and it didn't work out… Well, where would they be then? Parents living in separate houses, meeting in rooms where the tension would be so thick it would need to be chopped with an axe, not sliced with a knife.

She knew that was what happened. She'd experienced that when her mother had broken up with her many boyfriends. When Lucas had broken up with girls in school and he'd confided in her about how awkward a particular class had been.

It never went well. People would *say* they'd remain friends, but that never happened in her experience. They separated. Pretended for a while and then drifted apart. Far apart.

She could never allow that to happen with Lucas.

Callie pulled back and stared into his eyes. Absently, she touched her swollen lips with her fingertips and then she stood up quickly, putting physical distance between them as she pulled her scrubs back over her stomach and put her hands solidly into her pockets.

'We shouldn't do that.' She sounded breathless. 'We can't risk it… There's a baby now—we have to think about that.'

Lucas looked hurt, but then the shutters came down. 'Sure.' He licked his lips. 'Not a problem. I'd better get back to work.'

She watched him go, her heart breaking, wishing she could take back her words but knowing that she couldn't. But he must have thought the same thing as her. Why else would he have backed off so easily?

We have to be sensible about this. We can't risk what we have...

The baby began to swish again with all the excitement. Callie laid her hand on her stomach. 'I can do this,' she said.

Callie wished she could be sure of that. She was certain Lucas would make a good dad—she believed in him. Knew he would be.

It was her own maternal instincts she doubted.

Lucas stood in Theatre, suturing a wound, his face a mask of concentration. Anyone on the outside looking in would think that he was simply concentrating on the task at hand—and he was. It was just that he was also thinking about what had happened with Callie.

She let me kiss her!

She'd more than *let* him. She'd *welcomed* it! Hadn't she? At first? Just after the baby had started kicking and he'd been touching her belly?

His hands had felt alive at the softness of her skin and the roundness of her belly, each nerve-ending dancing with excitement. Not just from feeling the baby move, but from touching *her*.

When had he ever touched her so intimately?

Never.

Callie didn't invite touching. Never had. He'd always known to keep his distance in that way. But with the baby moving…

They'd been able to share a wonderful, cherished, delightful moment—each of them feeling the child they had created together. But it had also been the first time he'd ever properly laid his hands on her.

The way she'd looked at him! He would swear blind she'd had something akin to desire in her eyes! Her pupils had widened, her breath had hitched in her throat and he'd sensed her pulse beating rapidly… It had been too magical a moment *not* to kiss her.

And what a kiss!

He'd never felt that way from just a kiss before. It had been like waking up from a deep sleep and realising that after all this time, all the years with Maggie, the kisses meant nothing compared to this one. With Callie it had been so special, so tender—as if his lips had discovered what they were truly meant to do. They were meant to be connected to Callie. They were for her and her alone.

His whole body had come alive. Each nerve-ending tingling, every synapse in his brain firing away like a space rocket. His heart had pounded and adrenaline had rushed through him, awakening every muscle, every intention, daring him to touch her more, to wrap his arms around her and pull her close, to envelop her as much as he could.

Fighting that had been difficult. Because there'd been fear there, too. Fear that she would stop him. Fear that she would break away. And if she did what would she say? What would she do? She was so afraid of losing their friendship and he…he was afraid she'd push him away. She'd already done it once, broken his heart once, why wouldn't she do it again?

And she had.

She'd stopped the kiss, shut them both down, before he could get carried away.

Perhaps that had been wise? Perhaps it was good that she'd put the brakes on? After all, he had no real idea of what she actually *felt*. Hadn't he already rushed into one relationship? Look how that had turned out! Wouldn't he be foolish to do the same thing with Callie? The one person who mattered the most to him.

The suturing done, he snipped the stitch and pulled down his mask. 'I'm done.'

The theatre assistants nodded and watched him walk away.

But as he stood at the sink, firmly scrubbing his arms with iodine soap, he knew—just knew in his heart—that this time, no matter what, he would treat Callie better than he had his wife.

The kiss—though heart-poundingly amazing—had been wrong. Callie had been right to stop it. They could never be together in that way and no matter what he felt for her he had to get over it—or he knew he'd get hurt again.

CHAPTER FIVE

OVER THE NEXT couple of weeks Callie realised that the baby's movements were going from being 'swishy' to definite kicks. Their baby liked moving. *A lot.* She knew she had to keep track of the movements and make sure she felt ten or more each day—and as the days passed she had no problem surpassing that total.

She had a very active baby, and she enjoyed nothing more than lying in the bath and watching the somersaults going on inside, as her belly wobbled from one side to the other, or was poked up in one area as the baby stretched its legs. There were times when a foot would press up against her belly and she could push it back down with her finger. Other times the foot would keep pressing out, as if the baby were playing with her.

Every evening they were at home together Lucas would sit with her, his hand on her belly, and talk to the baby. They were moments that she treasured, not knowing for how much longer this closeness might last, so she eked out every last second of the time.

They jokingly referred to the baby as 'Bean', and there was nothing she enjoyed more than to have Lucas tell the baby a story. He'd once read *Jack and the Beanstalk* to it, and every time he'd got to the *fee-fie-fo-fum* the baby had kicked madly and wriggled, making them laugh with delight and joy.

They both thought they were having a boy, but the discussion came up as to whether they ought to find out at the next day's twenty-week scan.

'It might be nice to know for sure,' Callie said. Then she'd know what she'd be giving away. A son? A daughter?

'I don't know. I kind of like the surprise.'

'Well, it's going to be one or the other, isn't it? If you find out what sex it is then you can start thinking about names and how you might want to decorate the nursery.'

The nursery was going to be the room that Callie was currently staying in. It was currently a pale blue, but they both knew that babies preferred strong colours to pale ones, so it would need redecorating.

'Don't you want to know if you're having a son or a daughter?'

'I'll be overjoyed either way.' He shrugged. It was a simple matter for him, it seemed. 'And *we* will pick names and *we* will think about how *we* want to decorate the nursery. I don't want to hear any more of this "you" stuff.'

'But it's *your* baby, Lucas. I was never meant to be involved.'

He shook his head defiantly. 'But you *are*. Things are different now and I want your input.'

How could she explain? If she got involved—if she started making choices—then she might get too attached. What would happen then if it all went pear-shaped? If it all went wrong? She couldn't bear to lose him.

'I'm not sure that I should give it.'

He looked at her sideways. 'Why are you afraid, Callie?'

'I don't know! Because I'm not sure how good I'm going to be for the baby. What role model did I have? A lying drunk who couldn't even be bothered to think of a proper name for me. A sly, selfish monster who loved alcohol more than she did finding food for our table. I don't know how to connect with a child—'

'Ridiculous! So Maria was an awful mother? You think that will make *you* a bad one too? You see women at work every day from all social backgrounds, having been through neglect and abuse and poverty, and they prove that they can be the best mothers *because* they had such an awful time themselves. Look at how Jenny was. She didn't even have parents, and yet she knew she was going to be the best parent she could for her little girl. You can do that too.'

'I know. I know you're right. But I still worry. I never thought that I'd have a child, and now that I am I need to know that I'm doing the right thing for it.'

'If you really were such a cold fish—if I thought in any way, shape or form that you were a cold-hearted, selfish monster—do you think we would have stayed friends as long as we have? You're *lovely*, Callie. You're kind, and you have the biggest heart of anyone I know.'

He was looking into her eyes so intently it was difficult to stop the somersaults in her tummy. Ever since they'd kissed that time his close proximity, his intensity when he looked at her, sparked her awareness of him. The way he moved, his scent, the way he gazed at her when he thought she wasn't looking… She knew there was the possibility of something else developing between them. And that scared her too.

'Really?'

'Do selfish people offer to have babies for someone else?'

She could see his point. But she'd never told him that she'd once entertained the idea that they *could* get together. That she'd thought if she was ever going to have a baby with anyone she would have chosen him. She'd not told the clinic. Had deliberately lied to them all. Because when he'd asked her out it had been the toughest thing for her to turn him down. Because she'd known she had to do something she didn't want to do. To the one man she'd wanted to say yes to!

But she'd not wanted to lose him as a friend if anything had gone wrong. All his relationships with women up until that point had been short ones. They'd all started with passion and *'Isn't she amazing?'* and then they'd all ended.

Callie couldn't have borne to be one of those girls.

Couldn't have borne to lose the one rock who had always been there for her through her childhood. Her one shoulder to cry on. The one person who would actually listen to her. Comfort her. Hold her.

Did he know that he was the only person who had ever held her? Properly? Just to enjoy holding her and not want something else?

It had been a big thing for her to offer to be his surrogate—especially when she'd known she'd be using her own eggs…that the baby she'd be giving away would be biologically half hers.

'Talking of Maria—she rang this morning and left a message. I think you ought to go and see her. She clearly wants to make amends.'

Callie visibly sagged. 'I can't bear to be let down again, Lucas.'

He touched her hand and she squeezed his fingers in response. 'But if she really has turned a corner—if she really has been off the booze for six months—you could have that relationship with her you've always wanted.'

He was looking at her strangely again. Was he thinking about *them*? About the relationship that he'd once wanted?

But he was right. Her craving for a relationship with her mother had been long buried, but it was still there. If there was any chance at all that Maria had turned a corner…

'Would you come with me?'

'Of course I will.'

There was an intensity in their stares as their gazes locked, and suddenly Callie was aware of how close Lucas was. It would be so easy to lean forward and kiss him again, to allow themselves to lose each other in the moment again, but she knew she couldn't let that happen.

She pulled her hand free and stood up. 'Cup of tea?'

He looked disappointed at her putting distance between them, but then his face went serious, and she hoped he realised she was doing a good thing by keeping her distance.

We can't be together like that, no matter how much we want it. But, damn, it's so hard to get to sleep at night, knowing he's just next door...

By the next morning, the day of the scan—a day off for both of them—they still hadn't reached a decision. They sat in the same chairs they'd sat in at the first scan, waiting nervously.

'Can you remember the last time we sat here?' Lucas asked.

She nodded, watching a mother opposite them try to play with her toddler, who'd found a set of bricks and was stacking them rather unsuccessfully. 'Seems such a long time ago. So much has changed since then.'

He reached over to grab her hand. 'Good changes?'

She smiled back and squeezed his fingers. 'Definitely. But if you'd told me weeks ago that it would end up like this...I would never have believed you.'

He smiled. 'But I'm happy it has. Aren't you?'

Callie shrugged, noncommittal. 'Just...you know...at the beginning the set-up was different, wasn't it? I went into this pregnancy knowing I was going to give away the baby, and then everything got thrown up into the air. That was what I meant.'

'So *are* we finding out? The sex?' he asked. 'I'll let you choose.'

It was a nice gesture. But she knew he didn't want to

know and so decided to side with him. 'We'll leave it as a surprise.'

'Okay.'

They waited another ten minutes or so before they got called through, during which time the toddler tottered over, grinning and dribbling, grabbing on to Lucas's legs for stability.

'Hey, hello there.' He smiled at the little boy and Callie loved watching them interact.

He's so good with him! Lucas is going to be a great dad! But how does he make it look so easy?

She was glad the toddler hadn't come to *her*. She'd have felt awkward and the toddler probably would have cried—she knew it. She still wasn't sure what type of mother she'd make as she had no frame of reference as to what a good mother was.

Lucas had told her once that she didn't need a frame of reference. That she could learn as she went and that, seeing as Callie wasn't an alcoholic or anything like her own mother, the likelihood of her being a good mother was strong.

'Being a parent doesn't come with an instruction guide, Callie. People learn as they go. You think no one else is afraid?' he'd asked her once. He'd really got angry. Frustrated that she just wouldn't agree to the possibility that she might be a good mother.

She hoped beyond hope that he was right.

Eventually, her name was called and they went in. It was Sophie again.

'Hi, guys, nice to see you again. You're looking well, Callie. Blooming.'

Callie smiled and heaved herself onto the bed. 'Bigger this time.'

'Definitely. You've been okay? Everything normal?'

'Oh, yes.'

'Baby moving lots?'

'Like a trapeze artist.'

Sophie grinned. 'That's what we like to hear. Okay, same procedure as before. Lie back, I'll put the gel on and then we'll have a look around. It'll be a longer scan this time, because we use this one to check for any anomalies or soft markers that might indicate a problem.'

'Sure—I know.'

'Of course. I'm so used to explaining everything I forget this is probably old hat to you.'

'Not really. It's all quite scary when it's your own.' She reached out for Lucas's reassuring hand, surprising herself. Where had 'hands-off' Callie gone?

Sophie nodded and tucked paper towel into the top of Callie's underwear.

'Right…we'll have a general look round first, then I'll take four measurements today. The biparietal diameter to measure the baby's head, the abdominal circumference, head circumference and femur length. We'll check that against gestation and decide which percentile your baby is in. Do you want to know the sex today?' They looked at each other to confirm what they'd decided earlier. Lucas gave her a nod. Callie turned back to Sophie. 'No, we don't. We want a surprise.'

'Excellent. Okay. And so we begin…'

As before, Sophie kept the screen to herself until she'd found the heartbeat and could see the baby moving, and then she turned the screen so that both of them could see.

Callie gasped aloud. 'Wow! It's so big this time!'

'Baby's grown beautifully,' Sophie agreed.

Lucas squeezed her hand. But Callie couldn't take her eyes off the screen. There was their baby! Their beautiful baby! Moving and tumbling and sucking its thumb. It was all so clear! A real person. A new human being. *Theirs.*

Sophie was clicking and moving the mouse around, looking at the head, the brain.

'Beautiful butterfly patterning—just what we'd expect to see.'

Then she went down through the baby's body, checking various organs and pointing them out: the kidneys, the heart. Even their baby's bladder, which had some urine in it, was sweet to see! She checked legs and feet, then arms and hands, and then she turned to the blacker parts of the scan.

'I'm just going to measure the amniotic fluid around baby first.' She moved a small white cross from one side of the expanse of black across to the other and clicked again. Then she moved the transducer and took another measurement. 'Fluid's good.' As she worked she kept clicking to print the pictures. 'No soft markers that I can see. I'll do the measurements now.'

Callie gazed on in awe.

You're my baby. Our baby. The last time I saw you I had no idea if you'd be mine. Now... Well, now I'm allowing myself to think that you might be.

The thought didn't surprise her. Which *did* surprise her. It seemed natural to want this baby.

'So, how far along are you now, Callie?'

'Twenty weeks and six days.'

'Okay. That's good. I can use that against the measurements in a minute. I just need to check where the placenta is lying.'

Callie knew this was very important. Not that the other measurements weren't important too, but if there was a problem with the position of the placenta it might jeopardise her chances of a normal delivery. If, for example, the placenta was low down and covering the cervix, the baby would not be able to come out of the birth canal. What they needed to hear now was that the placenta was posterior, or placed high.

'It's just slightly covering the cervix, but you've got time for it to move up, out of the way. We'll keep an eye on it. Arrange for another scan.'

Callie let out a breath she hadn't known she'd been holding. 'Right.'

They both watched intently as Sophie carefully skirted around the pelvic area of the baby—without giving the game away—and took abdominal and femur measurements. Then she did the head, taking the two measurements she needed to check for proper growth.

Sophie wrote everything down in Callie's notes and then plotted the measurements onto a graph. She showed the results to them. 'Everything's perfect. Baby's on the seventy-fifth percentile for all of these, so he or she is growing properly in all the right places, and for the right gestation.'

'Good.' Callie took the long stream of photos that Sophie had printed off for them. 'Thanks.'

'Do you want a 3D picture of baby's face?'

They looked at each other. Then Callie turned back to Sophie. 'Yes, please.'

Sophie pressed a button to change the scan picture from two-dimensional to three. The grainy black and white disappeared and was replaced by a sepia-type colour as Sophie brought the transducer up to their baby's face. Part of it was obscured by a hand and the umbilical cord, but most of it could be seen.

'Oh, my God!'

Sophie clicked and a picture slid out of the machine.

Callie held it so Lucas could also see. He couldn't stop grinning.

He leaned down and kissed Callie on the cheek. 'Beautiful—like you.'

She flushed at the compliment—and at the burn of his lips on her skin.

Sophie smiled. 'Everything's normal. Progressing as it should be. Now, do you have any questions?'

They didn't.

'Can't think of any.'

'Okay. So we'll arrange for another scan in a few weeks—just to check the placenta has moved off the cervix. But if you have a bleed you must come straight in. Although at the moment I couldn't see any reason why that might happen.'

'You have to warn us just in case. Don't worry—we understand.'

Sophie nodded. 'Okay. Have a nice day, you two.' She stood and opened the door once Callie was cleaned of gel and covered up again.

They walked out into the light of the waiting area and hugged each other. The moment had been perfect.

'Do you think s*he* knows?' Lucas asked.

'Knows what?'

'The sex of the baby.'

'Probably.'

'Hmm, I thought so too. Seems kind of odd that she knows and we don't.'

Callie looked at him thoughtfully. 'Do you want to go back and ask? I won't mind.'

Briefly it tempted him, but then he shook his head. 'No. We agreed on a surprise and a surprise we'll get. Let's get home and have something to eat. I'm starving.'

'I thought we could go over to Laurie Park. The weather's nice—we could go out on the boating lake.'

'Sounds good.'

Lucas drove them home and they packed a picnic for Laurie Park. It was a beautiful place, filled with fruit trees and harvest bushes. It was a 'free food forest'—following an idea that had started in Seattle, America, and travelled across the pond. It had been specifically created and designed to be filled with fruit-providing trees and shrubs and plants, so that people could pick and harvest for free. Callie thought it was an ingenious idea, but hadn't been there yet.

In the centre of the park there was a boating lake, with an island at its centre established as a nature reserve, where you had to keep to certain paths and picnic areas. This was where they headed.

The weather was beautiful and sunny, and Callie couldn't help but admire Lucas's muscles as he rowed the boat. His short-sleeved shirt showed off his tanned skin and muscular arms to perfection and it was nice to see him relaxed—not the intense Lucas she usually saw at work, with a stethoscope draped around his neck.

They moored the small rowing boat at one of the wooden jetties and Lucas got off first, then reached down to help her out so she didn't slip or fall. She tried not to pay too much attention to how she felt whilst he held her hand, deliberately ignoring the wish that he would continue to hold it.

The boat wobbled as she stood, scaring her for a moment, but Lucas kept hold of her firmly until she was off. He took the picnic basket in one hand and walked beside her as she delighted in the different berries and fruits she saw, picking some for their meal.

The sun was hot and it was the type of weather in which you might easily burn. She was glad she'd chosen her summer dress. The dress was the first bit of maternity clothing she'd ever bought, knowing she would be carrying her baby through the long, hot summer months.

There weren't many people about on the small island, and no one else in the picnic area they chose. They spread a tartan blanket on the ground and began to lay out their food.

'It's beautiful here.' Callie remarked, looking out over the fresh green grass and through the woodland glade to the calm water of the lake. There were swans gliding smoothly over the surface, two grey cygnets behind them.

'It certainly is. You'd never imagine we were in London.'

'No.'

He reached out to smooth a tendril of hair away from her face and she awkwardly tucked it behind her ear, flushing slightly at the intimate touch. What was he doing? Didn't he know he shouldn't touch her like that? They'd kissed once, but that had been a mistake. It couldn't happen again. They were just friends.

Callie finished laying out the picnic: baguettes, cheese, fruit, fruit juices, deli meats and strawberry jelly—her current craving. Lucas laughed when he saw she'd brought it.

'I couldn't come out without it.'

'Our baby is going to have a sweet tooth.'

'Oh, I don't know…my mum drank all that alcohol and I'm not an alcoholic.'

She knew she shouldn't have said it. It had put a dampener on things as soon as it was out of her mouth.

'Sorry. Forget what I said.'

'We can talk about it if you want?'

She shrugged. 'I was being flippant.'

'But it's important to you. It's part of your history.'

She poured out some fruit juice. 'Okay…where do I start?' She shielded her eyes from the sun, wishing she'd brought sunglasses. 'Well, I guess I was lucky I didn't have foetal alcohol syndrome when I was born. I was small—only about four pounds, though I was full term—and they reckoned I had a small heart murmur, but that was it. The murmur's gone now, thankfully, but I was so worried about today's scan.'

'Even though you don't drink?'

'Even though I don't drink. I was worried that because I got away with it as a child there might be a problem with *your* baby instead. Jump a generation—that sort of thing.'

He smiled. '*Our* baby.'

'Yes.' She nodded quickly, feeling awkward.

'But you know that's unfounded?'

'I know, but I can't help myself worrying.'

Lucas wafted a fly from his leg. 'You never raised this at the clinic.'

'I did. I told my counsellor when we had one-to-one sessions.'

'And what did she say?'

'Same as you. That it doesn't work that way, and that, besides, when they choose the egg and the sperm in the dish they pick the healthiest, best-developed ones. The chances of us having a problem was going to be minimal. And they'd done the genetic testing, too. I'm just an old worrywart.'

He leaned forward. 'It's because you care. You're going to be a great mum, Callie, because *you* have that quality. Your mum didn't for a reason. Her alcoholism is a disease which you don't have. Please don't worry about what sort of mum *you'll* make. I *know* you'll be fine.'

It was sweet of him to say it, but he was her friend—of course he'd say that. There was still that deep-down worry that she would be an awful mother. Like Maria had been. It didn't matter that she wanted to make amends. She'd still got it badly wrong to start with.

'We'd better eat before the wasps beat us to it.' She laughed, but the laughter tailed away when she saw the stern look on his face.

'Why do you always change the subject, Callie?'

'I'm not sure I know what you mean.'

'Your being a mother. I give you a compliment, tell you you'll be fine, and you change the subject. Or you argue with me. Tell me I'm wrong.'

She shrugged. 'I was taught avoidance by a master at the craft.'

'For someone who's so afraid to be like her mother, you frequently admit her influence on you, happily accepting it.' He sounded annoyed.

'I'm not happy to accept it, Lucas. It's just the way my life was. You wouldn't understand.'

'Wouldn't I? You weren't the only one with a difficult childhood.'

She looked at him askance. 'I don't remember *you* having an alcoholic mother.'

'Don't be pedantic, Callie. I meant my father. I hardly ever saw him, and as a boy I craved that connection. When he did come home he would be angry and resentful, and smack me more times than I could count just to "make me into a man". He hated the fact that I was surrounded by nothing but women, and knew how to sew and cook rather than fish or hunt. Even my best friend was a girl, and my father hated that too. He couldn't understand why I wasn't this football and rugby-playing army cadet, ready to follow in his footsteps. Instead he'd come home from Malaysia or Singapore and find me cooped up in the kitchen with my mother and sisters, covered in flour and other baking ingredients.'

Callie looked upset. 'I'm sorry. I didn't mean to be flippant.'

'I'm just saying you weren't the only one with a bad childhood.' He sighed. 'I craved my father's approval and attention just as much as you craved your mother's. Neither of us got what we wanted.' He looked at her as the wind billowed her hair around her face. 'Or *who* we wanted.'

There was an awkward silence filled only by birdsong and the gentle humming of nearby bees.

Lucas got up and walked to the water's edge, his hands in his pockets.

Callie looked at his back as he stood by the water. So alone and remote. She felt bad, and knew she ought to go to him and apologise. This was supposed to be a nice day out for both of them. A day off from work. A day off from pressure. Time to give them both the opportunity to talk about what would soon happen.

And I've messed it up.

Callie got up from the blanket and went over to where he stood. There were some ducks happily paddling, and further along a moorhen. She reached out to touch his arm and slid her hand into his.

'I'm sorry.'

When he turned she could see the anguish on his face.

'I am too. I didn't think anything could spoil today.'

She was going to make a comment about being taught how to do that, too, then realised that it was just the sort of thing Lucas had been referring to.

'We need to talk, Lucas. Properly. About everything. The baby, the surrogacy… Everything.'

'The future?'

She nodded, blinking in the bright sun. 'Yes.'

He looked her straight in the eye. 'I want you involved, Callie. I want you to be there for our baby. I know you can be. I know you're capable. I just want you to persuade *yourself* that you can do it just as much as I know that you can.'

She wanted to believe him. She really did. But years of doubt and second-guessing everything she'd ever known was a hard habit to break. 'When you say "involved", what does that mean? Occasional visits? Being a godparent?'

'Being a *mother*.'

There. He'd said it. Out loud. Asked for a huge commitment from her. A commitment she'd not expected when she'd first gone into this surrogacy.

'But what if—?'

He grabbed her arms. 'No "what ifs", Callie! Okay, you were only going to be the surrogate to start with, but that's all changed now. We're in this together and we're best friends. I don't see why we can't do this!'

She looked deep into his eyes, aware of how firmly he was holding her, aware of the proximity of his broad chest, those strong arms that had rowed them across the lake, the healthy brown glow of his sun-drenched skin. How could she tell him she was so afraid? Afraid that she'd lose him as her friend if they took their friendship to the next level and it didn't work out.

She knew she'd just die if she didn't have him in her life, and if he stayed just a friend then she could keep him there. Anything more than that would put them at risk.

She shifted her gaze and focused on his lips. His beautiful mouth, his strong jaw. He was gazing hungrily at her, like a man who couldn't bear not to touch, and before she knew what was happening he'd pulled her against his chest and pressed his lips to hers.

She sank into his embrace, tasting him, submitting to him, sinking against his body and feeling his arousal as they kissed.

Why have we been fighting this?

It felt so natural. It felt so *good!*

Kissing Lucas felt so damn *right*, and her hands went into his hair, clutching him to her as their mouths opened, deepening the kiss, their tongues entwining. A fiery heat spread up her body, electrifying her skin with his every tender touch.

The sun beat down upon them as their own fires burned within them.

She could barely breathe. She didn't want to stop kissing him just to breathe but she had to, and as she pulled away she saw the dazed look in his eyes and knew he'd been just as physically affected by the kiss as she had.

'Lucas, we—'

He shook his head and kissed her again. More tenderly

this time, cupping her face, sliding his hands down her neck, over her shoulders, down her arms, until he pulled her firmly against his arousal once more.

Callie groaned his name as his tongue wrapped around hers searing his touch into her memory banks for evermore.

Oh, God, why can't I have him like this?

She felt dizzy. Hot. Swept away on a tide of passion that she'd never felt before. The heat deep within her began to burn, awakening after many years of being kept hidden, trapped inside, bursting forth to scream its very nature to the world.

Everything around them was forgotten. The lovely island, the beautiful warm sunshine, the romanticism of the lake. All there was—was his kiss.

Her need for Lucas was frightening, overwhelming, and suddenly she felt scared by what they were doing. She pulled free and stepped back, breaking their contact.

'Callie—'

'We should stop.' Her hands hung limply at her sides, her hair was ruffled by his hands, and the memory of his touch was burning a trace across her heart.

He looked at her, hungry for more. 'Why?'

She couldn't answer him. Why *was* she stopping them?

Because you're my friend, Lucas, and I dare not lose you if this goes wrong! I couldn't bear to be without you.

'I need time to think.' She saw the disappointment in his face, so she reached out for his hand and took it in hers. 'I'm not running away. I just…need time to absorb this.'

He nodded, reluctantly, and they went back to the blanket together. They sat and nibbled at their lunch, no longer hungry for food, looking over the water, talking about nothing. But the atmosphere was strained by what was not being said.

A mallard glided by followed by six young ducklings, all brown and yellow and chirping. Squirrels jumped from tree to tree above them, and all around was birdsong and sunshine and warmth and bees flitting from flower to flower.

It should have been perfect. It should have been easy.

She'd ruined it and hurt him again.

Eventually Lucas broke the silence. His face was grim. 'If your heart isn't in this, Callie, then I'd rather you stepped back.'

'What?' She wasn't sure she'd heard him correctly. What did he mean, 'step back'?

'If you can't commit to this one hundred per cent, then I'd rather you didn't commit at all.'

'Lucas—'

'I mean it.'

He stared at her. His eyes were telling her he would not budge on this. He would not make allowances for her. She had to decide. She had to let him know what her plans were.

A cooler breeze came along and Callie felt cold. She'd not brought a jacket or cardigan and neither had Lucas.

'We ought to head back,' he said.

'I'll gather together the picnic things,' she mumbled, but he blocked her with his arm and said he would do it.

She watched him tidy away. He was so good. He'd been so patient with her. She knew he wanted more for them and that she was unable to give it. Or too scared to give it. But she hoped that in time he would understand. Surely he valued their friendship as much as she did?

'I'm glad we came here today,' she said, trying to brighten the mood.

He nodded. 'Me too.'

'Perhaps another day we could go to Windsor Castle? I always wanted to go there, but my mother never took me.'

He sat back on his haunches, blinking in the sunlight. 'I remember. She always let you down, didn't she?'

He wasn't just talking about the castle, though, was he?

He was letting her know that he understood. About how hard it was for her.

'I'll definitely take you.'

Their eyes met and she wondered if he was still talking about taking her to the castle or *something else*? Feeling all hot and bothered suddenly, she smiled and helped him pack away the last of the things.

It would be nice to go to Windsor Castle one day.

Perhaps they'd make it?

As friends, if nothing else.

Back at the flat, Callie unpacked the picnic, put the things they hadn't used into the fridge, then headed into her room for a cardigan. As she stood by her wardrobe, deciding which one to choose, she became aware of Lucas filling the doorway.

'You okay?'

He was looking at her strangely. His beautiful blue eyes all intense and serious and dark.

'I need to tell you something, Callie. Something I wanted to say at the park, but…'

Callie closed her wardrobe and threw on the cardigan, then sat down on her bed, rubbing her abdomen as the baby kicked. 'What is it?'

He came in and knelt down in front of her, looking up into her face. 'I'm getting strong feelings for you, Callie. Feelings I never thought I'd feel again. And I want us to be honest with each other at all times.'

She nodded slowly, afraid of what he might say. He'd said 'again', reminding her of the first time he'd asked her out and she'd turned him down. But she'd been so young! As had he. It had been too scary to take that step with him then and it was even more so now! So much was at stake—not just their friendship, but the baby. Their innocent baby.

'You can be honest with me.'

'I think you ought to go and see your mother. Get some closure. See if she really has turned a corner.'

She sighed. 'I'm not sure I can cope with any more of her lies, Lucas.'

'I know. But if she's *not* lying, Callie…if she really has been on the wagon for six months and this new man has made a difference in her life…you'd be a fool to let that relationship go.' His voice softened. 'She's your *mother*. And that's a bond that can never be broken. Besides…people can change.'

He let her go and went back into the lounge, leaving her thinking over his words.

He might be right. If Maria *had* been dry for months, then didn't she owe it to her to give her another chance? Even after all her lies? After all the let-downs? If she turned away now, when there was the chance of reconciliation…

But what if Lucas was wrong? If she was still lying…?

Then I won't have lost anything. It'll just be the same as before, won't it?

But she knew he'd also been referring to her. Saying that *she* could change. That she could be the mother he believed she could be.

CHAPTER SIX

THE BANANA TASTED odd in her mouth, and after a brave attempt to finish it she pushed it away, half eaten. Life was beginning to bother her. Thoughts were keeping her awake. Feelings and physical pangs kept her hungry in more ways than one.

Lucas had said she needed closure with regard to her mother. Well, maybe she needed closure in other ways too.

When Lucas came in from work he was exhausted and needed a shower. She found herself twiddling her thumbs, then cleaning out a cupboard and reorganising a bookshelf before he emerged, hair wet, a towel around his neck and another at his waist, his bare chest and legs pebbled with moisture.

What are you doing to me?

He looked delicious. Delectable.

Edible, even.

Licking her lips, she tried to calm her twitchy fingers and the pang in her stomach that cried out for some physical contact from him. Perhaps another kiss like that one at the park, by the lake?

That had been a toe-curler in all the right places!

He had a nice flat stomach—nothing too ripped, but not flabby either. And from his belly button there was a smattering of dark hair leading down to…

To distract herself, she tried to think of Maria. Memories of her were usually perfect for dampening her mood. She spotted her favourite teddy bear, lying at an awkward angle on the table, and she reached for it to straighten it, remembering another teddy bear she'd once made.

As a child, when she'd outgrown a nightdress, rather than throw it out she'd cut it up into squares and circles and hand-sewn it into a teddy-type thing. It hadn't been pretty, or neat, but it had been girly and pink and she'd stuffed it with filling from her pillow, hoping her mum wouldn't notice the crudely cut hole in the pillow covering.

Of course her mum hadn't noticed.

Callie hadn't named it, but she had cuddled it. And for a long time she'd thought she'd known what it was to cuddle.

Until Lucas had held her.

Stop it, Callie!

Then the importance of being held by someone who loved you had suddenly became important, and she'd realised just how much she'd missed as a child.

'I'm glad you're home.'

He looked at her face and frowned. 'Sorry. I got called away. You got my note?'

'Yes. Thank you.'

She stared at him, wondering how to start, but with him dressed like that he was too much of a temptation and she took a step back.

He raised his eyebrow, then grabbed the towel around his neck and began to ruffle his dark hair.

'We've never really discussed Maggie properly, have we? When she left, I mean?'

That was it. Best to come straight out with it. Not beat around the bush.

'I didn't want to burden you with my issues about Maggie.'

'I'd like to talk about her now, if that's alright?'

He nodded. 'Okay. I'll make us some tea and bring it through. You go and sit down—put your feet up.'

'Will you...erm...' she licked her lips and eyed that smattering of hair on his abdomen '...get dressed?'

He looked down at himself and then back at her, raising a sardonic eyebrow. Then he smiled and nodded. ''Course.'

Callie waited for him in the lounge while he disappeared off to his room. Soon enough he came back through—dressed, thankfully, in jeans and a white tee. He moved into the kitchen and came back with a tray of tea and a small plate of biscuits.

'Hungry?'

Definitely. But not for food...

'I couldn't eat.'

'I could make you an omelette?'

She shook her head. 'This is fine. I'll eat properly later.'

Callie inhaled a deep breath. She wasn't sure she wanted to hear some of the answers, but there were questions and she had to ask them.

'So tell me about you and Maggie.'

'What do you need to know?'

'What went wrong?'

He shook his head as if he didn't know himself. 'We should never have married. Plain and simple.' He shook his head, disgusted with himself. 'I was stupid. On the rebound. When we first got together, everything seemed fine. Or I pretended it was, I guess. I was so determined to make it work with her, and love her, and give her anything she wanted to make her happy.'

On the rebound? 'So what went wrong?'

He shrugged. 'I really thought I loved her. I thought I was proving it to her every day. She seemed happy, for a few years, at least, but then she started looking at me strangely and asking me weird questions.'

'Like what?'

'Questions about you. Us. Our friendship. There was a distance coming between us and I panicked. I didn't know what to do. I knew she felt that there was something missing, and when she mentioned children I was determined to give her the child that she wanted.'

'But that didn't happen.'

'She learnt she couldn't have children. When we couldn't conceive the distance between us became greater. Because of her infertility, I believed. She was so sad, and I so wanted to make her happy. When you suggested the surrogacy I leapt at the idea.'

'*You?* Not both of you?'

He shook his head. 'Not at first. But I persuaded her it was a good idea. She had doubts, but she agreed to let us look into it. When she started to have counselling at the infertility centre...that was when it all started to go wrong.' He took a sip of his tea. 'There were issues in our relationship from the start. I truly believed I loved her, and she insisted that I didn't. But that wasn't true. I *did* love her...in a way...just not in the way I should have.'

Callie nodded in understanding, sad that he'd never confided in her about this before. 'When I worked with Maggie on the ward she kept questioning me about the surrogacy. About my feelings about it. My feelings for you.'

Lucas looked at her. 'Did she? What did you say?'

'That of course I was happy to do it. That I loved you. That I couldn't imagine not giving you the greatest gift a friend could give. She looked so sad.'

'It's hard to work in Maternity and then discover you can't have what's in front of you all day long...' He shook his head. 'I felt so sorry for her.'

'Perhaps you shouldn't have?'

Lucas nodded. 'I know. She told me the night she left that my pity was so obviously just for *her*, not for us as a couple. That I was truly showing her I wasn't connected to her in the way I should have been.'

Callie felt sick. Why hadn't he confided in her about all of this? She could have helped them both! Given them space, distance, time. Whatever it was they'd needed.

'And then she had her affair?'

'Yes. She told me she'd found love in the arms of someone who put her first for once. That she'd found someone who was willing to treat her right.'

'But you *did* treat her right.'

'No. I didn't.' He looked at her and smiled sadly. 'I thought I had. I truly did. But she was right about me, and I feel terrible for treating her in such a way. I know now that I'll never do that again. It's all my fault.'

He slid over to the couch she was sitting on and put his arm around her shoulders.

Callie sank into him. 'But it *wasn't* your fault! She should have said something! She had a voice. You were trying to make the best of what you had. You acted with good intentions—'

'I so wanted to put it right. In all of this I was trying to prove something. To myself, to my parents, to Maggie. I should have been thinking of you, and I want to put that right too.'

'You haven't hurt me, Lucas,' she said gently.

'I never want to—'

Callie heard the crack in his voice. Her heart swelled with concern and she hated the fact that he was hurting over what he might have done to her. She turned to hold him, comforting him, hoping her arms around him would convince him of her forgiveness. She kissed the side of his face, his cheek, his jaw.

Her lips were moving ever closer to his mouth and he pulled back, looking at her, searching her face with his eyes. 'Callie, don't do this if you're going to stop me again—'

But she leaned in and closed her eyes as his lips brushed hers. A fire ignited within her and she didn't fight it this time. This time she welcomed it, falling into his arms, falling into his strong embrace.

He kissed her as if the world was going to end, and when he stopped she was gasping for breath.

'I should have been stronger. I shouldn't have allowed you to be dragged into my mess.'

'But we're working it out, aren't we?'

He stroked her hair back from her face. 'Yes. But I need you to know, Callie.' He held her hands in his. 'I will never hurt you. I will never lie to you. I will be here for you, always.'

She had to blink back tears at his words. 'I still have doubts.'

'Why?'

'Because…because you've never had a relationship work out! At school, at college. Plenty of girls, plenty of dates, but never a commitment. And then with Maggie…even that was wrong…even that failed.'

'But I was so young then! You can't hold relationships I had at sixteen against me? They were all wrong for me. And I've just *told* you about Maggie…'

'And the others?'

He looked at her, his face a mask. 'I was a teenager. A young teenager. Hardly anyone has successful relationships at that age. Besides…the one woman I truly wanted turned me down.'

Callie stared, his words echoing in her skull, accusing her, blaming her. Asking why she had turned him down? She'd told him why! Did he not realise? Understand? Did he truly not appreciate just how much he meant to her?

He leant back against the chair and sighed. 'You should hate me,' he said quietly.

'But I don't. You can't take all the responsibility here,

Lucas. We went into this process with our eyes open. So you knew things weren't great between you and Maggie and you didn't say? Well, what about what *I* knew? What *Maggie* knew?'

'What do you mean?'

'You weren't the only one in that relationship—she knew how bad it was, too. She was even sleeping with someone else, for goodness' sake! And I was her husband's best friend and she still allowed me to get pregnant with a baby when she was messing around with someone else! You didn't do that.'

Lucas lifted her hands in his and kissed them, his lips caressing the backs of her fingers with a tenderness that broke her heart. 'We were all in the wrong. I'm sorry. With all my heart, I'm so sorry.'

'Don't be. Because you're *you.* Because you're truthful. Without this situation I would never have had a baby. I would never have been able to consider the possibility that I'm able to be a mum. I would never have tried to be. And I can only contemplate it because you'll be at my side. There are no doubts in my mind about what a committed father *you'll* be.' She stroked his jaw. 'You're nothing like your own father.'

'You'll be here with us?'

His eyes lit up with hope, and the realisation that he wanted her to be there so much almost broke her heart.

It was terrifying to say it, but she knew in her heart that she could. 'I'll try. If you want me to be.'

'I want nothing more than for you to try. Because I'm living my life for *me* now. Not for Maggie. No one else. Me. And this baby.'

As they sat next to each other Callie circled the few hairs in the middle of his forearms. 'I love it that we can be honest with each other.'

'Me too.'

'I don't regret the surrogacy, Lucas. I knew then and I know now that you're going to be the best dad in the world to this baby.'

She looked deep into his heart and saw that her words meant the world to him.

They decided to paint over the pale blue with a pale green, so that they could paint a jungle mural on the upper parts of the wall: tree foliage, brown monkeys hanging down from the branches holding bright yellow bananas, snakes with red and blue stripes wrapped around tree trunks, a bright yellow sunshine in one corner and some red macaw parrots flying from one side of the room to the other.

It was an ambitious project, but Callie had agreed to it after seeing Lucas's draft drawings. He was a pretty good artist and could sketch what he wanted to perfection.

'You weren't kidding about having an inner interior designer, were you?' Callie laughed. 'I don't suppose you've got an inner chef, too?' She was starving.

She was wearing an old shirt of Lucas's, tied in a knot below her bump, with some old jeans. He wore an old tee shirt with jeans and both of them were pretty much covered in paint. They'd been working hard on the room for hours.

The nursery was really beginning to take shape and Callie could picture herself there, holding the baby. She could imagine looking down and feeling something. Love, devotion… That bond that had always been missing from her daydreams before.

Everything seemed to be coming together. It was all starting to look rosy.

Lucas flicked some paint on her. 'Hey—planet Earth to Callie?'

She looked at him and smiled. Could a man look more delicious, wearing scummy old painting clothes with a smear of green paint across his forehead? 'What?'

'I said I've made arrangements for us to visit the castle. Didn't you say you wanted to go?'

Windsor Castle was one of the oldest castles in Britain, and it still stood in its entirety in the centre of London. Queen Victoria had gone there on her honeymoon with Prince Albert. The pictures she'd seen of the inside on the internet made the place look so romantic—like a real life fairytale castle, right in the heart of the capital. People could hire it out for celebrations, and last year couples had started getting married there.

'That's great! When?'

'After the next scan. I thought we could go as a treat—before the baby's born. I'm not sure we want to negotiate turrets with a baby buggy in tow.'

No. Those turrets looked narrow.

'That's great! Oh, I can't wait! I was always asking my mum to take me and she never did, and then one day at school we were all given a letter to take home about a school trip they were organising to go there.'

He listened intently. 'I think I know what's coming.'

She nodded. 'You're right. She gave me two pounds for the deposit, which I paid, finally thinking I'd get to go on a school trip, but then she never paid the rest. I stayed at school, doing algebra and factoring equations, whilst everyone else had a lovely time.'

'Oh, Callie…'

'My classmates came back full of it. Since then I've always meant to go, but when you live in the heart of somewhere you tend not to go to the touristy places.'

He put down his paint and held both her arms, looking her straight in the eyes. 'Well, we're going. After the scan to check the placenta we are most definitely going to the castle.'

She smiled at him, and this time she hoped he would kiss her. She wanted it to happen. If he did she wouldn't fight him or step away. Not today. Today she deserved to be kissed.

Lucas didn't disappoint her. He pulled her closer and dipped his head to hers.

Callie closed her eyes in expectation. This felt so natural to her now, and she wanted him so much! She'd denied herself years ago and kept Lucas stored in a box marked 'friend' for too long. She wanted his lips on her, his hands touching her, caressing her. She wanted to feel the love that he could give. To have that release. Just once.

As their lips met sparks flew. A barrage of sensations ripped through her body. It was like waking up after centuries of being asleep—every nerve-ending was alive and just waiting for him to caress it.

His hands cupped her face as their lips made sweet music and she inhaled him as if he were her only life's breath. Tenderly and slowly he removed her clothes, as if he expected her to stop him at any moment. He didn't rush her, but moved at her pace.

Callie helped him pull off his tee shirt to reveal his broad, muscular chest and she ran her hands over parts of him she had never seen, as if privileged now to do so. He was so perfect—so right. A delight to look at and to touch.

Briefly she wondered why she had denied herself this for so long. She wasn't thinking about what she was risking any more. Somehow she'd pushed those worries to one side, as if she was allowing herself this one night. Those thoughts were too burdensome, too disappointing, to let them rule her head now.

Her heart was in charge and she wanted Lucas. Hadn't they both wanted each other for too long? Well, dammit, this time it was going to happen!

Callie's fingers undid his jeans and they dropped to the floor. Lucas scooped her up to take her to his bed. This room smelt of fresh paint and they didn't want any distractions.

She laid her head against his chest as he cradled her to him before gently lying her down on the bed, lowering himself onto her, holding his weight off her round belly.

'You're so beautiful, Callie,' he murmured, kissing her skin in feather-light touches, trailing his lips down her body to envelop her peaked nipples. 'If you're going to stop me, then do it now.'

She gasped at the sensation, gripping his back, hungry for more. More than anything she wanted him inside her… To feel him filling her, to enjoy that ultimate surrender…

She wasn't going to stop him. Not today. Not any more.

He took her gently, but still she cried out his name. He stopped briefly to check she was okay and then he was moving. Rhythmically. His mouth claiming hers. Her body was his to control and she cried out in ecstasy as he brought her to her peak.

Her hands gripping his back, pulling him tighter against her, she went with him on his own journey to climax. When he finally collapsed above her, spent and sweating slightly, he kissed her once again and then just held her, as if she was the most precious thing he'd ever owned.

Callie kissed him back and he fell asleep in her arms.

CHAPTER SEVEN

IT TOOK CALLIE a while to fall asleep, and when she did she dreamt in fits and starts. Dramatic, terrible dreams in which she was on a small boat out at sea in rough weather. High waves kept crashing down into the boat and all she had was a small delicate china teacup to bail out the water. Just when she thought the boat was safe from sinking another wave would crash down, or she'd notice shark fins in the water and the music from *Jaws* would inexplicably be heard.

In the dream, her panic was rising and rising, and then in the distance, beyond the high waves, she spotted another boat—a larger, stronger boat. Lucas was aboard, with all his sisters, and they were waving and calling at her to come to them. But no matter how hard she rowed her stomach would start to hurt and she would have to stop.

When the biggest wave of all came crashing down upon her head Callie woke with a start and sat up, gasping, her eyes taking in the familiar room. She was safe and on dry ground. Beside her, Lucas slept peacefully, his face relaxed, his hair tousled and gorgeous.

Thank God for that. Just a dream…

She ached in places she'd never ached before, and she remembered last night and how Lucas had touched her… Why had she made them both wait for so long?

She wiped the sleep from her eyes and ran her fingers through her hair. Glancing at the clock, she saw it said six-thirty a.m. She had to be at work for eight a.m. Throwing back the covers, she went to swing her legs out of bed—but stopped when she saw all the blood.

'Oh, my God! *Lucas!*'

Lucas leapt up beside her. 'What is it?'

'You need to call an ambulance.'

'What?' Then he noticed the large pool of blood beneath her. 'Are you okay? Are you in pain?'

She hadn't thought so, but now that he asked she was aware of some cramping. 'A bit…'

Lucas leapt from the bed, pulling on his jeans and throwing his old painting tee shirt over his head. He grabbed his mobile from his jacket pocket and dialled 999. 'Ambulance, please.'

'What is the nature of your emergency?'

'My partner's bled overnight. She's twenty weeks pregnant.'

In both their minds they knew that twenty weeks was much too early for their baby to survive if he or she arrived now. They needed to remain calm, but it was hard.

'I need to put on some clothes.' Callie said, about to get up.

'No! I want you to lie still. I'll give you one of my tee shirts. Do nothing until the paramedics get here.'

'Am I losing it, Lucas? Am I going to lose the baby?' she asked in a timid voice. This was the most frightened she'd ever been in her life.

He came to sit beside her on the bed and laid his hand on her belly. 'We can't know. But you do know as well as I do that this can mean nothing. Just a breakthrough bleed.'

'But there's so much…'

Callie began to cry. What had they done? She knew they should never have done what they had—knew they should never have overstepped that mark. Look what had happened!

'Hey… Shh… Come on.' He leaned into her and put his arm around her. 'Have you felt the baby move?'

She thought for a moment. Had she felt anything since being awake? 'No—nothing.'

'That still doesn't mean anything.' But his face hardened, his mouth a bitter line.

It was the worst seven minutes of their lives, awaiting the ambulance. When the two guys in green made their way into the flat, carrying their big packs and smiling reassuringly at her, Callie couldn't help but burst into tears again. It was all so scary. She had no idea what was happening to her baby and wouldn't know until she got to hospital and got them to do a scan.

The paramedics were very kind, and they tried to keep her spirits up as they wrapped her in a cream blanket, strapped her into a portable chair and wheeled her down to their vehicle. In the ambulance they attached monitors and checked her blood pressure. It was a little low, but nothing significant that would indicate a major blood loss, which gave them a little hope.

Callie lay on the trolley after they'd transferred her over, concentrating like mad on her insides, hoping and waiting for baby to kick, to give her a sign that it was all right. That it was still there…that its heart was still beating.

Why won't you kick? You're always kicking me…

But she felt nothing, and by the time they wheeled her into the St Anne's Hospital, she was despondent and very upset. Convinced that because she'd slept with Lucas she had somehow killed her baby.

'This is my fault.'

'It's not.'

'I'm being punished, Lucas. It's because I never wanted to be a mother. It's life's cruel trick.'

'No, Callie, it's not. It's nothing to do with that.'

'How can you know? I never wanted to be a mum, and just when I manage to persuade myself I could be one life strikes a blow and takes the baby away anyway!'

'You don't know that.'

'The baby hasn't moved! And it's always kicking me. *Always.*'

Lucas felt helpless. And angry… Angry at the world. He knew what she'd be thinking. How she'd be blaming herself.

All he could do was hold her hand, when what he wanted to do, as a doctor himself, was take over and order a fast scan so that they could get the status of the baby. She hadn't continued to bleed, which was a good sign. The bleeding had happened overnight and then stopped for some reason.

But inside his rage was building. Rage at life playing cruel tricks. Finally he'd been allowed to have Callie and now they were being punished for it. He knew what she'd start to think. Start to believe. That their lovemaking was somehow to blame. That it had been wrong. He cursed the world for doing this to him. Letting him have a taste of her. A taste of what it could be like for them together. And then swiping it away before he could hold on.

The doctors took her blood pressure again and it had stabilised. They also brought a portable ultrasound machine to Callie's bedside.

Lucas took hold of Callie's hand and gripped it hard. He was trying to tell her through touch that he would protect her, that no matter what the result he was there for her and they would get through it.

The doctor added some gel to the transducer and slowly drew it over Callie's abdomen. It seemed to take an age, and then the doctor turned the screen for them to see.

There was a heartbeat.

'Oh, thank God!' Callie began to cry again, with relief,

and Lucas reached to embrace her and kiss away her tears 'So it's all right?'

'Baby's fine. Heart-rate is good—about one hundred and forty a minute, which is average.' He swirled the transducer around some more. 'Placenta is still in position—no sign of early abruption.'

Abruption would mean that the placenta was coming away from the uterine wall early.

'It's possible you had a breakthrough bleed—dramatic as it was. If it's okay with you I'd like to do an internal and just make sure the cervix isn't opening.'

Callie nodded. 'Check everything. I don't mind.'

She was happier now that she knew her baby was safe, and as if in response to her strong emotions the baby kicked.

She laughed. 'Ha! So *now* you start! You couldn't do that earlier?'

Lucas had felt the kick too and audibly exhaled, his own heart reassured that he wasn't about to lose the two most important people in his life.

'I'll call everyone—let them know it's okay.' By 'everyone' he meant his sisters and his mother, as he'd called them earlier from the ambulance, to notify them that they were on their way to hospital.

He left the cubicle, so Callie could have privacy for the examination, and used his phone.

Callie meanwhile was reassured to hear that her cervix was tightly closed, was not effaced or thinning out in any way, and that she was showing no signs of labour.

'There is a small spot of cervical erosion. That could have been the cause of the bleed.'

'Erosion? Right…' Lucas had been so gentle, though, and careful. Had she bled because she'd slept with him? Was this her punishment?

But of course it could just be 'one of those things'. Unfortunately for her, and everyone else who experienced it, 'one of those things' could be quite dramatic.

'Is it because the placenta was covering the cervix?'

The doctor seemed undecided. 'It hasn't yet moved up off the cervical opening, so it's a possibility, but with erosion we can't know for sure. It does look like it's recent.'

The doctor suggested that she stay on the maternity assessment ward for the day, just to make sure she had no further bleeds. It would also allow her to rest.

'You have a stressful job, Miss Taylor, and you said you were decorating the nursery. Perhaps you just overdid it a bit?'

She accepted the admonishment. She *had* been up and down the stepladder a lot. And she *had* made love with Lucas. What had she been thinking? A day of rest was probably a good idea. Though she felt a little embarrassed that her colleagues would have to look after *her* when they were overworked already.

They soon dismissed that silly idea. They were overjoyed to be looking after one of their own.

'It's so special!' one of them said.

Callie wanted Lucas to get some rest too, so she asked him to go home.

'No, I'll stay with you,' he insisted.

'No, Lucas. Go and get some rest. I mean it. I'm fine now, and everyone else will look after me. Please.'

She didn't tell him it was because she wanted him to go. She felt so guilty about having sex with him. As if they'd been punished for something they should never have done.

Would she have felt different today if there'd been no bleed? Possibly. But she *had* bled, and they *had* slept together, and it was clearly a sign that what had happened was wrong. It could never happen again.

Lucas did feel tired. So he agreed and kissed her goodbye. Their lips lingered as they kissed each other, not wanting to part. But part they had to, and he stroked her face, deep in thought, his fingertips tracing the soft curves of her skin as if memorising the contours of her face.

She watched him go and closed her heart once again.

By the time he got back to his flat Lucas was exhausted. He changed the sheets and then lay on his bed for ages, hoping to sleep, but the last few hours kept running through his mind. Hearing Callie's scream, the fear in her voice when she'd called his name. Maybe on the outside he'd looked calm, but inside he'd been a mess.

The fear of losing either of them had almost killed him and the knowledge of that had made him realise something.

He loved Callie. Not just because she was carrying his baby. Of course he cared for her because of that, but this felt deeper. Something that had been awakened after a long time. Something that had always been hidden there inside him, but had masqueraded as his friendship with her.

Lucas loved being her friend—yes, he did—but…he wanted more than friendship with her. He wanted to love her properly, in the open, not just as friends but as lovers, as a couple, as a committed partnership.

He'd seen her darkest days. He'd seen her go through so much. And each time it had hurt him and he'd been there for her—if only to hold her hand or to listen as she'd cried, wept with despair or anger. They'd shared good times too. Her getting into university, then qualifying as a midwife; himself qualifying as a doctor.

They had a shared history. Had shared so much together.

Now they were having a baby.

Surely two people could not be connected more than to have created a life together?

He got up and began to pace. Wanting Callie home.

Home.

They lived together. They were best friends. Were having a baby.

And he loved her.

But he knew she was afraid. Afraid of jeopardising their friendship. How could he make her see that she meant the world to him?

There had to be a way.

There had to.

Just thinking about her and the baby made him feel good, and his heart soared so high it might have been up in the stratosphere.

The baby meant so much to him. He loved it—he knew he did—that was without question.

I love Callie too. I do.

But could he have her in the way he wanted?

He needed to know that she would give him the commitment he needed. Not just to him but to the baby too. He'd lived his entire life wishing his own father would be more committed to him, rather than just being a disciplinarian and an occasional parent who swooped in from overseas for a week or two at a time…

Lucas needed to know that Callie would be there one hundred per cent. Not a weekend mother, not a godparent, not an 'aunt'.

A mother. A wife.

My first marriage might have been a dreadful mistake, but I could damn well be sure my second won't be.

He picked up his phone and dialled a number. A number he'd put into his phone just a few days ago. As it rang he hesitated, just for a moment, and wondered if he were doing the right thing. But then he thought of Callie and he just *knew.*

This was the right thing to do. But he'd keep it a secret for now. Surprise her.

As the phone was answered at the other end he grabbed his car keys and walked down to his car, making arrangements as he went.

He'd had a very productive evening with Sienna from the castle. Walking through the doors of the hospital the following afternoon, he felt less anxious. Hospital could be a frightening place for most, but for him, it almost felt like home. He liked working there—liked the people, the place. His work. He knew the team and he knew that Callie would be looked after well.

Upstairs in the maternity assessment suite Callie was sitting upright in bed and looking much better. There was colour to her cheeks and her face lit up when she saw him.

His relief at seeing her was overwhelming. 'Callie…' He kissed her and sat down in the chair beside her bed. 'How are you doing?'

'All right. I've had lunch, and the doctors say if I don't have any more bleeding in the next few hours I can come home.'

'That's fantastic.'

But he was looking about the ward, not looking at her. Distracted. Something had changed with him. What was it?

She looked at him, concerned at the odd tone in his voice. He didn't seem his normal self.

Something was wrong. Lucas was hiding something—she knew it. She could always spot someone lying to her or hiding something from her. She could smell a woman's perfume. She could also smell alcohol. On *Lucas*? What did that mean? Had he been drinking?

For some reason Callie chose not to say anything, but inside she hurt. Had Lucas been drowning his sorrows? Self-medicating with alcohol? Why would he turn to booze? She'd never known him to drink before.

She'd confront him later. Not here. Not in the hospital where they both worked.

'Did you get some sleep?'

'A bit.' He changed the subject. 'Have you spoken to your mum?'

Callie looked at him with a raised eyebrow. 'No. I figured because we're going to see her in a few days I could tell her then. If she's interested.'

'I'm sure she will be.' He squeezed her hand. 'Can I get you anything?'

The truth… 'You can get me out of here.'

He laughed. 'Soon. I *have* missed you, you know.'

Have you? 'I've only been gone a night.'

Lucas nodded. He knew that. They'd been the most unbearable few hours he'd ever spent.

Although Callie had her suspicions, she had to let them go for now—even if they *were* eating her alive. She would remain friendly until she had proof. She couldn't believe he was making her think like this! Making her suspicious. How *could* he? After all this time, after all her worrying about losing him as a friend, now he'd slept with her he'd gone out and celebrated, or something, and probably hadn't done so alone! That had to explain the perfume smell. The aroma of alcohol on him.

Why wouldn't he? He was a good-looking man. Charming. Women gravitated to him, didn't they?

She hoped her suspicions were wrong. Because if they were right then that meant Lucas was keeping things from her. *Lying to her.* She'd been lied to her whole life by the one person who shouldn't have. She couldn't do that again.

Not with him.

Not ever.

Lying was the worst kind of betrayal she could imagine.

* * *

They were just about to leave the hospital to go home, and were standing by the midwives' desk saying their goodbyes, when the telephone rang. One of the midwives answered it, listened and then put her hand over the speaking part of the phone.

'Callie? I know you're not actually on duty, and you're going home, but it's someone called Rhea on the phone and she says it's urgent. She's been trying to call you on your mobile.'

Callie's mobile had been left at the flat. She reached over the counter for the phone while Lucas rolled his eyes in dismay. She shouldn't be working.

'Rhea, it's Callie. What's up?'

'You said I could call you any time, but I couldn't get hold of you on your mobile.'

'I left it at home. Is something wrong?'

'I've been having some pains. Tightenings, really. I don't know what to do.'

'Have you had a show or anything?'

A 'show' was part of the mucous plug that sealed the cervix, and it could sometimes be seen before labour started to show that the cervix was beginning to soften and dilate.

'No. I had a bath, though. It didn't help.'

'Well, are these tightenings strong? Are they painful?'

'More achey. A couple of them have taken my breath away.'

Callie thought for a moment. 'It could be Braxton Hicks, but you're very early on for them. Is the baby moving?'

'Like a trooper.'

'Well, that's good. It's up to you, Rhea. You can come in and let us monitor you for a bit—maybe run a trace to be safe—or you can stay at home and see what happens.'

'I think I want to come in.'

'Okay, you can do that.'

'Will you be there when I get there?'

Her heart sank. 'I'm sorry, Rhea, I'm on my way home now—you've just caught me. But the other midwives here will look after you just as well as I would.'

'But you *know* me. Know my situation.'

'I'll tell them.'

She got off the phone and explained the situation, and then she and Lucas headed home.

He was happy in the car, whistling or singing along to the radio. She couldn't be sure of what was going on, and she needed evidence before she confronted him. Besides, she felt so tired from the last twenty-four hours that she didn't want to ask.

When they got home she went straight to bed, on Lucas's orders, and fell fast asleep.

Lucas watched her sleep. He was glad he'd stripped the bed earlier and replaced the sheets with fresh ones. Callie looked as snug as a bug in a rug, her face relaxed and free of the worry lines she'd had over the last few days.

She'd seemed a bit odd in the car, and he'd thought about asking her if everything was all right, but he'd decided not to push her. He didn't want to hear that maybe she was having second thoughts about their having slept together.

That night had meant so much to him, and he loved her even more if that was possible. It had been a real fright to think that they might lose the baby, but everything had turned out fine in the end. Besides, if he started asking questions she might tell him what he didn't want to hear. Not now. He'd be giving her ample opportunity soon to declare her intentions. Fully. For the whole world to know.

Just thinking about that churned his stomach. Everything would change on that day. Either his world would fall apart or he would get everything he had ever wished for. And by arranging a surprise proposal at Windsor Castle he would know for sure whether Callie's commitment to them both was a hundred per cent. He didn't want a part-time parent for his child. He wanted a mother.

But he also wanted Callie for himself. As his wife. As he'd wanted her years ago. If she turned him down...? Well, he'd be devastated, but he'd survive. He'd done it once before and he supposed he could do it again. Though it would be harder this time.

But he couldn't see how she *could* turn him down. Weren't they perfect together? Hadn't they always been great together? And some of the best relationships came from being friends first... By being committed to each other they could know that they would always be together. As Callie wanted. She'd never lose him.

Unless she got cold feet.

What if she panicked? What if she backed off? What if the proposal scared her?

He was trying to arrange the perfect conditions, so that there wouldn't be a crowd to pressure her into saying yes. He wanted her honest answer. If she said yes it would be because she truly wanted to be with him—great—but if she said no...

Lucas tried to imagine hardening his heart. Being stoic at the disappointment. But he couldn't. It would just seem so devastating.

Was he ready to endanger himself like that? Was it worth the risk? What if she *did* say no?

It was like being on swings and roundabouts. One moment his heart was all for it, the next his need to protect himself swung into play.

But it's not just about me any more. This is about our child too!

He *had* to do right by his child.

His secret plans were starting to come together and he

could only hope she didn't suspect what he was doing—because he wanted it to be the biggest surprise of her life.

The stress that the bleed had caused both of them had been awful, and he knew she'd not been sleeping well lately. But as he sat looking at her now, the woman who was carrying his beloved child, he vowed not to lose her. To prove to her that they had a future together.

Lucas switched off the small bedside lamp and curled on to the side of the bed next to Callie. The last forty-eight hours had been awful. Terrifying. But they'd got through it—and they'd got through it stronger than they'd been before because they'd pulled together. It was what people did. People who loved each other.

A few days had passed since the bleed, and Callie and Lucas were sitting in Maria's lounge. Callie felt awkward. The strained atmosphere between her and Lucas had developed more and more, and once when he'd been in the shower his mobile had rung and she'd seen the name 'Sienna' when she'd looked to see who was calling.

Who was Sienna? Callie didn't know of anyone at the hospital with such a name, and she'd not heard him mention a patient called Sienna. None of his sisters or family was called Sienna, and it was hardly an *old* woman's name, was it? Sienna was a young woman's name. A *pretty* young woman's name. How did he know her? How involved were they?

She'd been tempted to look at the contacts list in his phone but had quickly put it down, not wanting to be that kind of woman who checked her partner's phone.

But then a text from the lovely Sienna had popped up. It had read: Fabulous! You're brilliant! Can't wait to meet again. Sienna xx

Her heart had been ripped in two. Had he cheated on her? The night she'd been in hospital?

Although grief-stricken at the thought of having lost him already, she'd pulled herself together, determined to get through the rest of her pregnancy with dignity. She would have this baby and give it to Lucas and then she'd walk away.

It was what she'd been going to do in the first place, wasn't it? Lucas and this Sienna woman could play happy families. It was nothing to do with *her*.

She must have been in a weird mood since, because Lucas had kept asking her if she was all right. She'd kept answering that she was 'fine', and now she had to get through this visit to her mother.

As Callie was having difficulty driving, and not feeling comfortable behind the wheel, she'd had to let Lucas bring her.

She hadn't been to her mother's home for years and, truth be told, the last time she'd seen it, it had been a bit of a dive. Clutter and rubbish had been piled up everywhere, as if she was a hoarder, with surfaces overflowing with empty cans and bottles. The odd plate of food mouldering. They'd had a massive row the last time Callie had been here.

The last time I was here I stormed out.

But now the flat looked totally different. It was clean…it was neat and tidy. The walls had been given a lick of paint—'Gareth did them…'—and the hallway had been freshly wallpapered. There were pictures of Maria and Gareth up in frames, and one of Callie as a baby in her cot had been given pride of place in the centre of the mantelpiece.

'The place looks great.'

Maria smiled, inordinately pleased that her daughter approved. 'We've worked hard to change it around. Money's tight, but it's amazing what a bit of spit and polish and a dozen or so bin-liners can do.'

Maria placed a tea tray on the low coffee table and poured them all drinks, offered round a plate of biscuits.

'I'm just sorry Gareth couldn't be here, but he got called to work on an emergency.'

'What does he do?' Lucas asked, thinking someone ought to show an interest, and Callie was oddly quiet. She'd been strange for days now, and he wondered if she suspected what he was up to. He hoped it *was* that. Because she was starting to pull away from him. The way Maggie had in the last few days of their marriage.

'He works for a counselling line. For ex-alcoholics. Because of his background he's got a lot of experience with helping people, and sometimes when they get a crisis call he goes in and helps out.'

'A counsellor? Wow…' So Gareth was used to helping out people in crisis? What had made him fall for Maria?

'Gareth is an alcoholic too,' Maria explained, seeing the question in Callie's eyes. 'But he's been on the wagon for twenty years. He still goes to AA meetings and that's where we met.'

'Two alcoholics together? Is that a good idea?' Callie asked.

'A lot of people may say two dependents living together is a recipe for disaster, but we don't think so. It's down to the individuals at the end of the day, and Gareth was determined to help me kick the sauce. And he did. Over six months now, Callie.'

She nodded. 'That's good, Mum. Long may it continue.'

Maria smiled, looking at both of them. 'It's a new start for me. Like this baby is for the pair of *you*. I'm so glad you two got it together in the end. I don't know why it didn't happen earlier.'

Callie and Lucas looked at each other. But it was awkward. Uncomfortable, somehow.

Lucas spoke. 'Things are complicated. We're taking it slow—not rushing into anything. We don't want to get it wrong.'

Callie rolled her eyes. It was twice now that Lucas had told people he and Callie were together, and each time she heard it she still felt scared by it. Did he still think everything was okay? There was a baby involved here—they couldn't afford to screw this up!

'How are you anyway, Callie?'

It was the first time Maria had shown concern for her and something inside Callie softened. She had to fight tears for a moment as the one thing she'd craved from her mother—attention and concern—was finally given.

'I'm all right. We had a little scare and I was in hospital for a few days, but I just needed to rest.'

'Oh…I do hope you're okay? Having a baby is a truly life-changing event—one that I got badly wrong. But I'm sure that you two will love this baby in a way I never could.' She turned to her daughter. 'I need to apologise to you, Callie. For everything. For the way I mistreated you. The way I put alcohol first. The way I neglected you. But it was a disease I couldn't fight at the time. Thank God for Lucas, here, because without him around as your friend I don't know how you might have turned out.'

'Wow…' She'd never expected an apology. She'd never expected this. 'Thanks… I guess I turned out all right…'

'All right? You're an amazing person, Callie, and I can't say enough how proud I am of you, and how sorry I am that alcohol took me away from you and stole the mother you deserved.'

Callie swallowed back tears. 'Well, thank you for the apology. It means a lot.'

The rest of the visit was spent with Maria showing Callie a scrapbook she'd managed to put together with scant pictures of Callie through her childhood and some of Maria and Gareth together. They spoke of the years of Callie's childhood, telling stories, sharing snippets of what they remembered.

There were lots of tears.

But there was lots of forgiveness and love too.

Callie got into Lucas's car for the drive home, feeling that bridges were now being forged that would hopefully never break. There was some hope for the future with her mother at last, but even though she'd made a good start today there were still many more days when it could all still go wrong.

Past experience had taught her that.

And present experience.

But she was hopeful.

And yet cautious.

I may be losing Lucas, but I'm getting my mother at last.

More weeks passed and Callie didn't have any more bleeding. But she made it quite clear that they would not be sleeping together again. She kept Lucas at arm's length.

Lucas understood her reticence and accepted it, though it was killing him not being able to touch her. He had even accepted her explanation of why, but he'd seen that she was being quite clipped with him, and sharp. He was beginning to fear that she was putting distance between them in time for the big day, so that she could still disappear and leave him holding the baby.

She was at thirty-four weeks' gestation and that day was getting closer. She had two more weeks left at work before she went on maternity leave. The nursery was all done and painted, a pram had been bought, and lots of tiny baby clothes in neutral colours. Lucas had bought some cuddly toys to go inside the cot which he'd spent the previous night building—with much swearing and cursing and dropping the Allen key constantly, or catching his knuckles on the wood.

The future was looking good for baby Gold, even though

he wasn't sure if Callie would be a part of it—and that broke his heart.

He knew he ought to be resigning himself to her leaving. All the signs pointed to it. His dad had been the same when he'd been at home and was about to leave again for foreign climes. He'd get sharp with everyone, snappy, find reasons for arguments. Callie was behaving the same way. Maggie had done it—why wouldn't Callie?

Everything was going really well pregnancy-wise. She'd even been receiving calls from her mother every week! Asking how she was and everything! Maria was certainly making an effort and trying to prove what she'd said to Callie.

'I'm going to be dry now, Callie. For ever. You can depend on me.'

'Wow. That's great, Mum. That would be amazing, in fact. But you've got to do it for yourself—not for anyone else.'

'I *will* do it for me. And for you. I know I wasn't the best mum in the world to you. I was no mum at all.'

Callie's eyes had welled up at that point and she'd found it difficult to speak.

Lucas had wanted to lay his hand on hers, to offer support, but that was difficult now. He knew Callie wouldn't appreciate it.

'Well, I'm behind you. You have my support. And I think I'd like to meet this Gareth who's made you like this.'

Maria let out a breath. 'I'd like to come and see you. When the baby's born. Perhaps I could bring him then?'

Callie had agreed. 'That'll be nice. I'd love that.'

When she'd told Lucas of the call he'd been just as shocked as she'd been, at first, but then he'd been so pleased! Especially when she'd mentioned that she'd invited Maria and Gareth to come after the baby was born. He'd picked her up and whirled her around the room, with her shrieking and squealing at him to put her down. How could he not know that it hurt for him to touch her and try and kiss her?

'Is everything okay?' he kept asking.

'It's fine. I'm just hormonal,' she'd reply.

When he wasn't looking she'd glance at him and feel sad. He'd let her down so badly. She'd not got an opportunity to look at his phone again for more messages from this Sienna person, but occasionally a text message would pop through and he'd look at it and smile before texting back.

Each time her heart would break a little more, and she'd dread when the time would come for them to part.

CHAPTER EIGHT

WHEN CALLIE GOT into work the next day she was informed that her teenage patient, Rhea, had been admitted in early labour.

'She had a show last night, and then her waters broke this morning. She's in Room Two and she's waiting for you,' said Sarah, Callie's supervisor.

Callie was surprised. Rhea was at the same gestation as she was—thirty-four weeks. That was six weeks earlier than expected. Not drastic—the baby would more than likely be fine, although depending on its condition when it was born they would decide whether it needed to go to the Special Care Baby Unit or not.

Premature labour in teenagers was common. More common than most people knew. Lots of people assumed that teenage mums were healthy because they were so young, and would easily be able to carry a pregnancy to term, but unfortunately statistics and evidence didn't bear that out.

Callie grabbed Rhea's notes, quickly skimmed through them and saw that she'd been four centimetres dilated at her last check, which her colleague Donna had done only twenty minutes ago. Rhea had had a good night, had managed to get some sleep and was not using any medication—not even gas and air just yet.

She headed on down the corridor and got to the door of

Room Two. She tapped on the door gently and then popped her head in. 'Hiya—it's me. Can I come in?'

She was shocked to see a woman seated in the corner of the room, writing in a file. Who was *she*?

But Rhea was sitting on the bed in a beautiful red night-shirt and pink bed socks, one ear plugged into an iPod. She pulled the earphone out and smiled when she saw Callie.

'Thank God you're here! I was beginning to wonder if you'd ever make it.'

'I had no idea you'd come in.'

'I came in first thing.'

'Well, I only discovered that about twenty minutes ago. How are you doing?'

'All right. They don't hurt too bad at the moment.'

Callie nodded, then turned to the woman who was now smiling at her. 'Hi. I'm Callie, and I've been looking after Rhea throughout her pregnancy.'

The woman smiled politely. 'I'm Jessica. I'm the social worker assigned to Rhea's case.' She indicated Callie's bump. 'You look ready to have one yourself.'

Callie ran a hand over her burgeoning bump. 'Six weeks left. Looks like Rhea's going to beat me to it.'

'You can't stop babies when they decide to come, can you?'

Callie smiled. 'You certainly can't.'

Callie went over to Rhea and began to prepare the CTG machine. 'We need to run a trace for a little while. About thirty minutes. Is that okay? It's just with you having gone into labour early we need to make sure baby's okay.'

Rhea nodded and lifted herself so that Callie could get the straps behind her before applying the sensors to her abdomen and strapping them tightly. The baby's heartbeat was registering in the one hundred and thirties and the lower sensor measured the contractions.

She gave Rhea a push-button device. 'Record any movements you feel, okay?'

Rhea nodded, looking nervous.

'Don't be scared. This is all normal.'

'I bet *you'll* be scared when it's your turn.'

She laughed and smiled in sympathy. 'I probably will. And they always say medical personnel make the worst patients. I'll probably be a nightmare for whichever poor soul has to look after me.'

Rhea smiled nervously. 'What if I can't do this?' she asked in a small, terrified voice.

Callie sat herself down on the side of Rhea's bed. 'You? Not do this? Rhea? The brave girl who faced me off in her booking visit? What you've been through makes you the strongest girl in the world. You're here, you're a survivor, and you can and will do this.' She patted Rhea's hand, but Rhea grasped it, and Callie could feel her nerves. 'It's okay.'

Rhea met her gaze and nodded. But there were tears in Rhea's eyes.

'Look, I have to go and fill in your notes and then get Lucas. So I'm going to leave you for a bit whilst we get the trace. Try to use the time to relax. You'll need all your strength later. Can you do that for me?'

Her patient nodded.

'Put your head back, listen to some music, close your eyes. We'll be back in a jiffy.'

She quietly left the room, sighing deeply. Her own stress was building on Rhea's behalf. The time for her delivery was getting closer. Time for her to make a choice about her baby. They should have had more time. Another six weeks to get her to see that there were other options open to her. But time had been taken from them all. Was Rhea going to give her baby over to Social Services?

Sitting at the midwives' desk, she was writing up the notes when she felt Lucas's hand come over her shoulder.

She froze. Lucas had continued to try and touch her these last few weeks. It was baffling. Their relationship was seemingly just the same to him. Had he not noticed that she was trying to break away? So that when they did part her heart would remain in one piece?

She shrugged off his hand. 'Rhea Cartwright is here. Remember her? She's gone into early labour. Waters have broken, she's four centimetres, and she's in Room Two as scared as anything.'

'Don't you want to be with her?'

She nodded. 'She's got a social worker in there. I think she's going to take the baby if Rhea sticks with her decision. But whilst she's on the trace I thought I'd give her a break, you know?'

He looked at her, curiously. 'Give *her* a break or *yourself* a break?'

'How do you mean?'

'Well, I know how you feel about her case. Her giving the baby away. It has to resonate with you—it was what I was asking you to do.'

'But for completely different reasons. I hadn't been through what she'd been through.'

'So it would have been less traumatic for you to give away a baby because you hadn't been raped? Come on—you know that's not true. It would have been hard and difficult and heart-breaking, no matter what the circumstances.'

Callie rubbed her belly, feeling their child move and tumble around. There was less room inside now, so she felt every little stretch, every little movement, every little hiccup. It still could be heart-breaking. She had no idea if she would try to keep the baby herself now or give it to Lucas. She would most probably be giving it away. Unable to keep it or even be in its life.

Best not to think about that right now.

Was Rhea still okay about giving her baby away? Or was

she getting attached? Having doubts? Did she feel pressured to give up her baby because Jessica was in the room with her?

'I need to get her out.'

'Who?'

'The social worker. I need time to talk to Rhea.'

I may not be able to keep my baby, but Rhea could still keep hers.

'You can't persuade her to keep it, you know. That's not your decision.'

'I know, but I at least need to know that she's looked at all her options.'

'So what do you want to do?'

She looked to him for back-up. 'Come with me. Into her room. We'll say we're about to do an internal, or something, send her for coffee—anything to get her out of the room. I need to know that Rhea has thought through *everything* before she gives that baby away.'

Lucas breathed in deeply through his nose, thinking hard. 'Okay.'

They headed into Rhea's room and managed to persuade Jessica to go for a coffee whilst they ran some tests and examinations. Callie sat once more on Rhea's bed whilst Lucas stood by the CTG, looking at the trace.

'Hello, Dr Gold.'

Lucas smiled back at her. 'Hi.'

'Rhea, I'd like to talk to you,' said Callie.

'What about?'

'Your decision. About what happens after the baby has been born.'

'Oh.' Rhea looked down at her lap, fiddling with her earphones.

'Have you had any more thoughts about what you want to do?'

Rhea shrugged. 'I don't know.'

Callie didn't understand. 'You don't know? Whether to give it up?'

When Rhea looked up her eyes were full of tears. 'I don't know what to do! I was doing fine to start with. I was going to give it away—end of story. You know what I was like.'

Callie nodded.

'But then you bloody well made me see the scan! In 3D! I saw her *face*! Her sweet face... And you know what it made me think? That she *didn't* look evil. That she *didn't* look like a monster. It'd been so easy to think that she was.'

'Easier to separate yourself from it?'

Rhea nodded and sniffed. 'Yeah. But by then I'd got *them* involved, hadn't I? The Social.' Rhea wiped at her eyes with the back of her hand, then was gently handed a tissue from the box by Lucas. Rhea took it and blew her nose, wiping her face clean. 'I don't know what to do.'

She looked at Callie.

'How did *you* know you wanted to be a mother?'

Callie knew that was too long a story to go into. And if she was truthful about her own doubts that wouldn't help Rhea with hers.

She glanced at Lucas. 'I don't know... I guess it happened quite slowly. I had to get my head around the idea. It was frightening.'

'You were scared? But you're a midwife.'

'Worst patients, remember? I don't want to be flippant. It's an individual decision. But I think you know if you want to be a mother deep in your heart. Sometimes you think that you don't—that it'll be too hard, or it'll be too painful—but that's just a reflex reaction. It's not until you think about it...and I mean *really* think about it...that you know for sure. What's in your heart, Rhea?'

A contraction hit then.

They waited whilst Rhea breathed through it, and when she was done she let out a huge breath. 'Whoa! I think...I think I might like to try. When I imagine her life, lost in the system…'

Callie looked at Lucas hopefully. This was the sign she'd been after.

Rhea had another contraction then. A painful one.

Callie and Lucas looked at the CTG and saw that it was strong, lasting a lot longer than the others—nearly a full minute.

Callie got the Entonox ready and asked her if she wanted it for the next one?

'Are they all going to be like that?'

She smiled. 'They might get worse.'

'Then give it to me.'

Rhea took the tube and mouthpiece and waited, and another contraction came hurtling along, only thirty seconds since the last one.

Lucas looked at Callie. 'Things are moving on?'

She nodded. 'Definitely.' A glance at the clock told her that technically there were still two more hours to go before Rhea needed to be checked internally once again, but if she continued to have contractions that quickly, and for that length, they might not have them.

Rhea groaned. 'Here comes another one!'

She started breathing on the mouthpiece and Callie laid a hand on Rhea's stomach to feel the contraction. It was strong. *Very* strong. Rhea was gasping and panicking now, rolling around on the bed.

Lucas glanced at Callie, then whispered, 'What you said just now…about knowing in your heart whether you want to be a mother…'

She looked uncertainly at him. 'Yes?'

'Don't *you* know?'

Callie was saved by a knock at the door and Jessica was there, poking her head in. Callie asked her to wait outside for a moment. 'She's just about to have an examination…'

Jessica happily stepped back into the waiting room.

Callie asked Rhea if she could do an internal to check her progress.

Rhea nodded, and Callie began her examination to feel for the cervix.

But that wasn't what she reached first.

There was part of the umbilical cord visible.

'Prolapsed cord!' she stated.

Lucas quickly hit the emergency button. An alarm sounded and the bed was tilted backwards.

Callie warned Rhea that she was going to have to keep her hand inside her to keep the baby's head off the cervix.

'What?'

'You've got a prolapsed cord—we're going to have to take you to Theatre and do a Caesarean section.'

'Why?' Rhea began to cry.

'If the baby's head presses on the cord it'll cut off the blood supply and oxygen. I need to support the head and keep you tilted back so that gravity will help until we get you into the operating room!'

'But, Callie…'

There was no time for more conversation.

Other midwives came pouring into the room, along with maternity support workers and any paediatricians who'd happened to be present on the ward at the time. The general rule on Maternity was that if an alarm bell sounded you responded—no matter *who* you were!

They raced Rhea through the corridors, past a confused and shocked Jessica. Callie called out to her, to try and explain what was happening, but they were going past her so fast there wasn't time to check whether she understood what was happening.

Rhea was crying and gasping and trying to fight another contraction. 'Callie, what's going to happen?'

'We're going to give you a general anaesthetic.'

'Can't I stay awake?'

'I'm sorry, Rhea, it's an emergency.'

'But I want to *see* her! Don't let her take her away!'

She meant Jessica.

Callie nodded her understanding quickly and promised Rhea. 'No matter what, I won't let anyone take your daughter—not until you've seen her first.'

'And I hold her first. No one else gets to do that.'

Callie nodded. 'No one,' she agreed.

The anaesthetist quickly got a general anaesthetic into Rhea, and inserted an artificial airway to keep her breathing properly during the operation. Callie still knelt on the bed, holding the baby off the cord. She ached and hurt, and her belly was being kicked and punched from the inside by her own baby. All she wanted to do was sit back and relax and breathe a sigh of relief, but she knew she had to stay there until the baby was lifted out by C-section.

Lucas was scrubbing up, along with another consultant, and it wasn't long before he strode into the theatre. They made their incision, the seconds ticking away as they cut through the layers, burst her bag of water and lifted out the baby.

Rhea's daughter screamed her head off indignantly at being brought out into the very brightly lit room. She continued to cry until she'd been thoroughly wrapped in blankets and a towel and had her hair dried. Only then did she settle and go to sleep.

Callie climbed off the bed and went to the station where the paediatricians were working to see how the baby was getting on. Her knees hurt. Her lower abdomen ached from the position she'd had to be in. But none of that mattered. Rhea's baby was fine—only needing a little bit of oxygen to assist with her breathing. She looked a good size too: maybe even four or five pounds already. She didn't expect her to stay in SCBU for long. Not if she had the same determination and grit as her mother.

Lucas peered over at her. 'Is she okay?'

'Doing well.'

'And you?'

She turned and beamed a big smile at him. 'Fine.'

His eyes crinkled in the corners and she knew he was smiling back, even if she couldn't see it.

She informed the SCBU nurses that Rhea had insisted that Social Services were not allowed to see or touch the baby before Rhea had done so first.

'Social Services are around, and I don't know how pushy they'll be, but Mum gave strict instructions,' Lucas said, and Callie was glad and proud that he'd insisted on Rhea's wishes for her as well. He knew how important it was to Rhea.

'Don't worry—we'll look after her,' one of the nurses replied.

Callie discarded her gloves and washed her hands. Then she went to see Jessica.

'Everything's fine. Rhea's doing well—as is the baby.'

Jessica smiled and nodded. 'That's wonderful.'

'Rhea will be asleep for some time. She's insisted that she wants to see and hold her baby first. You won't be able to see her until she has.'

'I thought Rhea didn't want to see the baby?'

'It's Rhea's wish. She changed her mind and made it quite clear,' Lucas stepped in. 'We have to honour the wishes of the mother.' *As should you,* he wanted to add.

Callie went to get a drink, and had just made herself a cup of tea when Lucas joined her in the staffroom.

'Rhea's in Recovery. Doing well.'

'Excellent. I almost can't believe she's had her baby. We were going to be in it together until the end.'

She rubbed her stomach, aware that this was her last

few weeks of being pregnant. Would she ever experience being pregnant again? Was this going to be her only baby?

Crikey, I'm thinking too far ahead, here!

Lucas cocked his head. 'What's the joke?'

'Nothing. Just thinking about these last few weeks. Only six more weeks of being pregnant. It's scary.'

She chose not to mention all the other terrifying things. Losing him…

'Because you know all the things that can go wrong?'

'Because it's something I denied myself, not even considering it for so long. Now it's nearly at an end and I'm not sure how I feel about it. Whether I really *can* do it.'

He frowned. 'Be a mum? I thought you'd got your head round that?'

'What if I've been kidding myself? I'm good at doing that. What if this *doesn't* work out?'

'Why wouldn't it? So what if you get things wrong? Mothers do that all the time. So do fathers. But they carry on because they know that no one is a perfect parent, and that no one can do parenting without making mistakes.'

'Why are you so knowledgeable? You seem to know what you're talking about.'

'Because I believe in you. If you didn't care then you would have something to worry about—but you *do* care and so you don't. If that makes sense.'

She could see the pulse throbbing in his neck. He was clenching and unclenching his jaw. What she wouldn't give to touch him once more. Feel his lips on hers. The physical ache of longing for him almost knocked her off her feet.

'So, what are you going to do with your morning off tomorrow? Put your feet up? Knit bootees?'

She sighed. 'I thought I'd go into town. One last look around before I'm burdened with a buggy and have to hope people will hold doors open for me.'

He laughed and offered her a biscuit from the packet

on the table. 'Shall I meet you in town? I could be free around lunchtime? Maybe we could make it over to Windsor Castle?'

His face was flushed and she looked at him oddly. Why did he seem uncomfortable mentioning that place? Had he been there before? With this Sienna person? Maybe he'd met *her* there?

Maybe she *should* meet him tomorrow. There were a few things they needed to discuss. Time had not given her any answers. Any explanations. And it would be good to be on neutral ground.

'I'll meet you at the coffee shop opposite Laurie Park.'

She munched down four more of the biscuits before realising they weren't hers. They were *so* yummy.

'Oh, God,' she said, changing the subject. 'I'll buy some tomorrow. Replace the packet.'

'They're mine. Don't worry.'

But she *did* worry. She worried a lot.

Rhea was soon sufficiently awake and well enough to be wheeled down to SCBU. Lucas and Callie went with her.

They had to wait for someone to let them in, and then they manoeuvred Rhea round to the unit that contained her baby.

Baby Girl Cartwright.
Born: 2.37 p.m.
Weight: 4 pounds, 13 ounces.

'She's a good size,' Rhea said, peering through the plastic. 'Can I touch her?'

'How about holding her?'

The SCBU nurse got Rhea's daughter out of the unit and laid her in her mother's arms.

Rhea's face was a picture. It was a delightful mix of love and confusion and fear and excitement. And hope.

Rhea ducked her head to inhale her daughter's scent and examined her thin fingers and tiny nails. 'So little. So perfect.'

'And totally healthy for her gestation,' the SCBU nurse said. 'She's only here until we can be satisfied her oxygen levels are being maintained without assistance.'

'What is she on?' asked Callie, wanting to know the amount of oxygen assistance. The lower the number, the better.

'Only ten per cent.'

'That's good, Rhea. She won't be here long at all.'

Rhea smiled, but couldn't take her eyes off her daughter.

Callie reached out and touched the baby's cheek, wondering if *her* baby looked like this inside her. 'She looks like you.'

'She does. She's…beautiful. How could I ever have thought she was a monster?'

'You don't have to make any decisions you don't want to, Rhea. You can change your mind. You can ask for time. Social Services will hold off until you're ready to make a firm decision.'

Rhea's face darkened. 'I already told them, though. That I wanted to give her up.'

'But that was before. This is now.'

Rhea looked up from her daughter's face. 'But I'm on their radar now. Won't they think I'm a bad mother for wanting to give her up?'

'Of course not!'

Lucas knelt down in front of them. 'Have you thought about a name for her?'

Rhea looked shy. 'I thought of some. After the scan, when I knew she was a girl, I played around with a few names—you know, just in case.'

'No matter what path you choose for her, you can still name her,' Callie said.

Rhea smiled. 'Yeah? Okay. Then her name's Rosie. Rosie May Cartwright.'

Lucas smiled. 'That's beautiful. She's clearly a Rosie.'

'We'll leave you alone with her for a while. Let us know when you want to go back to the ward,' said Callie.

Rhea nodded.

Callie and Lucas walked away, standing at a distance in the corridor beyond the room where Rhea and Rosie were.

Looking through the window Callie saw all the other incubators, some covered with blankets to protect the babies' eyes from the overhead lights, and all the tiny babies—the ones fighting for life, the ones so small they were almost transparent. She saw the parents beside them, the fear on their faces, the grit and determination in the furrow of their brows that their babies *would* get better. She hoped that they'd all have positive outcomes for their stories. Unlike her.

'Look at them, Lucas. We're so lucky not to be in there. It must be horrible for some of them.'

He put a reassuring arm around her shoulders and she wanted to shrug him off. 'A lot of them will have been prepared for it. But you're right. And we shouldn't have to worry about coming here. Our baby is happy and well.' He reached over to rub her stomach and felt a reassuring kick in response. 'See?'

'Rhea's got a big decision to make. I hope she makes the right one. For her *and* for her daughter.'

'What do you think she'll do?'

'I honestly don't know. But I do know she's finally connected with her. It's what she needed to do. She needed to see that what she was giving away wasn't evil. I wish her well. I wish her happiness in whatever she decides, and I'll support her. She knows that.'

'And you know that I'm here for *you*, don't you?'

He turned Callie's face with his finger on her chin and made her face him. Looking into his blue eyes, she knew that she could never get tired of looking at them. They were a vibrant blue, like the down of a kingfisher as it sat above the water. The glint of sunshine was always reflected in them, no matter where he was.

'You've been odd with me ever since the bleed and I need to know, Callie, if you're here for the long haul or not? If you can't be—if you have any doubts—then tell me now, so I can be prepared. It's all of you or nothing. No half measures.'

She had to say something. Now was the time.

So she was blunt. 'I don't trust you,' she said, as simply as that.

Her doubts about him overwhelmed her. She couldn't stand it anymore! Keeping up this pretence, this façade that everything was okay and hunky-dory. She *had* to know if he'd lied to her! She needed to ask him. Because they couldn't move forward unless he told her the whole truth.

There could be no other way for them.

'Have you lied to me, Lucas?' She turned to face him, a whole yard of empty space between them. Her stomach was churning in anticipation of his answer. Would he try to lie even more to get himself off the hook?

'What?' Lucas looked shocked at her question.

'Did you *lie* to me?' Her voice rose slightly and she saw him glance around to see who might be listening.

'No!'

He sounded angry. With himself…?

But she could *see* the lie in his eyes, and the knowledge that he was keeping something from her broke her heart. She physically felt the pain in her chest.

'You have, haven't you?'

'No, Callie!'

'And now you're lying about lying! That's what happens when people tell untruths. They twist themselves into knots and show those around them that they have no respect for them!'

'I respect you more than anyone!'

'But not enough to tell me the truth? Why not, Lucas? Is it because you're afraid to tell me? You haven't been honest with me. I thought you cared for me…I thought…I began to believe I was good enough for you!'

'You are—'

'No! I'm *not* good enough for you because you've lied to me. Easily, it seems. My mother did that. I wasn't good enough for her to bother about and she lied to me. Every single day. Do you know how that feels? To be worthless?'

'I have *not* lied to you! And if we're going to play the blame game, what about you?'

'What *about* me?'

'You know I needed one hundred per cent commitment from you—but could you give it? Ever? You blow hot and cold, like a bloody kettle, and I never know where I stand from one moment to the next! One day you want to be a mother—another day you doubt it. You let me sleep with you one minute, then push me away the next.'

'You're blaming *me*?'

'Well, who else is there?'

She laughed harshly. '*You*! You and bloody Maggie, for getting me into this mess in the first place. If you hadn't been so keen to prove your marriage to yourself none of this would have happened!'

'None of this would have happened if you'd said yes to me in the first place!'

She stared at him. What he'd said… Was that true? Had him asking her out all those years ago truly meant something to him? She'd thought he'd asked because he'd been out with most of the girls he knew and she was the only one left!

He shook his head, upset, and then something came into his eyes. Knowledge. Knowledge of what she was talking about—about his keeping something from her. He tried to hide it.

'All these weeks you've been off with me…I thought it was because you've had second thoughts about us sleeping together…'

'Oh, I have. I regret it completely!'

'Callie—'

'I never thought that *you* would lie to me. *Ever*!'

'Callie, it's not what you think—'

'No? You came to the hospital stinking of booze and perfume! There were strange messages on your phone! Who's Sienna?'

His face blanched white. 'She—'

'No! I don't want to hear it! I can't bear to look at you right now…leave me alone!'

She turned from him and began to run away, back to SCBU. Lucas called her name, then ran down the corridor to grab her arm.

She shook him off. 'Leave me alone, Lucas!'

People were looking, watching them, so Lucas hung back, his jaw clenching, frustrated with himself for answering her with a knee-jerk reaction and saying he hadn't lied. He knew he should have told her the truth.

I will *tell her the truth. I'll tell her the truth and make her listen to me.*

Rhea waved at Callie through the glass to come in and she entered slowly, taking in the lovely sight of mother and daughter. 'Are you ready to go back?' she asked, and sniffed, determined not to show Rhea that she was upset.

'I've made a decision.'

'Yes?' Callie's heart was in her mouth. Whatever Rhea decided she would back her one hundred per cent, but there *was* one direction she was hoping Rhea would take more than any other.

'I'm keeping her. Even though I have nothing. No equipment. Nothing. I'm keeping her.'

Callie gasped with delighted surprise, letting out all the pent-up breath she'd not known she was holding. Then she was smiling and laying an arm around Rhea's shoulder, hugging her, trying her hardest not to cry even more.

'Well done. I'm so pleased for you! Do you want me to tell Social Services?'

'No, it's all right. I'll do it. They need to hear the truth from me.'

'I'm sure it'll be fine. They can still help you.'

'I hope so. My daughter is going to know her family. Be loved. That's what matters at the end of the day, isn't it?' Rhea looked up at Callie.

She nodded.

Yes it was.

More than anything.

Callie hadn't come home. He'd waited and waited, but there'd been no sign of her. He'd called her phone, but it either kept ringing or was switched off. He'd thought about going round to her mother's to see if she was there, but anger had stopped him.

Why was he so cross?

Okay, so he'd kept a secret—but it was a small secret, and it was one worth keeping for the surprise it would cause. It was a *good* omission of truth. He couldn't tell her he was going to propose!

And what had she done? Overreacted. That was what.

Instantly blamed him, not giving him a chance to explain himself, and then running off like...like someone in a dramatic movie.

Well, this wasn't a movie—this was real life. And he was mad at being tarred with the same brush as her mother.

One tiny mistake. Just one. That was all he'd made, and now Callie was using that to punish him for someone else's mistakes.

It was more proof to him that she couldn't commit the way he needed her to. Was she so frightened of commitment that when she actually had the chance of it she threw it away? Was she unable to recognise just what he'd been about to do for her?

There was no other way he could prove his commitment to her. Apart from being there every day. And he couldn't prove that ahead of time until he was actually doing it! But by proposing marriage, by showing her that he wanted that commitment from her...

He loved her! Plain and simple. That was how it had always been with him. But after that time she'd pushed him away he'd been cautious about showing it. Yes, there had been girlfriends at school. But he'd been so young! There had even been Maggie. But that had all been a façade to hide the fact that there was only one true love that he'd always wanted and craved.

Callie.

And she was unable to see it.

Why couldn't he make her see it?

Lucas lay in his bed and stared at the ceiling. Sleep wasn't coming easily.

By morning he was exhausted, and desperate to talk to her, but he had to go to work. He'd been paged with an emergency and had no time to try and find her. Hopefully she'd call later, because he *had* to get this sorted with her. He had to know whether she wanted to be with him or not.

Because he wouldn't lay his heart on the line a third time.

CHAPTER NINE

THERE WAS A book in her bag and Callie began to read as she waited, but she was so tense and nervous none of the words would go in. She kept reading and re-reading the same passage over and over again, until she gave the book up as a bad job and put it away again.

She was just closing the zip on her bag when the doorbell sounded as someone entered the café and she looked up, hoping to see Lucas, but it wasn't him.

She wondered if he'd remember that they were supposed to meet today in this little coffee shop opposite Laurie Park.

He probably wouldn't arrive. Not after their argument. She'd run out on him and not gone home, instead getting a taxi and going to her *mother's*, for crying out loud!

When had her mother ever been there to support her? Never. And yet…the world had gone topsy-turvy. Lucas had lied and let her down and the one person who'd never been there for her suddenly was. Life was screwed up and she couldn't possibly see how it would ever right itself.

She missed him like crazy. This was her most dreaded situation. To have lost Lucas. To have lost her best friend. Her pillar. Her rock. Her heart. She would give him his baby and then leave and go…where?

She wrapped her hand protectively around her baby, her feelings torn.

Where did you go when your heart was torn in two? Was there a place that could heal that? She didn't think so.

Her coffee sat untouched and cold on the table and she stared at her phone. Perhaps she could ring him? He was meant to be at home, unless he'd been called in to work, so he should answer. Perhaps she should hear his explanation? Though she couldn't imagine how he'd wriggle out of this one!

But she'd dialled his number without thinking.

He didn't answer for ages. She could imagine him standing in the hospital corridor, or at home, his hand rubbing at his eyes, pacing the floor, staring at nothing as he focused on the terrible question she'd posed.

Was he going to answer? It was taking him a long time…

'Callie?'

'Lucas.'

'Where are you? You didn't come home last night.'

'I stayed with my mum, but I'm at the coffee shop now.'

There was a pause. 'Of course. We were meant to meet there today. Before we went to Windsor Castle.'

She nodded, hearing the sadness in his voice.

'I don't know how this went so wrong. I want it all back to how it was before.'

'You mean before you lied to me, Lucas? You had an affair—'

'An *affair*? Hang on—what are you talking about?'

She closed her eyes in despair that he could still be trying to wriggle out of it. 'I know about Sienna.'

A shocked pause. His silence spoke volumes.

'You do?'

'I saw her message on your phone. The day after you came to me in the hospital, stinking of alcohol and her perfume.' Her voice broke and she hiccupped back a sob. She was *not* going to let him hear her cry.

'Oh, Callie, you've got it all so wrong!'

'I don't think so…'

'Callie, listen to me. I am not having an affair with Sienna! I was planning to propose to you! At Windsor Castle. She's the events manager there and she arranged for us to have a private part of the castle opened just for us so I could ask you to marry me! She served me champagne—that was why you could smell alcohol on me!'

What? A proposal? To *her*? To Callie?

'I was meant to be proposing to you today, Callie! At the castle! I was going to meet you at the coffee shop and then suggest we go for a walk around, only to surprise you!'

'But—'

'Everyone else knew about it! My family, your mother—they were all going to be there. But I had to cancel because I thought you'd fallen out with me.'

Oh, no!

Could it all be true? Her mother had kept trying to get her to call Lucas, but Callie had ignored her…

The baby gave Callie a hard kick to her bladder and she held her stomach, gasping… She felt sick. To her very core. She dropped her mobile. It began to ring again and she could see it was Lucas, but…

The whooshing noise in her ears was getting louder and she leant against the table as the world began to grow dark.

'I…'

She'd leapt to conclusions. Terrible conclusions. Because that was what she was used to! People letting her down. Lying to her. Treating her like a fool. And she'd accused him of having an affair…

She'd been so wrong. How could she have got it so wrong? She should have trusted him, given him the chance to explain… He'd promised he would always be truthful to her…

Her face grew hot and as she lifted up her hand to wipe at her forehead she stumbled forward, hoping to go outside to get some fresh air. But her legs were weak and jelly-like, and before she knew it she'd gone crashing down in the café, smacking her head violently on one of the tables.

Lucas was suturing in Theatre when the internal phone rang. A theatre assistant answered it, and Lucas expected it to be a quick reminder from his lead consultant about their meeting that afternoon. He really wasn't in the mood for it and he didn't want to go. All he could think about was that call from Callie.

Callie had rung off and then hadn't answered his calls. The urge to go and find her and right the wrong of having lied to her was strong, because he knew how she felt about liars. Her own mother had lied to her throughout her life and it was something she couldn't tolerate. He knew that.

I should have told her the truth from the beginning.

But he'd been trying to protect her and had thought a little white lie wouldn't hurt. How wrong he'd been! And now he hadn't been able to get away. There'd been emergency after emergency in Maternity that day. He was hoping for a break after he'd finished up here, so that he could grab a coffee and try and see if Callie would answer her phone yet.

When the assistant brought the handset of the phone over to him and held it to his ear he got a call he'd never expected.

'Dr Gold?'

'Yes? Who is this?'

'My name's Dr Alan Carter. I'm an emergency doctor down in A&E.'

'Yes?' Perhaps he had a maternity emergency down there and wanted some advice?

'We've had a patient brought in, thirty-four weeks, who's received a serious blow to the head and abdomen. There's internal bleeding and we need to deliver.'

'Right. I'm just finishing up in Theatre…'

'The ID in her bag states her as being Callie Taylor, and you're the ICE number on her phone.'

The ICE number was an 'In Case of Emergency' number that police officers liked everyone to have on their phones in the event of situations such as these.

'Oh, my God…how is she?'

'She's currently unconscious. We're having her rushed to Theatre Two now.'

'The baby?'

'We have to deliver the baby or she could bleed out. The trauma has caused a heavy bleed and we've had to rush her in for an emergency section.'

Lucas stared at the needle and suture in his hand. Two more stitches and he could be gone. But he didn't have time for two more stitches. He looked up at his foundation year one doctor and passed him the tools. 'Finish off.'

He ripped the mask and scrubs from himself, flinging on new ones and scrubbing his hands clean, then dashed from the department and hurtled down the stairs, not bothering with the lift. The doors banged as he slammed them open and raced down the long corridor. Staff and patients stared in wonder. It had been maybe five minutes since the call.

Lucas grabbed a nurse—any nurse who was walking by—and explained who he was. 'Callie Taylor. In surgery. Where?'

She seemed to look him up and down, saw his ID tag, noted he was an actual doctor and not just some weirdo off the street and pointed down towards where the emergency theatres were. 'But you can't go in!'

'Try and stop me.'

He pushed past her but was stopped at the security doors. There was a viewing window, and he planted both hands on the glass like a prisoner and stared through.

He could see Callie. Well, her head, anyway. One eye was swollen and starting to blacken and her other eye was taped over. She had a tube down her throat, helping her to breathe. An anaesthetist sat by her head, measuring all her responses and saturations, and by looking at the monitor Lucas could see she had very low blood pressure. Anything beyond that, he couldn't see.

The surgeons were beyond a green scrub screen, but he could see a baby monitor in the corner, manned by two women, and there was a flurry of theatre staff, all doing various things, concentrating hard on their patient.

There was a speaker button by the glass and he pressed it. 'I'm Dr Gold. The patient is my partner. How is she?'

The surgeon turned and peered at Lucas over his mask. 'She's in a bad shape, but we're doing our best.'

'How's the baby?'

'We're just about in. We'll let you know in a moment or two.'

It was an agony of waiting. They seemed to be moving so slowly at times. There didn't appear to be any urgency and it was all he could do to fight the urge to get scrubbed up and go in there himself! But he knew, sensibly, that he'd be no use. In fact he'd be a gibbering wreck!

I can't lose them. I love them.

I love her too much to lose her! And I never got the opportunity to show her!

What if she died? What if he lost her now and he never got the chance to prove to her that he'd been committed to them working out?

There was a weak cry and Lucas looked up, hope flooding him. The baby! The baby had been born!

It was handed over to a nurse, who took it away into the far-off corner. The staff stood over it whilst they worked. Lucas could see them using suction and oxygen and towels to rub some life into it. But the baby looked floppy. Unresponsive.

No! No, come on, baby! Cry again! Cry! He jabbed the communication button hard. 'What's going on?'

'She's weak, but we've got a heart-rate,' the nurse said.

She? I have a daughter?

'And Callie?'

The surgeon didn't look at him. 'We're still working on her. If the bleeding doesn't stop we may have to do an emergency hysterectomy.'

The baby let out a louder cry and Lucas exhaled heavily, slumping against the glass. He'd literally not been able to breathe and was winded now, as if he'd taken a sucker punch to the stomach. On shaky legs, he stood once again, just in time to see the baby wheeled out of Theatre.

He stopped them. 'Is she okay? I'm the father.'

She was a perfect pink bundle, wrapped up and swaddled in towels within a large incubator.

'She'll be okay. But she needs to be kept warm.'

'Where is she going? SCBU?'

They nodded and pushed past him. He let them go.

He was thrilled she was fine—thrilled to be a father finally, after all this time—but what mattered to him right now was Callie. He had to know she was all right. He had to be able to talk to her. To get a chance to put things right between them. He sensed they could have a great future together and he wanted to ask her something. To let her know that he would look after and love her always.

But it was awful to stand there and see her looking so lifeless and broken on the table.

But I will bear it. If she can, then so can I. Fight it, Callie. Fight it like mad.

He rested his forehead on the window and waited.

They fixed her skull and her womb before wheeling her through to recovery. He sat beside her bed, holding her hand and staring at her pale face, willing her to wake up.

Lucas kissed his beloved's fingers and reached over to kiss her face. 'Come back to me, Callie. Come back to me so I can tell you the truth. I love you. Do you hear me? I love you. We have a daughter who needs you. As do I.'

The machines continued to beep as Callie slept on. Her vital signs were good, he convinced himself of that, though he wondered how Callie might cope with a newborn *and* a bad head. It wouldn't be a problem the first two weeks, when he was at home, but he'd have to go back to work eventually… Perhaps he could get his sisters round to help? They loved babies. They'd fight each other for the opportunity.

He smiled and stroked Callie's hand. 'We're all waiting for you. And your daughter is waiting for you to hold her. She's waiting for her mum to name her, though if we could refrain from naming her after items in the room…' He laughed and felt tears as he recalled Callie's memory of how her mother had named her.

It would all be so different for their daughter. She was loved already. She was wanted. She would have a beautiful name and a beautiful mother.

And if Callie gave him the chance, then they could have a beautiful future together too.

After a few hours in Recovery, they decided to wheel Callie up to Maternity. The neurosurgeons had offered to visit her there, to monitor her, thinking she'd prefer to be by her daughter when she woke up.

Lucas had visited their baby briefly and put his hand through the little round window. His daughter had clutched his finger, breaking his heart and then swelling it to twice its size with love for her. She truly was a beautiful baby, and showed no signs of being harmed in the collapse—which was a miracle. She had dark hair that was quite thick, like Callie's, and when she'd briefly opened her eyes to squint at the world Lucas had seen they were a beautiful dark blue. Violet-blue, he thought to himself.

The staff had weighed her and discovered that she was six pounds four ounces—a good size for her gestation. The small birth-card read *'Baby Girl Taylor'*. He wanted to get that changed. He wanted to name her. Give her an identity. But he still *knew* her. Here was the little girl who had kicked him through Callie's abdomen, who had responded to his voice when he'd leant over Callie's belly and read her bedtime stories.

'I know you!' he'd whispered. 'Remember? *Fee-fie-fo-fum*!'

He'd not been there but a brief moment when he'd felt a gentle hand upon his shoulder. Expecting a nurse, he'd turned round, then smiled in surprise. 'Rhea! How are you? How's Rosie?'

'Doing well. They say she can go home soon. Is this yours? Is it Callie's?'

He'd looked back at their baby and nodded, unable to speak.

'She had a section, then?'

'Unexpectedly.' He couldn't say any more as his throat clogged with a lump.

'She'll make a great mum, Callie.'

'She will.'

'What are you calling her?'

He shrugged. 'We haven't decided. I said Callie could choose. To right a wrong from her past.'

Rhea frowned, not knowing what he meant, but she wasn't about to pry. 'Well, I'll probably be gone by the time she's come round. Will you thank her for me? Tell her how much I appreciate her? I got her this card.'

Rhea handed over a small pink envelope.

'Of course,' he said softly.

If she'll let me.

CHAPTER TEN

SLOWLY, SOUNDS AND sensations began to become clear. There was the beep of a heart-rate monitor and occasionally the cuff around her left arm would be inflated.

Measuring my blood pressure.

Hmm... Why's that?

And then, as she opened her one good eye and began to see the interior of a hospital room, she began to remember details.

She'd been at the coffee shop and then… Callie blinked and looked down. Her pregnancy bump was gone, though there was still some roundness, and by the side of her bed, fast asleep, sat Lucas, his hand still holding hers.

Where's the baby? Is it okay?

Her need to know about the baby made her speak.

'What's happened?'

Callie inhaled deeply through her nose. She could feel a small nasal cannula there that she hadn't noticed before. More and more sensation was coming through now. Looking at his sleeping face, so innocent, only made her feel like weeping. He'd lied to her, yes, but it hadn't been what she'd thought. Years of being messed about by her mother had made Callie instantly think the worst! But she'd been so wrong. So terribly wrong!

He mumbled slightly, then blinked slowly and looked up, his gorgeous blue eyes widening at the sight of her awake.

'Callie…'

'Where's the baby?'

He reached for her hand again and clasped it tightly, kissing her fingers. 'In SCBU. We have a daughter, Callie. A little girl. And she's beautiful, like you.'

Tears pricked at her eyes at the thought of a daughter. A baby girl! Oh, how differently she would do things! Her daughter would be loved and cherished and know deep in her soul that she was the most precious thing to her mummy.

I'm a mum…

'Callie, I'm so sorry I tried to keep the proposal a secret. I just wanted to show you how much I love you and want to be with you. For ever.' His eyes were dark and full of love. 'That you'll never lose me. That we'll always be together.'

He's never let me down in all the years I've known him.

'I do love you, Lucas…'

'And I love *you*—more than words can say. Can you trust me? Can you believe in me?'

She thought quickly, knowing in her heart what her answer was.

Yes… I can believe in you. I do believe in you.

'I'm so sorry!'

The pain lifted from her heart at her words. She reached out for him.

Lucas took her hands in his and leaned forward to kiss her.

She closed her eye, accepting the kiss. His lips touched hers so lightly it was as if he was afraid to kiss her harder in case she broke. She had to laugh, and then winced as a pain stretched across her stomach.

Of course. I must have had a Caesarean.

'Callie, I—'

'Shh. Don't talk. Let me speak. I'm sorry I got angry with you.'

'I'd never—'

'I know! I know. But back then… I should have trusted *myself* more. I'm so used to being lied to by people who are supposed to love me. When you told me about Sienna it was my fault I didn't give you chance to explain.' She sighed heavily. 'The fault was with me. I'm sorry. I should have trusted you more.'

'*I'm* sorry… We should never have secrets from each other. Planning the proposal the way I did, in secret, was a bad idea.'

Callie smoothed the hair on his head and cupped his face. 'It was a wonderful idea.' He was so gorgeous. So handsome. And he was all hers. Mind, body and soul. She knew that now. 'So…we have a daughter?'

He nodded, smiling, his eyes lighting up. 'She's gorgeous and she's absolutely fine. When you're stronger, we can go and see her.'

'I want to see her today. I need to hold her. Feel her in my arms.'

'I'll check with the nurses—see if we can arrange it.'

'I love you, Lucas Gold. But you're going to need to know that I may just love our daughter a bit more.'

He smiled. 'I can deal with that. But there's something *you* need to know too.'

'What?' she asked sleepily.

'I'll be damned if I'll have a baby with the woman I love and not marry her…spend the rest of my life with her.'

Callie smiled, her grin stretching her face. 'Are you asking me to marry you?'

He slipped from his chair and got onto one knee. 'I am. Calendar Taylor…I love you more than the world can ever know and I would be the proudest man alive if you would agree to be my wife.'

She nodded, smiling, her face aglow from happiness and the assurance of trust. 'I will.'

Lucas got up and kissed her again. Her mouth, her cheeks, her neck, her mouth again. 'You've made me so happy.'

'Me too.'

After that, she didn't remember much. The anaesthetic was still in her system and she must have fallen asleep again.

When she woke, some hours later, it was dark outside and Lucas still sat beside her bed. He reached into his pocket and pulled out a small box.

'I was going to give this to you when you went into labour, but seeing as you skipped that step…' He opened the small velvet-covered box to reveal a beautiful platinum ring, with sapphire stones set in an oval shape, surrounded by diamonds. Callie held up her left hand and let him slide the ring on. It was a bit small, so she had to put it on her little finger.

'Wait for the pregnancy fluid to disappear. It'll fit then,' she said.

'The nurses say if you give them the nod we can go and see Baby Girl Taylor.'

'Baby Girl Taylor-Gold,' she corrected.

'I like that.'

It was a bit of a squeeze, getting Callie's bed into SCBU, but they were used to adjusting the space for mothers in beds or wheelchairs who were eager to see their babies.

Lucas propped some pillows behind Callie's back so she could see into the incubator properly.

'Oh! She's amazing!'

Lucas looked through the little cot. 'Isn't she? Do you want to hold her?'

She looked at him. 'Have you?'

'No. I wanted her mother to be first.'

Callie smiled with happiness. 'What shall we call her?'

The SCBU nurses helped them open the incubator and they delicately laid their daughter in Callie's arms.

'You name her. I think it's only right.' Lucas held his daughter's foot, fingering her small toes as they peeked out of the blankets.

'She's so pretty.'

'I know. We make good-looking babies, me and you.'

Callie gazed at her daughter's face, seeing similarities with herself and Lucas. The eye-shape was all Callie, as was the nose, but she had her father's mouth and ears.

'So much hair, too… I'm so glad this worked out between us, Lucas, because I'm telling you now I don't think I'd ever have been able to give her away.'

He kissed Callie's cheek. 'You don't have to worry about that any more. You've given me a gift so wonderful I can never thank you enough.'

Face to face, they looked down at their daughter. Callie could feel the roughness of his stubble against her cheek and smell his familiar aroma, and she felt safe and secure, despite the fact that her head was throbbing and she had a wound across her stomach that would make bikini choices in years to come an interesting challenge.

'What do you think of Isabella?'

He nodded. He liked it. 'It's beautiful.'

'Isabella Marie.'

'After your mother?' He'd not expected that. But it was a measure of how much was changing now. Even Callie's mother had changed since meeting her new man.

'Isabella Marie Taylor-Gold. I love it. I love *you*.'

She smiled, and then bit her lip in surprise when Isabella opened her eyes and snuffled, her mouth opening as if searching for something. 'Do you think she wants a feed?'

He shrugged. 'You could try.'

'Her suck reflex might not be ready.'

'But the skin-to-skin will be good for her.'

Lucas helped Callie undo her hospital gown, so that she could lay Isabella inside her clothes, against her skin. Isabella seemed a lot happier and was soon rooting around, searching for the nipple.

'Amazing.'

Isabella managed a quick feed and then dropped off to sleep.

Callie just wanted to hold her for ever, and Lucas just *knew* he'd get to hold them both for ever. He would get to make Callie and his little girl the happiest people alive.

He'd prove it to them.

Every second of every day.

EPILOGUE

THEY PICKED A date in June for their wedding. They'd planned to get married as soon as possible, but Callie wanted the bruising gone from her face first. Then when they did enquire at the castle about dates, they had to wait another year to get the perfect summer wedding Callie dreamed of. Mother Nature smiled down on them with beautiful sunshine, warmth and birdsong. The little chapel in Windsor Castle was bedecked with white flowers, and the place was filled to capacity with family, friends and work colleagues.

Everyone was there to share in their happy day.

Callie walked down the aisle in a simple off-white dress, strapless, with a tight bodice and flowing skirt, and behind her toddled their daughter, just short of two years of age, assisted by Marie Taylor, her grandmother, who held the basket of rose petals that Isabella was tossing all over the chapel floor.

Lucas looked at them both as they entered through the archway and knew that he could never be happier. Coming towards him was the woman of his dreams, gliding along the floor, her hands holding a delicate posy of pink roses.

She looked gorgeous, and when Callie stood by his side he reached out to take her hand. He laughed with delight as Isabella took her place next to Callie and peeked out at her father from beyond Callie's skirts.

'Boo!' she said, making everyone laugh.

The vicar intoned her solemn words as the sunshine shone brightly through the stained glass windows and filled the chapel with bright light and blessing.

They turned to each other and said their own vows, staring deeply into each other's eyes. Callie's voice broke at the beginning, but she ended strongly. Lucas was the other way round. His vows rang out loud and true and steady, and then, as his thoughts focused on how he'd nearly lost her and Isabella once, he faltered. He had to take a breath, take a moment to gather himself, before continuing on in a quieter, but deeply determined voice.

No one had any objections to their marriage.

No one burst through the church door at the last minute to protest.

No one laughed or gasped at Callie's actual name.

They exchanged rings, held hands and looked deeply into each other's eyes. Callie wondered how she could be so lucky. If someone had told her a few years ago that she would be marrying a man with whom she had a daughter she would have laughed in their faces.

What? Me? Married? A mother? Don't make me laugh.

Yet here she was, and she was happy beyond imagining.

Lucas looked so handsome in his wedding suit—a dark charcoal-grey. He had matched her pink posy with a pale pink tie and pink rose buttonhole. As he looked down at her she could read every emotion in his face. Happiness, love, joy, devotion.

It was how it was meant to be, but there was one more secret she had to tell.

The vicar pronounced them husband and wife. When Lucas leaned in to kiss her Callie closed her eyes and allowed herself to sink into the bliss of their connection as their lips touched.

The congregation cheered and clapped, and after they'd signed the register they walked down the aisle together, this time as man and wife. They stood outside as confetti rained down upon them.

Isabella ran around their feet in delight at the cascade of fluttering paper in pink and yellow and white, scooping it off the floor and throwing it back into the air. Lucas bent down to pick her up, not knowing she still had a handful, and when he had her in his arms she let the confetti go above his head.

What could he do but kiss his beloved daughter and then his wife?

As the photographer snapped pictures Callie leaned in to her husband and began to whisper something.

He didn't quite catch it and had to ask her to repeat herself.

'I said, I'll be damned if I'm going to be married to you and only have *one* child.'

He hefted Isabella into a more comfortable position and frowned, his brow furrowed in an amused question. 'You want us to have another?'

Callie leaned in close and whispered in his ear. 'We already are.'

Lucas stared at her as the realisation sank in. Overjoyed, he leaned in and kissed her, passionately this time, as if he could consume her. The crowd of onlookers cheered and whistled.

When they broke for air he looked into her pale blue eyes and told her he loved her. 'More than words or actions could ever prove.'

'And I love *you*—and Isabella—and whoever is yet to come.'

He grinned and nodded his head at the crowd. 'Should we tell them?'

Callie shook her head. They were already sharing this wonderful day with the people they loved. This new secret was one she wanted to treasure for themselves just a little while longer. 'Soon.'

'All right. At least you're not sick yet.'

She laughed. 'Oh, yes. I must admit I'm not looking forward to *that* part again.'

But she didn't have to worry. This time her pregnancy didn't make her regret her decision. There was only a little nausea—no clutching of toilet bowls for Callie Taylor-Gold.

And when their baby boy, Benjamin, was born, seven months later, they knew their family and their happiness were finally complete.

* * * * *

THE SURGEON'S BABY SECRET

AMBER McKENZIE

To all my female physician friends. Heather, Kate,
Jaclyn, KP, Erin, Allison, Rebecca and Kristen,
it has been amazing being your friend and colleague.
Thank you for sharing your lives and friendship
with me. You are all both talented and beautiful,
like the perfect romance novel heroine.

CHAPTER ONE

WAS SHE RUNNING away from her problems? Yes—and who could blame her? Erin thought as she ventured farther up the hills that comprised Arthur's Seat. Was it working? No. Her trip across the Atlantic to Edinburgh had done nothing to change her circumstances or block the thoughts and feelings that had been tormenting her. The message that had awaited her at hotel check-in had confirmed that.

She looked around her at the lush greenery of the hills, the blue of the sky and the distant sparkle of the ocean. It was breathtaking, even with the signs warning of the dangers of severe wind gusts. She wished everything in life could come with such warnings. Then maybe she would have seen the hidden danger that had been disguised as her dreams coming true.

Erin stopped to catch her breath and smiled ruefully to herself. She felt as if she spent every day running from one delivery to another as an obstetrics resident, but maybe she wasn't as fit as she'd thought, as she took in another deep breath. She looked up the path and saw a bench and made her way toward it. Maybe this hadn't been her best idea. She hadn't even dressed for a hike, her gray blazer and heeled boots a poor choice for any athletic pursuit. But this hadn't been her plan. Nothing had been her plan. But another message from her now ex-husband had pushed her into the open air before she had even set sight on her hotel room.

She felt another wave of anger pass through her just as another gust of cold wind hit. She wanted to still be angry with him. Anger, indignation, hurt, she had felt them all when the truth had first come out, but now all those emotions she had once felt toward Kevin Dufour, her newly ex-husband, had long ago burnt out and had been replaced by disappointment in herself.

She reached back into the pocket of her blazer and pulled out the printed message that had interrupted her attempt at escape.

Erin—Divorce finalized. I think we can agree that you don't belong at Boston General. Kevin

Was he right? Was it worth having to deal with the aftermath of Kevin to stay where she loved to work? Damn, she was doing it again, letting someone else make her doubt herself. Why was she so weak? How had she been so naive?

She felt the gust as she watched the note slip from her hands and tumble down the slope. Instinctively she lunged for it, not wanting Kevin's cruel words to sully the beauty of the landscape surrounding her.

He watched, as if in slow motion, as the woman jumped from the steep hilltop over the edge. For a split second he froze before he sprinted to the spot where he'd last seen her. In the short time before he got there he prepared himself for what he might find and felt relief at the sight of her holding onto the last small outcropping of rock before the hill's cliff. He couldn't make out much of her face as she hugged her body close to the almost vertical ground beneath it, but he saw her tremble with fear. "Don't move," he yelled down to her.

But she did move, her head tilted only slightly to look back up at him, and once again he felt shock at what he was seeing. She was both young and beautiful. Her shoulder-length dark blond hair was being flung around her face as the wind continued to battle with her. Through the wisps of hair he could make out the beautiful large eyes that stood out even more against the pallor of her complexion. He was sure that he would never forget the way this woman was looking at him right now, at this moment.

"Stay still," he reminded her, not wanting to be a distraction to her.

"I'm scared," a small voice came back to him.

He wasn't surprised. Even though he had watched her willingly throw herself from the hilltop it was normal to have last-minute regrets. He needed to keep her calm and establish trust between them. "I know. I'm going to get you out of there. What's your name?"

"Erin."

"Okay, Erin. My name is Ryan and I'm going to help you."

How could he appear so calm and confident? She was literally on a ledge, facing death. Just as she had been reaching for the message a large gust of wind had blown it—and her—over the cliff. If she had thought she had hit rock bottom before, she had been wrong. This was truly it. She had let Kevin's words literally drive her over the edge, and for what? What did it matter? What did he matter? Nothing that had come before this moment mattered except she had never wanted a second chance more than she wanted one now.

She looked up again toward the reassuring voice from above. The sun was shining brightly and she was too afraid to move any further, so all she could take in was the man's muscular silhouetted outline. It immediately instilled confidence in her and she felt some of her fear dissipate. If anyone could help her it was this man.

She watched as he lowered himself to the ground, lying prone, hanging his head and shoulders over the cliff's edge. He extended one long muscular arm toward her. "Erin, when you are ready I want you to reach up and take my hand."

"I can't." The idea of letting go of any of her grip on the limited ground beneath her was impossible.

"Yes, you can, Erin. Trust me."

It was an even more impossible request. She didn't trust anyone, not even herself. "I can't."

"You can't stay where you are forever. Reach up and take my hand."

He was right. She had no options. Still, she couldn't help but marvel at the complete lack of frustration in his voice. When was the last time someone had been patient with her? Or even acknowledged her feelings? Trust? She had sworn against that. But right now she had little more to lose so she took a deep breath and reached out her hand. The moment her arm was fully extended she felt his hand pass hers and grip strongly around her wrist; instinctively she did the same. Then, as if she weighed nothing, she was being lifted until he could grasp her under her shoulders and they both went tumbling toward the ground.

But instead of the ground, she landed on him and felt herself being raised and lowered with his breath, her body lax against his firmness. She was too dazed to move as she took in everything that had just happened. He had saved her, this man, Ryan. Ryan, who appeared to have Herculean strength. Ryan, who smelled like a combination of sunshine and sweat. Ryan, whose whole body she was in contact with.

She rolled herself to his side and for the first time got a good look at the man who had saved her. He was more impressive up close. He was tall and there was no muscle on his body that wasn't defined. His black tech running shirt and blue shorts showed off the golden bronze of his skin. His hair was a light brown and he had a scar that extended from above his deep blue eyes toward his thick cropped hair. She could see at least one tattoo revealing itself from the short sleeve of his left arm.

"Are you okay?" His voice cut through her mental inventory of his assets.

Was she? No, but that wasn't what she wanted to say and likely not what her hero wanted to hear. "Yes."

"Are you disappointed?" he asked, his voice softer than before.

Disappointed? Had he sensed her evaluation? Truth

be told, he was the first man she had felt attracted to in over a year and his raw sex appeal and heroism left little room for disappointment.

"No," she answered, embarrassed.

"Good," he replied, appearing relieved. He deftly sprang to his feet and then reached out a hand, which she took, and he helped her do the same. He was tall, her head coming up only to the top of his shoulders as she had to tilt upward to look at him.

"Thank you. I don't know what I would have done if you hadn't saved me." She heard her voice tremble at the end, the direness of her previous circumstance even more apparent now that she was out of it.

"I'm just happy you wanted to be saved. Now, let's get out of here before the wind picks up."

She was shocked when he reached out to take her hand. So shocked that she didn't pull away, not that she could have even if she had wanted to. His grip was as tight as it had been when he had pulled her up. It was as if he was locking her beside him and didn't want her to get away. She should have felt fear. This man, Ryan, was a stranger, but instead she felt taken care of. It was a feeling she hadn't felt in a very long time and she was in no hurry to lose it. So instead she followed his lead and walked with him toward the base of the hillside.

"You're American." He finally broke their silence after several minutes.

"Yes." And she realized from his accent that he must be, too.

"What brings you to Scotland?"

"I'm running away from the disaster my life has become. You?" She almost gasped as she realized the answer that had run through her mind at high speed had also escaped from her mouth.

"Work." He answered as though her response had been completely normal and she welcomed his tact.

"What do you do?"

"I'm in the military."

"That explains it." She covered her mouth with her free hand. What was wrong with her? What was it about this man that made her lose her ability to filter? She turned her focus from the path ahead to look at him and was met with a similar appraisal.

"Explains what?" He had stopped and she felt his blue eyes question her more strongly than his words had.

"I just meant that..." Was it that he was the only man with scars and a tattoo that she had ever found sexy? Or that his bravery and strength in saving her had seemed so effortless it wasn't surprising he was a professional hero?

"It's okay, you don't need to explain yourself." He began walking again and she followed, still linked with him. Time went by as they made their way toward the hill's base and she marveled at how comfortable the silence was between them.

"It's a beautiful country." His words finally broke through.

"Yes, it is," she agreed, more comfortable with the neutral territory their conversation had achieved.

"Have you ever been here before?"

"No, but I feel like I have. My father grew up here and when I was little he would tell me stories from his childhood or sometimes just about this faraway country with princess castles and green grass and blue ocean as far as the eye could see."

"I'm not sure the Scottish would take well to having a strong part of their heritage referred to as 'princess castles.'" She looked back toward him and he was smiling. If she had thought he was handsome before, now he was devastating. She was shocked by the powerful wave of attraction his smile evoked and had to check herself against those feelings. Fortunately they had reached the end of the path, a natural place to say goodbye. She let go of his hand and was surprised by the feeling of loss. All the more reason to get away now before she let her attraction make her life more complicated.

"Thank you again."

"I'll walk you back to your hotel."

She wanted him to, but knew better. "Thanks. But I'm okay from here. I can find my way."

She knew he was going to argue with her so she didn't give him the chance. Instead she turned and headed toward her hotel and never looked back at the kindest, most handsome man she had talked to in years.

She looked nothing like Sabrina but she reminded him of her nonetheless. Both women were beautiful, but that wasn't the similarity that was troubling him. It was the look in her eyes that brought back familiar haunting memories. At first those large round eyes that he'd later learned were a deep blue had just seemed scared, but after she had been returned to safety their depth of emotion had changed from fear to sadness. A sadness he had seen in his sister Sabrina's eyes years ago and which had set off warning bells in his head—not that she hadn't already rung those bells hard by leaping off the hill's edge. What would she have done if he hadn't been there? Would she have followed through with her intention and let go?

He physically recoiled at the thought of losing her and stopped in his tracks. How could he already feel a connection to this woman he barely knew? Most people would blame the dramatic nature of their encounter, but truthfully, to him, that drama had been minor. He was a military trained physician and for the past five years had had a decorated career as a trauma specialist. Pulling a beautiful woman to safety was a nice day at the office compared to the horrors he had witnessed.

It must be the emotional resemblance to Sabrina. The first time he'd seen that look in Sabrina he had missed it. He had been away for too long and hadn't noticed the sadness in his little sister's eyes. His role as a big brother had circumvented his role as a physician and he'd missed all the warning signs of depression his sister had been experiencing. She had been thinner than he'd remembered, with dark rings of fatigue under her eyes. She had rarely smiled and when he had tried to arrange activities to cheer her up, she had gotten no pleasure out of things that had previously made her happy.

Classic depression, and he, her big brother, the physician, had missed it and had just thought she'd been heartbroken and would get over it. That she had been better off. But in the end that hadn't mattered. Instead, Sabrina had suffered for over a year before she'd hit rock bottom and he had never stopped blaming himself. He should have been there for her. He should have recognized the signs and gotten help for her earlier. He had failed her. He hadn't protected her from the man who had broken her heart and he hadn't realized how badly she'd needed help to be put back together.

The thought monologue snapped him back to Erin. She had thanked him for saving her. He wished that it was enough to reassure him. Hadn't Sabrina always smiled politely through her pain? The one thing he was certain of was that this was not their last encounter. Was it a sense of responsibility he felt to her? Intrigue at the cause of her sadness? Or the fact that she smelled of wildflowers and had felt soft and right pressed against him. At this point it didn't matter, his mind was made up. This was not the end of their story, it was merely the beginning.

CHAPTER TWO

Erin spooned another morsel of the warm decadent bread pudding into her mouth and let both the food and the ambiance overwhelm her senses. The local pub she had ventured to for dinner had been everything she'd been looking for; the noise and activity were a perfect distraction from the constant replay of her own thoughts. She had almost died today. She might have died had Ryan not saved her. The worst part was it would have been a stupid reason to die.

She needed to take responsibility for inadvertent actions. For her constant ability to let people, mainly her now ex-husband, manipulate her. But today it stopped. When she'd got back to her hotel room, she had torn up the new messages that awaited her and instead lounged in a hot bath and thought about what she wanted in life. She wanted to make a difference to the lives of others, just as Ryan had done for her today. The best way to do that was through her work as an obstetrician-gynecologist. So there was no way she was going to leave her training at Boston General, no matter what demands her ex made.

"Is this seat taken?" A deep voice interrupted her

repetition of the earlier inner pep talk. She looked up and saw Ryan. He had changed from his running clothes and was flawless in a button-down navy collared shirt and charcoal-gray dark denim. How was it possible in a city of five hundred thousand people she would run into Ryan again? Attraction followed by fear coursed through her. She wanted to say yes and protect herself from once again being swayed by a handsome man, but how could she? Ryan had saved her life. The least she could do was agree to let him join her table.

"No, go ahead," she agreed, gesturing to the single chair opposite her.

"Are you staying nearby?"

"Yes. You?"

"At the Glasshouse." She felt her eyebrows rise and her eyes widen as he named her hotel. It felt as if they were being drawn together and that was a tough feeling to reconcile in the face of her newfound decision to take charge of her own life.

"How long are you going to be in Edinburgh?" Maybe he would be gone before she had to worry about her feelings toward him.

"A few days. You?"

"The same." Of course, she thought to herself. She took a long sip of the local rhubarb cider she had nursed throughout her meal.

"So you are not running away from your life permanently?"

She looked up to meet his eyes, surprised that he had raised her impulsive comment. "No, I'm afraid that is not an option."

"Glad to hear it." The waitress arrived at their table and took Ryan's order. She was a gorgeous Scottish redhead, tall with a body as luxurious as her hair. She waited for Ryan to notice but he was polite and otherwise unconcerned with the other woman. "I hope you don't mind sticking around for a bit. It's been a long time since I've had good company."

"How do you know I'll be good company?"

"Because you're beautiful to look at and you speak your mind, making you interesting to talk to. It's a rare but highly sought-after combination."

He thought she was beautiful. When had she last heard that? She tucked a lock of her hair behind her ear before finally looking up to meet his eyes. "I don't know what to say to that."

"You don't have to say anything, Erin. That's the benefit of having dinner with a stranger. You don't owe me anything."

"I think I owe you a lot," she acknowledged.

"So tell me something about yourself and we'll call it even."

She thought of all the things she could tell him. She was a physician. She worked at the same hospital as her stepfather and ex-husband. She was recently divorced from the only man she had ever been in a serious relationship with. None of those topics she wanted to discuss. "I was born in Scotland."

"You don't sound Scottish." He was smiling at her and she couldn't help but feel a sense of warmth from him.

"We moved when I was one. This is my first time back."

"Your father never brought you here when you were growing up?"

"No. My father died when I was ten."

He reached across the table and rested his hand on hers. "I'm sorry."

This was where she normally said "That's okay" as casually as she could muster, but something about Ryan changed her response. "Thank you."

His hand lingered on hers until the waitress returned with his dark draft beer. "So tell me something about yourself," she said, genuinely interested in the man before her.

"What do you want to know?"

"Am I the first woman you have ever pulled off a hillside?"

"First, and hopefully last. What else?" He leaned back in his chair and looked completely relaxed with opening his life up to her questions.

"Where are you stationed?"

"I've been mainly in combat zones in the Middle East for the past five years."

"Do you like it?"

"Combat?"

"Being in the military."

"Yes. I originally joined to help pay for school but found myself drawn to the hard work ethic and structure. When I finished school I decided to stay for the challenge."

"You like a challenge?" She was surprised to hear her own voice almost coy, teasing him.

"I've found that everything in life worth having you

have to work for." The smile that followed was enough to make her heart begin to race. Was he flirting with her? A second later a horrible thought flashed through her mind and in a moment it also left her mouth.

"Are you married?" She alternated her gaze between the look in his eyes during his response and an examination of his left hand, looking for any hint of an outline of a ring.

"No, never have been." It seemed as if he was telling the truth, but would she know if he wasn't? He didn't seem at all disturbed by her question. "Are you?"

She thought about her new label, hating the way it made her relive all her mistakes every time the label was used. She took another sip of her cider and rested the glass back on the table before answering. "Divorced."

"That bothers you."

"You're observant," she acknowledged.

"I've built my career around paying attention to the subtle clues people give me."

"Then you're lucky. I'm so naive that I miss even the most obvious of signs people give me."

"You don't strike me as naive."

"I'm not anymore." Or that was her new resolve anyway. She still needed to prove it to herself.

"I get the feeling there is a story behind that."

He was more than observant, he was perceptive and he was right. There was a long story behind the loss of her innocence, but not one that she felt like sharing—especially with Ryan. It had been years since she had been a stranger to anyone and she enjoyed the freedom of talking to someone who wasn't privy to the backstory of her life. "Are you always this inquisitive with women you have barely met?"

"No. But considering how we met I think we're already beyond the superficial, don't you?"

It wasn't his words that implied an intimacy between them. It was the way he was looking at her. She again took in the man sitting before her. He was as handsome as he was confident and, as silly as it felt, it felt as if he was on her side. She wasn't sure which feature she found most attractive but attraction was definitely coursing through her body.

"Yes," she answered. "What exactly are we doing here, Ryan?"

She was direct. He'd known that already but he still wasn't prepared for her question, because he didn't know the answer. He had thought about little other than her since they had last parted. Relief had been just one of the emotions he had felt when he'd seen her tonight. If it had only been relief he would have just been happy to see that she was all right and left her alone, but more than relief he felt a complete fascination with the woman he had spotted the moment he'd entered the restaurant.

She looked more mature and somehow more desirable than she had on the hillside. Gone was the young frightened girl and instead, walking past him, was a confident woman. Her blond hair appeared freshly washed and accented perfectly against the blue silk of her shirt. She once again wore heeled boots to add to her height and they clung to her legs in the same fashion as her flesh-hugging gray denim.

Once in the pub he waited for over an hour before he ventured to her table and now he was being asked point-blank about his intentions. Intentions he still didn't even know or understand.

"I'm getting to know a person who has captured my attention and I hope you're doing the same."

He watched as her flush spread from the valley between her breasts that her shirt exposed upward toward her face. She reached this time for her iced water and he watched her bide her time before answering.

"You have definitely captured my attention. But I'm not sure about why we're bothering to get to know each other."

"You really know how to flatter a man." If he'd thought she'd turned red earlier, she had darkened two shades with his last comment.

"What I meant was that neither of us lives here. We may never even see each other again after tonight."

"Do you want to see me again?"

Another long pause before he heard the small sigh escape her lips before she answered. "I've learned the hard way it doesn't matter what I want."

"It matters to me." And it did. He hated seeing the look of defeat in her eyes and felt as if he would do anything to make it go away.

"And if I did want to see you again?"

"Then we would want the same thing."

He waited for her response, or more so her verbal response. He didn't miss the way her pupils dilated or the slight tremble in her response to him. "I want to see you again. I just don't know if it is a good idea."

"Why wouldn't it be?"

"Because things I thought were right for me in the past have been anything but."

"You don't think you can trust me?"

She wasn't ready for this. She wasn't ready for Ryan. Why now? Except she couldn't really begrudge his arrival in her life, because without him there was the possibility she wouldn't be alive. Could she trust him? Her instincts said yes, but she had been so wrong before that the person she really couldn't trust was herself.

"I don't know what to think about any of this."

"What does your gut tell you?"

Her gut told her that she wanted more. More of Ryan and more of the feelings he was bringing out in her. That even talking to him felt so different from her beginnings with Kevin. She didn't feel that sense of being charmed and swept off her feet, which ironically felt better. Ryan made her feel as if this was less about him and more about her and him liking what he saw in her. What would be the harm in spending more time together? To indulge in the feelings he brought out in her? Her first fling and in less than a week they would go their separate ways, and at best he would become a beautiful memory to carry with her as she carved out her new life. At worst, well, really, what couldn't she face after everything she had already been through?

"It's getting late and it's pretty dark out. Would you mind walking me back to the hotel?"

"I think I can do that."

He signaled to the waitress and paid their bill, silencing her objections to his generosity. She also wasn't able to slip past his gallantry as he helped her put on her jacket and held the door for her as they ventured into the slightly cooled night air.

"It is beautiful here, both day and night," she remarked, feeling relaxation take hold of her for the first time since arriving earlier that day. A yawn escaped her as the jet lag she had been waiting for did the same.

"Careful, these roads are charming but a bit uneven." His words were followed by his arm brushing past hers to take hold of her hand. It was the second time she had felt held to him and she allowed herself to enjoy it.

They walked the few blocks toward the hotel and her mind began to quiet as she enjoyed the evening and her time with Ryan. "It's nice to have someone to look out for me," she thought and said simultaneously.

The hand that had so strongly held hers pulled her toward him as they stopped still in the darkness a few meters from the hotel's entrance. "I wish I could say that all I want to do is look out for you." His voice, sounding slightly anguished, made the short voyage to her ears.

"What do you want to do with me?" she asked, surprised, with no essence of the "come-hither" that question would normally hold.

"This," he answered, as his hands moved even closer to hold her against him as his lips descended on hers. His lips were hard yet so soft against her own and she welcomed the contact. She reached up, letting her hands rest against his chest, loving the feel of his firm chest as much as she enjoyed the pressure of his kiss. She felt his desire for more and she wanted the same, opening her mouth to his for him to explore. She wasn't sure how long they stood like that, in the night, kissing, but she was certain that she had never been kissed like that before.

When they finally broke apart she felt breathless and dizzy, both in a very good way. "Thank you," she murmured against him.

"Thank you?" he said, puzzled.

"I needed to be kissed like that."

"I'd be happy to do it again."

She laughed and she enjoyed the sound echoing through the night.

"Really, Erin. I have full intentions of kissing you again," he stated outright, and she had no doubt of his plans.

"Can you meet me tomorrow?" she asked with a little hesitancy, hoping for the response she realized she desperately wanted.

"Yes."

"Then I have no doubt you will make good on your promise. Good night. I'll see you in the morning." This time she initiated the kiss as she closed the gap between them once again and softly pressed her lips to his, before breaking away and moving through the hotel courtyard to the entrance. He didn't follow her, which was good as she wasn't sure she would be able to resist any further advances.

Ryan walked onto the balcony of his suite, which in the daytime gave him both a clear view of old Edinburgh and the sea. He sipped from a short glass of Scotch and tried to organize his thoughts and motivations.

He could no longer pretend that he was spending time with Erin to protect her from herself. Did she have a hint of sadness to her—yes. But after tonight he couldn't make the argument that she was depressed and needed saving from herself. Maybe he had misinterpreted what had happened on Arthur's Seat. What he hadn't misinterpreted was his attraction to her. Tonight in the restaurant with every word that had come from her perfectly formed lips and every small move of her body toward him he'd felt a pull toward her. He had meant what he'd said to her—she was beautiful and she said what she meant, and he valued both qualities equally. So much so that he had kissed her and now wanted more.

He looked out into the night and had to blink before he believed what his eyes were showing him. On the balcony a few rooms away he saw Erin. She had changed into a dark-colored nightshirt that seemed to come just to the tops of her bare legs. It was loose on her but between the V-shaped cut of the neckline, its short length and the way a mild wind was pressing it against her he thought it was the sexiest bedtime apparel he had ever seen on a woman. He watched her, half mesmerized by her appearance and half concerned about her choice of location. What was she doing on the balcony? He exhaled a sigh of relief as she reached for a large blanket and wrapped her body in it before taking a seat in one of the balcony chairs, where she stayed staring out into the night.

Ryan, Erin thought, was she ready for Ryan? She had only said goodbye to him a few minutes ago and she already missed him, a man she just met. It was hard to reconcile all the feelings she was experiencing. One of the emotions she had felt during her divorce had been fear. Fear that outside her relationship with Kevin she had no experience with other men. Would another man find her attractive one day? And would she ever trust another man enough? And even if he did and she did, would she ever want the man she loved to suffer the same cruel fate she had been dealt? No.

But Ryan. Did she trust Ryan—yes. But were they ever going to be in a relationship—no. This was a brief and fleeting opportunity and one she didn't feel she could turn away. Because she liked Ryan and the way he made her feel and because she was not going to let Kevin take one more thing from her.

Kevin had been a mistake from the beginning. She had just been too young and naive to see it. She had been a medical student on her first clinical rotation in Orthopedics when she'd met him. She had been nervous and excited, wearing her white clinical jacket for the first time and being called student intern. Everyone had seemed more important than her—the nurses, the residents, the staff physicians—and all she had wanted to do was to impress.

Then she'd met Kevin, or Dr. Dufour, her supervising resident, and he had seemed godlike in comparison to her lowly medical student ranking. He would single her out from her colleagues, giving her more opportunities and one-on-one time than any of the other students on the rotation. At first she had been flattered and had done her best to impress him, going that extra mile to stay late and check bloodwork or making food runs to bring to him in the operating room in between cases. Looking back on it, she had been more his slave than his student, but she had been so in awe of everything he'd represented.

Then his attention had become more personal than professional. Subtle touches, comments on her appearance, and she'd continued to be flattered. She had never been involved with anyone older than her and the attention of an older accomplished man had been absorbing. And he'd been a charmer, a snake charmer, really. It hadn't been long before she'd fallen for him and he'd been making late-night appearances at her apartment. She had been in love with the man she'd thought he was and he had been willing to take advantage.

Until—until she'd become pregnant. And until he'd realized that while her last name was the same as her birth father's, Madden, her stepfather was Dr. Williamson, the hospital's chief of staff. That had been when she'd started getting glimpses of the man he really was, but she had been so overwhelmed with concern over her own life and how the pregnancy was going to affect her career that she'd pushed them to the back of her mind.

The same was done with her hesitancy over getting married. Her parents had made it clear that she had already disappointed them and it had been crushing knowledge, so she'd gone along with their demands, thinking that once Kevin got used to the idea of their upcoming family he would settle into their life together.

She had been so wrong. Once they'd married he'd become resentful and disinterested and she'd become trapped and alone. He hadn't even been there when she'd almost died from complications from her miscarriage. To him it had been the final nail in the coffin that was his marriage. He'd felt unable to leave her now, not if he wanted his career. So he'd stayed. She had tried to make him happy. Tried to regain what they had lost, spending months—years—trying to conceive again, but she couldn't.

Then had come the women. She'd met his first girlfriend shortly after they'd married, learning that he had been involved with the other woman at the same time as her up until their wedding. When she'd confronted him he'd told her what she'd wanted to hear and had promised his fidelity. Soon she had been too caught up in her own pain from her pregnancy loss to care whether he was telling the truth.

But as she had risen from her grief and begun to face her reality, she couldn't hide the signs. By then she had graduated medical school and was now the resident at Boston General and Kevin was a staff orthopedic surgeon. When she walked the halls she would notice people taking more notice of her than was normal. When she entered the emergency department she would see nurses turn and speak quietly to one another. Then finally after three years of marriage she received a written note in her locker from "a friend" who wanted her to know that her husband was sleeping with one of the hospital pharmacists.

He didn't even deny it. Instead he blamed his infidelity on her inadequacies as a wife. In some ways Kevin still won in their divorce. She filed for divorce citing irreconcilable differences, too embarrassed to have her husband's cheating and her deficiencies aired publically. His professional reputation remained intact and he was able to carry on at Boston General as if nothing had happened. Meanwhile, she was struggling to gain her own reputation outside her infamous failed marriage and position as the chief of staff's stepdaughter.

Kevin wanted her gone, completely, and communicated more with her postdivorce with his badgering than he had in the year prior to their ultimate divorce. And it would be easier for her just to leave and start over somewhere new with all her baggage left behind, but there was something about Boston General that felt like home and she wasn't ready to give up anything else in her life.

The wind picked up again and she felt the corners of the blanket lift. It was time to try to sleep, to force herself onto Scottish time. She rose from her chair and peered into the night, instinctively turning to her right, looking away from the ocean and at one of the neighboring balconies. She recognized Ryan. The backlighting of his suite and the darkness of the balcony created the same effect as when she had first seen him and the image of masculine perfection was unchanged. They were too far apart for words, so instead she pressed her hand to her lips and extended it toward him before walking back into her suite and closing the balcony door.

CHAPTER THREE

NERVOUS ANTICIPATION FILLED her as Erin dressed for the unknown in the day ahead. Somehow in the heat of her moment with Ryan they had not made true plans for today, she had just asked him to meet her. When? Where? She had no idea, but she had complete faith that she would see him.

She ran her fingers through her hair, deciding to leave it down, and took a look at her appearance in the mirror. It had felt great that morning, getting ready and knowing that there was someone waiting for her who would be appreciative of her effort. Her cream tunic top had a crocheted design that while it covered her it also revealed her shape beneath. The same went for her gray slim-fit summer pants that ended a few inches above her ankles. She had small slip-on shoes that matched and would be perfect for exploring Edinburgh. She hoped she would see Ryan sooner rather than later.

He was waiting in the hotel lobby when the elevator doors opened. He looked up and smiled, sipping from a takeaway cup of coffee. He looked as good as when she had twice previously seen him. He was freshly washed and shaved and the V-neck of his red polo shirt revealed the hint of another tattoo on his chest. She walked toward him and he rose to greet her, and before she could wish him good morning his lips were against hers. The kiss was brief but no less exciting. "I've been waiting to do that."

"I hope I haven't kept you waiting too long."

"You're worth waiting for. I brought you a coffee. I hope you drink coffee."

"I live on it, thanks."

"So what is your plan for the day?" he asked.

"My plan?" Her only plan had been to be with Ryan.

"Well, my plan was to be with you, which I have now accomplished, so now we move on to your plan."

She knew she was smiling like a fool, but still couldn't change the way she felt. "Ah. Okay, then. Today is my only free day and my plan was to explore Edinburgh. I would be very pleased if you joined me."

"Lead on."

With a genuine smile she led them back outside the hotel, where Ryan took her hand. "Let me guess, we're going to the princess castle."

"Of course," she replied, and felt by the time the day was done her whole face was going to hurt from the happiness Ryan seemed to be able to bring out in her. "But don't worry, the princess castle also contains the military museum, which should appease you."

They made their way through the irregular streets toward the Edinburgh Castle entrance. She knew not to object as Ryan paid their entrance fee and they passed through the castle gate. "Look up," he instructed.

Above them was a spiked portcullis designed to protect the castle against siege. "Not exactly a fairy-tale castle feature," he added.

"I don't believe in fairy tales."

"Another thing we have in common, because neither do I."

Ryan held her hand as they passed in and out of the buildings that made up Edinburgh Castle. She had always enjoyed history and was happy that Ryan also seemed fascinated by the depth of history within the castle walls. They took their time exploring the National War Museum and she was impressed with his knowledge as he took the time to explain to her the nuances of past wars. At the end of the museum was a new exhibit dedicated to war veterans with amputations and the use of prosthetics.

"Amazing, isn't it?" Ryan remarked, as they examined the cabinet filled with examples of modern bionic limbs.

"It is."

"I should have been an orthopedic surgeon," he remarked, not knowing the effect his words would have on her.

"No, you shouldn't have been," she blurted, not able to censor herself yet again.

"Why not?" he asked, confused by the shift in her demeanor.

"Because I like you just the way you are," she answered, trying to cover the real meaning behind her remark.

"Why do I feel like there is something you are not saying?"

She sighed, realizing that her deflection hadn't worked and she was going to have to bring her past into what was already the best day she'd had in years.

"Because there is. My ex-husband is an orthopedic surgeon and I would like to think that you have nothing in common."

"Ah. So you have a thing against doctors?" She could tell he was testing her and she hoped she didn't sound like a bitter, scorned woman.

"That would make my life very hard, considering I am one. I've just learned the hard way about the dangers of mixing personal and professional lives and would never risk that again." She watched him, waiting for his reaction, and didn't miss the conflict in his face. Was he so surprised that she was a physician or was he just as bothered as she was that her ex had entered into their time together. She wanted to go back and take away her comment. "Besides, the only type of man I could now ever imagine being attracted to is one in the military."

She smiled, and her smile only grew as he smiled back at her.

"Is that so?"

"Absolutely and completely."

"So doctors are not your type?"

"Nope, I only have eyes for ruggedly handsome soldiers who save my life and come with no strings attached." As the words left her lips even she didn't doubt her sincerity. Ryan was the complete opposite of Kevin and the possibility of something between them felt more and more right with every moment they spent together. He was what she needed, a couple of days of abandon to restore everything her failed marriage had taken away from her.

The way he looked at her she had no doubt he was feeling the same attraction she was. "Well, Dr. Erin, I think we are both fortunate that you have equally opened my eyes to the appeal of female physicians. So I take it you are not in orthopedics. What do you do?"

"Obstetrics and gynecology."

"That would be the opposite of orthopedics," he remarked, and she appreciated that he, too, was trying to lighten the mood.

"It's less complicated than taking care of men." She laughed.

"Ouch." He feigned injury.

"It is actually amazing helping women and being there for one of the most special times in their lives."

"Did you know that Mary Queen of Scots gave birth in this castle?"

"No, I didn't."

"Then let's go check out the birth chamber of James VI." He once again connected his hand with hers and she marveled at how the same action brought even more excitement each time he touched her.

She had been right. Her face hurt from smiling. As they toured the entire castle she felt completely at peace and in her element, learning about Scottish history and with a man she respected and whose company she enjoyed. Not to mention an attraction that was growing exponentially. Every time he reached for her hand it felt as if they were connecting and throughout the day she was holding her breath, waiting for the moment when he would kiss her again.

She felt the first drop hit her shoulder as they once again passed through the castle gates. Then the second, then the third. Within seconds the sky had opened and rain was pouring down on both of them. She felt a tug on her hand as he pulled her into the protection of a narrow corridor between the old brick buildings. The small space necessitated being pressed together and any thoughts she had of being cold immediately vanished. Ryan's hand swept her wet bangs from her forehead before his lips came down on hers.

Finally, she thought as she met him with equal passion. His lips were wet with the rain and added to the freshness of his taste. She opened her mouth to him, wanting more, and was rewarded by his response. His tongue met hers until she didn't know where he ended and she began. At the same time his hands trailed from his initial position on her face along the sides of her body until she felt them on her bare back underneath the dampness of her shirt. Another point of heat between them.

She wanted more. Wanted him to move his hands over her and caress her aching breasts. Wanted to feel the ultimate fulfillment that the rigidity pressed into her abdomen promised.

"Not here," he murmured into her ear, when they finally broke apart.

She looked into the pouring rain. "Want to make a run for it?"

"Yes," he agreed with the same smile she had become accustomed to.

She kissed him once more, pressing her lips to his with the firm passion that had ignited inside her, before they broke apart and made their start on the sprint back to the hotel. It took them ten minutes but on arrival in the hotel's lobby she was completely soaked through and panting from the exertion of their run.

She followed Ryan's lead and they said nothing to each other, the understanding already present between them as they entered the elevator and Ryan pressed the button for his floor. As soon as the door closed they were once again wrapped around each other. His lips were on hers. His hands were covering her body. And she was burning up despite the cold, wet clothing covering them both.

As the doors opened they broke apart and with one mutual look their sprint continued hand in hand. One swipe of Ryan's key and they were tumbling into his room. They reunited in their embrace, but this time there were no restrictions from being in a public place to hold them back. She watched as he pulled away from their kiss and peeled his soaked shirt from his body. It felt like an unveiling as she got to see firsthand what lay beneath.

Nothing disappointed. Every muscle on his body was defined. The tattoo she had seen hints of on his chest was a serpent entwined on a single rod along his right pectoral muscle. It reminded her of the caduceus, the symbol she recognized for medicine, but it was slightly different. Encircling his right biceps was another design.

Either way she had never considered tattoos attractive but on Ryan they were explosive.

Before she could enjoy him any further she felt herself being stripped of her drenched top. She had previously been shy about her body, but not with Ryan. The minute she was exposed she wasn't because he pressed back against her. His mouth rejoined hers but it wasn't long before he was trailing his lips down her neck to her shoulder. She threaded her fingers through his wet hair and felt her body melting into his.

His hands skimmed her back before she felt the clasp of her bra release and the weight of her breasts released from their confines. Yes, she thought, this was what she wanted. He stepped back from her and she was rewarded by the look in his eye and the knowledge that he was every bit as enthralled as she was. With painstaking precision he eased the garment from her shoulders, down her arms and completely off, before he skimmed her breasts with the back of his hand. It was seduction at its finest. Then without pause he was against her, lifting her, his hands cupping her bottom before resting her on the dresser's edge. The move had made up for their foot difference in height and she felt even closer to him.

She was finally rewarded with the feel of both of his hands, each cupping a breast and causing electric shocks of want to course through her body to her core. His hands gently caressed her as his mouth returned to her neck, his thumbs occasionally brushing against the peaks of her rigid nipples. She loved every touch, welcomed it as she felt the anticipation of what was still to come.

He paused his tactile exploration and she opened her eyes to see why he'd stopped. His hand was able to completely cover her own tattoo, a small willow tree on her lower left hip. She blinked hard, thinking about what it represented, not wanting to explain its significance, especially now.

"You're beautiful."

And she believed him. "Thank you."

A weeping willow, he thought to himself, and instantly the memory of her vulnerability on the hillside played in his mind. What was he doing? He thought to himself. He wanted her, desperately, but was this fair to her? When he knew she was vulnerable? No, it wasn't fair to her, and from what he had learned about her so far she both needed, and deserved, someone to be on her side.

"I think we should slow down." The words were torn from him because it was what his rational thought wanted but not what his body wanted.

"What?" she said. Her eyes dilated in both passion and disbelief.

He couldn't repeat himself so instead he reached into one of the nearby dressers and pulled out a T-shirt, which he proceeded to cover her with. He needed to cover the temptation she represented—it didn't work. She still turned him on and now she looked hurt and that was the last thing he wanted.

"I don't want us to do anything you are going to regret."

"Why would I regret this?"

He wanted to be as honest as she had been. Because

he was a physician and she didn't know. Because maybe her deeply hidden sadness was making her vulnerable to him. "Because I'm worried I'm taking advantage of you."

He watched as her arms crossed protectively across her chest and she ran a hand through her hair, which had become wild as it dried from the rain. "In what way?"

"In that I saved your life and maybe you feel indebted to me."

"I don't. I'm grateful, but I don't."

"Okay, but what about the fact that you admitted you were running away from a disaster in your life?"

"I think that's for me to worry about."

"Not just you, Erin."

"I think I should go."

He instinctively lifted her down from the dresser he had perched her on and backed away. He watched as she looked at the wet heap that was her shirt and bra on the floor before deciding to leave it and making her way to the door.

She shut the door of her room and collapsed against the back of it before sinking down on the floor. He hadn't stopped her and he hadn't followed her, and how she had wanted him to. The worst part was that she believed him and understood why he had stopped.

Ryan saw her as fragile and he didn't want to take advantage of her. Where had he been three years ago? And how she wished he had been wrong, but the truth was she was still vulnerable. And maybe she would always have that vulnerability that had been born from being broken.

Was she making a good decision with Ryan? She knew she wanted him and wished he hadn't stopped what had been the most sensual encounter she had ever experienced. But she also couldn't deny that she wasn't in a good position emotionally to be making major life choices. But was Ryan that? She had convinced herself last night that he was a holiday indulgence to be enjoyed but after today he felt like more. And what was worse, she actually respected and trusted him more for turning her away. So where did that leave them now?

CHAPTER FOUR

A KNOCK AT HER hotel room door roused her from the late-afternoon nap she had been indulging in. After she had lifted herself from the room's floor and showered the chill from her body she curled up in the hotel-provided terry-toweling robe, thinking of all the questions she had no answers for.

She fastened the robe's sash tightly and then made her way to the door. She opened the door slightly to see Ryan, who also looked drier than the last time she had seen him. She opened the door wider and stepped aside to allow him inside. Both her eyes and her nose spotted the bag of food he was carrying.

"I thought I would bring dinner to you."

She glanced at the room's clock and realized that her late-afternoon nap had spread well into the evening and it was past eight.

"Thank you," she said cautiously, not knowing where they stood. "How did you know which room I was in?"

"I saw you last night on your balcony and you're welcome." He went ahead and set up his offering on the round table adjacent to the glass balcony doors and she took the seat intended for her.

"Smells delicious," she remarked, trying to keep their conversation neutral but realizing she was more than happy at his reappearance.

"It's nice to see you smile. I was worried I had ruined things between us."

His confession brought out an instant relaxation in her and the awkwardness of the aftermath of the previous encounter dissolved.

"You haven't."

"I hope you like traditional Scottish fare. It was what the restaurant recommended and it seemed fitting. Plus they had the bread pudding that you seemed very fond of last night." He was smiling to accompany the gentle familiarity of his teasing.

"You know what they say about holidays—it's the time to indulge."

"Yes." His voice had changed and contained a masculine huskiness as she realized the other meanings of her words. It was clear that, whatever had happened between them, he still wanted her, too.

"So what are your plans?" she asked, trying to shift the focus from their almost sexual encounter.

He choked on the glass of water he had been sipping from. "Excuse me?"

"For the rest of your time in Scotland," she amended, realizing he'd thought she had been asking about his plans for her.

"I have a commitment the day after tomorrow and then I have to return to the base. What are your plans, Erin?"

"Today was my last free day."

"I refuse to accept that."

"I'm afraid it's true. I have two days of meetings then I'm flying back to the States the next morning."

"But your nights are free?"

"That depends. Why did you stop earlier?" She needed to know. She wasn't prepared to spend more time torturing herself by being with Ryan and wondering how he felt about her and what his intentions were.

"I thought we had covered that."

"What if I wanted to readdress it?"

"Your tattoo."

"What?" She didn't understand his comment.

"Your tattoo."

"Considering your own ink, I'm surprised you have a problem with a woman having a tattoo."

"I don't. I actually think it's beautiful. You can tell that you had it placed for only you to see."

"I did." How did this man read her so well?

"It's a weeping willow, and it reminded me that the one thing I don't want to do is hurt you."

"So don't." She was rewarded with his smile. "Did you know weeping willows are known for their tenacious roots that continue life, but the trees themselves are also a symbol of compassion? My tattoo symbolizes tenacity and compassion, both qualities of the weeping willow and both qualities I strive to possess."

"You don't think you already do?"

"I think, to be the person I want to be and the physician I want to be, I need to work on both."

"I like you the way you are."

It was what she needed to hear after years of being not enough for a husband who hadn't valued or loved her. Ryan's words empowered her. "Thank you. I feel the same way about you. What if I told you you were what I needed? Would that change your mind?"

"Explain." She saw him shifting in his chair and knew she had gotten through to him.

"Maybe what I need is time with a man I respect and who actually renews my faith in men and maybe myself."

"I'm a soldier, first and foremost. I couldn't promise you anything."

"I don't want you to promise me anything. I've been promised the world by a man and it didn't work out. So you don't need to worry about not giving me a promise for forever because even if you did I wouldn't accept it."

"Are you sure?"

"Yes."

He stood from his chair opposite her and she took a deep breath of anticipation until he started walking away from her. "If you are still sure tomorrow then I'll pick you up at seven tomorrow night. If you change your mind, please just stand me up so that I don't try to change it back."

She watched mutely as he walked away and then was surprised when he suddenly turned back. She felt him lift her from her chair and gather her in his arms before his lips made contact with hers. It was hot, it was hard and it was every bit as passionate as she wanted. When he broke away she was gasping for air but still not wanting it to have ended.

"Just in case you needed a reminder. Good night, sleep tight."

How was she ever going to make it until seven tonight? A restless night, thinking of the possibilities, had left her completely devoid of sleep. Added to that, she seemed to have forgotten the skill of being able to sit through hours of seminars and she had no ability to focus on the lectures being presented. The International Society of Obstetrics and Gynecology conference had been her original reason for the trip to Scotland but now it was the furthest thing from her mind.

She had been elected to sit on a discussion panel throughout the conference to provide a perspective on both the American experience and the experience of the younger generation of obstetricians and gynecologists. At the time it had been an honor, but now all she could think of was Ryan.

"Dr. Dufour." A voice cut into her thoughts and she instantly recoiled inwardly. She had registered for the conference before her name had legally returned to her maiden name of Madden.

"Yes," she answered reluctantly.

"What has been your experience in the States with single embryo transfers to reduce the rates of multiple births in infertile couples?"

She did her best to shift her focus away from the nervous anticipation of the upcoming night and back to her original purpose for being in Scotland. She needed to focus on her work, particularly as infertility was her area of interest and she was looking for a fellowship in that area after graduation.

She straightened her navy blazer and took a sip of water before turning on the power to the microphone in front of her. "The single embryo transfer program is a much better option for women whose treatment cycles are funded through government insurance programs. In the United States women still pay out of their own pockets for their cycles, most of the time taking on significant debt for the chance at a baby. Given those circumstances, it is hard to convince them to transfer just one embryo."

"What about the ability to reduce the rate of multiple births?"

She thought back to the aftermath of her miscarriage and the months, years, she'd spent trying for another baby. If she had naturally become pregnant with twins she would have cried with joy. It would have felt as if she was being compensated for the baby she'd lost and the suffering she had endured. Instead nothing, every month nothing, and instead she had felt punished. Punished for unwittingly being the other woman. She should never have been with Kevin. She didn't deserve a baby.

"As obstetricians we have firsthand knowledge of the risks of twins and most of us would not want to roll the dice with the risks of extreme prematurity and the resulting possibility of lifelong complications. Women with infertility feel very differently. They would take any risk for the chance at a child and no amount of counseling from us on the risk of multiple births is going to change that."

She tried her best to actively follow the panel discussion and not fall back into her own thoughts. But she was speaking from personal experience. She knew the risks of twins and still she would have happily rolled the dice for a baby. Babies. It had taken a long time before she had accepted that the life-threatening infection she had experienced after her miscarriage had permanently damaged her so that she would never have a child.

Acceptance of that harsh reality had been one of the reasons she had finally gathered the courage up to leave Kevin. She had realized that one of the reasons she had looked the other way from her suspicions of his infidelity was because she'd seen him as her way to have a baby. When her dreams of being a mother had been lost, she'd no longer had any need to pretend, even to herself, that she was happy in her marriage.

"I'd like to thank the panel for their experience and participation in today's discussion. We will resume tomorrow morning with our special guest speaker and headline symposium 'Postpartum Hemorrhage—Tales from the Battlefield,'" the moderator announced.

Erin snapped back to the present and glanced at her watch. It was four-thirty. That left two and a half hours until Ryan met her. How was she going to make it till then without going crazy?

She left the conference center and made her way to a nearby café. The sun was setting and the streets of Edinburgh appeared enchanting before her, as if they had a promise of something to offer. She ordered a latte, hoping the caffeine would help ground her, before settling into a corner table and dialing.

"Hey, Erin," the voice on the other end of the phone welcomed her warmly, and she instantly felt her nerves settle. It was hard to be infamous and make friends. Most of her fellow residents were intimidated by the fact that she was the chief of staff's stepdaughter. The others were too busy enjoying the gossip her dysfunctional marriage had created to get to know her. But Chloe Darcy was different. She was unthreatened by all Erin's baggage and instead Erin felt as if she had really gained a true friend.

"Hi, Chloe."

"I'd like to think you are calling just to chat and tell me how wonderful Scotland is, but I have a feeling there's something more."

"I met a guy," Erin confessed.

"Um, not what I was expecting to hear, but I'm absolutely thrilled!" Erin could tell she was being genuine. "So who is he?"

"His name is Ryan, he's in the military and he saved my life."

"Are you being literal or figurative?"

"Literal. I was walking on a hillside known as Arthur's Seat when the wind blew me right off. Ryan found me clinging to the hill's edge and pulled me to safety."

"But you are okay now?"

"Yes."

"Wow, that's scary and also incredibly romantic. So, aside from being a hero, what is he like?"

"Honest, kind and interested in me and not himself."

"Sounds perfect."

"It's not forever."

"He sounds perfect. Why don't you just see how things go and not worry about forever?"

"Because not worrying has previously been my downfall."

"I'm not going to disagree with that one. I'm actually not sure you could have picked a more horrible man to marry."

"Has he been hitting on you again?" Erin asked. Chloe was easily one of the most beautiful women Erin had ever met and was often on the receiving end of unwanted attention. Erin knew that Kevin had made passes at her even before they'd separated.

"Don't worry about it. It's nothing I can't handle. So what is the plan with hero Ryan?"

"He's coming to my hotel room tonight."

"And?"

"And anything beyond that is my decision. He's afraid of taking advantage of me, and quite frankly I'm worried I'm not ready. I might get hurt."

"But you don't want forever and this guy makes you feel happy and valued, right?"

"Yes."

"Are you wanting me to tell you what to do?"

"Yes."

"Well, then, that's easy! Go for it. If you didn't want to you never would have called me. I'm your enabler friend."

Erin smiled and felt herself nodding in agreement, even though Chloe couldn't see her. Maybe her life was coming around. In Chloe she had a friend she needed and now she was on the verge of a romantic liaison with a man who enthralled her.

"Thanks, you're a great friend."

"So are you. Do what feels right and if you want to talk I'm always only a phone call away."

Erin said her goodbyes, hung up the call and finished her latte, then made her way back to her room. Once inside she slipped into the bathroom and drew herself a hot bath, which she soaked in for another hour. Once the water had cooled considerably she forced herself to get out, and proceeded through all her typical rituals, drawing them out as much as she could. She applied lotion to her entire body. She dried her hair in sections, curling the ends under with her round brush. For makeup she decided to keep it neutral and applied only a layer of mascara to her eyelashes and a gloss to her lips. When she looked up in the mirror she liked what she saw.

She moved toward the closet and examined her options. She had packed for a conference, not for this, whatever this was going to be. She selected some of the clothes she had brought for travel. A pair of black footless tights over which she layered two tank tops, black with blue over top. Given her short stature, both ended over her hips. She had a long string of silver beads, which completed the outfit, and Erin was pleased when she saw her reflection. She glanced at her watch. Six fifty-eight.

Two minutes passed slowly, but it was only two minutes, because exactly at seven a knock sounded on the door. She took a deep breath before slowly making her way to the door. Ryan stood there, his white dress shirt layered with a black cable sweater. There were leather patches on the elbows and he had an overall look of sophistication, which she appreciated.

"Hi," she opened hesitantly.

He walked toward her, placing his hands on her arms and his lips on hers. He tasted of mint and felt like heaven. The kiss was romantic and passionate, true bliss. If this was how they would spend their night together, even this would be enough.

"I'm glad you're here."

"It's my room. Where else would I be?"

"You could have gotten cold feet."

"That was you, not me." She watched as he understood her meaning.

"Yes, but you need to know it won't happen again." He was giving her one last warning. One last chance to back out.

"Glad to hear it," she whispered, as this time she leaned toward him and pressed her lips against his. What she meant as sweet acceptance quickly changed. He matched the pressure she had exerted and her mouth opened to his instinctively. He tasted her and she reveled in his exploration. She ran her hand down his slightly raspy cheek and his hands slipped around her, pinning her to him and settling on her lower back. She was shocked when she heard herself purring against him and felt the smile that came to his lips.

"This wasn't my plan," he murmured against her.

"It wasn't?" She couldn't keep the disappointment from her voice.

"Well, it was, but later in the evening after I'd had the opportunity to wine and dine you."

"Then wine and dine away, as long as you and I are both clear on how this is all going to end tonight." She wasn't sure who was more surprised at her words, him or her. Gone was the shy, inexperienced girl she had been a few years ago. Ryan made her feel like a mature, confident woman and it was a feeling she found herself very much enjoying.

"Wow" was all Ryan could think. The small part of him that was still warning him that Erin was more vulnerable than she was letting on was being slowly eroded by the confident, sexual woman before him. When had been the last time he had been this enthralled by a woman? The answer was never. Everything about her—her honesty, her beauty, her open sexuality—was causing havoc with his cautious conscience.

"You are doing your best to ruin my good intentions." In more ways than one, he thought to himself.

"Good," she purred.

He had to force himself to take his hand from her back and instead grab her hand as he quickly guided her out of her hotel room and away from temptation.

They fell into a comfortable silence as they strolled through the night's dusky streets toward the restaurant he had chosen. Once inside the warmth of the dining room he dismissed the restaurant's host for the pleasure of slipping Erin's light trench coat from her shoulders and pulling out her chair himself.

They both read through the menus but, to be honest, he could have ordered dirt and not noticed tonight. "You pick."

"Me?" she asked, looking at him, puzzled.

"You. I want to get to know your tastes."

"I would have thought they were obvious by now. I like men in the military with tattoos and sexy scars on their foreheads."

He instinctively touched the thin silver line that ran on his forehead. "You noticed my scar?"

"It's part of the appeal." She beamed back at him. "How did you get it?"

It was a question he had been asked multiple times and he knew what response she was anticipating. Like everyone else, she probably assumed it was a combat-related injury.

"I was involved in an altercation," he started.

Erin leaned toward him and he could tell she was waiting for the excitement of a battle story. He could see her almost holding her breath as the gentle rise and fall of her breasts ceased.

"With my little sister when I was seven."

Her face froze and then broke into a larger smile as she burst out laughing. She didn't seem at all disappointed by the truth.

"What happened?" she asked.

"I was teasing her and she had enough."

"And…"

"And she threw a solid plastic castle at me. I needed twelve stitches."

He was rewarded again with Erin's laugh, which

sounded like soft musical notes. "The worst part was she took it harder than I did and cried for hours."

"Are you close with your sister?"

"Yes, one of the hardest parts of being in the military is the time away from my family. Do you have any brothers or sisters?"

"No. I'm an only child."

"Do you like it?"

He saw the slight change in her as her shoulder fell and her head tilted downward. She took a sip from the water glass in front of her before she answered. "No, it's hard to have all your parents' expectations fall on you."

"But you're a successful physician." And so much more, Ryan thought to himself. How could anyone not be proud of Erin?

"I'm a divorced obstetrician-gynecologist." She said it as if it made perfect sense but nothing about her words seemed condemning.

"So?"

"My parents are Catholic and don't believe in divorce."

"And?" He could tell there was more she didn't want to say.

"And my stepfather is an orthopedic surgeon and the chief of staff at the hospital where I'm completing my residency."

"In the same department as your ex-husband."

"Yes. And as you pointed out yesterday, orthopedics and obstetrics are about as polar opposite as you can get. I think I disappointed them both with my choice in husband and in my choice of career."

There it was again, that vulnerability. A need for approval. Part of him was pulling back, wanting to be cautious, but the majority of him wanted to help make her see everything he saw in her. "But you have no regrets?"

"About my marriage? Yes. About my career? Never."

"Well, in the end, it sounds to me like you made two very good decisions, since both of them have brought us together."

CHAPTER FIVE

SHE'D NEVER THOUGHT she would ever smile when it came to talking about her marriage, but Ryan had the ability to make her feel differently about her past. His praise was much needed and valued. It didn't feel like pointless flattery. It was obvious respect from a man she felt the same way about.

The waiter came to their table and looked at Ryan expectantly. He gestured toward Erin and she ordered for them both.

"Perfect," Ryan commented, and she felt even more relaxed in his presence.

She spent the rest of the meal conflicted between never wanting it to end and wanting it to end so they could be alone together. Her sense of nervous anticipation only returned as Ryan signed the check and she once again felt her jacket being slipped over her shoulders.

They left the restaurant and she started walking but Ryan, whose hand she was holding, didn't move. She stopped and turned back to look at him, not missing the serious look on his face. "I'm leaving the day after tomorrow."

"I know," she admitted. She found herself not looking forward to the end of their brief romance but wasn't going to dwell on it.

"I just needed to remind you."

"I know." She knew the type of man Ryan was. Everything he was he put out for the world to see. She closed the distance between them and kissed him, reveling in his response. She didn't know how long they stayed that way, kissing in the moonlight. It was wonderful and only the desire for a different kind of more had her break away.

He seemed to read her mind. "Let's go."

She wasn't sure she even exhaled during the short walk back to the hotel. As they rode up the elevator and hurried down the hall where both their rooms were located, she glanced fleetingly at her hotel room door as they passed it without slowing. Finally the door to Ryan's room was closing and she felt herself let go of the breath she had been holding.

Within seconds she was gasping for air for a different reason as she found herself pressed against the wall, every inch of her body covered with Ryan's. She opened her mouth to his, once again entangling her fingers in his hair as his mouth sealed with hers. As his lips finally left hers and started kissing down the column of her neck he whispered against her skin, "Last chance, Erin."

She reached down under the hem of his sweater, pulling it away from him to allow her hands access to the dress shirt below. She spread her fingers to feel his tight muscles and the radiating heat of his body beneath her hands. "I'm staying."

"Thank God, because there is nothing I want more right now than you."

His comment made her feel bold and she wrenched the sweater over his head and moved her hands to the small shirt buttons. Slowly she started working them open. The most arousing part was Ryan watching her, his pupils dilated, tracking her every movement. The instant she was done he returned the favor, stripping her of her layered tank tops.

His hands tangled in her hair, lifting it and exposing her bare neck. His mouth returned to her neck and she pressed so hard into his body she didn't know where he began and she ended. She felt the tips of his fingers brush upward just below her breasts. Her breasts ached in desperation for his touch. The clasp of her bra opened and she felt just the slightest release of her breasts before Ryan's hands replaced what the white lace had been poorly concealing.

His cupped hands allowed his thumbs to slowly graze her nipples. His lips brushed against her collarbone before she felt her breast being lifted, his lips gentle against the raised mound.

"Perfect." She felt his word vibrate against her sensitized skin. Before she could respond she felt herself being lifted, with Ryan's hands strong against the backs of her thighs as he carried her across the room. The hard wall that had been pressed against her back was replaced with the softness of the linen-covered king-size bed. But she didn't lack for firmness for long as Ryan drew over her.

His attention returned to her as he once again kissed

her softly parted lips, drawing her into him. As much as she hungered for the intense escalation of their passion, she also felt her entire body liquefy with the slow pace that Ryan was setting. His mouth was close to her breasts and as soon as she thought she might die if he didn't, his mouth closed over one nipple as his fingers rolled its companion.

She arched her back in pleasure and she could feel Ryan's upturned smile against her skin. Her nipple felt cold as his mouth left her but her other one was then treated to the same pleasure as he switched sides to give both breasts equal consideration. When she felt as if she could bear no more she reached for his hand and placed it where she wanted him most. She could feel the heat and moisture at the heart of her and hoped he got the message she was desperately, and not so subtly, trying to send.

He did. He pulled away and his hands gathered in her tights, peeling them away until she lay bare before him, aside from the small white lace bikini briefs that matched the previously discarded bra. She pushed herself up on her elbows to watch him undress, the act accomplished in mere seconds as he shed every article of remaining clothing until he stood naked before her.

"Wow." The word left her mouth before she could filter her feelings. It sounded naive even to her ears but she'd had no idea a man could look like that.

"That's what I was thinking about you."

Instantly her embarrassment at her momentary gaucheness fled and her connection to Ryan intensified. He kneeled on the bed before her and without breaking eye contact pulled at the lace of her panties until she was as bare as he was. He braced himself on one arm as his hand laced through her hair and began its gentle caress down her body. His hand was rough against the softness of her neck, the side of her breast, her abdomen, her hip, as it moved inward toward her thigh. She parted her legs, waiting and wanting. With the softest touch she felt him, his fingers first gently parting her and then a gentle stroke.

"Oh," she gasped, not ready for the wave of electricity that passed through her. He responded by reclaiming her mouth and kissing her deeply. Then she felt it again, the wave of pleasure that came as he stroked her, this time in an unending circle. She felt herself wriggling against him but not wanting to get away. A strange tingling intensity was building inside her and she wasn't sure she could bear it. She cried into his mouth until finally every nerve ending from her core exploded outward and she felt beautifully broken. Finally she realized what she had been missing.

"You're beautiful."

"Thank you, but we're so not done here."

"No, we are just getting started."

She watched as he reached into the nightstand and retrieved a small foil packet. "May I?" she asked.

His eyebrows rose, but he agreed by passing her the condom. She carefully opened the packet but before she sheathed him she took hold of him in her hand, wanting to feel what she was visually devouring. He felt hot and hard against her and she squeezed lightly and he hardened further in her hand. "You need to hurry."

She looked at him and felt every bit the temptress.

She gently rolled the condom along his length, looking forward to the moment when she could feel him more intimately. As soon as she reached his base she felt herself being pushed back against the blankets, Ryan's hand pulling her leg around him before he surged into her.

It felt like a completely new experience, an experience that was all pleasure. It was as if he had the ability to stretch and mold her into the most perfect state of arousal. She wrapped her other leg around him as he began to move back and forth within her, each time pushing her to a further level of bliss. Then that intense feeling came back, every stroke setting off a chain of sparks that was building a fire at her core. An all-encompassing need for more grew ever stronger within her until she thought she would die if he stopped. But he didn't. He pushed her harder and further until she burst into flames, screaming his name, not even aware of the marks she simultaneously scored down his back.

He cried out against her and she knew it was a cry of pleasure and not of pain as he collapsed against her, his breath rapid and hot on her neck. He appeared as shattered as she was and she ran her fingers more gently up and down his back in a soothing rhythm.

"You're more than perfect, you're amazing," he whispered in her ear.

"I…I…" But she couldn't think.

He kissed her fumbling lips and she closed her eyes in happiness.

She felt him pull away from her and was hoping and waiting for him to return to hold her. What would it feel like to be held in the aftermath of such bliss?

"Erin, we have a problem." Ryan's voice was as grave as his words and her eyes opened wide. He looked stricken, staring back at her.

"The condom broke," he explained, and she exhaled with a sense of relief.

"It's okay," she tried to assure him.

"No, it's not okay. As much as I care for you, this isn't forever."

It wasn't just what he was saying about the temporary nature of their relationship that burst her bliss bubble, it was the private information that she didn't want to think of and now had to share.

"I can't have children."

"What?" It was now his turn to be taken aback. How she didn't want to talk about this, but she also knew she needed to put his mind at rest so their night together could return to where it had been.

"I had a miscarriage during my marriage. Afterward I developed a severe infection that scarred my Fallopian tubes and uterus. I can't have children."

"Are you sure?" It was a natural question. One she had asked herself over and over again until she had accepted her fate.

"Yes. I wanted a baby very badly and have spent the past two years trying to get pregnant. It's never going to happen. I've accepted that. So you don't need to worry about the condom breaking."

"I'm sorry." It was exactly what she didn't want to hear. She didn't want tonight to be about her past or what she would never have in the future. She just wanted it to be about them and their night together.

She moved herself from the bed and started looking for her clothes.

"What are you doing?"

"I'm..." *Running from a painful truth and your pity.*

"You're not leaving me, not now, not when both you and I know what we can be together."

She looked back at him, looking for any traces of pity left on his face, but she saw none. All she saw was want and so she stayed.

Ryan reached out an arm and was met with air. He opened his eyes and searched for her, but it was clear she wasn't there. He had planned on telling her more about himself and why he was in Edinburgh, but the moment had never presented itself.

Between making love and holding her as they'd rested between bouts of rapture he had let the night slip away. When he had awoken that morning she was gone and all that remained was a note.

Ryan, thought you deserved the rest. Please come and find me tonight for a last night together—Erin.

Now he had no choice, he glanced at the clock and knew he wouldn't have time to talk to her privately in person. Still, after their night together he had no doubt that nothing could break the bond and trust they had formed.

Erin couldn't recall when she had last felt this happy. She had slipped from her lover's bed in the early hours of the morning and had hopes of returning to it as soon as she completed her work.

She straightened the black blazer that overlaid a cream lace camisole and her favorite strand of pearls. She had one more symposium before she knew Ryan would find her. She had never felt this free before. A feeling of wild recklessness filled her as she glanced nervously around the room. She hadn't prepared for today's session. Every thought and action had been about Ryan last night and she had forgone any thought of reading through the presentation or even the speaker's background information she had been provided with. She took her seat on the stage, sipping from a glass of the iced water before her to chill the heated thoughts Ryan provoked.

"Ladies and gentlemen, thank you for joining us for our final session, 'Postpartum Hemorrhage—Tales from the Battleground.' Our special guest speaker today is Dr. Ryan Callum. Dr. Callum is a medical officer in the American military. Having served on front lines for the past twelve years, he has developed firsthand experience in the management of massive bleeding and transfusion. This knowledge is becoming more and more relevant to the field of obstetrics, where acuity is forever increasing and particularly our management of postpartum hemorrhage, which, despite our best efforts, we have not been able to decrease the incidence of. Today Dr. Callum is going to shift our attention beyond prevention to optimum management to ensure patient well-being. Everyone, please welcome Dr. Ryan Callum."

All of a sudden the moderator had her absolute attention as she replayed everything he had just said. His name was Ryan, he was in the military… She watched the entrance, desperately hoping to see someone other than her Ryan. But as the door opened her sense of dread ballooned into extreme hurt as her Ryan walked through the doors. Dr. Ryan Callum was just that, a doctor. Why hadn't he told her? How could he have held something back when she had bared her soul and innermost pain to him?

Had he just told her what she'd wanted to hear, just as Kevin had? He had to have known the conference was why she was in Edinburgh and that she would find out that he was also a physician. Why wouldn't he have told her instead of the public humiliation of learning who your lover really was in front of hundreds of people? It didn't bother her that he was a physician; it bothered her that she felt she had been lied to, even if by omission. The trust that had built between them vanished in an instant and her heart, body and mind felt instantly on guard against this man whom she had briefly let in. She had been a fool, again.

Ryan took his place at the podium and she could feel his eyes on her, but she couldn't turn to look at him.

"Dr. Callum," the moderator continued, "allow me to introduce your panel. Dr. Nicholas Richter. Dr. Richter is the head of Maternal Fetal Medicine at St. Bishop's Hospital in London. Dr. Mary Ellison. Dr. Ellison is a community obstetrician-gynecologist from Canada and also has an extensive background in global obstetrics and gynecology, spearheading multiple international projects around the world. And Dr. Erin Dufour. Dr. Dufour is a resident in obstetrics and gynecology from

Boston, Massachusetts. She has been kind enough to provide us with insight both from the American and the younger generation's experience."

At this point she could no longer stare ahead and forced herself to turn her eyes to his. She saw something she had never seen before in his eyes—anger. Confusion and an equal anger set in. What did Ryan have to be angry about? He was the liar. He was the one who had betrayed her trust.

It was the longest ninety minutes of her life. As Ryan talked she had the utmost difficulty focusing on his words. She was aware the panel had started talking and any minute she could be called on to comment.

"Dr. Dufour, do you think there is a need in American centers to adopt the massive transfusion protocol Dr. Callum has discussed today?"

She wanted to refuse to have anything more to do with anything related to Dr. Callum but she managed to swallow her personal feelings and focus on being professional. "As we heard from the outset of today's lecture, we have not been able to reduce the incidence of postpartum hemorrhage in the past ten years. Even when we know the risks are present, all we can do is hope that it doesn't happen to our patients. Having more options for treatment is something every obstetrician would embrace in order to decrease the morbidity we often feel helpless to prevent."

A discussion continued on optimal implementation and the availability of resources in smaller centers. Erin was thinking of her own words. Had she known she could get hurt becoming involved with Ryan? Yes, and no. Yes, it was always a possibility in any relationship, but she had never considered it to be a real possibility, not with Ryan. He had seemed so honest, so genuine in his interest in her best interests. And the things she had told him, everything about her marriage, her infertility, what had he told her in return? Hardly anything. And definitely not the entire truth in what little he had revealed.

An ache settled at the center of her chest. She had told herself he was just a fling, but last night had felt like more and it made the hurt and betrayal all the harder to endure.

Applause broke out as she felt a merciful end to the continued strain of keeping up appearances. She watched as numerous physicians approached Ryan, no doubt congratulating him on a job well done. Perfect, she thought. She had no need to hear any more lies. She gathered her bag and made her way to the door. She had just entered the corridor when she felt herself being pulled into another room. Before she could think she was staring at an empty conference room, empty aside from Ryan.

"Your last name is Dufour?" he demanded more than asked.

She was too taken aback to do anything but answer. "Dufour was my married name."

"Is your ex-husband Kevin Dufour?"

She felt as if she'd been slapped and recoiled. Just hearing Kevin's name on Ryan's lips meshed two realities that she never wanted joined. How did he know Kevin? And what on earth gave him the right to be this angry?

"Yes," she answered defiantly. She wasn't at all proud of that fact but she still was not deserving of whatever was summoning Ryan's anger.

"So you're the one." Ryan ran his fingers through his hair and she had the feeling that he was as disturbed by this conversation as she was. It made no sense to her but she wasn't going to let him continue to attack her.

"I'm the one? The one who lied? No, that would be you."

"I didn't lie to you."

"I consider significant omissions lies, Ryan. Unfortunately I am used to being lied to. I'm just sorry I didn't realize the type of man you were earlier."

His eyes blazed at her as he stepped one step closer to her. "Don't compare him to me."

"Why not?" The realization that Ryan was very familiar with her ex had dawned and she had no problem comparing them in her anger, even when deep down she still sensed that they were very different men. "You are both liars who say what a woman wants to hear, no matter what the truth really is."

"People who live in glass houses shouldn't throw stones."

"What is that supposed to mean?"

"It means I don't believe your victim act. I know the truth."

"The truth about what? What is the truth, Ryan? Do you even know the meaning of the word?"

"I know you had no problem destroying the life of an innocent woman to get what you wanted. You got what you deserved."

She rapidly processed everything he'd just said. *You got what you deserved.* Wasn't that what she had thought when she'd lost her baby? When she couldn't conceive again? It had taken a lot of healing to accept that that wasn't how life worked. She had taken care of enough other infertile women to know that being infertile wasn't the fate of the unworthy.

She was on the verge of leaving this conversation and him before she suffered any more abuse when the rest of his words came through to her: *destroying the life of an innocent woman to get what you wanted.* She thought back to the confrontation she'd had with Kevin's girlfriend after their marriage. She could see the woman perfectly in her mind and the connection became clear. The nose, the eyes, they were the feminine form of Ryan's. "Sabrina..."

"Sabrina Callum, my sister."

Had he known? Had he always known who she was? Was this some sort of revenge for the pain she had caused his sister? Had he seduced her just to hurt her because she had hurt his sister? She blinked hard but when she opened her eyes it was still Ryan and he still looked at her as though she was nothing.

She thought back to her conversation with Sabrina and the pain she had felt on learning for the first time of Kevin's infidelity. To think a part of her had still clung to hope for her marriage. In the end she had been the loser in the love triangle because as much as Sabrina had been hurt by Kevin's betrayal, at least she hadn't had to endure the continual infidelity and emotional abuse Erin had over the years of their marriage.

"She was lucky." She spoke her mind, not meaning to anger him further but also not holding back.

"Lucky?" He seemed stunned.

"Yes, lucky."

"Do you know what you did to her? What it was like for her to one day have the man she loved and had been with for years, the man she was engaged to marry, drop her completely and marry another woman within weeks?"

He was yelling at her now but she couldn't respond. Had she thought about Sabrina—yes, but only after she and Kevin had married because that had been when she'd learned of her. But to be honest she hadn't agonized over the other woman's pain because she had been deep in her own, first learning that her husband had not been faithful and had cast her in the role of the other woman, then struggling with the pain and complications from her miscarriage.

Erin looked up at Ryan and realized there was no point. Nothing was as it seemed. He was no longer a fresh start, an honest man who would renew her faith in men. She honestly didn't know which was worse—the fact that he was a liar or that maybe he had seduced her intentionally to avenge his sister. Either way, it didn't matter. There was no point in arguing further. She didn't care to explain herself to him and there was nothing he could say to her to regain her trust.

"Goodbye, Ryan."

He watched as she walked away from him and tried not to notice that she held her head up. He was still reeling from the sight of her sitting on that panel and the introduction that had been made. As she had been introduced his mind had sparked from one connection to another until the final unfortunate conclusion. Her last name was Dufour, her ex-husband was an orthopedic surgeon and she was from Boston. She was the other woman.

He thought of the glimpses of Sabrina he had seen over the months she had been sick. Serving away, he hadn't been a continuous presence in her life, but even from a distance he had learned enough about the unsavory details of her breakup with Kevin. How he had been entranced and seduced by a woman named Erin, who had then trapped him with a pregnancy, giving him no choice but to leave Sabrina to marry her. Now, having met Erin, he felt torn. Part of him wanted to believe what he had learned of her over their two days together. But the other part of him knew the wickedness of her past actions and worried that she had conned him, as well.

Was he that transparent that she had managed to morph herself into exactly what he wanted? He felt his heart begin to pound at the other possibility. She had trapped one man into marriage, was that her plan again? The sadness she had expressed when she'd told him of her infertility had been so believable he hadn't bothered with a condom again. He was the only kind of fool. Never had he ever trusted a woman when it came to contraception and now there was the possibility of significant consequences for his first lapse in judgment. Time will tell, he thought to himself. He had no doubt that if Erin was pregnant she would make him pay for his mistake.

CHAPTER SIX

Two years later...

"PUSH," SHE ENCOURAGED the woman, whose mind and body spoke of true exhaustion. Erin glanced at the monitor displaying the baby's heart rate.

"Push, Allison. I know you can do this." She kept all sense of panic from her voice as she mentally formulated her backup plan if Allison did not have her baby in the next five minutes.

Another set of pushes and Erin finally saw the progress she had been hoping for. "Perfect, Allison, that's perfect," she encouraged softly.

She would never get tired of this. The experience of watching a couple who at that moment were as close as two people could be welcoming a child into their lives.

"I can't." A small plea escaped from the head of the bed.

"Yes, you can, Allison, and you are. Just a little bit longer and you will get to meet your baby. Now push."

She alternated her attention between the baby's head and the monitor. One-twenty, one hundred, ninety, eighty… The number and the graph descended below normal range.

"Allison." Her eyes were closed and her head tipped back. "Next contraction you need to have the baby."

The woman's eyes opened wide and Erin knew she had gotten through to her. "It's coming," Allison declared.

"Okay, let it build, take a deep breath in, hold it and push."

And a minute later Erin was holding a small, perfect person for just a brief moment before she put him on his mother's chest, gently rubbing him with a towel to stimulate breathing.

She exhaled when a small cry filled the room, followed by his mother's tears of happiness. "Congratulations, momma, you did it."

She finished everything she needed to do and completed her final checks in silence, not wanting to interfere with the couple's moment. After carefully disposing of sharp instruments and counting the sponges, she was ready to leave to complete the required paperwork.

"Congratulations again," she wished them both.

"Thank you so much, Dr. Madden, we couldn't have done it without you."

"Yes, you could have, but thank you for including me." She gave Allison a gentle squeeze on her foot before grabbing the chart.

Erin walked behind the desk on Labor and Delivery and began her charting. She glanced at her watch. It was almost midnight, but it had been worth it. She had followed Allison through her fertility treatments and her pregnancy, and now she had a son. Her pager blared through her peace. She glanced at the number. It was the emergency department.

Instantly her heart began to race, as it always did when she saw those numbers, and she had to concentrate on breathing. She didn't know why she was being paged. She wasn't on call tonight; she had come in on her own time for Allison.

She took a deep breath and let professionalism take precedence over her fear. She dialed the numbers and waited until the call was answered. "It's Erin Madden."

"Dr. Madden, we need you in the emergency department now," the unit clerk relayed to her.

There was nothing normal about the request. Usually she would speak directly with the consulting physician and hear the details of the patient consultation. Never had she been almost ordered to appear.

"What's going on?" She could hear chaos in the background.

"I don't know. Dr. Callum just yelled out that I needed to get you here as soon as possible."

The sense of dread she had been carrying around for the past two years solidified within her. The minute she had seen the announcement welcoming him to Boston General she had been waiting for this moment, but she had almost convinced herself she was going to be able to avoid it indefinitely. As chief resident, she made the schedule and before she assigned herself shifts she always looked at the emergency department schedule to ensure their shifts never aligned. Tonight she wasn't supposed to be here but she was and so was he and he was calling for her.

"Did he say why?" she asked quietly, wondering if Ryan having the unit clerk make the call was his way of making sure she didn't avoid him.

"No, he's tied up trying to stabilize Dr. Darcy."

Erin did a double take as she replayed the clerk's words in her head. "Do you mean work with Dr. Darcy?"

"No. Dr. Darcy was found unconscious in the women's change room. He's with her now."

"I'm on my way."

Erin ran. She rarely ran, but today she ran from the maternity unit to the waiting bank of central elevators. As she frantically pushed the button she tried to control her panic. Chloe. Something was wrong with Chloe and she needed her, and in order to do that she was going to have to see Ryan again.

The minute the doors opened she ran through the halls to the emergency department, going first to the trauma bays, where she feared she would find her. She came to an abrupt halt at the sight before her. Chloe lay on a stretcher, pale and barely conscious of the commotion around her. She was already hooked up to the monitors and Erin glanced at the screen. Her pulse was high at one hundred and fifty. Her blood pressure was low at eighty over forty. She was in shock.

"Where are we at?" she asked the group, needing an answer.

"She's received four units of packed red blood cells and two units of fresh frozen plasma from the rapid transfuser." The voice came from behind her and she didn't need to turn to recognize its owner.

"Can I speak to you alone for a moment, Dr. Madden?"

She could do this, she told herself. She had already been through so much that she could do this, too. She had no choice but to turn and confront the man she had been successfully avoiding until now. "Yes, Dr. Callum."

She watched as recognition flared in his eyes and for a moment he was stunned into silence.

"Dr. Callum, what's wrong with Chloe?" she asked, doing everything possible to bring him back to the professionalism Chloe needed.

"She was found unconscious in the women's change room. A bedside rapid ultrasound of her abdomen reveals a significant amount of free fluid and her beta HCG has returned positive."

She looked away from him back at Chloe. The presentation was classic for one thing, a ruptured ectopic pregnancy, which meant that Chloe was in serious danger and needed her entire focus.

"I need to call the operating room and have them get ready. Make sure she is prepped and ready to go in the next five minutes." She walked away from Ryan toward the nursing desk and one of the phones.

"This is Erin Madden. I have a ruptured ectopic in the emergency department. We need to come now. Set up for an attempted laparoscopic removal and possible laparotomy."

She moved from the phone back to Chloe's side, lifting the hospital gown and feeling her abdomen herself. It was distended and rigid beneath her touch. She pushed down just slightly and heard Chloe moan in response. "It's okay, Chloe. I'm going to take good care of you," she murmured as reassuringly as she could, when inside she was scared to death.

Ectopic pregnancies were still among the highest killers of women in pregnancy. Often they were caught early since women now had more access to ultrasounds in pregnancy and were able to be treated medically. But occasionally they presented without the woman noticing any warning signs and a perfectly healthy woman like Chloe could in an instant be on the brink of death.

She worked through her plan in her head, reminding herself she needed not to do anything differently just because it was her friend. She needed to use the same common surgical sense she would with any other patient. She walked back to the phone and called her supervising staff.

"Hello, it's Thomas."

"Dr. Thomas, it's Erin Madden. I got called to the emergency department for an unstable, probably ruptured ectopic pregnancy that I've just booked for the operating room."

"Erin, you're not on call tonight." The voice was questioning, but not with any misgivings.

"The patient is Dr. Chloe Darcy, the chief resident from Emergency. They called me directly."

"Say no more. I'll meet you in the operating room."

She made two more calls, first to the blood bank to arrange for more blood products to be dropped off directly to the operating room and second to the resident on call to assist. Out of the corner of her eye she saw Chloe being wheeled down the hall toward the elevators for the operating room.

She still needed to change into fresh scrubs, give handover to the awaiting anesthetist and check to make sure the right equipment had been picked, so she took off running. This time she took the single flight of stairs to the second floor, focused only on the task ahead of her. She had half pulled off her scrub top before even entering the change room and quickly completed the task before arriving ready in theater seven.

The anesthetist was at the head of the bed, preparing for Chloe's arrival. "What do you have, Erin?"

"A previously healthy thirty-year-old female with a probable ruptured ectopic pregnancy. She was hypotensive and tachycardic in the emergency department. She has two central large-bore intravenous, each in an antecubital fossa on her arms. She has received four units of packed red blood cells and two of fresh frozen plasma. No repeat CBC has been done yet. I've arranged for another four and two units to be delivered directly to the operating room. I'd like to start laparoscopically."

"Are you sure?"

It was the question she had been asking herself for the past ten minutes. No, she wasn't sure. Starting with the less invasive method might help Chloe in the long run but it also might not work or prolong her time to treatment. Would she be considering this if Chloe were any other patient?

"Yes."

The nursing team brought Chloe into the room and

Erin helped transfer her off the bed to the operating table. She watched as the anesthetist did his assessment and felt a small sense of fear grow within her when he called for a second anesthetist to assist him. Erin sat on a stool by Chloe's side, holding the cold hand that lay splayed on the arm board as she was anesthetized, and then it was back to work. Erin positioned Chloe for the planned less invasive surgery before turning to leave the room to complete her surgical scrub in the outside scrub sink. She saw Ryan through the threaded glass windows of the operating-room doors.

She pushed through the doors and he took a few steps back from her. "You need to leave," she stated without anger but with significant conviction.

She understood why he was there. Chloe was loved by everyone and she knew from conversations with her friend that Ryan had become a mentor to her in the emergency department, but still that didn't make a difference to her right now. "Ryan, I can't have any distractions right now. I have a job to do. Think of Chloe."

He seemed to understand. She almost wished she had a minute to look into his eyes and try to figure out what he was thinking, what he was feeling, but she didn't. She checked the ties on her surgical mask and hat before opening the sterile scrub packet and methodically rubbing the sponge up and down each exposed axis of her hands.

When she turned from the sink Ryan was no longer there and she felt a sense of relief, which she knew would only be temporary.

She gowned, gloved and draped Chloe, which made

things easier. It helped her separate her fear for her friend from the job she had to do.

"You can start," the anesthetist confirmed.

"Knife." And she held out her hand in anticipation.

Chloe's abdomen was flawless until the moment she made the five-millimeter incision into the base of her belly button. A minute later she had a camera inserted and was staring at the monitor across from her. Chloe's abdomen was a sea of red. She couldn't see anything; particularly she couldn't see where the ectopic was bleeding.

"Can I have her more head down, please?" she asked the anesthetist, hoping that tipping her would move some of the blood away.

"No, I can't move her from where she is now. Her pressure won't tolerate it."

"Okay." She took a deep breath and said the words she didn't want to say. "We are going to convert. Open the laparotomy set."

The nurses in the room scrambled to change the instruments as Erin sterilely repositioned Chloe. "Knife," she called again.

This time her incision was more than five millimeters. She grimaced as she drew the ten-centimeter line just above Chloe's pubic bone, but didn't stop. She worked quickly until she accessed Chloe's abdomen and started removing the blood. She was constantly aware of the amount present as the nurses and anesthetist updated her on the number of canisters she filled and sponges she soaked through. She needed to hurry to stop the bleeding. "Can we make sure that the second four units are on their way?" she directed.

Then she saw it, the continuous pouring from the frayed edges of the ruptured tube. She closed a clamp over it and the bleeding stopped. She felt as if she took her first breath.

"Okay, let's take a moment and finish evacuating all the blood then we'll reassess the tube."

She was buying time. A few minutes later she had to refocus on the Fallopian tube. With the clamp still on she carefully removed the pregnancy from the tube, nothing visible aside from placental tissue and blood clot. Every time she removed a piece the bleeding increased. She struggled in vain to be gentle and not injure the tube further. She tried cautery to burn the edges, but more bleeding ensued. Then she asked for a fine suture for a tension stitch, but the tube was too shredded from the rupture.

"Erin," she heard Dr. Thomas's voice break through her concentration.

"Yes," she answered, already knowing what he was going to say.

"You know what to do." She did. She'd been thinking it for the past five minutes. She nodded in agreement.

"Curved roger." She held her hand out, waiting for the larger clamp. Two steps later she held the Fallopian tube in her hand and felt sick. She hadn't rendered Chloe infertile as she still had her other tube, but still she felt awful about the possibility that Chloe might have difficulty having children in the future.

She looked around again, cleaning things up, until she was aware of a shift in the room. "Do you need help?"

It was the voice of Dr. Tate Reed, one of the hospital's most prominent surgeons.

Erin had no idea why Tate was there, but the one thing she was certain of was that she was in control and the only other thing she could do for Chloe was protect her privacy. "You need to leave, Dr. Reed."

"Dr. Thomas?" He was going over her head and Erin held her breath, praying that Dr. Thomas would back her decision.

"Dr. Madden is right. This is not a vascular case, Tate. We are going to have to ask you to leave."

"Okay," Erin heard him concede, but she was also very aware that he did not venture farther than the operating-theater doors and was watching her every move.

"What is her hemocrit?" she asked, wanting to know if Chloe needed more blood.

She waited as the anesthetist drew a sample and put it in the machine. "Sixty."

"Please give her the next four units and the two fresh frozen plasma."

"If we do, we'll have to keep her warmed and intubated in the intensive care unit."

"She needs the blood. Once she redistributes the rest of her fluid her hemoglobin is going to be much lower than that."

She stared again at where the tube had once been, wanting to be sure Chloe was absolutely dry before she started to close her. The operating-room doors pushed open again. This time she didn't feel any tension at the sight of Chloe's best friend and her friend, Dr. Kate Spence.

"Hi, Kate." Erin acknowledged her presence but didn't change her focus from the surgical pedicles.

"She's going to be okay. We have evacuated the hemoperitoneum and have stopped the bleeding. We are going to be closing in the next few minutes and then she will be going to Recovery, followed by a short stay in the intensive care unit in case she runs into any massive transfusion complications."

"Uh-huh." Kate seemed as stunned as she had been when she'd first got the call. Still, Erin was friends with both women and knew that Chloe was protective of Kate and would want her comforted.

"I'm sorry we had to open her. We tried with the laparoscope but she had too much blood in her abdomen and was too unstable to tolerate it." She felt self-conscious about her choice, knowing that Kate was a general surgeon with excellent laparoscopic skills.

"But the bleeding has been stopped? Kate asked.

"Yes."

"What happened?" Kate finally asked.

She couldn't answer that. Her job right now was as Chloe's doctor, not Kate's friend. "That's not for me to disclose to you. Chloe will be able to tell you herself later, if she chooses to. I think you should go now and take Dr. Reed with you. She is stable and we'll take good care of her. You can see her in the intensive care unit in a couple of hours, once she's settled in."

"Okay," Kate said, resigned. "Thank you."

Ryan paced the halls of the operating rooms, waiting. His mind flashed with images of the night. Chloe lying lifeless on the change-room floor and all the ways he had seen Erin. First it had been when she had turned around in the emergency department. He hadn't known she'd still been there. Before he had agreed to take a position in the emergency department he had checked the resident listing for the department of obstetrics and gynecology. There were no Dufours listed, or even Erins, for that matter. He had assumed she had left following her divorce and he had taken the job pleased with the knowledge that she was a complication he could avoid.

Then as Chloe had been transferred to the operating room he had assisted and followed her to ensure her well-being. He had seen Erin again, rushing into the change room, her shirt half pulled off before the doors had closed, and that had been when he could no longer have doubts about who he was dealing with. For a moment he had forgotten everything except for the memories of the last time he had shared that intimate a view.

Now he had no choice but to trust Erin with the care of one of his closest friends and he felt absolutely gutted by everything that was happening around him. From the moment he had heard the nurse screaming for help, to holding Chloe unconscious in his arms, realizing that the person he needed to make this right was Erin Dufour, he'd had no control. A career in the military had prepared him for a lack of control, but tonight every coping mechanism had abandoned him. He had already run into Tate Reed in the hallway and lost his temper, something he never did.

The sound of the operating-room doors swinging open got his attention and he looked at Chloe, who was being wheeled out, still intubated, the anesthetist intermittently squeezing oxygen into her. Erin was at the foot of the bed, assisting with the transfer. Her blue eyes met his and she nodded slightly and he knew that Chloe was going to be okay.

After they passed he stood undecided in the hallway until he could resist no longer. He walked into the recovery room and to the desk where Erin sat.

"You're not on the resident list."

Her eyes flashed back at him and he watched as she pulled a blue flowered scrub hat from her head, running her fingers through her hair, which was a darker blond and longer than when he had first met her. "Yes, I am."

"No, you're not. I checked before I came to work here."

She sighed, pulling her nametag from her pocket and laying it before him to read.

"Alexandra Erin Madden," he read aloud.

"My mother's name is Alexandra. I've always gone by Erin."

"And Madden?" he asked, still wondering how he could have not known.

"My maiden name. Sorry to disappoint you." It was a throwaway comment and he knew by both her reaction tonight and the conversation they were having that she was not surprised to see him.

"You knew I was here?"

"Yes," she confirmed.

He thought about all the time he had been at the hospital and realized that he had never seen her. Through his role as an emergency-room attending physician he knew most of the residents across all the programs, which meant one thing. Erin had gone out of her way to avoid him. He had no idea why that angered him, but it did. "You've been avoiding me?"

She stood from her seat and even though she barely cleared his shoulders the effect was still there. "No different than your attempt to avoid me. I was just more successful. If you want to you can pretend you never saw me tonight."

He didn't stop her as she walked away.

Her heart was pounding. She had made it so far and now with less than three months left before her departure from Boston General she had come face-to-face with the one person in the world she had never wanted to see again. She remembered the feeling of betrayal she had felt in Edinburgh and felt uneasy, not knowing who she was dealing with. For the rest of the night she found herself looking over her shoulder, waiting for another encounter with Ryan. She would be a fool to think it wasn't going to happen again. It was just a question of when.

She returned to Labor and Delivery and checked on Allison and then looked at her watch. She had a desperate need to go home and had enough time to do so before Chloe was conscious and ready to talk.

CHAPTER SEVEN

ERIN STOOD OVER the crib and marveled at the miracle it contained. Not one trace of blanket covered the sleeping baby inside. She reached down and pulled the blanket over her again, knowing the action was futile, but it gave her the maternal reassurance she needed right now.

She had thought that seeing Jennie would stem the panic that had started the minute she had seen Ryan, but it had only made it worse. Everyone who had met her little girl had always exclaimed how much she looked like Erin, but only Erin, who was privy to more intimate information, knew how much Jennie actually looked like her father.

She brushed the wisps of brown hair gently, not wanting to disturb the baby but also needing to touch her. If she had woken up, Erin would have had to face Ryan's eyes staring back at her and she wasn't ready to face that reality. How long would it be before he found out about her baby?

She should have left Boston the minute she had heard of Ryan being hired. Certainly the misery of being in the same hospital as Kevin, a torment that had only increased when she'd become pregnant, had been reason enough to leave. But she had needed help. There had been no way she could be a single mother and continue her training in a specialty as demanding as obstetrics and gynecology without the help of her family and friends, so she had stayed.

She hadn't concealed her pregnancy. At the time there had been no reason to, and it was common knowledge she was a single mother. Most people assumed it was her ex-husband's child and that he just regarded the child the same way he had his marriage—with indifference. As much as she didn't like the connection, she had never bothered to correct the assumption. Jennie was the love of her life and she would do anything to protect her miracle.

After some lengthy time had passed, she forced herself to move away from the crib and out of the nursery. It wouldn't be long before her eighteen-month-old daughter would be out of the crib and Erin wanted to hold on to these moments as long as possible.

It had taken her ten positive pregnancy tests even to consider the possibility that she might be pregnant. Stress, she had thought to herself as her cycle had stopped, nausea had begun to rule her life and her abdomen had become uncharacteristically bloated. She'd even thought she might be going crazy, developing symptoms of a phantom pregnancy that she desperately wanted but was never going to have. So she had taken the test to force her unconscious self to face reality and had been completely unprepared for the positive result that had appeared.

She had never heard of a false-positive pregnancy test, so she'd bought another, and another. Then absolute fear had set in when she'd considered the possibility of having a hormone-secreting cancer that had been making the tests positive. It had taken another two weeks of positive tests before she'd forced herself into action and had asked for help from Dr. Thomas, one of her favorite staff obstetricians.

He had been very gentle and kind when he had broken the news of her pregnancy to her. It had been almost laughable that as an obstetrics resident she hadn't diagnosed the obvious, but it had taken so long to accept that she would never have a child that she hadn't allowed herself to even consider the possibility. Even after he'd convinced her that she'd been having a healthy, normal pregnancy she hadn't let herself really believe it.

Every milestone, every change in pregnancy had both amazed and terrified her. Despite the growing contour of her abdomen she'd still had trouble with the reality that she was going to be a mother. It had felt as though if she believed it, it would hurt more if it all went away.

Then one morning she'd gone into labor and as the hours had passed she'd become ever closer to becoming a mother. She had delivered Jennie with her mother by her side and amid the tremendous joy that had flooded her she couldn't help but feel a small amount of sadness that she hadn't had "that moment." The moment that she loved most when delivering babies. The moment when a man looked at the woman he loved, amazed at what she had done and more in love with her than he had ever been. Instead, while holding Jennie, the moment with her baby's father had been a memory of how she had misplaced her trust yet again and the anger and disdain Ryan felt for her.

The moral part of her had thought about finding him, letting him know they had a daughter. But the protective mother in her had said no. She couldn't say she knew Ryan, not after he had made it clear how he felt about her. She'd known enough to know he wouldn't just thank her for the news and move on. He would want Jennie; who wouldn't? And given the feelings he had for her and his view of her as a person there had been the chance that maybe he would even feel that he was the better parent and try to take full custody. That risk was one she had decided she was not willing to take.

Now that question was reopened. It wasn't a secret that she had a daughter. How long could she last before he put together the puzzle?

Her pager buzzed against her hip and she recognized the number as being that of the intensive care unit. Chloe must be awake. She moved back into the nursery, gently pressed her lips to her hand and onto Jennie's cheek before leaving quietly.

Ryan walked to the bank of computer screens and stared at the images. Black-and-white images filled the screens and he searched for the fracture. He knew it was there. There was no way the cyclist's wrist and arm was that swollen and tender without a fracture, but why couldn't he see it? Because he was distracted. Thinking about Erin. His stubborn pride kept him from simply waiting for the radiologist's report and finally after several minutes the subtle thin line became apparent.

He walked back to the nursing desk. "Who's on for Orthopedics?"

"Dufour."

Perfect, thought Ryan, clenching his jaw to keep his teeth from gritting. He hadn't avoided Kevin since coming to Boston but he also hadn't gone out of his way to make contact with him, either. He had never been close with the other man. When Kevin had been engaged to Sabrina he had seen him socially on one or two occasions when he'd had leave from the military. Each time he had seemed charming and the perfect match for his sister. When Sabrina had talked about him it had been nothing but praise and happiness.

Even when their relationship had ended Sabrina had placed minimal blame on Kevin. He had been lured away. Enticed and trapped by another woman. Now he knew that woman was Erin. He had blamed Kevin more, seen him as weak. But that had been before he, too, had fallen for her charms.

After Edinburgh he had struggled for months to reconcile how he felt about Erin. He would replay all of the time they'd spent together, trying to find the crack, the hairline clue that she had been pretending to be something she wasn't. Trying to appeal to everything he wanted in a woman. Had she intentionally thrown herself from the hillside, knowing he would save her? It seemed ridiculous but he felt as if he couldn't put anything past her. Unlike the fracture today, he had never found that crack, and that frustration he'd felt toward her had only increased because of it.

The confrontation after he'd discovered her true identity had been enough, though. Just hearing her acknowledge his sister, what she had done to her and calling her lucky had been enough to make Ryan want to turn his back on her and walk away forever. Now he no longer had that luxury. She was in Boston, at Boston General Hospital, and the past was simply not going to be able to remain just that.

"Please page him," he told the nurse.

A few minutes later she handed him the phone.

"This is Dufour."

"This is Ryan Callum. I have a wrist fracture in Emergency I would like you to see."

"Page my resident." The reply was both arrogant and irritating. If Kevin had any memory of Ryan it wasn't apparent by his tone.

"Your resident is three consultations behind and seeing them between operative cases. We need to clear the backlog in the emergency department."

"That's not my problem," Kevin dismissed.

"I'm making it your problem." It was a tone he didn't use often, but he wasn't in any frame of mind to take any condescension from Kevin Dufour.

"Who is this?"

"Dr. Ryan Callum, staff emergency physician. We've met."

There was no response on the other end of the line. It was almost as if Dufour was searching his memory for when he had met Ryan. "So are you coming to see the patient or should I call another orthopedic surgeon?"

"Be my guest."

"I will. I hear Dr. Williamson is interested in keeping his hand in clinical practice." The conversation could not have gotten more antagonistic. He had known exactly what he was doing, bringing up the chief of staff and Dufour's former father-in-law. The phone clicked and a few seconds later he heard the empty dial tone.

"Is he coming?" the nurse beside him asked. He could tell that by the small uplift of the corner of her mouth that she had heard and approved of his handling of the conversation.

"I think so."

Ryan continued his charting, sure in his assumption. Dufour would come, not immediately but he would come. Thirty minutes later he saw the other man, striding arrogantly toward him. He took in his appearance, which hadn't changed much since their last meeting, his all-American pretty-boy good looks still at their finest.

"Just exactly who do you think you are?" Apparently their conversation was not over.

"At this moment I'm the senior staff physician responsible for the emergency department."

"Let me make something clear—you don't tell me what to do."

Ryan smirked slightly. It was almost comical watching Dufour make an attempt to intimidate him. He had spent over a decade in the military, including combat experience, surrounded by superiors who had been the essence of intimidation and fellow soldiers who had all been volleying for promotion. Dufour's obvious peacocking was nothing to him, except that it once again challenged his past perceptions of the other man. He was nothing like the charmer Ryan had once met. And with his attempt at dominance neither was he the weak man he had envisioned being seduced by Erin.

Erin. Despite the fact that he couldn't claim to know her, not really given what he knew about her past and the facade she had presented in Edinburgh, he still couldn't picture her with this man. Never mind be married to him.

"The patient is in exam six." And he walked away, having heard enough from Dufour. He came to a dead stop when the idea in his mind penetrated his thoughts. Sabrina was lucky not to have married him. He thought of her life now. She had since married, had a son and settled down for a quiet life in the suburbs that she loved. Discomfort tore through him when he realized he was thinking exactly what Erin had said to him. When she'd said it he had been furious. But, still, even if that was the case, Erin hadn't known that back then. Not when she'd been seducing another woman's fiancé. But after a few moments with Kevin he was certain that Sabrina had had a lucky escape. But had Erin gotten what she'd deserved?

Erin felt exhausted as she finished her clinic day. Infertility work was 10 percent happiness and 90 percent emotionally draining. Talking to couples about their options, none of which had any guarantee, was a hard conversation. Then there was Chloe.

She had followed up on her twice daily in hospital. Their first conversation had been very hard. Telling her friend that she had been pregnant and had then lost the pregnancy had brought back old memories of the feelings she'd had when she had been in Chloe's position. That feeling of "Why me" and all the possible answers to that question. She had done her best to be Chloe's friend but also remain professional, when truthfully all she'd wanted to do had been to cry along with her.

Now she was busy juggling the demands of her regular work, taking care of Chloe and living with the constant threat of Ryan discovering her secret.

She drew in her breath as she saw him. She wasn't surprised to see him—she'd known it was inevitable. There was no way she could turn around and walk away; she didn't want him to think she had anything to hide. Besides, other than their daughter, she had nothing to hide from him and nothing to be ashamed of. He had accused her of immoral behavior when she had been nothing but honest about her life and past with him. She hadn't even lied by omission, not then, because she'd had no idea Ryan was connected with her past. Now she had no choice. She would lie. She was going to do everything she needed to do to protect her family.

They met outside Chloe's door at the same time.

"Ryan."

"Erin. You're here to see Chloe?"

"She's my patient," she replied, hating that she felt a need to defend herself against such a simple question.

"She's my friend."

"Mine, too."

"Chloe never mentioned you." He was staring at her with suspicion in his eyes.

"Why would she?" She knew he was getting at something and felt a need to emotionally brace herself.

"Did you tell her?"

"About?"

"Scotland."

Chloe had asked about Erin's romantic Scottish love affair when she had returned home and without giving any details Erin had been firm about not wanting to discuss it and Chloe had been gracious enough to not ask anything further. As far as Erin knew, she had never put together that the Ryan Callum in the emergency department was the same military Ryan Erin had met in Scotland.

"No, I didn't. Enough of my mistakes are public knowledge. I didn't think my latest poor choice in men was worth mentioning." She knew she shouldn't antagonize him, but now, outside the life-and-death scenario Chloe had presented, all of the hurt she had felt as a result of Ryan had come flooding back.

"It probably would have been difficult to explain that you passed yourself off as something you were not and then the truth came out."

"Are you talking about me or you?" She pushed past him and into Chloe's room. She didn't make it far. Chloe's room was filled with their friend Kate and Dr. Tate Reed. She remembered how she'd had to be firm with Tate in the operating room and had asked him to leave. She hoped he realized she had done what had been best for Chloe and wasn't angry with her, because she didn't need another confrontation right now.

"I just came to see if you needed anything," Erin said, deciding to focus on the only person who mattered in the room—her patient.

"I'm good, thank you." She still looked tired and wary but, considering how she had looked a few days earlier, Erin would take it.

"When do you think Chloe will be discharged?" Tate asked, his entire attention focused on her. She quickly glanced at Chloe, who didn't object to Tate's question and appeared to be waiting for the answer.

"She can be discharged tomorrow if she feels well enough to go. But she can't stay alone for the first few weeks."

"She can stay with me," Kate volunteered.

Erin had assumed that was what would happen so hadn't addressed discharge planning with Chloe prior to this conversation. She was shocked when Chloe declined the offer. She was about to offer her own home when Ryan interrupted her.

"Chloe, you are welcome to stay with me." His offer rang with confidence. Erin looked back at him, stunned by his offer. Chloe had never mentioned anything beyond a professional mentor-mentee relationship between them. She knew they were close professionally but not personally. Their lack of personal relationship outside the hospital had provided comfort to Erin, knowing there wasn't a possibility she see Ryan socially through her friendship with Chloe.

"I don't think that's a good idea," Tate replied, before

anyone else could interject. Erin was forced to look at both men and the same feeling she had gotten the other night from Tate returned. He obviously cared very much about Chloe and she felt a small twinge of pain at what she didn't have.

She was lost in her own thoughts so that it wasn't until she heard Kate's and Chloe's simultaneous gasps that she realized the conversation had escalated and it felt as though Tate and Ryan could come to blows at any moment.

"I agree with Tate," Erin interrupted the men's discussion. She wasn't sure exactly what had been said, but she knew from personal experience that staying with Ryan was not in Chloe's best interests. All eyes turned to her.

"I don't think *you* are the right person to comment on propriety," Ryan rebuked.

She heard the gasps again, and she would have gasped, too, if she'd had any higher expectations of Ryan's opinion of her, but she didn't. If anything, it reinforced her decision to keep the knowledge of Jennie to herself.

"*Enough.* I appreciate everyone's concern, but I am an adult, capable of making my own decisions and deciding what is in my own best interests. Erin, are you sure I can't go back to my apartment as long as I don't overdo it?" Thank goodness for Chloe. Erin did her best to let go of Ryan's barb before turning back to her patient.

"Yes, I'm sure. With your low hemoglobin and naturally low blood pressure I think you are at high risk for dizziness and fainting and you shouldn't be alone." There, she had done what she had come to do, take care of Chloe. It was decided that Chloe would go and stay at Tate's and, to be honest, Erin was pleased. Tate was a good man. He cared for her, and maybe, just maybe, her recovery would bring them both together. Just because she was unlucky in love, it didn't mean that her friend couldn't find happiness.

She casually said her goodbyes and left the room, trying to make her escape without it being obvious.

"Erin."

She heard Ryan call out her name before she had made it a few feet from the door. She knew she had no choice but to stop for fear that their pending conversation became even more public than it was about to be.

"Ryan," she acknowledged, as she turned and watched as he quickly made up the distance between them.

"What did you think you were doing in there?" It wasn't hard to read the anger in his voice.

"Being insulted in front of my patient and my friends," she replied, before she could stop herself. What was it about Ryan that made her speak her mind and her feelings so freely?

Her words seemed to penetrate through him and the tension between them lowered. "I'm sorry."

At that moment she was more shocked than she had been in Chloe's room. She had been expecting an attack, anger, not the return of the Ryan she thought she'd once known, albeit briefly. "Thank you." She accepted his apology as best she could. "It wasn't about you. I think Chloe would be better off with Tate personally and professionally. It would hurt her professional reputation if she moved in with one of her staff physicians, no matter what the reason. Tate has nothing to do with her career."

She hoped he accepted her explanation and they were done talking. It hurt more than she would have liked it to—to be reminded of how perfect she had thought he was in Edinburgh.

"I talked with your ex-husband this morning." She was acutely aware of him waiting for her reaction to his statement.

"And..."

"And what?"

"There is something you are either waiting to say or are not saying. Either way, I have nothing to do with Kevin and am not responsible for his behavior, past or present. Are we done here?"

He paused and she could feel his visual assessment of her. The black pencil skirt and turquoise blouse she had chosen now felt more revealing than it had looked in the mirror that morning. She tucked her hair behind her ear before looking him in the eye with raised brows.

"You were right about Sabrina being lucky," he confessed.

Before she could respond to what had almost sounded like an apology, he walked away from her.

CHAPTER EIGHT

ERIN WALKED THROUGH the emergency department with her normal sense of unease heightened. She hadn't had time to check who the attending emergency physician was. She was still counting the days until she was done at Boston General and holding her breath that her secret would remain hidden from Ryan.

As the chief resident, Erin ran her own clinic, filled with patients she took primary responsibility for. Tara, an infertility patient, had called that morning with all the classic symptoms of hyperstimulation syndrome, a condition in which as a result of fertility treatments, overstimulated ovaries caused excess fluid all over the body. Normally she would see all her patients in clinic, well away from Ryan in the emergency department, but Tara had sounded sick on the phone and Erin was worried she was going to need to be more closely monitored.

That morning she had chosen a fitted, knee-length yellow dress with a boat neck, which she had paired with her favorite string of black beads and black slingback low-rise heels. It was perfect for clinic, but she looked and felt out of place in the emergency department.

"Has Tara Compton arrived yet?" she asked the main unit clerk.

"Yes, Dr. Madden, she's in treatment room four."

Erin's assessment had been right. If Tara's symptoms had been mild she would have been placed in one of the lesser acuity rooms. She shook her head. She shouldn't have triggered her ovaries and done the retrieval. She had known throughout Tara's treatment cycle that this was a risk. Her ovaries had responded too well to the medication she'd received and had swelled beyond normal size. But Tara had begged her. Her husband had severe infertility problems and in vitro fertilization had been their only hope of pregnancy. They had saved for five years and this cycle was their only shot at a family. So Erin had persisted and performed the egg retrieval earlier in the week, doing everything she could to lower the risk, but it hadn't been enough.

She walked into the room and struggled to keep her feelings inside. Tara looked very unwell, sitting upright in bed and leaning forward as she struggled to catch her breath. Her abdomen was visibly swollen, so much so that she already looked six months pregnant. Erin glanced at the monitor screen displaying her patient's vitals. Tara's blood pressure was low and her respiratory and heart rates were both above normal.

"Hi, Tara," she greeted her, trying to keep any sense of alarm from her voice.

"Dr. Madden, I don't feel well." Erin noticed that she sounded breathless trying to complete the simple sentence.

"I know," Erin empathized. She already knew Tara

and her history well, so she directed her attention to the immediate problem. "When did this start?"

"Yesterday."

"What is bothering you most?"

"I can't seem to catch my breath and my stomach is hard and swollen."

Erin listened to her chest, noting the decreased breath sound at her lung bases. She tapped her fingers on the base of the lung fields, noting the fullness. With the help of Tara's husband she lowered her onto her back. "I won't keep you here long," she reassured her, aware of the panic in her patient's eyes.

She placed her hands on Tara's abdomen. Uncovered, it looked worse, and Erin estimated there were at least five liters of fluid present. She was able to feel the shift of fluid against her hand as she pushed on one side. With care she helped Tara up again, trying to ease her labored breathing.

She peeked out of the room's curtain and got the attention of one of the nurses assigned to the treatment area. "We need to get some bloodwork and a chest X-ray, stat."

"What would you like, Dr. Madden?"

"Complete blood count, electrolytes, creatinine, prothombin time, prolonged prothombin time, liver enzymes and three views of the chest. Once the blood is drawn and X-ray is done, we are going to set up for an abdominal paracentesis and bedside ultrasound." She held her breath for a moment. "Who is the attending physician in Emergency today?"

"Dr. Callum is on until four this afternoon."

It wasn't what she wanted to hear, but she had few other options.

"Thank you."

She went back into the treatment room to explain the plan to Tara and her husband and then went in search of Ryan. She didn't have to look for long before she found him. He was standing at the physicians' desk, charting.

"Dr. Callum," she addressed him, her only goal to keep this conversation professional.

She saw the muscles in his back and shoulders tense before he turned to meet her eye. She couldn't help but notice how the dark navy of his hospital scrubs complemented his eyes.

"Erin, you can call me Ryan."

"I need your help with a patient."

"What do you have?"

"A twenty-eight-year-old woman with severe ovarian hyperstimulation syndrome She has significant ascites and I need help with a paracentesis."

"What do you need me for?"

"I can't do the procedure blind. I can't risk accidentally puncturing one of the ovaries. I need another physician to do a simultaneous bedside ultrasound so that I can see where I'm going."

"Okay, call me when you're set up and ready."

Thirty minutes later she reviewed all the results and made plans to admit Tara to hospital. She had ordered supplemental oxygen and intravenous fluids to make up for the fluids that were accumulating in her abdomen. She had all the supplies ready and she asked the nurse to get Ryan.

He walked into the room and took his place on the opposite side of the bed from her. "Hi, I'm Dr. Callum. I'm going to be assisting Dr. Madden with the procedure."

Erin wasn't sure why, but the anxiety reaction she had felt for the past two years with regard to Ryan didn't reappear. In fact, the trepidation she had over the upcoming procedure was dissipating. "Okay, Tara, I'm just going to wash your abdomen with this sterile solution. It's really important you keep your hands by your sides and not touch any of the drapes I'm going to cover you with."

She performed the described actions and then looked at Ryan, who nodded his understanding. With the ultrasound probe sterilely draped, he scanned her abdomen. Erin interpreted the black-and-white images on the screen for both Ryan's and Tara's benefit. She could see the black of the accumulated fluid and the outlines of the enlarged ovaries.

"Can you measure the ovarian cysts, please?"

She watched as he did what she asked. "The left side is twelve centimeters and the right side is ten centimeters."

"Thank you."

"Is that big?" Tara asked, an obvious look of fear present in her eyes.

"It meets the criteria for severe," Erin answered. "Now you are going to feel the small burn of the freezing before I do the poke to drain the fluid. Dr. Callum, can you stay centered on the pocket on the left?"

"Yes."

With a precise and quick motion she inserted the needle into Tara's abdomen, quickly enough to limit the discomfort but slowly enough that she could see the opacity of the tip of the needle as it appeared on the screen. As soon as she confirmed placement she removed the sharp tip, leaving the thin plastic catheter that had overlain the needle, and set up the tubing to the suction canisters. She was rewarded as straw-colored fluid began to drain. Then all there was to do was to sit at the bedside and wait.

"Dr. Madden," Tara's voice interrupted her thoughts.

"Yes?"

"Are we still going to be able to do the transfer?" Tara asked, though her tone made Erin believe she already suspected the answer to the question.

"No, we can't. You are pretty sick right now. If we put your fertilized embryos back, it is only going to worsen your condition."

Tears filled the other woman's eyes and began to fall down her face. "I don't care about me. I want a baby." It was an explanation Erin understood perfectly.

Holding the catheter, she contaminated her other hand by taking Tara's. "You will have a baby. It's just going to take a little more time. We'll freeze these embryos and when you are better and ready we'll transfer them back. The most important person to a baby is its mama, and we need to think of you first."

"Are you sure?"

"Yes, I'm one hundred percent sure."

It took twenty minutes, but eventually Erin had removed the bulk of the fluid. Afterward Tara was able to breathe more easily and appeared much more comfortable. She still needed to remain in hospital, but with supportive care was on her way to recovery.

"Thank you, Dr. Callum," Erin said to Ryan, as she pulled the catheter. He nodded at her and left. She stayed with Tara for a while longer, reviewing her plan for her hospitalization and also her future fertility treatments.

"You were good in there." Ryan's voice met her as she left the room.

"Thank you."

"I think we need to talk."

"I thought you had said everything you needed to say to me in Scotland." She needed him to know that he had hurt her and she wasn't prepared to let it happen again.

"Meet me at five in the lobby?"

She felt lost for words to respond to his request and he took her silence as acceptance as he walked away from her and back to work.

She couldn't believe it herself as she strolled into the lobby of Boston General. She had tried to talk herself out of meeting Ryan but hadn't been able to do it. She felt as though she owed him something, her guilt over keeping Jennie a secret from him growing with every kind word and reminder of the man she had once thought he was. But she still couldn't get past the way they had ended in Scotland. The one-hundred-and-eighty-degree turn from the man he had been had left her lost for how to feel about him. She had memories of the time they had spent together before the symposium, but everything that was happy in her mind had been colored by what had come after.

She saw him sitting in a chair by the large glass wall that defined the atrium's entrance. He had changed and for the first time since she had seen him the night of Chloe's collapse he was not in scrubs. She stopped halfway to him and let her mind process the effect, and at that moment he turned and it was completed. It was the same man she had been with in Scotland and she had to mentally give herself a shake to remind her that he actually wasn't. She couldn't move from her spot as she watched him come to her.

"Let's get out of here."

She needed time to sort herself out so she mutely followed him.

Ten minutes later she slid into a booth at a wine bar a few blocks from the hospital. It wasn't the Irish pub frequented by most of the hospital staff and Erin was grateful for the privacy. They both ordered from the server and again Erin was reminded of their night in Edinburgh and she couldn't help but feel the difference at the jarring discomfort she was feeling at that moment from the ease of that long-ago night.

"I thought we should say what we need to say to each other, as it seems we are going to be working together," Ryan opened.

"You have more you want to say?" Erin asked, still feeling intensely defensive from his previous attack on her.

He drew in his breath and seemed to put her comment aside. "I was surprised to learn who you were in Edinburgh. I didn't handle it well."

"How should you have handled it?" Why was she waiting for a certain response?

"I should have just walked away. I shouldn't have waged a personal attack on you."

So he hadn't known who she was. A sense of relief passed through her but she still couldn't get past his words. It felt like the classic feedback you got in medical school, a good comment mixed with the bad. Funny how, despite the good, she always focused on the negative part. "But you still would have walked away?"

"Yes." There was no hesitation in his response.

"Why?" It was the question she had asked herself after her anger toward him had left enough room for other emotions.

"I can't be with a woman like you."

"Like me?" She knew she was prying words out of his mouth that he didn't want to say, but she hadn't opened this door, he had.

He took a sip from his beer before he looked her in the eye. "A woman who is willing to be the other woman."

Part of her wanted to tell him her side. That she'd had no knowledge of his sister until she'd already been trapped on a path she had never intended. But it bothered her both that she wanted him to think better of her and that she had to defend herself. In the end what had happened between them hadn't all been about her. "You were not entirely honest with me."

"Yes. I'm sorry"

"Why?"

"At the time I had no idea how important it would be."

She wanted to tell him how much she valued honesty. How it was the most important thing to her, but she couldn't take that stand now when she knew she was prepared to lie about their daughter. "You are walking on a slippery slope."

"I know. That's my punishment."

"I don't see how that is a punishment."

"You're making it hard to stand my ground. Even now, just sitting here talking to you, I have to constantly remind myself of the pain you caused my sister."

"And if you don't?"

"If I don't all I see is the woman I met in Scotland who seemed so perfect and with whom I spent the best night of my adult life."

She felt heat rise through her body and she pulled at the neck of her dress before stopping the telling movement and instead reaching for a large sip from her chilled white wine. Ryan felt the same way about that night as she did. What would happen if she did explain her past with Kevin?

When she looked up he was staring at her and she felt lost in the blue of his eyes. As if it were a different time, he reached out, his hand covering hers. "But it is a different time and we are different people, Erin. No woman, no matter how tempting, would ever lead me to betray my sister."

And just like that his hand was gone and she felt the loss as intensely as she had in Scotland. The thoughts of telling him the truth about her past and the truth about her present evaporated. He had just told her that, no matter what, she would never have a place in his life, his family, and she wasn't prepared to take the risk of her daughter being taken to a family she would be excluded from.

"You don't have to worry for long. Temptation has less than two months left at Boston General and then I'm moving for a fellowship in California with no plans to return."

"You don't have to move because of me."

How could he not understand? "I have to move precisely because of people like you. I'm not going to let the mistake of my marriage to Kevin ruin the rest of my life. Thank you for the drink."

She rose from the booth and left the restaurant, not wanting to hear any more. She was a few meters from the restaurant's door when she heard him call her name and she stopped. She felt his hand on her shoulder and she turned toward him. She didn't even recognize his intention before his mouth was on hers and her face was being cradled between his hands. While the kiss started hard and passionate, it progressed to a tender touch before his lips left hers.

"I'm not sure what we were, but I still felt we deserved a proper goodbye."

She looked up at him, wondering if it was worth the risk, hoping they had another outcome, but then panicked. No man was more important than her daughter. "Goodbye," she said, and with strength she hadn't known she had she walked away from him.

CHAPTER NINE

"Dr. Callum."

Ryan looked up from the chart he had been completing. Amanda, the triage nurse for the evening shift, was standing in front of him.

"Emergency Medical Services has just brought in an eleven-year-old girl with ten out of ten abdominal pain. She's tachycardic, but stable, but overall looks really distressed. I've put her in treatment room two and I was hoping you could see her as soon as possible yourself."

It wasn't often he got requests like these. He normally gave the medical student or resident he was working with the opportunity to see the patient first then review his or her findings. He could tell, though, that Amanda was really worried, and he knew that she didn't worry often.

"I'll see her right now."

He walked the short distance to the treatment area and to room two. He opened the door to find what Amanda had described: an eleven-year-old girl, crying, her whole body rigid in an attempt not to move.

"Hello, I'm Dr. Ryan Callum, the staff emergency

physician on this evening." He introduced himself as he shook hands with each of the girl's worried parents.

"What's your name?" he asked the girl.

"Lauren."

He could tell she was trying to be grown-up and answer his questions.

"Okay, Lauren, when did your stomach start to hurt?"

"At gymnastics," she answered.

He had already come to that conclusion judging by the leotard she was wearing.

"Did you have any pain before gymnastics?"

"No, it came on all of a sudden when I dismounted from the balance beam."

"Okay," he tried to soothe her, "have you ever had pain like this before?"

"No, but it hurts so bad." She started to sob and the minute the cry racked her body she sobbed harder with the movement, perpetuating a painful cycle.

"Does she have any allergies?" he asked her parents.

"No," they both answered.

"How much does she weigh?"

"She's about seventy-five pounds," her mother responded immediately.

"I'll be right back." Ryan walked to the drug room, using his security card to log in to the automated system. He selected Lauren from the list of registered patients and then typed in her weight, as she was a pediatric patient who required all her medication adjusted for her size. He selected the painkiller and waited as the correct drawer was unlocked before withdrawing the medication.

"Okay, Lauren, I'm going to give you some medication to help make you feel better." He waited to see her reaction and was worried when she didn't question the needle he was holding. Most children wouldn't agree to a needle for anything, so the fact that she was ambivalent was a sign of just how much pain the young girl was in. He injected the medication slowly through her intravenous line so she wouldn't have to feel any discomfort with the injection. He waited until he saw her face relax to know the medication had taken effect.

"Lauren, does it hurt more to move or to stay still?"

"Move."

"Can you point to me where you feel the most pain?"

With the most careful movement he had ever seen she moved her hand, not disturbing the rest of her body, and pointed to her lower left side. "I think I'm going to be sick." With a grimace of pain spreading across her face, she rolled to her side. He managed to move quickly for a plastic basin before she vomited.

He helped support her weight and when she was done gently rolled her onto her back, leaving her to rest before redirecting his attention on her parents.

"Does she have any medical problems?"

"No," her mother answered quickly, clearly alarmed by the state of her daughter.

"Any surgeries in the past? Does she take any medications?"

"No, she's always been a very healthy little girl." He could see tears of fear starting to well up in her eyes.

He nodded in acknowledgment and carefully uncovered the girl's abdomen. He touched the upper right half, as far from the spot she had indicated as he could. Her stomach was as rigid as her posture, and she flinched when he palpated gently, but jumped and cried out when he let go.

"It's going to be okay, Mrs. Connor. Lauren is right where she needs to be. I'm going to order a few tests, including an ultrasound, and we will keep on top of her pain and nausea medication so that we can get her as comfortable as possible. Please don't give her anything to eat or drink until I tell you it's okay."

He walked out of the room and found the attending nurse. He glanced at the clock before picking up the phone and dialing the hospital switchboard. "It's Dr. Callum from Emergency. Can you please page the chief resident from General Surgery urgently for me."

"Yes, Dr. Callum. Do you want to stay on the line?"

"Yes."

Two minutes later. "This is Dr. Kate Spence."

"Kate, it's Ryan Callum from Emergency. I have a healthy eleven-year-old girl with a surgical abdomen following sudden onset left lower quadrant pain. She's stable and we are starting with investigations now, but I wanted you to know before you went home for the evening."

"Thanks for the heads-up. I'll be down shortly."

Ryan paced the emergency department, checking on his active patients and waiting for Lauren's results to come in. Kate Spence had come and gone. She agreed with his assessment but wanted to wait for more information before rushing to the operating room.

"Ryan." Erin's voice cut through his thoughts of the girl and started a new one—how was it possible that she had avoided him for so long when now it felt as if their careers were throwing them together at every chance it got? She was wearing scrubs, her hair pulled back and covered by a scrub hat made with purple fabric.

"Kate called me. All pediatric consultations go direct to the chief resident. The scan of Lauren Connor's abdomen shows classic signs of ovarian torsion. She has a left-sided eight-centimeter cyst that has twisted on itself, cutting off blood supply to the ovary and causing it to swell. I'm going to go and talk to her parents and get consent for the operating room. I thought you should know."

"I'll come with you."

She didn't object and he followed her toward Lauren's room. Both parents stood as they entered. Lauren was still lying still, her eyes closed, with occasional moans of pain.

"Mr. and Mrs. Connor, I'm Dr. Madden, the chief resident from Gynecology. The CT scan of your daughter's abdomen shows that her left ovary has become twisted on itself, cutting off its blood supply. She's having pain because it can't drain or receive fresh blood. We need to take her to the operating room and fix it."

"Are you going to take out her ovary?" Mrs. Connor asked, her horror at the idea obvious.

"No. In a child Lauren's age we often untwist it and hope that it heals. If possible we can try to tack the ovary to reduce her risk of it happening again, but we won't proceed with anything that may compromise the health of the ovary."

Ryan alternated his gaze between Lauren, her parents and Erin. He found her words reassuring and his worry for Lauren dissipated. He knew that Erin would do everything she could to save the ovary, the same way she had struggled to save Chloe's Fallopian tube.

"What are we looking at for her recovery?" Mr. Connor asked.

"Hopefully two days in hospital and then a couple of weeks. We are going to try to get her surgery done using a camera and a few incisions that are all less than one centimeter. It will make her postoperative pain a lot less and she will have barely noticeable scars."

"Are you doing it?" the mother asked.

"Yes," Erin answered definitively.

"Good."

Erin crossed the room toward the head of Lauren's bed. "Lauren, I'm not sure how much you heard of what your parents and I just talked about. You're going to come with me and have a nap and while you're sleeping I'm going to take away the pain and make you feel better." She gently reached out and rested her hand on the girl's shoulder for a few moments before walking away.

"She'll be going to the operating room within the hour. There's a family waiting room outside the operating room and she'll go to the pediatric area of the recovery room so that you both can come in and see her as soon as possible."

"Are you a mother, Dr. Madden?" Ryan's attention rocketed to Erin. It was an innocent question. He was often asked if he was a parent when he was treating children, but he knew that for Erin it was a painful one. He looked over at her and she looked absolutely stricken by the question, her pallor evident against the dark blue of her scrubs, her eyes wide.

"Dr. Madden is an excellent surgeon. You're lucky to have her involved in Lauren's care. Dr. Madden, I'll help get Lauren ready for the operation if you want to go upstairs and organize the operating room."

He wasn't expecting a look of gratitude, but Erin just stared at him questioningly before she returned to her planned course of action.

"I'll see you both soon." And she left the room.

Erin exhaled for what felt like the first time since she'd met Lauren Connor. The young girl was slowly waking in the recovery room and the surgery had been a success. She had untwisted the dark swollen ovary and had waited patiently until she'd seen some evidence that the blood vessels feeding it were going to be able to restore it. Before the case she had called home to talk to Jennie's nanny and if she hurried she would still be able to give Jennie her bath and put her to bed.

"How did it go?" She turned and saw Ryan on the other side of the counter she was sitting at. His deflection of Mrs. Connor's question had taken her aback, both by his gallantry and by the guilt that had overcome her when her lie to him had come too close to the surface.

"Great. We did everything laparoscopically and I think the ovary will heal normally. We left the cyst and will follow her closely until it resolves. She's resting comfortably in the pediatric area if you want to see her." She hoped he would as she didn't feel she could face him much longer, knowing her secret.

"You would have been a good mother."

Her mouth felt completely dry as she watched Ryan walk away toward Lauren. She didn't like deceiving him and her doubts in herself were growing by the minute. It was easier when he was judging her, declaring her a lesser and immoral person. Now he was supportive and still attracted to her, she was at a complete loss at how to deal with all the feelings she had toward him. Was she still attracted to him? Yes. The kiss outside the restaurant had left no room for doubt. She also respected him—it was hard not to, knowing his professional reputation and having watched him take care of Chloe and his other patients. But above everything else she was still hurt by him. Hurt that he couldn't see the truth about who she was and that he thought the worst of her. Was she so hurt that she was keeping Jennie from him to hurt him, too? No, she had told herself and reminded herself again.

Erin looked down at her pager and dialed the number.

"Erin, it's Dr. Thomas. If you have a minute I'd like you to come see your friend Chloe in follow-up."

"Is everything okay?" It didn't make sense to her that she would be called for what should be a routine follow-up.

"Just come."

She headed directly to the hospital's outpatient clinic space. Dr. Thomas simply handed her the chart with Chloe's most recent bloodwork on the front page. "It would be a great case for your upcoming board exams. She's in exam room three. Why don't you go see her and do a bedside ultrasound and let me know?"

She nodded in agreement, still not believing what she was reading. She needed to calm herself before she panicked Chloe. She knocked on the door and waited a minute before letting herself in.

"Hey, Chloe. Dr. Thomas paged me to let me know you were in for your follow-up and asked me to come see you. It's hard to believe it has already been six weeks. How are you feeling?"

Chloe was sitting on the exam table, the paper drape drawn over her lap, looking tired but still considerably better than the last time Erin had seen her.

"Okay. Good days and bad days, I guess. I went back to work this week and that has helped. But I haven't been studying nearly as much as I planned and will be more than happy when this exam is done. I'm surprised to see you still at work. I would have thought you would have been off studying, too."

"You know what they say about the best intentions."

"Well, I'm here, aren't I?" She heard the sadness in Chloe's voice and recognized it as the same she had felt after her own miscarriage.

"How are you feeling *really*?" Erin asked, pulling the stool from the end of the bed so she could sit and talk to her friend.

"Disappointed, frustrated—take your pick. It's hard to admit that I made such a mistake, both in getting pregnant and then not even having the medical sense to realize it. I want to be able to move past it, but I can't seem to get back to normal. I still feel tired, nauseated, and I have no control over my emotions, which just leads to more frustration."

Erin looked down again at the bloodwork results. "You may be being slightly hard on yourself."

"I know."

"Chloe, would it be okay if I examined your abdomen and we did a quick bedside ultrasound?" She tried to be reassuring but knew that Chloe knew enough to know that this was not routine.

"Of course. What are you not saying, Erin?"

Erin couldn't answer. Instead she was trying to convince herself that she wasn't feeling what she was feeling. The elevation of Chloe's uterus two centimeters above her pubic bone was consistent with a fourteen-week pregnancy.

"Your bloodwork from this morning shows a persistently elevated beta HCG."

"What does that mean?" Chloe was as confused as Erin had been when she had seen the result.

"It shouldn't still be elevated. If we had performed a salpingostomy and removed only the ectopic pregnancy then some residual placenta might be present in the Fallopian tube, leading to the elevated hormone level, but..."

"But?"

"But your tube had ruptured and we were unable to control the bleeding from the rupture site, so we performed an open right salpingectomy, removing the entire Fallopian tube. The pathology report confirmed the presence of the pregnancy. So your beta HCG shouldn't still be elevated, unless..." She couldn't believe she was about to say this.

"Unless what?"

"Chloe, you may not be able to move on. I think you are still pregnant."

"I don't understand."

"I think your pregnancy was a heterotopic pregnancy. One inside the Fallopian tube and one in the uterus. It's a rare condition, occurring in only one in every five to thirty thousand pregnancies." She wasn't sure who was in more shock, her or Chloe.

"How do we find out for sure?" Chloe asked.

"We look."

And without further discussion Erin squeezed warmed jelly onto Chloe's abdomen and placed the ultrasound probe against her. She saw everything instantly. The uterus filled with amniotic fluid and inside a baby.

"A baby..." Chloe stated with awe.

"Your baby," Erin confirmed. "I'm just going to do some measurements to date the pregnancy."

"There is only one date possible."

Erin smiled as she went along her routine, measuring the baby's head, abdomen and thigh to estimate the gestational age.

"Which makes you about fourteen weeks along."

"Does everything look okay?" Chloe asked.

Erin thought through the complexity of Chloe's case, the heterotopic pregnancy and the complications and medications involved in her initial surgery. Dr. Thomas was right, she was like a hard board exam question. Still, her job wasn't to get lost in the academics; she needed to focus on supporting Chloe.

"As much as I can see right now, everything looks okay, but we're going to need to do some investigations.

You received a lot of blood products that they initially didn't have time to match against your own blood screen. You also received some medication we don't recommend in pregnancy, but right now you have a baby."

"A baby..."

"How do you feel about that, Chloe?"

They both turned to watch the monitor and the baby's activity. Erin remembered when she had first seen Jennie and how special it had been to hear her heartbeat for the first time. She moved the ultrasound cursor over the baby's heartbeat and the rapid sound filled the room.

"Wonderful."

"Okay, so we will just go from here. I am going to give you a requisition for prenatal bloodwork and another ultrasound in four weeks' time so we can look at the rest of the baby's anatomy."

"Erin, is it weird that I am excited and terrified at the same time?"

Erin thought back to when she had finally realized she was pregnant with Jennie.

"No, I remember that feeling well. You're going to be a wonderful mother, Chloe. Congratulations."

CHAPTER TEN

A WEEK OF sleepless nights had done nothing to strengthen Ryan's resolve. He hadn't seen Erin since she had taken care of Lauren Connor, but she still filled his waking thoughts and his dreams. He struggled with his feelings toward her.

Watching her take care of the young girl had shown another side of her he had never seen. Amid her professional behavior she had also managed to show her maternal side. It was one more part of her he found disarming. If everything he knew about her was true, it was as though her pros and cons were balancing on a scale and he was worried that any minute the scale might tip to the positive side and he would be forced to choose between Erin and his sister.

If he had never learned about her past with Kevin he would be doing everything in his power to make her his, forever. But he couldn't live life based on what-ifs. It had almost been a relief to hear that she was leaving Boston, enough that he had let his resolve slip and had kissed her again, knowing the temptation she represented would soon be gone forever.

He knocked at Chloe's door and waited. He had promised Chloe that he would help her study for her upcoming board exams and had agreed to come to her while she was still recovering. At first that had been at Tate's and after she had moved home last week they had decided it was easier to keep meeting at her home.

"Hi," she greeted him, as she led him into the living room.

"How are you feeling?" he asked, as he watched her make her way slowly across the room and ease herself back onto the couch. It was hard to dismiss the clinician in him and just be Chloe's friend.

"I have good days and bad days, but Erin says that is normal."

Erin. He had almost convinced himself that he was here just to help Chloe but the moment she spoke Erin's name he knew he had deeper motives. "Have you already seen Erin in follow-up?"

"Yes, last week, and she calls at least once a day to check in on me. Can I get you something to drink?"

"Water, please." He should change the subject. He had already resigned himself to the fact that Erin was not suitable in his life and he should have nothing more to do with her.

"I didn't realize you two were close friends." Damn, guilt washed over him as he realized he was using Chloe to get information on Erin, but he couldn't resist. Erin was still an enigma to him and he needed to know more. Maybe then he would be able to reconcile the past and move on with his life.

"Erin is a pretty private person. I would be, too, if I had gone through everything she has."

"You mean her marriage to Kevin Dufour?"

"I'm not sure I would call that a marriage."

"What do you mean?"

"I mean Kevin Dufour never for one day acted like he was married. I moved to Boston after they were married and the fact that he had a wife never once kept him from making advances on me or any other woman who walked by him."

Ryan inhaled and exhaled slowly as he processed Chloe's words. Did the fact that Kevin was a serial philanderer change things? Certainly it questioned the theory that he had been lured away from a happily committed relationship, as Sabrina had suggested. "Did Erin know?"

Chloe stopped, her facial expression changing, and all of sudden he felt as if he was the one being evaluated. What had started as casual conversation between friends had definitely changed. She paused before she finally answered him. "Eventually, but she didn't see it for a long time. I was with her the day she found a note in her locker anonymously telling her of her husband's affair with the hospital pharmacist."

He winced, both at Chloe's words and at once again wishing he could take back the words he had spoken in anger in Scotland. *You got what you deserved.* If he'd known then what he knew now he never would have spoken them. He murmured under his breath to himself, *"Callous bastard..."* That was how he had behaved.

"There are a lot more words I would use to describe

Kevin Dufour, but I don't waste my time and neither does Erin. I'm friends with her because I admire her, Ryan. She walked away from her marriage with her head held high and is an incredible mother to Jennie."

Water lodged in his windpipe and he coughed violently in response. Erin? A mother? Had he heard Chloe correctly? Confusion coursed through him and he felt as if his chest was being crushed with a vise.

"Erin's a mother?"

"Yes, she has a one-year-old daughter named Jennie. She's beautiful."

One. Erin's daughter was one. His mind flashed back to their night together and the broken condom and Erin's confession. He would have sworn on his life that her infertility had been the thing she hadn't deceived him about. "Did she adopt?"

If he hadn't gotten Chloe's attention before he definitely had it now and he had shown his hand, revealing his knowledge of her infertility. "I didn't realize you knew Erin."

"I know of her from her marriage to Kevin." As much as he didn't like lying to Chloe, he also knew that if Erin hadn't told Chloe about the two of them she would not appreciate Ryan being the one to do so.

"But you knew about her infertility?" Chloe asked skeptically.

"Yes." He wasn't prepared to fabricate a story so instead he acknowledged the truth.

Chloe was silent for a long time before she finally began speaking. "No, she got pregnant around the same time as her divorce became final. Not surprisingly,

Kevin has taken no responsibility for the baby, so Erin is a single mother and she's wonderful at it. Jennie is the happiest, most loved baby I have ever seen."

Ryan felt his mind and heart race. Kevin had taken no responsibility for the baby. Was there a reason for that beyond his obvious selfish character flaws? He needed to know more, and he needed to know more now. He looked up at Chloe and knew that she had no more answers for him. There was also no way he was going to be able to sit and focus on helping her study for the next hour. He needed answers now and to get them he needed to talk to Erin.

"Chloe, I just realized there is something I need to tie up back at the hospital urgently. Can I give you a rain check on today and we can try again later on in the week?"

"Sure," she answered, still looking puzzled but not questioning him further.

"Don't worry about getting up. I'll let myself out." He walked back to the large door and looked back at Chloe once more, wondering if she had just been the one to tell him he had a daughter.

Erin led afternoon rounds, her team of junior residents and medical students gathered in the ward's conference room giving verbal updates on the patients.

"How is Mrs. Campbell?" she asked one of the medical students who had just returned from seeing the patient. It was routine to allow the junior residents and medical students independent learning with the patients but she always laid her eyes on every single patient before leaving for the day.

"She's doing better. She was able to walk around the ward this afternoon and tolerated the introduction of food this afternoon."

"Great. Mrs. Gregg?"

"She'll be ready and wanting to be discharged by tomorrow morning," her junior resident responded.

The door to the conference room swung open and the discussion stopped as Ryan entered, walking directly toward her. He wasn't in scrubs but was dressed in a taupe fitted T-shirt and designer denim. He obviously wasn't working.

"I need to talk to you." She wasn't sure if it was clear to the others in the room but it was clear to her that this need did not stem from anything regarding a patient. She looked at her team and tried to figure out how to handle this, instantly worried about what Ryan wanted and his obvious sense of urgency.

"We're just finishing afternoon rounds. I can talk to you in about thirty minutes."

He didn't take her up on her offer. Instead he leaned closer, his voice quieter but no less insistent. "It needs to be now, and I think we should probably talk alone."

She looked out again at their audience, knowing she was powerless to stop this conversation from happening. The least she could do was have it privately.

"Ruth, please finish afternoon rounds while I speak with Dr. Callum. If you have any concerns, please let the on-call resident for the evening know."

She walked from the room, aware that Ryan was following her. She heard him inhale, about to begin their conversation, but she stopped him. "Not here."

She walked farther down the hall until she reached an empty patient room, waiting for him to enter and then closing the door behind her. When she turned back to look at him she knew he knew.

"Tell me about Jennie."

Blood rushed to her ears and she could hear each part of her heart beat as if in slow motion, though she knew it was racing. It didn't even matter how he knew—he knew and all her plans and her life changed now.

"Jennie is my daughter."

"I think you know there is a lot more that I am asking."

She wiped her palms against fitted black slacks before looking up at him. She knew he wasn't going to let this go. She had to make a decision now. How she handled things from here would make all the difference.

"Do you want a paternity test?" It wasn't what he had been expecting. But it was the only way she could buy some time until he found out the truth.

Ryan went from standing to sitting on the empty bed, his hand running through his hair. "So there is the possibility she's mine?"

"Yes." More than a possibility, she couldn't be anyone else's.

"And you didn't tell me?"

"You'd already told me you can't be with a woman like me."

"That has no bearing on whether or not you have been lying and keeping my daughter from me, Erin."

She knew he was angry and didn't want to antagonize him. After she had condemned him in Scotland for lying by omission, she had no ground to stand on.

"Jennie and I are a package deal, Ryan." He needed to know that. That she would never be separated from her daughter.

"You're not going to California."

"What?" She was shocked by the abrupt change in focus.

"You heard me. If Jennie is my daughter you are not taking her across the country away from me."

She wasn't surprised. Hadn't she known that if Ryan knew about Jennie he would want to be involved? Wasn't that one of the reasons she hadn't told him in the first place? She thought of her fellowship and how long and hard she had worked to earn it. She was amazed that she wasn't going to fight him; Jennie was the most important thing in the world to her and her career was a distant second. From this minute on she needed to do everything possible to prove to Ryan that she wasn't the immoral other woman he believed her to be. She needed him to see who she really was then maybe he wouldn't try to take Jennie away.

"Okay."

She could tell he was ready to argue with her and was not expecting her acquiescence.

"I want to meet her."

"Now?" she asked. "Do you want to wait for the test results instead?"

"No. If she is mine, I don't want to waste another minute apart."

This time she nodded her agreement. She knew she couldn't object because she knew the test results were going to reveal just that. From this moment on everything hinged on him seeing her for the person she was. Maybe even seeing her with Jennie would make him think twice about possible custody demands.

"I need to check on a few of my patients and then we can go."

"I'll wait for you."

She did her afternoon rounds in a daze, hoping that her team had done a good job because she felt as if today she could miss something. Would Ryan see what she saw when she looked at Jennie? His own smaller, feminine reflection looking back at him? It was a chance she was going to have to take.

She finished up in twenty minutes and met him outside the ward's doors. They walked in silence down the hospital corridor toward the parking garage. "You'll need my address. I live at 90 Winchester Avenue."

"I'll follow you there."

Boston traffic was typically heavy, but she wasn't surprised when he didn't lose her tail on the way home. She motioned toward visitors' parking and waited for him at her building's elevator.

"You live in an apartment?"

She found herself bristling at his question but reminded herself she needed to keep her cool. "Yes, I decided that it was better to live closer to the hospital so that I could spend more time with Jennie rather than commuting. The building has a lovely children's play park that Jennie goes to daily."

"Who watches her while you're working?"

"Her nanny, Carolyn. She's been with us since Jennie was three months old and is wonderful with her."

He didn't ask her any more questions as they rode up in the elevator together. She walked to the end of the hallway and unlocked the door to her three-bedroom apartment. From the entry she walked to the combined open dining, kitchen and living room. She saw Jennie playing with her wooden puzzle on her play mat in the living room and, as always, the best part of her day was watching her daughter's face light up when she saw her. "Mum, mum, mum, mum," Jennie repeated, as she pushed herself onto her pudgy legs and with her usual unsteady walk made her way to Erin. Her arms extended upward the moment she ran into Erin's legs.

"Hello, my sweetheart." She brushed her daughter's brown hair back and kissed her cheek.

Carolyn emerged from the kitchen, pausing only slightly at the sight of Ryan. Erin had never before brought a man home and she was impressed that Carolyn was handling the surprise so well.

"How was she today?" Erin asked.

"Great. She had her normal naps and we spent most of the afternoon at the park. Supper is ready in the kitchen for you both. I'll see you in the morning."

"Thanks, Carolyn."

The other woman let herself out and Erin turned back to Ryan, but his attention was entirely on Jennie, who seemed equally transfixed by the new person in her life.

Watching them together made Erin's heart cry and question every decision she had made since the moment she'd found out she was pregnant.

She shifted Jennie onto her hip. "This is mummy's friend Ryan."

His eyes broke from Jennie's and he looked up at her. She couldn't introduce him as her father, not yet. "Do you want to show Ryan your puzzle?"

She watched as Jennie evaluated Ryan and then nodded in agreement. She walked with Jennie over to the play mat, sitting them both on the floor and waiting for Ryan to do the same. He did, but he still seemed overwhelmed so Erin took the lead. "Show Ryan where the sun goes." And she handed Jennie the piece.

It was Jennie's favorite puzzle and she took no time to place the piece near its slot and then with the awkwardness of a toddler wiggled it in. She looked up at Ryan expectantly.

"You're a smart girl. Do you want to show me where the balloon goes?" He handed her the red, round puzzle piece. She reached out her little hand and took it from him, placing it in the same fashion as the previous piece and then looking back at him. "Good job."

Erin stayed silent as the two worked together to complete the rest of the puzzle. When they were finished two pairs of identical eyes looked up at her. "Would you like to stay for dinner?"

"Yes."

She lifted Jennie from the floor and carried her toward the eat-in kitchen, securing her in the high chair. Carolyn had prepared a large Cobb salad and Erin picked out small pieces for Jennie, putting them on her tray, and also served two plates for her and Ryan. She opened the fridge, holding up a bottle of wine, and Ryan nodded agreement and she poured two glasses, as well.

The meal was a typical one for Erin. Erin ate while at the same time watching Jennie get as much food on the floor and high chair as she did into her mouth. After dinner Ryan made no attempt to leave so she included him in their bathtime and bedtime rituals. "Good night, my love," she murmured sweetly, before gently covering her daughter. She closed the door and returned to the living room, where Ryan was seated on the couch.

She went to the fridge and refilled their glasses of wine before joining him.

"I don't know what to say to you. She's a happy, healthy, wonderful little girl and part of me is grateful and the other part of me will never forgive you for keeping her from me if she's mine."

It was honest and it was fair and she couldn't argue against his feelings. "I'm sorry."

"Why? How could you do something like this?"

She wished he would yell at her. Yelling would be better than hearing the pain come through his confused, calm voice.

"Do you know what Jennie means?" It wasn't the immediate answer to his question but the best explanation she had. "It means 'God is gracious' and ever since I found out I was pregnant that has been my only thought. Jennie is my miracle, the baby I desperately wanted and never thought I would have. Since the moment I found out I was pregnant I have been terrified of losing her."

"You thought I would take her away?"

"The last time I saw you you made it clear that I was the last woman in the world you would want to be the mother of your child."

"And that gave you the right to possibly keep me from my child?"

She did her best not to rise to his accusations. "It took away any sense of trust I had in you."

"So now we're even, except this time the consequences are considerably higher. Can you organize the paternity test?"

"Yes."

"I want answers, Erin."

Ryan stood in the hospital's large garden, waiting. It was the last day in June and the annual graduation ceremony for the finishing residents. The sun was hot but a breeze off the water dampened its effects.

As a member of the staff who was closely involved in resident education he had been asked to speak at the commencement, but his mind was distracted from his requested purpose. He looked through the crowd, waiting for Erin to arrive. Finally he spotted them. Erin was walking through the crowd, beautiful in a sleeveless midlength turquoise lace dress that was tied with a simple black ribbon belt. In her arms she held Jennie, who was wearing a vibrant red summer dress and was happily looking around the crowd. He had never seen Erin look more beautiful.

At his request Erin had sent him a photo of Jennie and since then he hadn't been able to keep his eyes off it. It would take time to do the paternity test and get the results back, and until then all he had were his gut instincts. Those instincts were telling him Jennie was his child. Her hair was darker than Erin's, more like his. She had Erin's nose and mouth but her eyes reminded him of his. Her smile was definitely her own. He couldn't imagine that a child so wonderful could ever be a part of Kevin Dufour.

When he wasn't thinking of Jennie he was thinking of Erin. He had heard her explanation and her apology, but that didn't change the anger he felt over missing the first one and a half years of his probable daughter's life. He still felt as if he didn't know her. He had thought he had known her in Edinburgh, but her past with Kevin had changed his mind. Now he had competing thoughts of her inside his head.

There was his first impression of the honest, caring woman he had taken to bed. Then she had been portrayed as the other woman, the image his sister had supplied. He had worked with her enough in the past few weeks to know she was a competent, dedicated physician, and he respected her for it. And now he knew her as a mother, which brought with it the double-edged sword of watching how wonderful she was with Jennie and knowing that she had deliberately kept her from him.

He walked up to the both of them. "Congratulations."

"Thank you."

"What are your plans now that you are no longer a resident?" He thought it was a casual question but he could tell that he had set her on edge.

"I did as you asked and declined the fellowship in

California. Very graciously Boston General has offered me a temporary position pending a formal hiring process."

He hadn't considered the ramifications to her career when he had insisted she not move to California. But it spoke volumes about her that the hospital had been willing to offer her a position on short notice. He hadn't been wrong about the type of physician he knew her to be.

She looked around before she resumed talking. "I talked to the laboratory and arranged the testing. You can go and give a blood sample at any time. All Jennie needs is a cheek swab that I'll do as soon as I can and then we should have the results in a few weeks."

He looked between the two, Jennie happy and content on her mother's hip, and knew what he needed to do. The two were a pair and he would never separate them for either of their sakes.

"I think we need to start again."

"I don't understand what you mean." Neither did he. What was it that he wanted from Erin?

"There was a time when both of us were very compatible and very much in sync. I think the best thing for Jennie would be if we tried to get back to a time where we trusted each other."

"I don't know if that's possible."

"It was once. Maybe it will be again if we actually take the time to get to know each other and put aside our joint pasts."

Erin wasn't prepared for Ryan's suggestion, but she couldn't fault his reasoning. There had been a time when she had trusted him, she just didn't know if it would be possible to get that back. Regardless, being given a chance to prove to him that she was a good mother before he learned for sure Jennie was his was an opportunity she wasn't going to let slip away.

"Okay, I think you're right but I have no idea where to even begin."

"What are you doing after this?"

"Jennie and I are going to the Hamptons. My parents have a house on the beach and now that I am done with residency I thought it would be the perfect time to take Jennie for a weekend away before I start my new position next week."

"I'll come with you."

"I don't know." She was hesitant. Was she ready to be alone with Ryan for that period of time? So far all their interactions in Boston had been centered around work or Jennie. The one and only time they had been alone together he had kissed her and even though it had been just once, every inch of her body remembered what she wanted from him. What would happen between them each night after Jennie went to bed?

"I do. We need this time together. When the results come back we need to have something to build on together."

He was more right than he knew so she couldn't disagree. "We are already packed and ready to go. If you don't mind driving with us, we can pick you up after the ceremony."

"Agreed." He looked down at the program he was holding. "You're speaking, as well?"

Erin smiled "Chloe and Kate nominated me to represent the chiefs. It's an honor."

"Then we'll pick up where we left off in Scotland. Hopefully this will go better than the last time we spoke in public together."

CHAPTER ELEVEN

ERIN PULLED UP to Ryan's brownstone townhouse and immediately became envious. The old brick facade and heritage trees that surrounded the yard were warm and inviting. She looked back at Jennie, who was playing happily in her car seat. This was going to be one of her homes and Erin felt emptiness at the possibility of Jennie and Ryan here together without her.

She saw Ryan lock the front door and head toward her with a small bag. He had changed into gray linen shorts and a teal-colored polo shirt. She could see glimpses of both tattoos and she knew without having to take a breath that he would smell of sweat and sunshine, just as he had the day they'd met. She wrapped her hair in her hands and lifted it from her neck to cool the heat from her body. She was happy she had changed into shorts and a loose-fitting thin cotton T-shirt.

She got out and met him at the hatch of her crossover. "Do you want to drive?"

"Sure." He took the keys from her outstretched hand. The brush of his fingers against hers was both surprisingly familiar and arousing. What had she gotten herself into?

The trip to the Hamptons was long, but not as arduous as she had worried it might have turned out to be. Jennie stayed content and they stopped frequently to let her move around and snack. She fell asleep and slept the last few hours as evening progressed into night. She and Ryan stuck to safe topics. Now that they had their careers in common there was a lot of shared experience to draw on for conversation. At times she even found herself forgetting that there should be awkwardness between them.

It was dark, the sky lit only by the stars as she directed them to her parents' beachfront house. "It's not large," she cautioned him. "My stepfather is a doctor, not the CEO of an international company."

Ryan laughed. "I know who your stepfather is, Erin. I believe he is my boss."

"True." And Erin joined his laughter.

As Ryan shut off the engine they both looked back at Jennie. Her head was tilted all the way to her shoulder and her eyes were shut, body relaxed. "I'll get her if you want to get the door," Erin suggested.

She unfastened the child belts and enjoyed the moment when the little girl relaxed back into her arms. Ryan held open the door for her and she went into the house, leaving it dark so as not to wake her. Ryan seemed to understand and he wordlessly emptied the back of her vehicle and brought in all their belongings.

The house had two bedrooms, a single bathroom and a combined living room and kitchen. Its interior was classic cape-side, with white wainscoting and wooden floors. It was furnished with comfortable light-colored furniture and accents of bright yellows and oranges. The best feature was the patio that looked out onto the beach and ocean. Most of Erin's happiest childhood memories had been made at the beach house and she had dreamed of the day when she could bring her own children here to share it.

"Where do you want her crib?" he asked. She had planned to take the master bedroom and set Jennie's portable crib in the other bedroom but she quickly realized that wasn't going to work with Ryan. His tall frame would never comfortably fit into one of the two single beds in the guest room.

"The room at the end of the hall on the left, please."

She waited until he reappeared in the hall before bringing Jennie to bed. She wasn't surprised that Ryan had had no problem assembling the complicated device and had found the sheets she had packed. She smiled at the turned-down blankets.

"I love you, my sweetheart," she murmured, as she kissed Jennie's cheek and laid her in the crib.

With a final look she left her to sleep. "She's beautiful when she sleeps," Ryan commented, still not making any move to leave the small bedroom.

Guilt swept her again. Should she tell him now that he was Jennie's father? For the first time since Scotland they'd had several hours together that had been not only pleasant but enjoyable, with no confrontations or accusations. What would happen if she told him now? Would he even believe her?

"Yes, she is," she answered simply.

He joined her in the kitchen. "Can I get you something? I had the caretaker stock the fridge for the weekend."

"I'll have whatever you're having."

She opened the fridge and discovered a bottle of champagne tied with a red ribbon and small envelope attached. She took out the bottle and opened the card.

Congratulations, Erin.
We couldn't be more proud of you.
Mom & Stephen.

She showed Ryan the card as a means of explanation. She didn't want him to think her plans had been to drink alone in the beach house for the weekend with a small child. "We should open it," he recommended.

She handed him the bottle and got out two wine glasses. Ryan opened the bottle, the pop and emerging foam reminding her that this was indeed an occasion to be celebrated.

"I should show you the patio. It's the best part of the house." She led the way through the French doors and took her place on one of the covered wicker patio chairs, drawing her legs under her. Ryan joined her, sitting across from her, in the still of the night.

"Congratulations, Erin. I know it hasn't been the easiest journey for you and you should be proud of your accomplishment."

She was stunned by the generosity of his comments. He could easily have argued that it didn't have to be as hard as she had made it if she had only made better choices, particularly asking for his help with their daughter. Instead he didn't and she felt proud of herself, as well.

"Thank you."

"You seem to be getting along better with your parents. The last time we talked you thought they were disappointed in you."

"It's amazing what having a child does to your point of view. I realized when I had Jennie that I could never be disappointed in her, just her choices. And looking back, I made some choices that were worthy of their disappointment."

"So being a single mother didn't add to their disappointment?"

"No, I was worried when I told them, but both Mom and Stephen were wonderful. I think, like me, they had lost hope of ever having a grandchild and they see Jennie as the wonderful miracle she is."

"You call your stepfather Stephen?"

"Yes. My mother remarried when I was fourteen. She was ready and I wasn't. I loved my dad—he was my hero—and there was only ever one of him."

Through the darkness she could see Ryan's face and knew what he was thinking. They were the same thoughts she was having now. How could she deprive Jennie of a father when losing hers had been so hard for her?

She took another sip from her glass and let the cool, dry bubbles pass down her throat. "I wasn't thinking clearly, Ryan. Maybe I'm still not. When I found out I was pregnant all I could think about was not losing her."

"I know, Erin. You've apologized already and you don't need to keep doing it. I need to accept my responsibility in this situation, too."

He walked over to the patio rail and faced the ocean with his back to her. She remembered what it was like to direct most of the anger inward. It was the same way she'd felt when she'd finally left Kevin. She knew she had to give him space, but also remembered how much that anger had turned to an aching pain. So she simply stood and joined him at the rail.

"One of my favorite things about the world is the sky, no matter where you are," Ryan shared.

She stared up with him, enjoying the pitch-blackness she never saw in Boston. "That must have been comforting when you were in the military. Do you miss it?"

"At times. But it was also time to move on with my life."

"Would you have come to Boston General if you'd known I was there?" She moved her eyes from the sky to the man standing above her.

"Honestly, no, I wouldn't have."

"I offended you that badly?" Now it was her turn to be hurt.

"No, you confused me. I didn't understand how the woman I had met equated with what I had learned about your past."

"And that was enough to keep you away?"

He brushed her hair from her face, his hand resting on her cheek. "No, I stayed away because, despite everything, I was still attracted to you. I still am."

She realized she had lifted herself and was straining

toward him only a moment before his head came down and his lips touched hers. She could taste the champagne on his lips as they brushed against hers. It was the softest of touches before a gentle pressure opened her to him and he deepened their kiss. If she had been capable of rational thought she would have wondered how this man, despite everything, could still cause her to feel such passion, but she couldn't think, not even when he broke away.

"This wasn't my plan." He shook his head slightly.

"I…I…" Still she didn't know what to think or say.

"When I said we should get back to the place we had been in Scotland, I didn't mean physically."

"Oh." And she was embarrassed by just how much disappointment she felt. She, too, had absolutely no plans for anything romantic or physical between them, deeming that dream well lost, but the reminder of what they had once experienced together was enough to make her feel bereft again as he pulled away.

"You should go to bed."

"Your room is the one down the other hall. I'll see you in the morning."

Erin walked quietly to the room she was sharing with Jennie, taking a moment to cover her daughter, who always managed to kick off her blankets. She looked at Jennie, the sight of their daughter giving her the strong reminder she needed—that this was not just about her and Ryan. The option for a fleeting love affair had ended in Scotland. She couldn't do anything that would jeopardize their relationship because, despite her attraction and growing romantic feelings toward him, he was Jennie's father first and foremost. Now Jennie had a father, and Erin remembered how she had treasured hers for the short time he had been in her life, Erin wasn't going to be responsible for taking that away from her daughter.

Erin awoke to the sun streaming in through the windows and the smell of the ocean in the air. She glanced at the clock and blinked. When had been the last time she had slept past eight? She immediately glanced at the crib, only to find it empty. Panic sparked inside her as she scrambled to find Jennie.

She didn't have to look far. Jennie was sitting in the center of the living room floor amid the toys Erin had packed for her, Ryan by her side. She exhaled, not even considering concealing the fear she had been feeling.

Ryan looked up at her and realized her alarm. "I'm sorry, I heard her playing in her crib and thought I would get her so that you could sleep. I didn't mean to scare you."

She was afraid and upset, but one look at Jennie and she knew she couldn't share any of those feelings. The little girl was beaming with happiness and she didn't want to upset her.

"It's okay. I guess I'm just not used to having help." She wanted to take back the words the minute she'd said them, realizing that the reason she didn't have help had been her own choice. She looked at Ryan and respected him even more for letting her comment pass.

"What are your plans for the day?" he asked.

"Not much," she confessed. "I really thought we would

just go down to the beach and play in the sand and then maybe check out the farmers' market this afternoon."

"Sounds great."

She walked to the kitchen to make a cup of coffee and noticed the pot was already brewed.

"I remembered," Ryan commented, from the living room.

She poured herself a cup and took a sip of the hot, dark, full-bodied roast. It wasn't until that moment that she realized what she was wearing. In her haste to find Jennie she hadn't had time to pull on her robe so instead she was standing in the kitchen in nothing but an oversize T-shirt, her legs bare. She looked up and saw Ryan watching her and she self-consciously slipped behind the kitchen island. The kiss from last night was still very much on her mind.

He smiled at her not-so-subtle move and she heard the faint laugh coming from his lips.

"It's okay. It's nothing I haven't seen before."

She blushed and then blushed harder, remembering in just what state he had seen her.

"On your balcony in Scotland. The first night we met you weren't very shy about your choice in pajamas then, either." His explanation should have been comforting, except that she realized he had offered it because of the alternative he had guessed she was recollecting.

"If you are okay with her, I'll go get dressed."

"We're fine. Take your time."

She showered and dressed quickly, not used to having the extra time. She had packed before she'd known Ryan was coming and looked down at the meager options before her. She didn't spend too much time thinking about what was making her want to look her best. In the end she didn't have much choice, so she settled on what she had planned she would wear when she had thought it was just going to be her and Jennie, her emerald-green bikini with its matching cover-up. She blew her hair dry and then looked in the mirror, forgoing any makeup in favor of sunscreen alone.

Jennie and Ryan were still playing when she finished. She picked out Jennie's protective sun shirt and shorts and dressed her, being careful to apply sunblock to all her exposed skin.

"Ready?" Ryan asked.

"Yes."

It was nice having the extra hands as they made their way down to the beach. Between beach chairs, a blanket, toys, snacks and Jennie herself, Erin would have had her hands full. They picked a spot on the sand and immediately Jennie dumped a bucket of sand in the center of the blanket.

"Nice." Ryan laughed before picking up the little girl and swinging her round. Her shrieks of delight filled the air.

The three of them played for the next two hours and Erin couldn't remember when she had been this relaxed or seen Jennie as happy. The look on her face when Ryan dipped her feet into the ocean for the first time was amazing. They ate a picnic lunch and then headed to the market.

A different time, a different place, but as the day went on Erin realized that Ryan had been right. This was what they needed. A chance, away from everyone else and their past, to get to know each other again. She also realized what she had been missing. What it would be like to raise Jennie with two parents, a partner for all the joys and challenges that lay ahead.

They made a light salad for supper and participated in the nightly bath ritual together. "It's a wonder there's any sand still on the beach!" Ryan commented, as the water drained and the entire bottom of the tub was full of sand.

Erin laughed but her attention was on Jennie. It had been a great day, a busy day, and Jennie had barely napped and showed no signs of willingness to sleep any time soon. She had a bad feeling about where this was headed. Sure enough, the simple act of putting her in her pajamas was the last straw and Jennie began to cry. The cry progressed to earsplitting wails as Erin struggled in vain to soothe her.

It was impossible as the little girl rubbed her head back and forth into Erin's neck and shoulder, large, wet tears streaming down her face.

"What's wrong with her?" Ryan asked, Jennie's complete meltdown a new experience for him, as well.

"She's overtired," Erin answered very quietly, begging Jennie to stop.

The more Jennie cried the more distressed they both became. Erin walked up and down the short hallway, whispering reassurances to her daughter, but nothing worked. It wasn't Jennie's first meltdown and normally Erin would have been more relaxed and let it run its course, but not in front of Ryan. She needed to prove she was a good mother and what kind of mother couldn't soothe her little girl?

More tears, only this time Erin's as Jennie's wailing continued. She put her down, but she only cried harder, her arms reaching up for her mother.

"Here, let me take her." Ryan's words broke through the cries.

She wanted to say no, that she could do it, but she couldn't and she wasn't in a state to argue that she had control of the situation. She passed Jennie to him and her wails increased for a minute before there was silence, a few more cries, and more silence. Erin wiped away her own tears and saw Ryan gently rubbing Jennie's back, her little face pressed against his chest as he walked the halls with her.

A few minutes later she was out cold, her body limp in Ryan's arms. Erin walked with him to their bedroom, watching as he laid her in the crib and covered her. "Good night, my sweetheart." She bent down to kiss the still-wet cheek softly.

They carefully closed the door and retreated, the house now eerily quiet in the aftermath of the meltdown. She took a seat on the couch, moving one of the orange pillows to hold it protectively in front of her.

"I'm sorry," she said, her nerves totally shot both from Jennie's crying and her inability to soothe her in front of Ryan. What must he be thinking of her mothering skills?

"Why are you sorry?" He sat beside her on the couch.

"I couldn't comfort her."

"That's okay."

"No, it's not. I'm her mother, I'm supposed to be able to comfort her."

"Erin—" he started, but she interrupted him.

"I don't want you to think I'm a bad mother." She moved her hand to her mouth the moment the words escaped. It was another example of her inability to keep her thoughts to herself in front of him.

"No one is perfect all the time, not you, not Jennie."

"I'm so afraid you are going to take her away from me." Now that she had started there was no stopping her and her own tears resurfaced.

He reached forward, taking away the pillow she held between them, turning his whole body toward her. He looked more confused than ever. "Why would I take her away?"

"Because you don't think I'm a good person, because maybe you won't think I'm a good enough mother. I wanted this weekend to go well, to prove to you I was a good mother to our daughter."

"That's the first time you've ever called her our daughter." Ryan's voice was soft.

She had, and there was no going back. Just spending the day with Ryan as a family, she'd realized that Jennie wasn't just hers, she was theirs, together. She also no longer just wanted Jennie as her family, she wanted it to include Ryan.

"She has your eyes."

"I know," he admitted.

She looked at him, feeling more vulnerable than she had when they'd first met on that hillside in Scotland. "What are we going to do?"

"What do you want?"

"I want to do what's best for Jennie."

"And what about you?"

"I'm not important."

"To me you are."

His words could not have been more perfect. As her feelings for Ryan had resurfaced one of her fears had been that she would be the consolation prize that came with his daughter. She needed him to tell her otherwise, to prove to her otherwise.

"Kiss me," she said quietly.

"I can't." She looked up at him and she started to pull away but he grabbed both her hands, keeping her facing him.

"I can't just kiss you. I want you too badly just to kiss you."

She understood everything he was saying so instead she leaned in and kissed him. Everything about the taste of his lips, the feel of his skin and the smell of him was familiar, so much so that it instantaneously sparked a fire inside her. The first time they had been together she'd thought she had wanted him, but she had been wrong then, because nothing compared to the desperate need she felt now.

He broke away and lifted her from the couch and into his arms. She didn't ask where they were headed as Ryan carried her to the master bedroom. He pulled off his shirt before coming down on her on the bed, his lips finding hers and his tongue exploring and tasting her. She wove her hands into his short hair, holding him to her. She never wanted the kiss to end but at the same time she wanted more.

She felt him rise slightly from her, his arm a study in flexed muscular perfection. The casual beach shorts and jersey halter top she had changed into after the beach gave him no bother as he quickly stripped her naked and then did the same with his own clothes. The bedroom window was open and she could smell and feel the night's ocean air against her skin. Between the slight coolness of the air and her anticipation she felt as if her whole body was trembling in want of him, every hair in every pore poised for his next move.

He didn't leave her waiting for long and soon there was nothing cool about the feel of his completely naked hard muscular body hotly pressed against her. He paused, looking into her eyes, and she felt she could drown in the depths of the blue. He wanted her, too. She arched her back, pressing herself even more against him, feeling every inch of him and his want for her.

His hand swept up her side and over her tattoo before his hand cupped her breast, his thumb stroking her nipple. She didn't have to wait long before he caressed the swollen tip with his mouth.

The more he touched her the more she wanted him and she could feel her body readying for him as she unconsciously spread herself more and more open for him.

"You're even more beautiful than I remembered," he murmured, his breath hot against her breast.

"I need you." And truer words were never spoken. She needed him to make love to her, she needed him to be a father to their daughter and she needed him to love her because she knew she was in love with him.

He broke away from her, reaching into his shaving kit to bring out a small foil wrapper. She didn't miss the look of irony on his face as he sheathed himself. He kneeled between her legs, his hand stroking upward from her ankle to the top of her thigh. Without thinking, she wrapped both legs around him moments before he pushed into her.

It had been over two years since she'd had this feeling. The last time she had been touched so intimately had been with Ryan and she had never wanted any other man. She found herself matching his every movement. Their rocking back and forth echoed the waves of the ocean heard through the open window. As she reached ever nearer to her climax she wanted even more from him and she moved her hands from their strong hold on his back to touch his hands. He immediately took hold, lacing his fingers through hers. Now with each movement she felt truly complete. As Ryan pushed deeper each movement moved her closer to the edge, his virile length hitting hard against her core, her breasts pressed hard against his chest, her hands in his being pressed into the mattress as each mini-peak was met with the sound of the waves crashing on the beach.

Then she could hold on no longer. She moved both her legs behind his back, locking her ankles, and with one final stroke she pushed herself hard against him as his mouth came down on hers, stifling both their cries of ecstasy.

They stayed like that for a long time before he finally pulled away from her, only briefly to discard the condom, before he pulled her against him and the sheet over both of them, their sweat-covered bodies cooling quickly in the night air.

"I think that is the only thing that hasn't changed between us," Ryan murmured against the back of her neck.

"Mmm..." she moaned, still in a satiated fog.

"The last time we were together was the most passionate night I had ever had, until now."

He had more of her attention now, as she thought back to the revelation she'd had right before they'd made love. She loved Ryan. She was in love with Ryan and she desperately needed him to love her, too. She waited, but her hopes of hearing those words were dashed as she recognized the gentle repetition of his breath signaling he was asleep.

The next few days were almost perfect. They spent their days as a family, going to the beach, exploring the public gardens, and after Jennie went to bed their nights exploring each other. Neither Ryan nor Erin did anything to ruin the budding relationship between them. They never spoke of their past, his sister, and Ryan didn't ask her any more questions about Jennie's possible paternity.

They celebrated the Fourth of July sitting together on the beachfront patio, watching the fireworks with Jennie, who barely managed to keep her eyes open in Ryan's arms.

The next day it was time to return to reality and Erin felt uneasiness build. They had been perfect together in Scotland. Perfect together again here in the Hamptons as a family. But what would happen when they had to face the realities of their lives together in Boston? What would happen when the paternity test definitively proved Ryan to be Jennie's father? Would he want to be a family? Could she continue in their relationship just waiting and hoping he fell in love with her?

Eventually they would also have to face their past. She knew he loved his sister and she had no idea how Sabrina would take the news of Erin's involvement in her brother's life. She had wanted to explain to him the truth about her past with Sabrina and Kevin, but was afraid to ruin the ideal of their family time together by bringing up such an unsavory subject. Was their relationship strong enough to overcome his family's disapproval, and what would happen if it wasn't?

CHAPTER TWELVE

THREE WEEKS AFTER their return Ryan felt sure about what he needed to do. Without discussion he had practically been living with Erin and Jennie and he had never been happier with his life. Every day he felt even closer to Erin and Jennie. He had done the bloodwork more to confirm paternity. He wanted the world to know that Jennie was his daughter.

The heat from the late July afternoon hit him as he opened his car door and walked along the stone path toward Sabrina's front door. Her house was a suburban family home in Cambridge only a few blocks from their parents' and perfect for her growing family. The neighborhood was filled with children running and playing outside and he thought about how much he wanted that for Jennie.

Ryan rang the doorbell and waited for an answer.

Sabrina answered the door and the similarity between Sabrina and Jennie struck him instantly. All of his features he saw in Jennie he also saw in Sabrina. She was dressed casually in capri pants, a loose-fitting T-shirt and with a beaded necklace his nephew, Simon, was struggling to grab and put in his mouth. "Well, this is a surprise!" Sabrina exclaimed, as she reached out and gave him a one-armed hug. "What's the occasion?"

"Can't I just stop by and see my little sister and nephew?" he asked her casually, knowing there was much more behind his visit, and that Sabrina knew that, too.

"You can, but you don't," she teased.

She was right so he didn't disagree. "Can I come in?"

"Of course." She walked with him to the heart of her home, the kitchen, and he took a seat at one of the barstools that lined her granite-covered island. "So are you going to tell me what is wrong?"

"How do you know something is wrong?"

"Because my very important doctor big brother does not just drop by on a weekday in the middle of the afternoon."

"I need to talk to you about something and I'm not sure you are going to like what I have to say."

"Then just say it. I'm not as fragile as you think I am, Ryan."

He was taken aback at her comment and took a moment to truly look at her. She was right. She didn't look fragile. She actually looked nothing like his memory of the depressed, broken woman she had been. Instead, she looked relaxed and at peace and he began to wonder if he had been making decisions to protect her when she didn't need his protection after all.

"I need to talk to you about Erin Dufour." He watched her carefully and she didn't appear anything but surprised.

"That wasn't what I was expecting to hear." She placed Simon in his baby swing and came around to sit on the barstool opposite him.

"I met her at Boston General. She goes by her maiden name, Madden, now."

"I know," she replied simply.

"You know?" He couldn't hide his shock.

"I met her a few months ago when I had Simon. She didn't recognize me with all the swelling from my pregnancy and my new last name but I recognized her."

"You never said anything." He still couldn't believe what he was hearing.

"You never asked. Why are we talking about Erin?"

"I had a brief relationship with her two years ago before I knew who she was." He looked at his sister carefully, trying to read her response. "When I realized she was Kevin's ex-wife I broke it off."

"Why would you do that?" Sabrina appeared genuinely confused and he felt frustrated at having to explain his motivation.

"Because of what she did to you. The pain she caused you."

"She saved my life. She saved Simon's life."

"What?" This conversation was reaching surreal proportions and his sister's revelations were doing nothing to ease the turmoil inside him.

"When I was pregnant with Simon and started feeling unwell she was the only person who really took me seriously when I said something was wrong. When the others tried to send me home she refused and she ordered the testing that diagnosed my preeclampsia."

"So you forgave her because she took care of you in your pregnancy?"

"There was nothing to forgive."

"What about her affair with Kevin?" He hated having to remind Sabrina of it, hated having to remind himself of Erin's marriage.

"It saved me from a serious mistake. When Kevin first broke off our relationship I was devastated. I wasn't ready to face the fact that the man I loved, whom I had built all my dreams around, had really cheated on me with another woman, so instead I placed all the blame on Erin. It wasn't until after she had married Kevin that I had the courage to confront her. She had no idea who I was, never mind that she had been the other woman. That was when I realized that that man I spent the past four years with had been a liar and a cheat. I felt used, and foolish, and ashamed, and those feelings were the catalyst for my depression."

He wanted to talk more about Erin, but this was the most Sabrina had ever shared with him about her depression and he couldn't dismiss her admission.

"I thought you still blamed Erin. I didn't realize you felt differently. Why didn't you say something back then? I still blame myself for not being there to help you."

"You were away saving the world and I didn't want to bother you with my problems. My feelings didn't seem as important as the wars that you were helping to fight and the lives you were saving."

"I wish you had." For all of their sakes, how he wished he had known.

"Is that why we are talking about Erin?"

"I've been fighting my feelings for her for the past two years, thinking I was betraying you."

"Oh, Ryan." Sabrina was gently shaking her head from side to side.

"She has a daughter, Jennie. She's a year and a half and I'm sure she's mine."

"Oh, my God! When did you find out about her? Why didn't Erin tell you about her?"

"Because before she had Jennie the last time we saw each other I accused her of being an immoral other woman who seduces and traps other women's men." Even to his own ears it sounded horrible and Erin's reaction in not telling him when she had learned of the pregnancy became more clear to him.

"You didn't!"

"Not in those exact words, but the point was made."

"I understand, then," Sabrina commented.

"You agree with her keeping Jennie a secret from me?" Now it was his turn to feel betrayed.

"I understand how on the heels of her divorce from a man who spent their entire relationship violating her trust, she wasn't keen to give you the benefit of the doubt. So what are you going to do?"

"I don't know. I still don't understand why she never told me the truth about her and Kevin."

"Maybe because it's humiliating and embarrassing to admit that you were in love with a man who not only didn't love you but also had no respect for you as a woman?"

He let Sabrina's words sink through him, but she didn't stop there. "Or maybe because it's even worse after going through that to put your trust in a new man, only to find out he thinks the worst of you, too."

"Okay, I get the point." He felt totally unworthy of having Erin in his life.

"So what are you going to do?"

"Tell her I love her and ask her to marry me." Something he regretted not doing sooner. If anything, his conversation with Sabrina had highlighted how lucky he was to still have Erin in his life. Jennie really was a miracle. If it hadn't been for her they wouldn't have found their way back to one another.

"Oh, Ry, you haven't even told her you love her yet?"

"No." He didn't need Sabrina to highlight how foolish he had been.

"Watch Simon. I'll be right back."

He looked over at his nephew and couldn't help but think of everything he had missed with Jennie. Over the past weeks Erin had shared with him her baby albums and videos but it hadn't been the same. Erin hadn't cheated him—he had cheated himself out of Jennie's first year of life.

"Here." She handed him a square velvet box.

"What's this?"

"It's Grandma's engagement ring. Mom gave up hope years ago that you would ever settle down and marry so she gave it to me. I think Erin should have it."

He opened the box to discover the platinum ring that was handcrafted with intricate trellis-like embellishments that led to a central circular diamond that was surrounded by a circle of smaller diamonds. "It's perfect. Are you sure?"

"Yes. I can't think of a woman I would want more as a sister and you need to secure her place in our family as soon as possible. Simon wants to meet his cousin and I want to meet my niece!"

"Thank you, for everything." He stood and hugged his sister, more grateful than she would ever know.

He left Sabrina's finally feeling as if he had the answers. Even after their weekend in the Hamptons he hadn't been able to put together who Erin was completely. He didn't understand how the woman he knew could ever have been the other woman, but now everything made sense. His only regret was not recognizing sooner that Erin could never deliberately hurt anyone. Erin was the same woman he'd fallen for in Scotland, the woman he'd fallen in love with in the Hamptons and the mother of his child. If he was lucky, she would agree to be his wife.

He looked at the ring box and wondered how he was going to make it through the weekend. Erin and Jennie had gone away for her friend Kate's wedding and it would be another four days before he could tell her he loved her.

Long weekends were notorious for the emergency department. Alcohol and an above-average sense of fearlessness typically led to at least a 20 percent increase in volume. Ryan was happy to be busy. His evening shift was taking his mind off waiting for Erin and Jennie to return home.

The emergency medical services dispatch radio

sounded. They were ten minutes away with a motor vehicle accident trauma.

"Activate the trauma team," he told the unit clerk, and she keyed in the single code that paged the eight-person team to the trauma bay.

He arrived at the trauma bay and looked around to make sure all the required equipment was there before donning a protective gown and goggles. Three nurses, a respiratory therapist and one of the emergency medicine residents gathered with him. One of the orthopedic and general surgery residents soon followed.

He could hear the sirens as they approached and could tell the ambulance was racing toward them. It arrived less than a minute later, driving through the bay and coming to an abrupt stop outside the doors. He went through the automatic glass doors and helped the team unload the stretcher, getting a good look at the patient.

He recognized the paramedic, who began to give report. "Restrained middle-aged male involved in a frontal collision. Lost consciousness at the scene and was intubated for airway protection. Obvious open femur fracture."

Ryan glanced down to the man's thigh and saw the protruding bone.

The team moved quickly into the trauma room, and each person specialized in their particular role began their assessment. He gave them three minutes before he intervened. "What do you want to do?" he asked his resident.

"Stabilize, transfuse for blood loss and get full-body

imaging to ensure that we are not being distracted by the femur and missing something worse."

"I agree."

He stood in the doorway for the next thirty minutes, being unobtrusive but also making sure the patient was receiving optimal care.

"Why haven't you booked the femur for the operating room?" he heard a voice yell down the hall. It was a voice he had no desire to hear. He looked down the hall to see Kevin Dufour yelling at the trauma team orthopedic resident and now making his way toward them.

"I want this patient in the operating room now," he yelled at the remaining residents and nursing staff. The team paused and looked at Ryan.

"Stick with the plan. Dr. Dufour, can I speak to you for a moment?"

"I want that patient in the operating room now," Kevin seethed.

Ryan did his best to remain calm, which was the opposite of what he really wanted to do. "The patient is still to be stabilized and still needs to have his imaging survey completed to ensure there are no more serious injuries before you spend three hours fixing his femur."

"His femur is his most serious injury, isn't that obvious?"

"No, it's not, which is why we have ordered a CT of his head, chest, abdomen and pelvis."

"I'm in charge here, and I want him transferred to the operating room."

"No, you are not. This man is a patient of the emergency department and under my care and will remain so until I choose otherwise."

"We'll see about that."

Ryan paid no attention to Dufour's exit and returned to his patient.

Twenty minutes later he received verbal report from the radiologist. The victim had an extradural hemorrhage in his brain, requiring immediate evacuation in order to help prevent permanent neurological injury. He called the neurosurgeon on call and made arrangements for transfer.

"Dr. Callum," the unit clerk called to him. "Dr. Williamson is on the phone."

"Sir," he answered, his respect for his superiors bred from his military training.

"Ryan, I'd like to see you in my office. Is there another physician who can watch your patients?"

"Yes, sir, but I would prefer not to leave right now. We are getting slammed and have already had two major traumas this evening."

"Are there any major traumas not managed at present?"

"No."

"Then I'll see you in my office now. This won't take long and you will still be in the building."

Ryan didn't have time to respond before the other man hung up. He walked up the three flights to the administrative offices, knowing what he would find. Dr. Williamson's receptionist showed him into the office, where Kevin was sitting, looking overly smug.

"You brought this on yourself." He snickered as Ryan took the place beside him.

Ryan balled his hand into a fist and then forced himself to relax. A few minutes later Dr. Williamson entered, looking unimpressed at both men.

"Gentlemen, I can't tell you how much it does not impress me to have to come in on a long weekend to deal with this complaint.

"Dr. Callum, Dr. Dufour has filed a complaint alleging you endangered a patient by refusing to transfer care following a motor vehicle trauma." He paused and looked directly at Kevin. "However, I am well aware that you have more trauma experience and are a better physician than Dr. Dufour will ever be so I thought it would be best to remind him of that in your presence. I trust you two can figure things out from here. Good evening."

Ryan tried hard not to smile as Dr. Williamson left the room.

"You may think you won but that had nothing to do with you. I should have known he wouldn't have been able to be professional."

"Because?" Ryan was waiting, waiting for him to say something about Erin.

"Because he thinks I fathered and abandoned his precious little bastard grandchild. Well, the joke is on him. His perfect little stepdaughter got herself knocked up again, but this time it had nothing to do with me."

"How do you know?"

"Because I had a vasectomy right after the first time she played that card to make sure it never happened again."

"So you are the reason Erin thought she was infertile?" He looked at Kevin and wondered if he had any idea how much pain he had caused the two most important women in Ryan's life, and realized he didn't care. Seconds later Kevin was on the floor, holding his rapidly swelling face with a look of sheer confusion.

Ryan looked over to the door that had just opened and saw Dr. Williamson standing in the entry. "I forgot my briefcase. You should have that looked at, Kevin." And he walked across the room, retrieved the forgotten briefcase and walked out with no further words spoken.

CHAPTER THIRTEEN

ERIN WALKED THROUGH the hospital's front entrance, eager to find Ryan. She knew that he had gotten the same call she had last night, confirming he was Jennie's father. Even though she'd known what the test was going to show she still felt hopeful that it would prove to be the turning point between them.

Her pager went off and she recognized the number of the maternal fetal medicine unit. She had continued to follow Chloe in her pregnancy and had arranged an urgent ultrasound for her that morning. If it was normal, they wouldn't be calling.

"This is Dr. Madden," she announced as her call was picked up.

"Please hold for Dr. Young."

Dr. Young was the perinatologist who was following Chloe in conjunction with Erin. "Erin, I just finished scanning Chloe Darcy. She's just past twenty-six weeks in her pregnancy but the baby has started showing signs of acute heart failure. There is also reverse flow in the umbilical cord. I think you need to get her delivered."

"Thank you. I'm in the building and will be right there."

Erin felt a panic she hadn't felt since her own pregnancy. She couldn't let anything happen to Chloe's baby. Not when she had already gone through so much. She knew that the finding in the umbilical cord meant that a stillbirth could happen at any moment and she had to act quickly.

She ran to the ultrasound unit and directly to Chloe's room. She could tell from the panic on Chloe's face that she had already been told the devastating news. She had to stay professional and do her job. "Chloe, when did you last have anything to eat or drink?"

Chloe knew the reason Erin was asking. She needed another surgery, and urgently. "Last evening," she answered. "The baby's in heart failure," Chloe declared, looking at Erin, obviously hoping she would say something different.

"Yes," Erin confirmed. "I'm sorry, Chloe, but we need to get you delivered."

"I'm not ready. The baby's not ready. I'm only twenty-six and a half weeks.'

"There's no other option, Chloe. The heart failure and the reverse blood flow in the umbilical cord shows that the baby is at high risk for stillbirth at any moment. Dr. Young is reviewing the images and she is on phone to the neonatal intensive care unit now, letting them know what to expect with the baby." She didn't want to scare Chloe any more than she was already scared but she needed her absolute cooperation and time was of the essence.

"Erin, what's going to happen?"

For the first time since entering the room Erin slowed herself and sat down next to Chloe.

"Right now the baby weighs about two and a half pounds, but some of that is swelling from the extra fluid that has built up in the baby's tissues. Following birth, the baby will be intubated for respiratory support and also given some medication down a tube and into its lungs to help the lungs mature and make breathing easier. We can use the umbilical cord to establish intravenous and arterial access so that we can both monitor the baby and provide medication and nutrition in a more direct fashion. There is at least an eighty percent chance of survival and a fifty percent chance of no major complications."

"I haven't exactly been doing great in the luck department this year, Erin."

"Chloe, we need to focus on the positive. We diagnosed the baby before anything really horrible happened and we are going to get you delivered right away."

"A Caesarean section?" Chloe asked.

"Yes. It's the fastest way, and the baby is still breech right now, making a vaginal delivery a poor option."

"Okay," Chloe agreed, and Erin felt a little relief, knowing Chloe was accepting of the plan.

"They are preparing the obstetrics operating room across from the nursery. We need to walk to the unit now and get you admitted so we can deliver this baby as soon as possible."

"Okay."

Erin reached over and grabbed the paper drape, wiping the jelly from Chloe's still-exposed abdomen. She helped her sit up and then walked with her as quickly but as calmly as possible toward the obstetrical unit.

"Chloe, when you get on the unit it is going to be chaotic. Everyone is going to be coming at you, asking you questions, getting you changed, poking and prodding you to get you ready. I have to make a call and get changed into my scrubs. Just remember that you and this baby are going to be okay. Do you have any questions about the plan or the Caesarean?"

"No."

"Chloe, do you want me to call Tate?" Over the previous weeks Chloe had confided in Erin about her relationship with Tate. Erin would never normally interfere in a patient's personal life, but Chloe was her friend and she knew that she would regret not having the father of her baby at her delivery. Erin had.

"Yes."

Once they stepped onto the unit the predicted chaos ensued. Erin squeezed Chloe's hand hard before letting go. She went to change and then quickly made phone calls to Tate and then the blood bank. Chloe's pregnancy had been complicated by blood antibodies she had created after she had received emergency unmatched blood products with her ectopic pregnancy. Now it was even harder to find blood to transfuse her with if she needed it.

She felt her whole body shaking as she watched Chloe being sat up for her spinal anesthetic. The last time she had operated on her she hadn't had time to think about the fact that her friend's life had been in her hands. At this moment she thought she preferred that. She watched as they laid her down. It was time.

She waited until Chloe's abdomen had been painted

with antiseptic and then covered her with surgical drapes. The room continued to fill as the neonatal intensive care team arrived. She found herself looking at the door, praying Tate would get here in time. She couldn't wait for him. Then he arrived and took the spot next to Chloe, where he belonged.

"Chloe, can you feel anything?" Erin asked, as she pinched her stomach hard with a pair of surgical forceps.

"No," Chloe answered.

"Patient is Chloe Darcy. She is having an emergency Caesarean section. She has no allergies. There are two units of blood in the room, and she received a gram of cefazolin at nine thirty-two. Does anyone have any concerns?" the circulating nurse asked, as she completed the presurgical safety pause.

"No," Erin answered, when in her head she had a thousand concerns. Would Chloe's baby be okay? What would she do if Chloe hemorrhaged again?

"You can proceed," the anesthetist confirmed.

She held her hand out for the scalpel and followed the line she had made months earlier. The room quieted and she focused on the technical aspect of her job and not her feelings for Chloe. Within two minutes she had made the uterine incision.

"Uterine incision," the scrub nurse notified the neonatal team.

"Chloe, you are going to feel some pressure on your abdomen as we help get the baby out. Tate, if you want to stand up you can watch your baby being born. The baby is breech, so you are going to see legs and bum first," Erin counseled both parents.

She cut the last layer of the thick muscle as gently as possible so as not to cut the baby. Clear fluid drained into the drapes and onto the floor. Two little feet protruded immediately and pushed against her hand and she found herself smiling, reassured by the little one's spirit. She went through breech maneuvers, being as gentle as possible with the delicate newborn. Once the baby was out she showed Tate that they had a son as the little one let out a small cry that was the best sound Erin could have asked for. She looked briefly at Tate, his eyes glassy as he looked down at Chloe, and Erin smiled, honored to be included in their moment. She handed the baby to her assistant, who took the baby over to the resuscitation team before she continued with her job.

Her sense of reassurance didn't stay with her long as Chloe started to bleed heavily from the uterine incision, the uterus too soft to close off all the blood vessels that had fed it while Chloe had been pregnant.

"Tate, I think I'm going to be sick," Erin heard Chloe mumble.

Erin looked at the blood-pressure monitor and saw that Chloe's pressure had dropped.

"Open and hang the blood," Erin ordered, as she tried to clamp the corners of the incision while massaging the uterus, begging it silently to firm up.

Her actions were in vain as the blood kept coming. She looked at the anesthetist and he understood that they were in trouble with no words spoken.

"We need another four units of packed cells and two of fresh frozen plasma crossed and in the room. Open the postpartum hemorrhage tray and have a hysterectomy tray standing by, please," Erin commanded.

"It's going to take at least an hour to cross her for more blood," the anesthetist responded.

"Then let's get on it," Erin responded, frustrated but knowing it was the truth.

"I'm going to put her out," the anesthetist declared.

"Agreed."

Erin injected the uterus directly with medication, with no effect. She was running out of options. It had been thirty minutes since the baby had been born and they were only getting further behind.

She looked at the hysterectomy tray. She had asked for it to be opened, thinking that if she opened it she would never have to use it. Now it was looking more and more likely that she would have to take out her friend's uterus to save her life. The fragile little two-pound boy that Chloe had just delivered would be her only child and he might not even survive.

She resolved to try one more option then she was going to have to move on, no matter how much she disliked the other option.

"Can I get the B-lynch, please?" She saw the nurse's brows rise beneath her mask as she put the hysterectomy clamp back on the table and instead handed her the elongated suture.

With care Erin sutured a tension suture through and around the uterus until it was physically forced to contract. She watched for two minutes and saw the bleeding was better. She closed the uterine incision and watched again. It was now dry.

"Dry?" she asked her resident, who looked more shocked than she did.

"Dry."

The anesthetist stood up and looked, too, his nod a subtle agreement with her assessment.

She watched and waited for another ten minutes, but there were no signs of further bleeding so she began to close the incision and in twenty minutes Chloe was being wheeled into Recovery. The baby was in serious but stable condition in the neonatal intensive care unit but was already showing good signs.

For the first time since she had been paged, other than the brief moment at delivery, Erin thought of Ryan and Jennie. She hadn't heard from him since he had gotten the results and that both surprised and bothered her. He had already accepted that Jennie was his daughter so she didn't understand why he was holding back now. She glanced at the clock—it was two in the afternoon. She dialed his cell phone and waited—no answer. She tried his pager, only to get the same response. She wanted to find him but she couldn't, not for the next couple of hours until she was sure Chloe was stable.

Her pager went off an hour later and she didn't recognize the number. Hoping it was Ryan, she dialed.

"Dr. Madden, this is Dr. Williamson's assistant, Beverly. Dr. Williamson was hoping you could stop by his office this afternoon."

It was an unusual request. She and Stephen had never interacted personally at work, and he certainly had never had Beverly page her while she was working. Was she in trouble professionally? She checked back in with Chloe before heading to the administrative offices.

"You can go right in, dear," Beverly directed.

Erin still stopped to knock at the door before letting herself in. Stephen was behind his desk, going through a pile of paperwork on his desk. "Take a seat, Erin."

"Okay." She did as she was told.

"I thought you would want to be the first to know Kevin handed in his resignation this morning."

Of all the things she had prepared herself to hear, that was not one of them.

"Why?" she asked, utterly surprised. Kevin had spent months, years, trying to force her out of Boston General. It made no sense that he would leave now.

"I believe it may have something to do with the black eye he received last night and a lack of support from hospital administration."

"What happened?" Erin was still in shock, and was that a twinkle in Stephen's eyes?

"Officially he walked into a door. Unofficially Ryan Callum from the emergency department gave him what he deserved."

"Ryan hit him?"

"No, he walked into a door. But I have to say I am very fond of Dr. Callum. I hope we will be seeing more of him."

She didn't know how, but Stephen knew about their involvement and she was surprised at how much his approval meant to her.

"Thanks for letting me know." She smiled and excused herself from their meeting.

Erin unlocked the front door of her apartment, anxious to see Jennie. Seeing Chloe's son today had only made her feel more grateful for her healthy child. She walked directly to the living room but Jennie wasn't there. Instead, the entire space was filled with long-stemmed red roses and Ryan. He was dressed in a gray pinstripe suit with a white shirt and matte red tie that matched the single rose he wore on his lapel.

She inhaled sharply, only to have her senses overtaken by the scent of the fresh-cut flowers.

"What is all this?" she asked in confusion.

"What you deserve. I know you like to focus on the meanings of things, your tattoo, Jennie's name, so I thought I would tell you what I need to tell you in every way I possibly could."

"With roses?" she asked hesitantly, her hopes growing by the second.

"With red roses."

"Ryan, do you know what red roses mean?" Oh, how she needed him to say it.

"They mean passionate love, which is how I feel about you."

It wasn't enough that he felt passionate toward her; she knew that from their lovemaking. She needed to know he loved her. "You love me?"

"Very much so, and I'm desperately hoping you love me, too."

"I do," she confessed, her words giving her a sense of freedom.

"Ah, that part I was hoping we would save for later, but if you insist." He reached into his pocket and pulled out the most stunning ring she had ever seen. "Erin Madden, would you do me the great honor of becoming my wife?"

"Yes." And she watched in absolute awe as he slipped the ring on her finger.

"You aren't just doing this because Jennie is your daughter and you want us to be a family?"

"I'm doing this because I love you and there is no other woman in the world I would want to be the mother of my children."

"We just have Jennie." She hoped that would be enough. She remembered the look on Tate's face when he'd seen his son.

"I need to tell you something and I hope it will give you more joy than heartache."

"Okay," she answered, wondering what else there could possibly be.

"I had a conversation with Kevin yesterday."

"A conversation?" she asked, with one eyebrow raised.

"It started as a conversation. He told me he had a vasectomy right after you two were married—that was why you couldn't have more children after your miscarriage."

She felt anger and joy at the same time. Anger for everything Kevin had put her through and joy at the possibilities that had just opened up for her. "We can have more children?" she asked him, as though she didn't know the answer to her own question.

"Yes, we can."

EPILOGUE

"PUSH—ONE, TWO, three, four, five, six, seven, eight, nine and ten. Take a breath."

She exhaled, her breath hot against her damp skin.

She felt the cool cloth being pressed against her forehead and the plastic of the straw against her lips. She took a quick sip of water, trying her best to relax every muscle in her body and not think about what was coming next.

"Okay," Erin managed, and she took the offered hand and squeezed it hard. An incredible pressure overwhelmed her as she tried to focus her efforts.

"You're doing great," Ryan murmured quietly.

As the contraction passed she looked around the room, knowing that any minute her life was going to change. The lights of the delivery room were low and aside from Dr. Thomas and the delivery nurse it was just her and Ryan.

She pushed again, and again with the next contraction. "I can't," she cried out, completely exhausted.

"Yes, you can. You've done it before and you can do it again," Ryan encouraged.

"That was different. Last time I had an epidural." She tried to argue, but had to stop when another contraction brought on an unbearable urge to push.

"And this time you have me. I know how strong you are and I know you can do this."

She opened her eyes, which had been closed from the pain, and looked at her husband. He was right. Last time she had felt alone despite her mother's presence. Now her life was completely different. Her pregnancy had been a complete time of joy, her fear of losing her baby not a dark cloud lingering over this pregnancy. Each milestone was new again as she got to reexperience it as if it was the first time through Ryan's eyes. She had a husband who loved her and was 100 percent devoted to her, and together they had a happy, healthy four-year-old daughter, who was with her mother in the waiting room, eager to find out if she had a new brother or sister.

"All right," she agreed, as she reached deep inside herself to find strength left she hadn't known she had.

She pushed harder, her focus on meeting their child. And then in an instant her cries were joined by their baby's. She opened her eyes just as she felt their baby being laid on her chest and she reached up to hold the baby against her.

"We have a son," Ryan murmured, bending down to their level. "Thank you for our son. I love you, Erin."

Tears of happiness streamed down her face. It was the moment she had always wanted and finally had.

Two weeks later, their home was filled with laughter and celebration. A baby "sprinkle" Chloe had named it when Erin had tried to dissuade her from hosting a baby shower. But she couldn't disagree with Chloe's argument that she had never had this with her first baby and their family deserved a proper welcome.

"I think he wants his momma," Ryan said, handing her their son. The nine-pound expression of their love snuggled into her arms immediately, recognizing her scent. Already Ian was the spitting image of his father, from his dark hair to the shape of his eyes, there was no doubting whose son he was.

"Did you have trouble picking his name?" Kate asked, her one-year-old daughter, Darcie, bouncing happily on her lap. Darcie, named after Chloe, even had the sense to look like her namesake, the surprising swath of red hair she had been born with sealing her name fate. As neither Kate nor her husband, Matt, had red hair, they had taken it as a divine sign.

"I've delivered enough babies to know what not to pick. Fortunately, Ian did not look like a Dynamite or a Twister so he was lucky there." She laughed.

"Come on," Chloe teased. "Think of the luck he would have had later in life with women with a name like Danger."

"True, it was a tough choice. But we knew we wanted a Scottish name and when we found Ian and learned it had the same meaning as Jennie's name we knew it was perfect. They both mean 'God is gracious.' Ian Madden Callum. My maiden name in honor of my father."

Squeals of delight erupted loudly and all three women turned to look as Jennie ran across the living room, her pants mysteriously gone, with Chloe's three-year-old son, Spencer, chasing her. Spencer, who had been born premature, was still a little on the small side but made up for it completely with his robust personality. He was completely fearless and spent most of his time scaring the life out of Chloe and Tate.

"She does that these days. Most of the time it's funny, except when we're in public," Erin explained, still smiling.

"I still can't believe that it all worked out. If you had asked me five years ago where I would be now, I would never have guessed this," Erin commented.

"I know. It's amazing, isn't it?" Kate agreed.

"It's hard to believe that at one time they all wanted to hit each other," Chloe commented, nodding her head toward the group of men who stood in the kitchen, conversing but also keeping a close eye on the commotion in the connecting family room.

"In Matt's defense he was insanely jealous of Tate." Kate laughed, now able to make light of the complicated path to love she and Matt had taken.

"And Tate didn't make things any easier on him, or Ryan, for that matter," Chloe agreed, knowing her husband and his protective nature.

"But it's all been worth it," Erin agreed, thinking back to the turmoil each of the women had endured on their road to love. "If we hadn't gone through all of that then we wouldn't have all of this."

She looked at Ian, then Ryan, and then at Jennie, who was carefree and happily playing in the family room, and knew she deserved this. They all did.

* * * * *